SILT

DENVER CEREAL, VOLUME EIGHT

Claudia Hall Christian

SILT

DENVER CEREAL, VOLUME EIGHT

Claudia Hall Christian

Cook Street Publishing
Denver, CO

Second edition © August 2021
Cook Street Publishing
ISNI: 0000 0004 1443 6403
PO Box 7247
Denver, CO 80207

What's happened so far

Denver Cereal is an addicting, fun, sweet and crunchy serial fiction filled with the tension, drama, and love of urban life.

The best way to catch up is to read the previous books. They are very affordable and available wherever you buy eBooks. You can also read *Denver Cereal* chapters online at DenverCereal.com

We used to write a section here that gave a synopsis of all of the previous books. Frankly, the synopsis wasn't very good. More than anything, they deprived you of the chance to hang out in Denver Cereal for a while. We were only be spoiling your fun

You deserve a chance to read all the crazy twists and turns, mischief, and wild adventures of Denver Cereal. These aren't books to be accomplished or checked off a list. They are stories to be savored and enjoys.

Get to it.

We'll be here when you get back.

~~~~~~~~~~~~~

Denver Cereal is provided free online due to
the generous support of our patrons and you, the book buyer.
This book was created because of your support.

Thank you to you, and all of our patrons

For all of you who risk yourselves, in public and private ways, to fight for a better world.
We salute you.

CHAPTER TWO HUNDRED & TWENTY-TWO

PERFECT

Saturday morning—5:15 a.m.
Somewhere over the United States

A little woozy from the airline champagne, Yvonne turned to look at Rodney. His airline blanket was pulled up to his chin, and his eyes were closed. She was about to touch him to see if he was awake when he opened his eyes.

"You okay?" he asked.

She nodded.

"What's up?" Rodney asked.

"I wondered if you were serious about being naked all week," Yvonne said. His eyes scanned her face. When he didn't say anything, she continued, "It just doesn't seem like you."

"How so? I've always had an intense desire for you, woman."

"I would expect you to have a big plan about how we're going to this museum and that one," Yvonne smiled. "We have to, just have to, see this other thing. I guess, if I were to imagine you in Paris, I wouldn't imagine you spending the whole time in bed. Some quality time, sure. Not all week. But, then, I don't know — maybe you go to Paris every weekend."

Rodney laughed.

"Do you go to Paris every weekend?" Yvonne asked.

"No," Rodney said. "In the summer, I work on Saturdays. In the winter, I split my time between Cañon City, Limon and Buena Vista prisons to mentor young men on Saturdays."

"You just go to Paris on Sundays?" Yvonne smiled.

"I spend my Sundays at church and with my daughter," Rodney

said. "Your mother fixes an afternoon meal. Bumpy and Dionne come. Miss T is there when she can make it. It's nice. Reminds me that I'm free."

"Oh." Yvonne looked straight ahead.

"You're saying you don't want to be naked all week?" Rodney smiled, and Yvonne turned her head to look at him. "Well, what do you think?"

"I think some naked time is definitely in order," Yvonne said. "But I want to see everything and eat all that delicious French cooking."

"Now that you mention it." Rodney smiled and took out his phone.

"You can't use that," Yvonne said. "The lady said that when we took off!"

Rodney smiled.

"What?" Yvonne asked.

"You remembered," Rodney said.

"I did!" Yvonne beamed.

"The phone's on airplane mode." Rodney showed her the setting, and she nodded. "I was going to show you."

He passed the phone to her. There was a map with detailed notes about what to see at each location. He pressed a button, which opened a spreadsheet with a schedule of everything he wanted to see.

"That's my Rodney," Yvonne said. "What's this and this?"

She pointed to time slots on the itinerary.

"Your friend Claire," Rodney said. "The woman who made your pretty dresses?"

"I remember her." Yvonne gave him a bright smile.

"Just checking," Rodney said. "I asked if she could help get appointments to buy you some clothes. She set up appointments for the both of us. She said that either she or her son Frederec would come with us to help."

Yvonne gave a happy clap.

"Perfect?" He raised his eyebrows. She leaned over and kissed him.

"Thank you," she said.

He smiled.

"Can I ask you a question?" Yvonne asked.

"Anything," Rodney asked.

"It's kind of a . . ."

"Just ask."

"Was the spider in the car next to your car? You know — in the parking lot of the 7-11?"

Rodney became very still. His eyes reviewed her face.

"The car was a US Government Fleet car," Rodney said. "There was a guy who was definitely some kind of cop watching us and the car. He wasn't wearing Kevlar, but he had a Glock 22 or 23 in a side holster like the Marshals carry."

"Smelled like him." Yvonne gave a little shiver. "I made myself not look."

"The windows of the car were dark-tinted and looked like they were bulletproof," Rodney said. "The way it was rocking and not moving, I'd say it was an armored car."

"You noticed all of that," Yvonne said.

Rodney nodded.

"Was he in there?" Yvonne asked.

"I honestly don't know," Rodney said. "If he was, it wasn't because I asked for him to be there."

"Then who?"

"Seth, maybe," Rodney said. "Your handsome Homeland Security agent, Senator Hargreaves . . ."

"You know some important people now," Yvonne said.

"I met most of them through you," Rodney smiled. "What if the spider was there in that car?"

"Well . . ." Yvonne sighed. "It didn't seem like he could get out."

"I don't think he can get out," Rodney said. "He's in witness protection. That's kind of like being in prison. He can't go where he wants to, can't see who he wants to; he has to work a real job..."

"What about his family?" Yvonne looked horrified. "That lovely girl I met today?"

"He traded everything for not going to prison," Rodney said.

"Everything?"

"All his money, his secrets, everything," Rodney said.

"I don't believe it," Yvonne said.

"Everything," Rodney said. "Bumpy said that his daughters just found out. They're quite distressed. The youngest was in college. She'll have to drop out. Seth's fiancée lost her job. So did her older sister."

"And he traded it all just to not have to go to prison?"

Rodney looked away from Yvonne.

"He traded it all for me," Yvonne whispered. "Then why am I here? Why didn't I have to go with him?"

"Because of your book," Rodney said. "Because you are not without friends. But mostly because the world is filled with decent people who used this opportunity to free you."

"So, I go free," Yvonne said.

"And he's locked up like you were," Rodney said.

"I'm sorry about his family, especially his children," Yvonne said.

"He's a monster," Rodney said. "Only an evil man would do such a thing to his family. But look at what he did to you. To us."

"Why do you think he was there in the parking lot?" Yvonne asked.

"I don't know," Rodney said.

"Any guesses?"

"To show him what he lost," Rodney said.

"Me?"

"Everything he stole was returned to where it belonged," Rodney said. "There's some justice in that."

Yvonne smiled and leaned back against her seat.

"What?"

"He never stole my heart."

Rodney smiled.

"That's what he really wanted," Yvonne said. "But he never could have it."

Rodney couldn't think of anything to say. He just smiled.

"Do I really get all new clothes?" Yvonne asked.

"Do you have any clothes?"

"No," Yvonne said. "But I really get all new clothes?"

"We'll have fun," Rodney said. "Do you want to go to all these boring old museums with me?"

"I'm never bored when I'm with you," Yvonne said.

Rodney smiled. Yvonne shut her eyes.

"Are you going to sleep?" Rodney asked.

"If I sleep, we'll get there sooner," Yvonne said.

Smiling at her logic, he closed his eyes. Yvonne opened her eyes to look at him again. He opened his eyes and reached for her hand. For a moment, their eyes held. She smiled, and he kissed her hand.

"Sleep?" he asked.

"Sleep."

~~~~~~~~~

Saturday morning — 5:15 a.m.
Denver, Colorado

Heather heard a sound and sat up in bed. She'd been sleeping with one ear open for Blane to come home. But this wasn't Blane.

After the ceremony, she'd taken Mack and Tink home. While Mack was used to sleeping at the Castle, Tink needed her medication and some real rest. Heather had to be super good and try to keep her on her schedule if they were going to be her forever family. So, they came home, had a snack, and went to bed.

Heather checked the crib in their room. Mack was sound

asleep, with his head on his favorite stuffed giraffe and his thumb was just to the side of his mouth. She put her hand on him to see if he was warm or sick. He seemed fine. She went out of her bedroom and into the hall.

She heard a noise from the room across the hall where Tink was sleeping. Having had a nosy, invasive mother, Heather debated with herself as to whether she should look in. She went back into her room to get her phone. Normally, she would just call Blane. They lived their life together and made every decision together. But tonight, Blane was with Honey, and Honey really needed him.

Which one of her girls was awake? Tanesha had left right before they did because she had to study. Jill was becoming a continent on her own. She was surely asleep. She heard the noise again. Unable to stop herself, she jogged across the hall and opened the door.

"Tink?" Heather leaned in through the door.

The girl was lying diagonally across the queen-sized bed. Her body was jerking, and she was making a low moaning noise. Her fist jerked as if she were trying to hit someone.

Heather blinked. She'd seen this before. She crept out of the bedroom.

In the hallway, she dialed Sandy and waited impatiently while the phone rang.

"Yeah," Charlie said into the phone.

"Jeez, Charlie, were you raised in a barn?" Sandy asked in the background.

"Yes," Charlie laughed. "Uh, Sandy's phone. This is Charles Delgado-Norsen. How's that?"

Sandy's voice was muffled.

"Can I talk to Sandy?" Heather asked.

"Who may I say is calling?" Charlie asked.

"You know who this is," Heather said. "It's kind of an emergency. And when did you become a Norsen?"

"I thought that would sound super fancy," Charlie laughed. He moved away from the phone and said, "It's for you."

"It's my phone," Sandy said. "Of course, it's for me. Sorry about that."

"Sandy, I need some help," Heather said.

"Just a second," Sandy said. "Okay, I locked myself in the bathroom."

"Tink's doing that thing that you used to do," Heather whispered. "They told us she had seizures, but that's not a seizure."

"It's a nightmare?" Sandy asked.

"Looks like those things you used to have," Heather said. "Night terrors."

"Poor thing," Sandy said. "Should I come over?"

Someone pounded on the bathroom door. A deeper voice, probably Aden, said something to the person pounding on the door.

"The natives are full of sugar and excited," Sandy said. "The outside party is just getting going, and Delphie wants them in the clothes she got for them. I hate to say it, but they actually look . . . civilized."

Sandy chuckled, and Heather smiled.

"I hate to ask . . . I know you have . . . but Blane, he's . . ."

"Give me five minutes," Sandy said.

The phone went dead. Heather went back to the doorway of the other room. She remembered, from Sandy's night terrors that, if she didn't do it exactly the right way, anything she said or did would get integrated into Tink's night terror. At this moment, she couldn't remember what the heck she was supposed to do. Her phone buzzed. She looked down to see that Blane was calling.

"How's Honey?" Heather tried to be breezy so he wouldn't know how worried she was.

"She's just starting real labor," Blane said. "Sorry it's been so long. We've had a tough time deciding what to do."

"Why?" Heather asked.

"Because the midwife wants Honey to fight through natural delivery," Blane said. "The doctor wants to do a safe C-section. MJ isn't able to talk, and Honey, well . . . I'm always amazed with her ability to handle everything."

"Can she deliver naturally?" Heather asked.

"Steve thinks she can, and he's her nurse," Blane said. "Anyway, I called because I just had that . . . twinge that you needed me. Are you all right?"

"I think Tink's having night terrors," Heather said.

"Not a seizure?" Blane asked.

"They look like what Sandy has sometimes," Heather said. "I know I can't say her name or touch her, but I don't remember what I can do."

"I'm so sorry I'm not there to help," Blane said. "You must be worried sick. Should I come home?"

"No," Heather said. "Honey needs you. And if MJ can't talk, they both need you to be their voice. Sandy's coming over, so we'll figure something out."

"You always amaze me too," Blane said. "You're awfully generous."

Heather blushed at his words.

"We do things together," Heather said. "I think Honey deserves your undivided attention."

"Call me if you change your mind," Blane said. "I'll call as soon as I can. Love you."

And he was gone.

Heather paced around in the hallway until she saw Sandy coming up the stairs. Sandy hugged her and went into Tink's bedroom. She was just there a moment before she came back out.

"Night terrors?" Heather asked.

"Looks like night terrors to me," Sandy said. "Come on."

Sandy went into the room and around the bed near Tink's head. Anxious, Heather lingered near the door.

"Get over here," Sandy mouthed to Heather. "You're her mother. Be the Mom you are."

Heather smiled at Sandy, and Sandy grinned. Sandy pointed for Heather to sit down on the bed.

"Say her name," Sandy said. "We need to comfort her."

"Tink," Heather said in a soft, comforting voice. Sandy gestured her to say more. "You're safe. You're here with us. Tink."

The girl's night terrors seemed to get worse. Her mouth opened in a grimacing, silent scream. Heather looked up at Sandy in desperation.

"Tiffanie," Sandy said.

The girl stopped moaning. Sandy gestured for Heather to continue.

"Tiffanie, you're home now, safe and sound," Heather said in her most comforting voice. "Tiffanie. Remember tonight? You went to the party and sat next to Charlie."

"Pan," Sandy whispered.

"Pan," Heather said. "Tiffanie, you are loved. You are safe. Everything is fine."

"Keep going." Sandy left the room. Heather heard the bathtub going.

"Tiffanie. Remember your pretty dress and Charlie's . . . uh . . . Pan's reaction when he saw you?"

The girl seemed to smile.

"You are safe. No one can hurt you now," Heather said.

Tink rolled onto her back and opened her eyes. Heather gave her a moment before touching her arm.

"Tink?" Heather asked.

The girl threw herself into Heather's arms and sobbed.

"Keep talking," Sandy yelled from the bathroom.

"You're all right," Heather said. "You're safe. Everything's fine. Everything's fine."

Heather softly rubbed the girl's back.

"Sandy's making a bath for you," Heather said. "She gets night terrors. She says that baths are the best thing to help get you back to the present and relax you. Would you like...?"

Tink pulled back in horror.

"I...I...Did I blow it?" Tink asked. "Are you going to send me back?"

"No way," Heather said. "Not a chance."

"Will Sandy tell Pan?" Tink's eyes seemed luminous with horror.

"Sandy, are you going to tell Charlie about this?" Heather asked.

"Not a chance," Sandy said. "This is private, girl to girl. Now, come on — the bath's almost ready."

Heather helped Tink out of her nightdress and led her to the bathroom. Sandy helped her into the bath.

"Try to relax," Sandy said. "Just feel the warm water. We'll be right outside if you need anything."

"I'm sorry," Tink said. "I..."

"You have nothing to be sorry about." Heather gave Tink a little nod and pulled the bathroom door closed.

"Are you all right?" Sandy hugged Heather. They went into Heather's and Blane's bedroom to talk.

"I think so," Heather said. "Do you think these are Tink's seizures?"

"We'll have to wait and see," Sandy said. "I know they got a lot worse for me when I started liking boys."

"You think..." Heather pointed to the bathroom. "And Charlie?"

"Remember how bad they were for me when I started dating Aden?" Sandy smiled.

Heather gave a little clap of her hands.

"You don't feel bad that they might be happy, and you don't have a romantic boyfriend?" Sandy asked.

"You mean do I feel like my mom does?" Heather smiled.

Sandy nodded.

"No, I don't feel jealous," Heather said. "I feel excited for them. Plus, I have a really great life. I'm happy."

Sandy smiled at Heather.

"I passed the test," Heather said.

"You did," Sandy said.

"Heather!" Tink called from the bathroom.

Heather went to see.

"I saw the time," Tink said. "Can we go to the party? I mean even though I . . ."

"Sure," Heather said. "But you have to be in the bath for at least twenty minutes. I'll get Mack up in a bit. We'll go over after he's awake."

Heather closed the bathroom door, and Sandy applauded.

"You're a great mom, Heather," Sandy said.

"Who'd have thought?" Heather beamed.

~~~~~~~~~

Saturday morning — 5:15 a.m.

Tanesha slipped out from under Jeraine's arm and went into the bathroom. Her parents were on their way to Paris, and Jeraine had to work all day. The only thing she had to worry about was studying for *medical school.* She felt almost giddy. The feeling evaporated when she saw the bald spot where the rapist had pulled out a clump of her hair. She made a sour face in the mirror, flushed the toilet, and went out into the bedroom.

Jeraine was sitting on the edge of the bed.

"I thought you were sleeping in?" she asked. Her speech slurred through the wire on her jaw.

"I wanted to talk to you first," he said.

"I've got to study," she said.

"I know," he said. "I wanted to talk to you before you started work, and I started work, and . . ."

"You can talk," she said. She pointed to the closet to indicate that she would get dressed.

His eyes followed her naked form to the closet.

"I write a lot of songs about love," Jeraine said. "A lot of songs about you and me and our love and ..."

She turned to look at him while she pulled on underwear.

"I was moved by the service yesterday," he said.

"I noticed," she wiggled her eyebrows, and he smiled. "Last night was fun."

"Not just sex," he said. "I mean the sex was great, but ... Ah shit."

He shook his head and stalked to the bathroom. She sat down on the bed to pull on her boots. When he came out, she patted the bed. He sat down.

"What are you saying?" she asked.

"Last night, in the middle of everything, and when your Dad broke down ..." Jeraine said. "I ... just kinda understood something I didn't before."

Tanesha watched him search for words.

"Love, real love, like what you and I have, like what your parents have, my parents ..." Jeraine said. "It's sacred ... from God or whoever. By whoring around, all the women and drugs ... I make profane something godly ... like sullying a holy gift from God. I definitely took the gift, married you, but then I messed up and ..."

Tanesha reached for his hand. He held her hand close to his heart.

"Your Dad is a great man," Jeraine said.

"So's yours," Tanesha said.

"I want to be a great man," Jeraine said. "Worthy of the real gift of your love."

Tanesha smiled.

"That's it," Jeraine said. "That's all I wanted to say."

"What are you going to *do*?" Tanesha asked. "It's nice to *say* something. Anyone can *say* something. You have to *do* something, Jeraine!"

Jeraine gave her one of his "gotcha" smiles. She shook her head at him, and he laughed.

"I'm going to do my work here," Jeraine said. "I'm going to focus on my head therapy and my mind therapy, and I'm going to love you. We'll do medical school together because I'll take care of you, love you, while you study. I don't think I have to *do* a lot of things differently. I think I have to receive all that I've been given."

Tanesha smiled.

"See? I'm not as thick as you thought," Jeraine said.

Tanesha leaned forward, and he kissed her.

"I'm cutting my hair off and going natural," Tanesha said.

"That's your response?" Jeraine looked offended.

"No, that was a test," Tanesha said. "To see if you were sincere about loving me or just being your old, charming, psychopathic Mr. It."

"Did I pass?"

"Do you have some snide comment to make about my hair?" Tanesha asked.

Jeraine opened his mouth and then closed it. He shook his head.

"Then you passed."

She kissed him.

"I love you, Jer," she said. "I always have."

"I love you, Miss T," Jeraine said. "Did you hear your Mom and mine at the party? They said I couldn't wait for you to be born."

"I'd be your best friend," Tanesha smiled.

"My mom said that when I learned you were a girl, I told her I was going to marry you," Jeraine said. "I told her you would be the best thing that ever happened to me, and you are."

She smiled at him.

"I'll make breakfast," Jeraine said. "The extra bedroom is all set up for you to study. The guys will be here in an hour for breakfast, but you can just ignore us."

She smiled.

"What?" he asked.

"I feel like I'm just starting *my* life," Tanesha said. "My parents are safe and together. You're off drugs, not whoring around, not in jail, and even happy! With me!"

She smiled.

"I'm glad we're still together," he said.

"Me, too," she said. Her eyes glanced at the clock. "Is that the time? Oh, goodness — I have so much to do!"

Without another word, she hopped up and jogged to the second bedroom. A few minutes later, he tapped on the door with her cup of tea. She opened the door, grabbed the mug, and closed the door in his face. Smiling, he went to shower.

CHAPTER TWO HUNDRED & TWENTY-THREE

HARVEST

Saturday morning—10:03 a.m.

Jill bit the cuticle on her right thumb and paced in front of her apartment door. Five steps to the window; turn; five steps to the wall. Back and forth, she paced.

Katy was outside with the Castle family at Yvonne'S and Rodney's big party. She had peeked out the bathroom balcony to see that everyone from Lipson Construction seemed to be at the party. Yvonne and Rodney had been smart to head out early, or they would still be here.

Jacob had stopped by the party early before heading into work. He, Aden, and their CFO, Tres Sierra, had planned to spend the day working on summer's-end financials. The Site Managers were meeting around noon. The party would probably go until the Site Managers left.

Jill had to be upstairs.

Jill needed her rest.

Jill couldn't go to the party because she was on bed rest.

She was so exhausted after the emotional ceremony that she hadn't argued about coming up here or missing a party. She was doing the hard work of building babies and needed her rest.

That was before Honey needed her.

She didn't know how she knew Honey needed her. She just did. She'd gained this "ability" when she became pregnant with her twins. And, for the record, the whole psychic thing sucked. Jill was at the place where she couldn't wait to have two gloriously healthy boys, to be able to see her feet again, and to be rid forever of this psychic curse.

There was a tap on her apartment door. Jill stopped pacing, thought for a moment, and then opened the door. MJ was standing on the top landing of the stairwell. Unable to speak under stress due to his traumatic brain injury, he held out a sheet of paper with a message in Blane's handwriting.

Blane asked me to come to get you. Honey needs help.

"H-h-h-on-n . . ." MJ looked so desperate that Jill hugged him.

"You get the water," Jill said. "It's too heavy for me to carry."

MJ gestured that he would carry Jill.

"My brother's right behind you." Jill pointed. Mike was standing on the landing of the stairs. "If you carry the water, Mike can carry me."

"A-a-a-n-n-n-y-y . . ."

"No," Jill said. "I don't need anything else. Mike will be there to help, and so will Steve. If we need more help, then we'll call my Mom."

"Sh-sh-she's . . ."

"Really?" Jill curled her lip. "She's waiting with Sam and Delphie?"

"G-gr-r-a-an-n-n . . ."

"She's there to see the birth of her grandchild?" Jill groaned. "But Honey's not her daughter."

"I-i-s-s-s n-n-n . . ."

"She's adopted Honey, too?" Jill asked. "Oh God, I hope that doesn't mean she'll be around for . . ."

Jill nodded behind MJ.

"Hi, Mom," Jill said.

"I heard that," Anjelika said. "And you'd better believe I will be there. Your father, too."

MJ gave Jill a knowing look, and Jill scowled.

"Now be very careful, Mikhail," Anjelika started.

"*Mom!*" Jill groaned.

Anjelika laughed.

"You have to come down for me to come up," Mike said.

Jill started toward the stairwell.

"Not you," Mike said.

"You can't take the stairs!" Anjelika gasped.

"The soldier," Mike said. "MJ, come down."

MJ turned in place and jogged down the stairwell. Mike came up and picked up Jill. He gave an exaggerated groan when she was in his arms.

"Jeez, are you gaining weight?" Mike asked.

Jill double-tapped the top of his head, and he laughed.

"Come along," Mike said. "We're on baby duty."

Mike carried Jill down the stairs, through the main kitchen, where the caterers were working on food for the party, and up the stairs on the other side. They passed Delphie's apartment and the one Mike shared with Valerie, before coming to the entrance to what Valerie had dubbed "The Birthing Zone."

"You ready?" Mike asked in a low tone.

Jill gave a quick nod.

"You'll let me know if it's too much?" Mike asked in the same low tone.

Jill nodded, and he pushed the door open. They walked through a short hallway and into the office space. In the time since Valerie had her baby, the space had gone from a 1950s doctor's office to a beautifully restored, clean, state-of-the-art medical office.

Mike set Jill down. MJ pointed to a stack of clean scrubs. Jill, Mike, and Anjelika dressed in scrubs as well. They followed MJ to the room where Honey was in labor. Honey was connected to a heart-rate monitor for herself and the baby. Steve, Honey's nurse and Jill's brother, was moving an ultrasound wand around so they could see the baby on the screen. Camille, the midwife, was standing between Honey's knees. Colin Hargreaves was standing at her head. Blane was moving around Honey to twist an acupuncture needle on her chest and remove one from her wrist. He looked up and smiled when they came in.

Jill leaned down to kiss Honey's cheek.

"How are you doing?" Jill asked.

"Good." Honey smiled.

"We're really at our last chance for natural delivery," Blane said.

"I'm sorry but I don't understand why you're pushing for a natural birth." Jill smiled at her little pun and took Honey's hand. "I'll probably have a C-section."

"Because she's in a wheelchair," Steve said. "C-sections are harder to heal for people in a wheelchair, and she'll have an infant to care for. She'd have to be admitted for at least a day, maybe two, just to get a head start on the healing."

"I don't want to go to the hospital," Honey grunted. "I've spent enough time there."

Jill nodded.

"How can we help?" Anjelika asked.

"Honey's getting tired," Blane said. He pointed toward the screen. "So is the baby. We thought you might be able to give them a little healing boost."

"Sure," Jill said.

Jill put her hands on Honey's belly and looked up at the monitor. The baby stirred. She felt something behind her as Colin set a chair behind her. Jill sat down. Mike stood across from her and put his hands between hers. Anjelika went to Honey's head and put her hands on her head. Steve put his hand on her shoulder.

"Ooh, I feel warm!" Honey said, before gasping. A contraction ripped through her.

"We're moving now," Camilla, the midwife, said. "Honey, can you wait for one . . .?"

Honey jerked up with the force of her contraction.

"This is our shot," Camilla said. "You do this now, or we'll get the doctor. *Si*?"

"Got it," Honey said.

"Blane?" Camilla said.

Blane removed a needle from her hand and placed a new needle in her head.

"Ready," Blane said.

"Go, Honey," Camilla said. "Push, push, push, push . . ."

Honey groaned.

"Help her!" Camilla pointed MJ to Honey's head. She nudged Jill with her shoulder. "Do more now."

Colin touched Jill's shoulder. Jill looked back at him to see that he was holding the vase full of salt-water she'd prepared. She lifted her left hand to touch the vase.

"Mike!" Jill said.

Mike looked up, saw the vase, and lifted his right hand from Honey's belly to hold the vase.

"Mom!" Mike said.

Anjelika leaned over to touch the glass.

"Steve," Anjelika said.

Steve set down the ultrasound wand and reached to touch the water. A connection seemed to be made the moment Steve touched the vase. Colin picked up the ultrasound wand so that they could see the baby again. Honey bore down, and the baby moved.

"Good," Camilla said. "Go, Honey, go! You can do this. Go!"

Closing her eyes to concentrate, Jill heard her own sons cheering for Honey and the baby they knew to be a girl. When she opened her eyes, the baby had crowned.

"One more time!" Camilla said.

Margaret Celia Scully was born.

~~~~~~~~~

Saturday afternoon — 2:03 p.m.

Humming to herself, Valerie cleaned the main Castle kitchen. Tomorrow was Delphie's annual Harvest Day. Valerie was in charge of making sure there was room in the refrigerator and kitchen to store everything they harvested.

Harvest Day was Valerie's favorite day of the year. She had been here at the Castle for every Harvest Day. Even when she wasn't getting along with Mike, she'd come home to help dig out a potato or whatever. Valerie loved the glorious experience of finding one treasure after another. Now that she was home, she loved the idea that the tiniest seed could multiply into a glorious vine that created a bounty of acorn squash or pumpkins or watermelon.

When Celia had purchased this house, Delphie's first task was to remove the asphalt. Valerie smiled remembering how Delphie had taken a sledgehammer to the black mess. When Delphie went to work the next day, Celia had paid a team from Lipson Construction to take out the asphalt. Delphie had come home, and the asphalt was gone. No one ever told her how the asphalt disappeared. But then, she'd never asked.

Valerie heard a sound and looked down. She was carrying Jackie next to her heart. Claire Martins had modified a Moby sling into a short-sleeved top that crossed over in the front to form a kind of baby sling. Claire showed Valerie how she could set Jackie on one side, with the fabric crossing from the other side. The third piece of fabric held Jackie tight in place. Claire had modified the wrap with a piece of lace to cover Jackie's face if they were assaulted by the paparazzi.

Valerie was wearing a pair of Mike's old overalls to make doubly sure that Jackie wouldn't fall out. Today was her first day trying this outfit, and, so far, it had worked really well. Valerie made a soothing sound to Jackie and kissed her face. Jackie went back to sleep.

Valerie grabbed the full trash bag from the can and went out the back door. From the deck, she could see Sandy's kids helping to clean up from Yvonne and Rodney's celebration. She was always amazed at the way Sandy and Aden could get these kids to do things. Sandy said it was a mixture of bribery and threat, but Valerie thought they were just nice kids.

"I can take that," Nash said. He held out his hand for the trash bag.

"Great," Valerie gave him the trash bag. "Thanks, Nash."

Nash blushed, nodded, and trotted off. He picked up a bag of trash near the end of the fence and went out into the alley. Taking in the warm day, Valerie stretched her arms and neck before returning to the kitchen. She had her head in the refrigerator when Nash burst in the backdoor.

"Mrs. Valerie! Mrs. Valerie!" Nash yelled.

Valerie stood up quickly. Nash's yell and Valerie's sudden movement woke Jackie. She gave a rousing wail. Valerie scowled at Nash and soothed Jackie back to sleep.

"Sorry," Nash said. "I didn't ..."

"I know," Valerie said. "What happened?"

"When I went out into the alley, there was a photographer on a ladder just behind the police video camera," Nash's voice came in one excited rush. "I threw out the trash and called the police. They must have been close because — bam! They were right there."

"Great," Valerie smiled. "Thanks."

"But ..." Nash's face clouded.

"What happened?"

"The photographer saw me and yelled that he'd already sent the photos off ..." Nash swallowed hard. "And Delphie told me to come in and tell you immediately. And Dad, well, he was really mad. He got Mike and Charlie, and they went around making sure there aren't more photographers back there. And ..."

"What did the photographers say?" Valerie asked.

"Now, I didn't say this," Nash said. "I'd never say this to anyone, but ..."

"The photographers are pigs," Valerie said. "What did he say?"

"He said he'd already sent in photos of . . . um . . ."

Valerie waited.

"That pig, Valerie Lipson," Nash said. "He made a rude gesture like you'd gotten really, really fat. They were putting him in the police car when he yelled that you should be on *The Biggest Loser*."

"He didn't get a photo of Jackie?" Valerie asked.

"You can't see her in the overalls," Nash said. "I mean, I knew she was there. Sandy wears Rachel like that sometimes, and, really, where *else* would Jackie be? But . . ."

"What?" Valerie asked.

"You look really fat in that outfit," Nash said.

Valerie looked down at Mike's old overalls.

"I know that's not a nice thing to say," Nash said. "Dad always says never tell a woman she's fat, and Sissy has an eating disorder, so we don't talk about it in our family, but . . . um . . ."

"I look pretty fat," Valerie said. "So what?"

"Delphie said you should call your publicist," Nash said.

"Why?"

"Something about the upcoming premiere and your next movie part?" Nash shrugged.

At that moment, Valerie's cell phone rang.

"That's probably them." Nash gave her a guilty look, and sped out the back door.

"Hello?" Valerie answered her phone.

"Have you gained five hundred pounds?" Jennifer, her publicist, asked.

"No, I . . ."

Her phone beeped with her agent.

"Hang on, Jen." Valerie clicked over.

"Are you insane?" her agent yelled. "Do you ever want to make another movie?"

As her agent ranted, Valerie looked up at the ceiling. Looking down, she saw Jackie and knew what to do.

"Listen," Valerie interrupted her agent. "At least they didn't get a shot of Jackie."

"What do you mean?" he asked.

"I'm carrying her under the overalls," she said.

"You are?"

"Of course," Valerie said. "And that's how you're going to spin this. Anyone who calls. You tell them I carry my newborn baby girl next to my heart in a hug hold, like I should."

"Good thinking," he said.

"And furthermore," Valerie said, "I'm going to bring her to the premiere."

"What? Are you insane?"

"No," Valerie said. "You're going to make it happen."

"But..." he started.

"Women bring their kids to European Parliament meetings. Premieres are a part of my work," Valerie said. "Why can't I bring her there?"

"Good point," he said. "I'll make some calls."

"Jen's on the other line," Valerie said. "I'm going to tell her the same thing."

"Go ahead," he said. "My phone's already ringing."

When he hung up, Valerie smiled. She was going to turn this thing around. If they were going to watch her, stalk her, she was going to use that attention to help other mothers.

Valerie kissed Jackie. Jackie should be able to bring her children to work. Her workplaces should support families. Her own mother had made this a reality at Lipson Construction. Valerie was going to do her part to help make it a reality for Jackie and the rest of the world.

Nodding to herself, she clicked over to talk to Jen.

~~~~~~~~~

Saturday night — 7:03 p.m.

Honey opened her eyes. Not sure where she was, she pushed her way to sitting.

"How are you?" MJ asked. He was sitting in an armchair by the bed. He looked like he'd been reading a book.

"Where are we?" Honey asked.

"Our new bedroom," MJ smiled.

"It's very posh," Honey said. "Where's . . ."

MJ lifted his arms to show Maggie sleeping on his lap between his knees.

"The LC's dad told me about this position," MJ said. "He said it was the only way they could get their twins to sleep. She's been out for a while. Do you want to try to feed her?"

"I didn't think I could breast feed, because of all the meds I'm on," Honey said.

"You can't," MJ said.

"Did you decide which formula to give the baby without me?" Honey's voice rose with indignation.

"No," MJ shook his head. "We didn't decide. So, I figured we'd breastfeed."

"But I can't breastfeed," Honey said.

"Sandy and Valerie filled up our freezer with extra breast milk," MJ said. "They both brought some by this evening after dinner."

"They did?" Honey blinked back her tears of gratitude. "That's . . . I mean . . ."

"Sandy said not to fuss about it," MJ said. "You're family, and they wanted to help our Maggie have her best start in life. Plus, Valerie said they'll meet you tonight at 2:30 a.m. for a moonlight feeding."

"Wow," Honey said.

"I'm a little jealous." MJ smiled.

"How long have I been asleep?" Honey looked around.

"Since right after we got back from the hospital," MJ said. "I wanted you to sleep because having a baby is a big deal."

"Are you saying the baby's a big deal because you have to go back to work?" Honey asked.

"No," MJ said. "I'm off for at least six weeks. I can stay off for up to six months, but I have to tell the LC midway if we need more time. They aren't going to replace me — or they're hoping not to. Anyway, she said we have a lot of work to do from Yvonne's notebooks. We'll be in town for a while. I'd just be going back and forth to the Federal Center or Buckley."

Honey smiled, and he returned her smile.

"How has Maggie been?" Honey asked.

"I think she misses you." MJ picked up the sleeping infant and laid her in Honey's lap. "I'll get a bottle."

Honey looked down at the tiny baby in her lap. The only babies she had been around were the ones in the family. Mack was big when he was born. He had clear white skin, bright blue eyes, a round face, and black hair. Everyone thought he was gorgeous. Jackie had a kind of European air to her. She had Mike's thick, dark hair and Valerie's darker skin tone. Her eyes had already started to darken to hazel. In the last month or so, Rachel had just started to look like a regular baby. Rachel might still not have any hair, but she had the prettiest smile. Of course, Honey had seen her little sisters, but she never really looked at them like she had with Mack or Jackie. She'd never kangarooed a baby before Rachel.

Little Maggie didn't look like any of them. She was small, like Rachel. She had a tiny tuft of reddish hair. Her skin was almost translucent white. She became red all over when she cried or squirmed.

Honey felt her heart swell with love.

Maggie was perfect.

CHAPTER TWO HUNDRED & TWENTY-FOUR

KISS

Monday morning — 5:40 a.m.

After seeing Sam off, Delphie knelt at her altar. Yesterday's sun and activity had put a glorious cap on what had been a wonderful weekend. Delphie lit a candle in front of her porcelain statue of Quan Yin, the Buddhist Goddess of Compassion.

The chapel was consecrated with love. Yvonne and Rodney's union had been reblessed. At dinner last night, Tanesha had shared a photo of her parents standing in front of the Eiffel Tower. They looked happy and in love.

Saturday marked the arrival of tiny Margaret. Delphie smiled and lit a candle to the Hindu God Ganesha. "Maggie," as her parents called her, might have been small, but she surely knew how to get what she wanted with her robust cries and charming smiles. While she had none of Jackie's innate Old World elegance, she had charmed everyone completely.

And yesterday's Harvest Day had been amazing. She lit the votive in front of the replica of a statue of Demeter, the God of the Harvest. Alex and Max had arrived early to help Delphie with her hives. They'd harvested more than a hundred pounds of honey. Members of Alex's team had spun and bottled everything, leaving Delphie with a closet full of honey bears. Sandy's kids and their friends had harvested the fruit from the trees. While the little kids and adults picked the vegetables, Mike, Jacob, and MJ made quick work of chopping the plants for the compost pile, turning the beds, and putting the garden to rest.

And the tomatoes! On tomato duty, Valerie had already made

two pots of tomato sauce. She enlisted Jill's help in juicing. Sitting at the kitchen table, Jill kept the juicer running late into the night. They had enough tomato juice and tomato sauce to last most of the winter.

She knew that she was responsible for the creation of this bounty. She had planted every seed, made sure it was watered, enlisted help to pull every weed, made sure the soil was ready, turned the compost, and dug the holes. Still, she knew in her very soul the bounty of love and babies and honey and vegetables were a gift from the benevolence of something much greater than herself.

Humbled, she lit a stick of incense at the feet of the statue of Saint Mary and said her thanks.

~~~~~~~~~~

Monday afternoon — 2:45 p.m.

Charlie waited for Tink outside the front entrance of East High School. They hadn't agreed that he would meet her after school, but he thought she might like it. After yesterday, she was definitely his girlfriend. Or, at least, *he* thought she was his girlfriend. Anyway, he knew they were coming this way because Jake was picking them up for martial-arts practice.

He glanced at his watch. He had only a few minutes before basketball practice, so he hoped she showed up soon. His basketball coach made him run laps if he was late. He didn't care about running laps. He just hated the look on the team captain's face when Charlie screwed up. Charlie didn't like that guy. Charlie felt stupid for even thinking it, but he didn't like the way the team captain talked about girls or moms or women teachers. The team captain didn't like him because Charlie was a better basketball player than he was. So Charlie figured they were even.

He saw Sissy and Tink near the door and waved. Sissy waved back. They waited until their friend Wade — *no Wanda* — came out before walking toward him. Sissy had given Charlie an entire

lecture on Wanda, so he should have known all about the guy —
no girl — but he hadn't been listening. He didn't really care if
Wade was Wanda or whatever. He was just glad Wade — *no
Wanda* — had nice friends and a family who supported him. Kids
like Wanda didn't do very well on the streets. When they got
close, he noticed that Wanda was actually starting to look like a
girl. As if he — no, she — could read his mind, she gave Charlie a
pretty smile.

Tink ran up and kissed him on the lips. He kissed her back.

For a breathless moment, nothing else mattered. Then sound
returned. Sissy was squawking about something. Wanda was
giggling.

Sissy cleared her throat and acted offended, but she smiled.
Sissy liked it that he was dating Tink.

"I have basketball," Charlie said.

"I have to go to counseling," Tink said. "Heather's going with
me today."

"How come?" Charlie asked.

Tink shrugged.

"She wants to help," Sissy said. "Heather is going to be Tink's
forever Mom, and that's what Mom's do."

"How would you know?" Charlie asked.

"That's what Sandy does," Sissy said.

"But she..."

Charlie started to remind Sissy that Sandy was their sister, but
Tink waved to someone, and he got distracted. Auntie Heather
waved back. He thought it was a little weird that his Auntie was
going to be his girlfriend's forever Mom. But he didn't say
anything. He didn't want to jinx it, and he really liked Auntie
Heather. He waved to her, too. Tink turned and kissed him again
before running to Heather's car. He looked up to see the
basketball-team captain sneering at him. The boy walked into
Charlie's shoulder as he passed.

"Hey!" Sissy said.

The team captain gave her a cruel look and continued into the school.

"I don't like that guy," Sissy said.

"Yeah?" Charlie raised his eyebrow to show her he felt the same way. "I'd better go."

He realized he hadn't said anything to Wade — no, Wanda. So, he smiled at her.

"You look nice today," Charlie said.

He groaned internally. Now he sounded like Nash. But Wanda smiled and looked less depressed, so that was worth it. Out of the corner of his eye, he saw Jake pull up. Sissy and Wanda got into his SUV.

Charlie went into the gym. His teammate threw him the ball, and they began warming up. Charlie was all business when it came to basketball. He and the other guy going to online school always warmed up together. They worked out for a while before the team captain and his crew joined them.

"D'you hear On-Line here is dating that slut?" the team captain asked.

"I saw him wid his tongue down da slut's throat," another boy said.

The idiots laughed. Charlie kept working the drill.

"Don' wanna date that girl," the team captain said.

"Seriously, man," a different boy said. "That girl's done everybody."

"Good to know you're virgins," Charlie said. "Are you all virgins or just our team captain here?"

"Ooooh," the crew of idiots said, while they laughed.

"Harsh On-Line, harsh," the team captain said. "I'd worry about what you say if I didn't know you can't read."

The crew of idiots laughed.

"Nah, dog, seriously," one of the boys said. "You don' wanna date that girl."

"Yeah?" Charlie looked at the boy. "Why?"

"'Cuz she don' nasty," the boy laughed. "Everybody knows."

"You mean like everyone knows you're a virgin?" Charlie asked.

"I ain't no virgin," the boy said. "Here — I can prove it."

The team captain and his boys stopped working out. A look passed between them. The team captain sneered at Charlie before nodding his head. The boy got out his fancy cell phone.

"Whaz your number?" the boy asked.

Not thinking much about it, Charlie rattled off the only cell phone number he knew by heart—Nash's cell phone.

"Der," the boy said. "You watch dat and see if you wanna date dat slut. We're doin' you a favor, dog."

"Yeah, a favor," one of the other boys said.

"Hey!" Their basketball coach looked up from his meeting. "What the hell is going on?"

"Coach, we're trying to help On-Line here," the team captain said.

"Why don't you help yourself to laps?" the Coach asked. "But only if you girls are done talking."

"Yes, Coach," the boys said.

Charlie followed the other boys out the door to the track.

~~~~~~~~~

Monday afternoon — 3:12 p.m.

Nash looked up from his book when his cell phone buzzed. He and Teddy were making quick work of their homework before martial-arts class. Mr. Colin had been on them about finishing their homework and getting good grades.

"Ninjas get good grades," Mr. Colin always said.

Nash and Teddy were on track to becoming ninjas, except for the fact that they didn't always get good grades. Teddy was living at his Auntie Alex's house this week, so Nash just went there after school. Nash's cell phone buzzed again.

"Shouldn't you get that?" Teddy asked.

"Nah, it's just Charlie," Nash said. "He can't remember anyone's number but mine."

"Why does he remember yours?" Teddy asked.

"It's the same number as his drug dealer's." Nash shook his head at Charlie's stupidity. "Different area code."

"Charlie is never going to be a ninja," Teddy said.

"You got that right," Nash said. "You done?"

Teddy nodded.

"I have one more problem set," Nash said. The cell phone buzzed again. "Can you make it stop buzzing?"

"Sure." Teddy picked up the cell phone. Teddy pressed the button, and a video started to play. "What the hell?"

"What is it?" Nash asked.

"It's a video." Teddy leaned over to show Nash. "A nasty video."

"That's Tink," Nash said.

"Oh, my God." Teddy dropped the phone on the table. "That's horrible."

"We have to figure out what to do." Transfixed by the violence, Nash stared at the phone.

"Awful," Teddy said. "Stop watching."

"I have to figure out what to do with it," Nash said. "These guys don't even care that their faces are on camera."

"Awful." Teddy put his hands over his ears to block out the girl's screams.

"Why the hell aren't you doing your homework?" Teddy's guardian, Captain Andrew "Trece" Rodriguez, said as he came into the room. A bodybuilder, the man took up all of the empty space in the small room.

"I finished, sir," Teddy said. He didn't uncover his ears.

"What is that?" Andy took the phone out of Nash's hand. Nash's head dropped to the table. "What are you watching?"

"It's not ours," Teddy said. "I swear. It's not ours."

"Where did you get this?" Andy asked. "Do you know what they're doing to this poor girl?"

Nash got up from his seat and ran to the bathroom. He threw up. For good measure, he threw up again. He stuck his entire head under the sink's cold-water tap to wash the images from his brain.

"Where the hell did you get this?" Andy filled the door to the bathroom.

"Someone sent it to me," Nash said.

"Did you ask them to send it to you?" Andy asked.

"No," Nash said.

"How did it get on your phone?"

"Someone sent it to me," Nash repeated.

Andy gave Nash a horrifying look. Nash's entire body shook. He turned around and threw up.

"Why would someone send *this* to *you*?" Andy asked.

"I don't know," Nash said. "I don't know. You have to believe me. I don't have any idea. I like Tink. I think she's pretty, and she's my brother Charlie's girlfriend, and Sissy's best friend, and . . . I would never . . . I have a sister!"

"Oh, my God! Noelle!" Teddy pushed Andy aside to throw up in the sink.

"What happened?" Colin Hargreaves asked Andy.

While Teddy was throwing up, Colin and Andy had a quiet, grown-up talk. Colin came into the small bathroom. He hugged Nash and Teddy. With his face mashed against Colin's stomach, Nash started to cry. Nash's tears brought Teddy's tears. The boys cried for a while. When they stopped, Colin let them go. Teddy hugged Nash.

"You will never speak to anyone about what you saw on that video," Colin said.

"Unless it's the police," Andy said from the doorway. "I mean, you can talk to us about it, of course, but . . . Ah shit — you know what I mean."

"He's trying to say that we're here for you," Colin said. "For anything, any time. We're happy to talk to you about this."

Nash and Teddy nodded.

"What are we going to do?" Nash asked.

"It's done," Andy said.

"You two are going to practice," Colin said.

"What about my phone?" Nash asked.

"We have to keep your phone for a while," Colin said. "You won't need it in class."

"But . . ." Nash started.

"I will personally replace your phone if anything happens to it," Colin said. "Do you get a lot of calls?"

Nash shook his head, "No."

"Then you won't miss it," Colin said.

"But Sandy . . ."

"I'll speak with your mom while you train," Andy said. "You'll have a phone by the end of practice. It probably won't be as cool as this, but it will be a ninja phone."

"A ninja phone!" Nash stood up a little straighter.

"Do I get one. too?" Teddy asked.

"Of course." Andy grinned. "Go train."

There was a noise upstairs.

"The girls are here," Colin said. "You are not to say a word to them. Got it?"

Nash and Teddy nodded in unison.

"Great!" Colin smiled. "Let's get to work. Jake's coming to teach you some jujitsu techniques. I think you'll get a lot out of them."

Teddy went down the hallway. Nash watched Mr. Colin and Andy share information in a long look. Not wanting to know, Nash jogged to catch up with Teddy.

"Teddy!" Noelle said. "Are you feeling all right? You look a little sick."

Teddy hugged Noelle tight. Feeling a little lost, Nash stood next to them.

"Nash?" Jacob touched Nash's shoulder. Nash threw himself at the man. Jacob held him tight.

"You did exactly the right thing, Nash," Jacob said in a low tone. "You have to be strong now. Charlie, too. But real ninjas work to make everything right."

Nash had to bite his lip to keep from crying again.

"Let's get started," Colin said. "Girls over here ,and . . ."

Jacob patted Nash's back and went to the front of the room. Nash waited for Teddy, and they went to the boys' side of the room. He saw the adults talk in low voices. Mr. Jacob took over the class, and Colin left the room. When Colin came back, he gave Nash a nod.

Mr. Colin had taken care of it.

Nash was terrified.

~~~~~~~~

Monday afternoon — 4:52 p.m.

Charlie knew something was going on.

He just didn't know what.

About an hour into practice, a uniformed police officer came into the gym. He tried to look natural, but Charlie could tell that he was watching the practice. The coach went over to talk to the officer. When the Coach looked up, he ordered the hardest set of workouts Charlie had ever done.

They ran suicides back and forth between the lines, touching every line on the court. After that, they had to bounce the ball against the walls for two full minutes and then run the lines again. They kept at the brutal drills until Coach changed it up and they were doing push-ups and burpees and all kinds of other body-weight exercises. The other boys groaned and moaned, but Charlie focused on the workout and the growing number of police officers. He pumped his urge to run from the cops into the drills and churned out exercises twice as fast as the other boys on the team.

Two more officers came in when the team had finished running suicides. A couple more were standing in the hallway, talking to the principal. Charlie felt a tingle up the back of his neck. Whatever was going down was not going to be nice.

He was halfway through his last set of burpees when Aden came into the gym and did something weird. He came over to where Charlie was working out. He didn't say anything to Charlie. He just leaned against the wall.

Coach blew his whistle to call practice. Instead of getting everyone together, he walked out of the gym. The other boys noticed the police officers for the first time. Charlie walked to where Aden was standing.

"What's going on?" Charlie asked under his breath.

"They're here for you, son," Aden said.

"Me?" Charlie could not have been more surprised. "What did I do?"

He looked up to see the uniformed police officers coming toward him.

"I don't know," Aden said. "They're being very quiet about what they want. They're going to take you downtown."

Aden hugged Charlie.

"I love you, Charlie," Aden said. "Go with them. Tell them everything you know. I'll be waiting for you in the waiting area."

"But . . ." Charlie said.

A man put his hand on Charlie's shoulder. Charlie looked up into the face of one of Uncle Seth's good friends.

"Can you put your hands behind your back?" the man asked. He acted like he'd never seen Charlie before. "I don't want any trouble."

Charlie looked at Aden.

"Just go with it," Aden nodded.

Charlie saw something in Aden's face. Aden was angry, really angry.

"What . . .?" Charlie started.

Uncle Seth's friend jerked Charlie's hands back. While his basketball team gawked, the uniformed police officers closed in.

The officers made a big show of cuffing Charlie.

His basketball-team captain said something snide under his breath, and his buddies laughed. Aden shot the boy a dark look.

Two officers grabbed Charlie's upper arm, which caused him to bend over. Someone threw a towel over his head. He felt himself being marched out of the gym.

He felt more than knew that they were outside. He heard the click and whir of cameras. Reporters were shouting at the police. Charlie could see only the pavement. The policemen put him in the back of a police cruiser. With the siren blaring, the car sped off.

Charlie counted the streets. They turned onto Colfax and raced toward downtown. The cruiser made a sharp turn on Broadway and a quick right down Thirteenth. They were going to the downtown station.

Charlie's mind raced. He tried to figure out what he had done.

He'd gotten up early, made breakfast for the kids, and helped Sandy with Rachel. He was trying to be extra good because Aden told him he could take Tink to the movies or dinner or something fun next Friday. He was trying to repay Aden's gesture by doing what he was supposed to do, helping make sure the privilege wasn't taken away.

He really wanted to go out with Tink.

He'd done every school assignment. He'd made sure everything was up to date before he went to school. He'd hoped for more than a couple kisses from Tink, but the kisses were nice.

The cruiser pulled into the parking lot, and Charlie remembered that Uncle Seth didn't work for the Denver Police anymore.

Charlie's heart sank. A sense of doom came over him.

The cruiser jerked to a stop. He felt the door open.

"Get out," the driver said.

Charlie felt the door open. He got out of the back of the car. Two uniformed police officers appeared at his side and escorted him into the station.

Chapter Two Hundred & Twenty-Five

GET OUT OF HERE

Monday night — 6:52 p.m.

Charlie felt like he'd been alone in this room forever. Every once in a while, he thought he could hear whispers and felt like someone was watching him. But he couldn't figure out where they were. He wasn't in one of those rooms with a mirrored-glass wall, like they show on TV. He was just in a small room. By himself. All alone.

He'd just remembered that Yvonne and Rodney had been stuck in this station. He knew the whole thing was a set up to catch some bad guys. He even knew that all the police involved were just acting. Still, he couldn't get over the feeling that he'd never leave this room alive.

The hair stood up on his neck, and he had the same creepy feeling that someone was looking at him. He got up, looked around the room again, and sat on the table. He put his feet on a chair. He decided he could last another half hour before he had to pee. He wondered if it was better to pee in the corner, or bang on the door and beg for help.

He was trying not to think about peeing when he heard a noise outside the door. The door moved, and he jumped to his feet. A small person ran into the room and threw her arms around him. He looked down and saw filthy blond hair. His nose picked up the distinct odor of alcohol, cigarettes, grease, and street filth.

"Ivy?" Charlie asked.

"Pan." The girl's voice came from his chest.

Charlie looked up to see a stocky policewoman standing next to the door with her hand on her weapon. With his eyes on the policewoman, Charlie pushed the girl off him.

"Ivy." Charlie had to bend over to see her face. Her eyes were squeezed closed. "Ivy."

He gave her a little shake, and she opened her eyes.

"You have to get out of here," Charlie said. "I don't know what's going on, but it's not good. This lady will take you away from here and . . ."

"Oh, Pan. I miss Jeffy so much." Ivy started to cry.

Charlie hugged the girl again.

"You helped them get the killer, right?" Ivy said. "At least that's what Tink said."

"Yeah, I guess so," Charlie said.

"Did you really kill Saint Jude?" Ivy asked. "You're sure he's dead and not just gone somewhere?"

"He's dead," Charlie said. "I saw it myself."

"Pan, why did Jeffy . . .?"

Ivy pushed away from him and stepped back. She started picking at her fingers. When she did, Charlie saw that she was high.

"Ivy, you have to get out of here before they . . ." Charlie leaned close, " . . .figure out you're high."

"I can't do it anymore." Ivy slowly closed and opened her blue eyes. She was bone thin, and the landmarks on her face looked like peaks and valleys. "I wish he had taken me. Saint Jude, you know. Why didn't he take me instead of Jeffy? No one would miss me, but I . . . I really miss Jeffy."

"Me, too," Charlie said. "But I'd miss you just as much."

"Tink said you live with that psychic woman," Ivy said. "Did you talk to Jeffy?"

Charlie blushed and nodded.

"I keep having this dream that he's being tortured, like Saint Jude, only worse, a lot worse, and Jeffy . . ." Ivy said. "I have it every time I sleep. He's calling for me, Pan, to help him. I don't sleep anymore."

Ivy raised her eyebrows to indicate she used methamphetamines to keep from sleeping. Charlie's stomach tightened with anxiety. He had to get the tiny girl out of there.

"Listen." Charlie put his hands on Ivy's shoulders, like Aden did when he tried to talk sense to Sissy. "My sister's husband is in the waiting room. Go out there, and tell him you saw me and that you want to talk to Delphie. She's nice. You can trust her. She'll give you dinner and a place to sleep. She'll even let you talk to Jeffy."

"She will?"

"I swear," Charlie said. "If you can talk to Delphie . . ."

"She's in the waiting area," the policewoman said. She gave Charlie a doubtful look.

"You're sure?" Charlie asked.

"Medium-sized white woman with a crazy flower skirt," the policewoman said. "Red hair."

Charlie nodded.

"She's out there with Sam Lipson," the policewoman said. "Plus, I've known Delphinium for a long, long time. She's good people. You can trust her."

"Go with her," Charlie said. "She'll take you to Delphie."

"But, Pan . . ." Ivy hugged him. "I miss you, too."

"Ivy, I don't know what's going on here," Charlie said. "I'm in some kind of trouble, and . . ."

"There's a bunch of chicks," Ivy said, under her breath so the policewoman wouldn't hear. "I saw four chicks. Nobody I recognize, but I saw Fawn in the parking lot. She's not on the streets no more."

"Good for her," Charlie said.

"She's in foster care," Ivy said. "Tink said she might have a forever home."

"One of my sister's best friend's," Charlie said.

"I heard you're dating," Ivy said.

Charlie knew the girl was trying to extend her time with him. But the more she talked, the more anxious he became.

"Yeah," Charlie said. "It's new."

"Tink's always loved you, Pan," Ivy said. "You guys are good together."

"You ready to see Delphie?" Charlie asked.

"Who?" Ivy looked up at him with a blank face.

"The psychic. You remember — to talk to about Jeffy?"

"I miss Jeffy, Pan," Ivy said.

Charlie's eyes shifted to the policewoman. The policewoman moved toward them to take Ivy.

"Me, too," Charlie said. "Go with this woman, Ivy. She'll take you to the waiting room."

The policewoman maneuvered Ivy toward the door.

"Bye, Pan." Ivy turned to look at him. "I love you!"

"Love you too, Ivy," Charlie said.

When the door opened, he saw a man he recognized but couldn't place. The man had dyed dark hair and a big matching mustache. He wore a deep-rust-colored cowboy sports jacket, boots, and jeans. He wasn't as tall as Charlie, or Aden, or even Uncle Seth. But he looked tough. The man gave Charlie a hard, assessing look. The door closing broke his stare.

Charlie was alone. He stared at the door for a moment and then went back to sitting on the table.

He hoped he didn't have to pee in the corner.

~~~~~~~~~
Monday night — 7:12 p.m.

"How did it go?" Blane asked, Heather when she came into the house.

"It was hell to drop her off at the shelter," Heather said. "Just hell. I cried the whole way home."

Blane hugged her, and she sighed.

"I feel like she's already our daughter," Heather said.

"That's because she is." Blane nodded and held her tight. "How was therapy?"

"Good," Heather said. "We talked about the night terrors. Her therapist thinks Tink is re-experiencing her assault in those dreams. He thinks there's something in Tink's daily life that makes her remember what happened to her. 'Triggers her.' Those where his words."

"God, how awful," Blane said.

"I guess they've talked a lot about it," Heather said. "Tink has no idea what might be affecting her. She's excited about Charlie and us. Her therapist — well, really a *counselor* — is through the shelter. We'd have to find a new one when she comes home."

"Did you eat?" Blane asked.

"I got fast food for Tink," Heather said. "She loves the shakes. I didn't eat there because of the baby, and I knew you'd give me hell."

"I would have," Blane smiled. He went around the bar in the kitchen and started getting her dinner together. "I waited to eat in case you wanted to talk. Plus, you know, I'm eating for two."

Blane patted his stomach, and Heather laughed.

"How's Mack?" Heather asked.

"He wanted to stay up to see you and Tink," Blane said. "But he crashed around five."

"Did you call our social worker?" Heather asked.

"I forgot." Blane set out a plate of herbed chicken, rice, and vegetables.

Heather didn't say anything. She let the silence pressure him.

"Okay, okay, I give!" Blane laughed. She smiled. "She said that she'll get a report from Tink's counselor, talk to Tink, and we'll see. She said that everything looked really good when she stopped by at the Castle on Sunday. She felt like Tink had found a 'nice village' to live in."

"*Village?*"

"That's just what she said," Blane said.

"Mmm," Heather said, because her mouth was full. "I'd hoped she would say that Tink could move right in."

"I think they like to move slowly," Blane said. "It's funny, though."

"M-hmm?"

"She asked if Tink said anything about her assault," Blane said. "She said the police think they have a break in the case. They called her to ask if Tink could come down to the station, but she wouldn't let Tink go."

"Oh? Why?"

"She thought it was too much," Blane said. "Especially if she's triggered. She said when they had a firm lead and a real case, she'd let Tink talk to them. She wasn't going to let Tink be dragged through it again on a 'maybe.'"

"I like her," Heather said.

"I do, too," Blane said.

"Do you think she likes us?" Heather asked.

"I don't know," Blane said. "I hope so."

Heather nodded. As if on cue, Mack began to wail.

"Finish up," Blane said. "I'll get him ready for our run. Do you want to come?"

"Just ate," Heather said.

Blane just looked at her. Most nights, Blane and Mack ran while Heather walked the running path. While she watched, her boys ran away from her and back again. Mack loved it. She really liked the walks, but now that she was pregnant again, she was harder than usual to get moving.

"Sure," Heather said. "I'll get dressed."

"That's my girl," Blane said. "We'll have cake when we get back."

"Bribes! I love bribes!"

Heather yelled after him as he ran up the stairs. For a moment, she stared off into space. She had the feeling that things were changing. She nodded to herself and got ready for her walk.

~~~~~~~~~

Monday night — 7:32 p.m.

The door opened and Charlie jumped to his feet. The guy Charlie had thought was a friend of Uncle Seth's was standing in the doorway.

"I have to pee," Charlie said.

The guy nodded and gestured for Charlie to come out. The guy didn't say anything as they walked down the hall, but Charlie had the distinct impression he was protecting him, not keeping him captive. Just for a little privacy, Charlie went into a stall and closed the door. He stayed there long after he finished because the stall was familiar and safer than the little room.

"Come on, son, we can't delay the inevitable," Uncle Seth's friend said. "Just no point."

Charlie blinked. MJ always said something like that. He always said, *"You know what the LC always says? There's no point in delaying the inevitable."* Charlie got up, flushed, and opened the stall. Uncle Seth's friend gave him a kind look and a nod. Charlie was going to leave, but then he remembered that Aden was trying to get him to wash his hands after he used the toilet. He stopped near the door and went back to a sink. If he was going to get into trouble, he may as well have clean hands.

They walked back down the hallway. Uncle Seth's friend opened the door to the room he'd been in. There were two men, cops, sitting on one side of the table. Uncle Seth's friend moved Charlie into a seat on the opposite side of the table. Then he did something weird. He stood near the door.

The guy with the mustache, the one Charlie remembered but couldn't place, didn't like that Uncle Seth's friend was there but clearly couldn't do anything about it. He cleared his throat as a way of indicating that this was his show. Charlie squinted.

He innately liked the guy with the mustache. He wasn't sure

why, but he did. The man had dark eyes and the brownish skin of someone from Mexico or maybe one of the tribes. His teeth were a little snaggled—like Charlie's had been before he started braces. He looked smart.

Maybe more than anything, he had a really great haircut.

Charlie leaned back in his chair. The man's eyes seemed to laugh.

"You seem to be at the center of a lot of my problems," Mustache Cop said.

"You sure that's not some kind of projection?" Charlie said. "Freud said that we project our anxiety and anger onto other people as a mechanism of defense against our own emotions. Are you anxious? Angry?"

Mustache Cop looked at Charlie and blinked.

"I knew your father," Mustache Cop said.

"Oh, yeah?"

"Never liked the man."

"Well, he's been dead a long time," Charlie said. "Maybe it's time to get over it."

Mustache Cop gave Charlie a steely look.

"Therapy works," Charlie said.

Mustache Cop laughed. Charlie smirked.

"I've had a number of threatening calls about you." Mustache Cop raised his eyebrows to ask Charlie what he thought of that. Charlie shrugged. "O'Malley might not invite me to his next party, which I don't care about, but my wife loves those music things. General Hargreaves told me if I didn't go easy on you, he wouldn't sign the recommendation for my next promotion. I got a call from your coach, who told me if you're injured, he won't let his kid mow my lawn anymore."

"Sounds rough," Charlie said.

"You know what hurt the most?"

"Sandy won't cut your hair anymore?"

"That's just mean," the man said. "Dirty."

Uncle Seth's friend covered a laugh with a cough. Charlie leaned forward.

"What do you want?" Charlie said in a low, intimate tone. "My family must be crazy with worry. The little kids have been through a lot. They can't handle this kind of thing. And that police lady said Sam was in the lobby. He's not young, and they go to work early. Can we just get this over with? And . . ."

The man looked up at Charlie.

"Don't I get a lawyer?"

"Yes, actually, you get another threatening Hargreaves," the man smiled. "She's in the lobby making the desk Sergeant's life hell. I wanted to talk to you first."

"Isn't that illegal?"

"How is it that you know both Freud and the law and . . .? I heard you were a drugged-out street kid." Mustache Cop put on some half-glasses to read from a file in front of him. "Can't read. Hep C positive. Uses meth, pot, tends to avoid opiates."

"I had a tutor all last summer," Charlie said. "Anjelika Roper."

The man raised his eyebrows as if Mrs. Anjelika's name was a threat.

"She's in Costa Rica right now," Charlie said. "Or she probably would have called you, too."

Mustache Cop cleared his throat and pulled on his collar. He nudged the younger cop sitting next to him. The younger cop started to lay pictures on the table. Charlie didn't dare look, in case it was something horrible, like pictures of Saint Jude's victims or worse.

"I wonder if you know these girls," Mustache Cop said.

Charlie glanced down to see the outlines of photos. He instinctively counted. Eleven photos. He looked up at the man.

"Can I touch them?" Charlie asked. "I don't have my glasses."

"Reading glasses?" Mustache Cop raised his eyebrows.

"I'm kinda blind," Charlie said.

"You look like the man and have the same eye problems," the

man said.

"My Dad?" Charlie asked. "Yeah."

Mustache Cop raised his hand to Uncle Seth's friend. He stepped forward with glasses that looked like Charlie's glasses.

"These belonged to your father," Mustache Cop said.

Charlie raised his eyebrows in surprise. Mustache Cop shrugged. Charlie put on the glasses and looked down. The prescription wasn't perfect, but it worked pretty well. For a moment, he debated whether to be honest. Then he remembered how what he knew could have saved Jeffy if he'd come completely clean with Uncle Seth when he'd asked. He started organizing the photos.

"I've never seen these girls." Charlie pushed four photos toward the man. "They look rich."

"That's good," Mustache Cop said.

"Why?"

"They've never seen you, either," Mustache Cop said.

Charlie nodded. There *had* been someone looking at him.

"How many of these other girls have you had sex with?" Mustache Cop asked.

"Uh . . ." Charlie squirmed.

Uncle Seth's friend stepped forward to the table. Mustache Cop looked up.

"I'll get his lawyer now," Uncle Seth's friend said.

CHAPTER TWO HUNDRED & TWENTY-SIX

PAN

"Don't say anything until I get back," Uncle Seth's friend said.

Charlie nodded, and Uncle Seth's friend left the room. Charlie sat back in his chair and crossed his arms. Mustache Cop leaned over to say something to the younger cop. The younger cop got up and left the room. He came back with three bottles of water.

Charlie drank his bottle dry. The younger cop pushed another bottle at him, and Charlie drank it down. He heard a harsh woman's voice coming down the hallway toward him. He had to force himself not to smirk.

"Your lawyer is upset," Mustache Cop said.

The door opened, and Samantha Hargreaves waddled into the room. Charlie instinctively stood up.

"I'd like some time alone with my client," Samantha said.

"I'd like a present from Santa," Mustache Cop said. "Neither one is going to happen."

"But . . ."

"Sit down, Ms. Hargreaves," Mustache Cop said. "We have a lot of ground to cover."

Charlie pulled out the chair next to him, and Samantha sat down. He sat down next to her. Under the table, she reached for his hand. She gave his hand a squeeze and let go. Charlie sat up a little straighter.

"Did you at least introduce yourself?" Samantha looked at the friend of Uncle Seth's. He shook his head. Samantha gave Mustache Cop a threatening look. He cleared his throat.

"See the problems I have?" Mustache Cop said.

"Therapy works," Charlie said.

Mustache Cop laughed.

"I'm Detective Ben Red Bear," Mustache Cop said. "This is Sergeant Aziz. We work in Major Crimes."

"What major crime did these girls do?"

As if to protect them, Charlie moved his hand over the photos and pulled them closer to him. They were photos of girls he'd known on the streets. While he had some idea of the crimes they may have committed, he didn't like the fact that these cops might, too. Detective Red Bear noted the response.

"Nothing," Detective Red Bear said.

"Then we can go." Samantha started to get up.

"No," Detective Red Bear said. He looked down at the table and up at Charlie. "I have a problem."

"I think we went over that," Charlie snapped.

"In the last three years, eleven girls have been brutalized, raped, beaten, and humiliated," Detective Red Bear said. "Their assaults were videotaped and photographed. The images sold."

Charlie gritted his teeth and stared at the man.

"Not unlike . . ."

Charlie jumped from his seat.

"Don't you *ever* say *anything* about my sister." Charlie raised his hand to point at the man.

For a moment, everything stopped. The cops on the other side of the table looked up at Charlie. Samantha Hargreaves tried to pull Charlie back into the chair. Detective Red Bear nodded, and Charlie sat down.

"What is the problem that you believe my client can help you with?" Samantha asked. "I remind you that he is *sixteen years old*. He hasn't *eaten* a thing after a difficult workout. He needs to be *home* with his family."

"A couple of the girls . . ." Detective Red Bear turned to look at Sergeant Aziz. He held up three fingers. "Three girls said that 'Pan,' and his friends, fought off their attackers and took them to the hospital. A couple others said that 'Pan' took care of them while they were healing."

"So?" Charlie shrugged. "What's that to me?"

"Until today, I've had no leads — zero," Detective Red Bear said. "The girls are too terrified to say a word. So, I've been looking for this 'Pan.'"

"Why?" Samantha asked.

"Because I think he can help. Maybe he saw something. Maybe he can stop . . ." Detective Red Bear pushed two photos toward Charlie. "These two girls killed themselves."

Charlie swallowed hard.

"These other two," Detective Red Bear pushed the other two photos forward. "These girls are in a residential treatment program out of state. But those girls? They're not great, but they're not killing themselves, either."

Charlie didn't say anything.

"And a couple of the girls, like your girlfriend Tink, have really nice haircuts." Detective Red Bear smiled for the first time. "What do you think of that?"

Charlie locked eyes with the police detective.

"I'm wondering how much we're going to sue the Denver Police Department for," Samantha said. "I think a jury would easily see the imprisonment of a sixteen-years-old boy without representation or due process for three hours as . . . what do you think Charlie? Three million?"

"Why don't you just go after the guys in the video?" Charlie asked.

"Their faces are altered, wiped out — not even the FBI can recover their images," Detective Red Bear said. "Until today. Did you send your brother Nash a video?"

"No," Charlie said.

"To his phone?"

"No," Charlie said. "I had an assignment due. I worked on it until I went to basketball."

"Let's cut the crap," Samantha said. "What video are you

talking about?"

"This afternoon, Nash Norsen received a video on his phone," Detective Red Bear said.

"How do you know that?" Samantha asked.

"It was forwarded to me by a Homeland Security Agent."

"My brother Colin?" Samantha asked.

"Uh..." Detective Red Bear blushed and looked down at the folder in front of him.

"I was at basketball," Charlie said.

"Nash Norsen indicated that you sometimes send things to his phone because it's the only number you remember," Sergeant Avis said.

"So?"

"Did you send something to Nash's phone?" Detective Red Bear said.

"No," Charlie said. "I was at basketball."

"Did someone else send something to Nash's phone?" Sergeant Avis asked.

"Like what?" Charlie asked.

"Like a video of your girlfriend being gang raped," Detective Red Bear said.

"What?" Charlie felt his face flush bright red. He had the immediate urge to cry or throw up. And for reasons he couldn't fathom, he wanted Aden. "Tink?"

~~~~~~~~~
Monday night — 8:32 p.m.

Flushed from her walk, Heather waited at the front door for Blane and Mack to finish their last sprint. Mack liked Blane to race toward the house and come to a screeching halt. Heather cheered her heroes.

"Is that your cell phone?" Blane asked. "Sounds like ... 'Rescue Me.'"

"It's our social worker." Heather rushed to get the door open and ran into the house. Her hand was almost to the phone when it stopped ringing. Blane came up behind her. "Missed it."

Fontella Bass belted out "*Come on and rescue me*," and Heather answered.

"Hi!"

"You sound awake," Risa, their social worker, said.

"We got home from our walk," Heather said.

"Well, I can't say I'm sorry you're awake," Risa said.

"What's going on?" Heather asked.

"I need a huge favor," Risa said. "I want to say first that you can say 'No.' I won't hold it against you or think you've done something wrong. It's late and . . ."

"Has something happened to Tink?" Heather's hand went to her heart. She pointed to the phone. Blane picked up Mack and leaned in closer to listen. Heather moved the phone so they could both hear.

"That's part of it," Risa said. "Tiffanie is hysterical. She's been crying since you dropped her off. Her counselor came in to help, and he called me to ask if Tiffanie could come back to your house. I was there when . . ."

"When?" Blane said.

"One of her friends from the streets was picked up tonight," Risa said. "She's at Denver Health right now. It's going to freeze tonight, so there aren't any free beds anywhere in town. Even if Tiffanie comes to your house, her bed will be taken by one of the kids asleep in the lunch area. The woman who dropped Ivy — that's her name — at Denver Health said she can come home with her, but . . ."

"They're not approved," Heather said.

"That's exactly right. Because of the cold, our emergency homes are filled and . . ." Risa seemed to sigh. "I wondered if you could take the girls tonight."

"Girls?" Heather asked.

"Tiffanie and her friend," Risa said.

Heather and Blane looked at each other.

"The girl goes by Ivy. Her legal name is Anna-Marie McDonald," Risa said. "I have to tell you that she's filthy and coming down from being high. She asked for Tiffanie, and . . ."

Blane nodded, and Heather smiled.

"Of course," Heather said.

"You won't have to keep Anna-Marie," Risa said. "She has an aunt and some grandparents who have been looking for her. We'll have to research the families, do home visits and stuff, but we expect them to pick her up . . . probably next weekend. The longest she'd stay with you is three months. We'll find a more permanent placement if she's there that long."

"They'd have to share a room," Heather said. "One of them will have to sleep on the air mattress tonight."

"That's fine," Risa said. "I was with Tiffanie when I got the call about Anna-Marie. We went to Denver Health to see if Tiffanie could help Anna-Marie. This was Tiffanie's idea."

"Sounds perfect," Blane said. "We can leave right now."

"Why don't I drop them off?" Risa said. "That way, I can review the room and make sure they're settled."

"Sounds great," Heather said. "We'll see you in . . ."

"A half hour," Risa said. "And, thanks. You really saved my bacon."

"Blane made cake," Heather said.

"I'll start a pot of coffee," Blane said.

"I was hoping you'd say that," Risa said. "See you in a bit."

Heather looked at Blane, and he beamed.

"You're sure you're okay?" Heather asked. "You've been sick, and . . ."

"Perfect!" Blane said. "Can you start the coffee?"

She took Mack from him, and he ran up the stairs to get the other room ready. Smiling, she went into the kitchen to start a pot of coffee.

~~~~~~~~~

Monday night — 8:32 p.m.

Charlie swallowed hard and looked down. He knew this was the kind of moment that he needed to "be a man." He heard the words in Anjelika's accented voice, and he felt better. He could do this. He looked up.

As if to start a rant or a lecture, Detective Red Bear took a deep breath. He took a look at Charlie's face and let out the breath. He glanced at Samantha Hargreaves.

"The guys on my basketball team don't like me very much," Charlie said. "They call me 'On-Line' and tell everyone I'm stupid. They saw me with Tink and said they were going to prove to me that I didn't want to be with her. I didn't think anything of it because they're assholes, and Tink, well . . ."

Charlie shrugged.

"Tink was a street kid," Charlie said. "These girls were all street kids. The only one who's still out is Ivy."

He pointed to the picture of Ivy.

"You mean Anna-Marie McDonald?" Sergeant Aziz asked.

"Who?" Charlie shook his head.

"That girl," Sergeant Aziz said. "Her name is Anna-Marie McDonald."

"I don't know anyone's real name," Charlie said. "They take fairy names out on the streets. You know, fairy names?"

The detective looked puzzled.

"From *Disney*?" Charlie asked.

"Anna-Marie is from North Dakota," Sergeant Aziz said. "Her mother died when she was a baby. Car accident. Her Dad left her here with her grandmother when he was called up. He went to Iraq and didn't come back."

"Her grandmother died a few years ago," Charlie said.

Sergeant Aziz nodded.

"She was a good friend of Jeffy's," Charlie said. "You know — the one Saint Jude . . . and he . . ."

Charlie dropped his head for a moment. The longer hair on the top of his head fell forward and covered his face. He had to breathe hard to keep from crying.

"What's so important about this video?" Samantha asked.

"It hasn't been digitally altered," Detective Red Bear said. "We can see the faces of at least five of the perpetrators."

"Was my client on the video?" Samantha asked.

"No," Sergeant Aziz said.

"Why are we here?" Samantha asked.

~~~~~~~~~
Monday night — 8:42 p.m.

Sissy waited until she thought Noelle was asleep before she crept from the room. She slipped out into the hallway and dug around in the hall laundry bag until she found one of Charlie's smelly basketball jerseys. She pulled it on over her head and tiptoed to his closet at the end of the hall. She slipped into his bed and pulled the covers over her head.

A few minutes later, Nash plopped down almost on top of her.

"What are you doing?" Nash said in an angry whisper.

"Sleeping," Sissy asked. "What are you doing?"

"Uh . . ." Nash said.

He lay down on Charlie's futon and closed his eyes. Sissy settled in between him and the wall. They lay there for a few minutes before Noelle lay down.

"What are you doing?" Nash sat up. He nudged Noelle over.

Noelle gave him a shove.

"What are you doing?" Nash pushed her back.

"She's doing what you're doing — missing Charlie and hoping he's all right," Sissy said. "Now shut up, or we'll get caught."

Nash lay down between Sissy and Noelle. A few minutes later, Sandy stuck her head into Charlie's room. The children pretended to be asleep. She smiled and left. She came back with a large comforter to cover the worried children.

"He's going to be all right," Sandy said.

"How do you know?" Sissy's heartbroken voice came from near the wall.

"I just know," Sandy said. "Should I wake you when he gets home?"

"Yes," Nash said.

"Okay," Sandy said. "Sleep tight."

She went out to the living room. After fifteen minutes, she crept back to Charlie's room.

The kids were sound asleep. Smiling, Sandy went to her room. She picked up Rachel in her bassinette and carried her to the kitchen. For a moment, she closed her eyes and smelled — flour, sugar, a touch of cinnamon that escaped Aden's morning coffee.

"What should I make Rachel?" Sandy whispered to her sleeping baby.

She opened the refrigerator and saw the apples.

"Pie it is," Sandy said and set to work.

~~~~~~~~~

Monday night — 8:42 p.m.

"I need a chain of custody for the video," Detective Red Bear said.

"Before my client comments on anything, I want, in writing, an agreement that my client has immunity from any crimes he might admit to during this investigation," Samantha said. "And by *any*, I mean *any and all* crimes."

Uncle Seth's friend stepped forward with a folded sheet of paper. He held the form out to Detective Red Bear. The mustached man gave Uncle Seth's friend a searching look. Uncle Seth's friend nodded. Detective Red Bear took the paper, looked it over, and signed it. He passed the paper to Samantha Hargreaves. She read it and signed it.

"Charlie?" Samantha asked. Charlie turned to look at her.

"They need you to tell them everything you know."

"You're saying those guys beat up Tink? Raped her? Broke her teeth and gave her seizures?" Charlie's face flushed. He stared at Detective Red Bear. "She almost died!"

"I need you to help me," Detective Red Bear said. "Did you ever beat up guys who were assaulting your friends?"

"Sure." Charlie shrugged.

"How many times?"

"Maybe three — no, four — times," Charlie said. "Me and some of the guys. I didn't do all the beating up. I'm not much of a fighter. I just don't have an interest in it. I mean, I'm taking martial arts now because Aden wants me to. I mean we all have to, even Sissy. And . . . never mind. The other guys usually did most of the fighting 'cuz they like it. I mean I'd throw a punch or two, and I'm big, so I can toss people around, but I'd usually take the girl away."

"So you could get laid?" Sergeant Aziz asked.

"I don't need to trick girls or beat them up or whatever to get laid," Charlie said.

"Answer the question," Detective Red Bear said.

"No," Charlie said.

"But you had sex with all of these girls?" Detective Red Bear asked.

Charlie turned to Samantha Hargreaves. "Do I have to answer that?"

"Why is that question such a big deal?" Sergeant Aziz asked.

"Because a gentleman never speaks about his sexual encounters," Charlie sniffed. He wasn't sure why, but he felt really indignant. "Whatever you think of these girls, they're good people. It's none of your business what we do or did in private."

Sergeant Aziz smirked, and Detective Red Bear gave him a long, assessing look.

"Do I have to answer that question?" Charlie asked Samantha.

"No," Samantha said.

"Why did you help these girls?" Sergeant Aziz asked.

"Why *wouldn't* I help these girls?" Charlie asked. "You're really pissing me off. I saw my friends in trouble, and I helped. And I didn't just help them just because they were my friends. And I didn't help them because I was going to get something from them. I helped them because they needed help. What kind of a person do you think I am? What kind of a person are you?"

Charlie got to his feet.

"I want to go home," Charlie said. Samantha Hargreaves got to her feet. "You don't want my help. Scum like you ... You really should work on yourself. Maybe if you were a better person, these girls would tell you what you want to know."

"Do you still want to help these girls?" Detective Red Bear asked.

"You don't have to do anything, Charlie," Samantha said.

Charlie didn't say anything.

"Or you can let these guys keep terrorizing young girls," Sergeant Aziz said. "They prey on virgins."

Charlie gave an involuntary shudder. He turned to look at them.

"What do I have to do?" Charlie asked.

"Help us identify the boys on the tape," Detective Red Bear said. "Give a statement about what you saw in situations you broke up. Get your friends to talk to us — the guys who broke up the fights and the girls — the ones you helped and the ... others."

"Let us know where it happened and when — time and day," Sergeant Aziz said. "We might get lucky and get security video."

"Can I think about it?" Charlie asked.

"What's to think about?" Detective Red Bear asked.

"If I do this, I have to quit basketball," Charlie said. "I really love basketball. Sometimes it's the only thing that's good about being sober and ... everything I have to do now."

"You can think about it," Detective Red Bear said. "But every hour you're thinking, they're planning their next attack."

Charlie swallowed hard.

"Okay, that's enough," Samantha Hargreaves said. "We're going home. You'll have our answer tomorrow."

With that, she walked to the door. Uncle Seth's friend opened it. Charlie turned one last time.

"You're Sandy's Detective," Charlie said.

Detective Red Bear gave a slight nod.

"That's why you don't like my Dad," Charlie said. "He used to ride you to find out who was involved, to get you to solve her case. You never did. Uncle Seth solved it last year."

Detective Red Bear gave a slight nod.

"Huh," Charlie said, and walked out of the room.

Samantha Hargreaves held onto his arm. He felt her hand as they walked through the maze of the police station and into the lobby, where he walked into Aden's arms.

"We're going home," Aden said.

CHAPTER TWO HUNDRED & TWENTY-SEVEN

BELONG

Monday night — 9:17 p.m.

"You haven't said a word since you got out of your interview," Aden said to Charlie.

Aden looked over at Charlie and turned left on Lincoln Avenue. He stopped his Saab at the light in front of the Colorado State Capitol Building before turning right on Colfax Avenue. Charlie grunted. Aden pulled into the McDonald's drive-through on Pennsylvania Street.

"Do *not* tell your sister," Aden said.

Charlie nodded, and Aden ordered the boy a meal deal, with a couple extra double-cheeseburgers on the side. Aden pulled into the parking lot, so that they would have a chance to talk. Charlie powered his way through the meal deal before he said anything.

"Hungry?" Aden smiled.

"Starved," Charlie said. "We had the hardest workout before... before..."

Charlie scowled and turned his attention to his French fries.

"What's got your goat?" Aden said. "You know that holding on to anger makes you more likely to use."

"I want to." Charlie punched the dashboard. "Ow."

Aden smiled. Charlie gave Aden an impish grin.

"Angry?" Aden tried again.

"They kept asking me if I'd had sex with these girls," Charlie said. "Like I was only friends with them because I wanted sex from them or like I'm a pimp or something... gross."

"Did you tell them?"

"No," Charlie said. "But they asked three times. Three times!"

"Hmm," Aden said. "What do you think that was about?"

"No idea," Charlie said. "I felt . . . stupid . . . ashamed . . . small."

"Do you think they wanted you to feel small?"

"Yeah, I guess so."

Charlie drained his soda. The straw made a slurping sound, and he shoved the straw down into the ice. Aden raised an eyebrow. Charlie nodded and set the cup in the cup holder. Sandy would kill him if she heard him making that "foul noise."

"Did you have sex with the girls?" Aden asked.

Charlie looked at Aden for a moment.

"You're as sick as your secrets," Aden said. Charlie nodded.

"Yes. No. I don't really know. Maybe. Probably." Charlie shrugged. "You remember how it was being out. You're cold, high, and there's no one telling you not to. The stuff you have to do just to stay alive . . . It was nice to have someone warm and there at night. But I never, ever raped anyone, or helped a girl because I wanted to screw her, or . . ."

"Even when you were high?" Aden asked.

"No," Charlie said. "Girls have always liked me. They called me 'Pan' and . . . Trying to help them, protect them, and the guys, too . . . It made me feel closer to my dad, I guess. And the sex was just . . . life, I guess. I didn't realize sex was a big deal for kids until I started playing basketball at East. I just thought . . . I don't know, whatever. You want to have sex, you have sex."

"Even for Sissy or Noelle?" Aden asked.

Charlie shrugged.

"Is it different for girls?"

"It's different for people who are sheltered, innocent," Charlie said. "But that's not me. I've seen . . ."

Charlie did a kind of hiccup. He looked away from Aden and began to cry. Aden put his hand on the boy's shoulder.

"I was out for years and years," Charlie said. "Hungry, cold. I was so alone, so alone. Predators everywhere. The homeless shelters are the worst. And . . . I guess it sounds *fun and free love* — drugs and lots of sex. But it was . . . lonely. I was so lonely. I wanted to help because it made me think I wasn't scum. Is that so weird? So wrong?"

"No," Aden said. "It's not."

Charlie slumped into his jacket and cried. When the storm passed, Charlie hit the dashboard again.

"They want me to build a case for them," Charlie said. "Get the girls to talk about what happened to them. Tell the guys to talk about beating up the bastards. And testify myself. It's so . . ."

"Hypocritical?" Aden asked.

"Stupid," Charlie said. "No one gave a rat's ass about me or any of those kids. I mean, Sissy did, and I know Sandy, and whatever, but you know what I mean."

"I do," Aden said.

"Now, I'm supposed to give up the only thing that makes me happy so they can . . . what? Add another star on their chest? It feels stupid and wrong."

"You'd have to quit basketball," Aden said.

"How did you know?" Charlie asked.

"Nash recognized a few of the boys in that video," Aden said.

"Oh," Charlie said.

"He was very upset," Aden said. "Threw up and cried. Both he and Teddy were freaked out by the video."

"God." Charlie hit his head against the passenger window. "I hope he knows that I would never . . ."

"Of course," Aden said. "He was upset by the violence and worried about you. He and the girls are sleeping on your futon. They're worried about you."

"I told them that this was bad for the little kids," Charlie said.

"Don't call them that," Aden said.

"What?"

"*Little kids*," Aden said.

"But they *are* little kids."

"It's demeaning, and they're not that much younger than you," Aden said. "It's a way of setting yourself apart from the family, a way of being alone while surrounded by people who love you. Is that what you want?"

"No," Charlie said.

Charlie had taken too much of a beating tonight to tell Aden he was right. Aden glanced at the boy, and Charlie gave him a "You're right" nod. He picked up one of his double-cheeseburgers and wolfed it down.

"Can we go home?" Charlie asked.

Aden smiled and started the car. They continued up Colfax and stopped at the light at Downing.

"I think you have to find a win for yourself. Something you can believe in," Aden said when they started through the light at Downing. "Do you believe in helping people?"

"I try to," Charlie said. "I like to. I help out at home and with Delphie and stuff."

"Would you be helping the girls?"

"I don't think so," Charlie said. "Most of them have moved on. Who wants to dig up all this crap?"

"Do you think these boys will continue hurting people?"

Charlie focused on his last hamburger, and Aden let the silence do the work.

"They will," Charlie said.

"Of course, they will. Do you really want to associate with boys like that?"

"No," Charlie said. "No way. But . . ."

Charlie fell silent again.

"What?"

"Can't they just arrest them, and I can play basketball?" Charlie asked.

"What did they tell you?"

"They said they have no one to testify, no case," Charlie said.

"They had no leads until Mr. Colin sent in the video."

"Are you angry about that?"

"No way," Charlie said. "I feel ... awful ... stupid for giving out Nash's phone number ... irresponsible ... like a bad brother. Did he really throw up?"

"He did," Aden said. "When he told me about it, he was shaking."

"God," Charlie said. He bounced his head against the passenger window a few times.

"You can get mad at yourself. I understand that," Aden said. "What strikes me about Nash is that he's a truly, deeply, nice person. It always shocks me to see what nice, good people Nash, Noelle, Sissy, and you are. It always surprises me that these are *my* children — you know? But I think you should take notice of how nice people react."

"Why?"

"Because these boys have a little industry of selling videos and photos of their encounters," Aden said.

"How do you know that?"

"Seth told me," Aden said. "He didn't want Sandy to know, but, of course, that's the first thing she thought of."

"So, everybody knows what I did," Charlie said.

"You didn't do anything," Aden said. "But now that you know about all of this, you know Sam would say, 'What will you do now?'"

"This life ..." Charlie said. "It's great but so hard. Basketball is the only thing that gets me through. I don't interact with those guys very much, and ..."

"Knowing what you know now, would you want to play basketball with them?" Aden asked. "I think that's the question."

Aden pulled the car into the Castle driveway and clicked the button for the gate.

"I was a lot older than you when I had a chance to meet nice people," Aden said.

"But these kids, my old friends — girls and guys — are really nice, good people," Charlie said. "They just lived outside because no one loved them."

"They *are* nice people," Aden said. "Why would you want to play your favorite sport with guys who aren't?"

Aden parked, and they went inside. Aden followed Charlie up the stairs to the second floor.

"I think everyone is asleep, so we should . . ." Aden said in a low voice.

The door to their apartment flung open. Sandy, Noelle, Sissy, and Nash were standing in the doorway. Charlie stepped into the hallway, and they didn't come out. For a moment, everyone just looked at him.

Nash broke free and threw himself at Charlie.

"I'm so sorry," Nash said. "I didn't mean to . . ."

"I'm sorry, too," Charlie said. "I never would have given them your number if I'd had any idea that they . . ."

Sissy joined the hug, and Noelle followed her.

"Let's get inside before we wake everyone up," Aden said.

"Did Charlie make it home?" Valerie's voice came from down the hallway.

They heard running feet, and Valerie appeared with a baby monitor in her hand. Delphie poked her head out as well. Sam appeared from downstairs to give Charlie a bear hug. MJ brought Honey up to see Charlie, and Jacob brought Jill down.

Soon everyone who lived at the Castle was standing in the hallway. There were lots of hugs and kisses and a few baby monitors.

For the moment, Charlie knew he was a real part of this family, and that being a part of something was pretty nice.

"Good thing I made a couple of pies," Sandy said.

"I have ice cream!" Jill said.

"Shall we?" Aden ushered everyone inside for a mini-celebration.

"I think that's about it," Risa, their social worker, said. She stood and gave Heather her coffee mug. "Thank you for the cake and coffee. After the day I've had, and the night I'm going to have, it was absolutely perfect. Mostly, thank you for being willing to help out at the last minute."

"It's our pleasure," Heather said.

"I'll walk you out." Blane looked at Heather, and she nodded.

She watched him help Risa with her coat. When Blane left to walk Risa to her car, Heather went upstairs to check on the girls. She peeked into the room that had been Blane's room but was now Tink's room.

Ivy was lying on the air mattress next to the bed, and Tink was on the bed. Both girls had their eyes closed. They looked like peaceful angels.

It had taken three washings to get all the muck off of Ivy. Tink helped her clean up and then shared her new clothing with the girl. Of course, Tink was twice the size of Ivy, but Ivy didn't seem to care that her clothing didn't fit. After Ivy was clean and dressed, they were too tired for cake. They went to bed without a fuss, which was good, because Risa was watching.

Heather smiled and began to close the door. The door was open just a crack when Ivy said something. Heather groaned at herself, but she couldn't help but stop to listen.

"Tink?" Ivy asked.

"Yeah?" Tink's sleep-filled voice came from the bed.

"Tink?"

"Okay." The bed groaned as Tink sat up to look at Ivy. "What's going on?"

"I just wanted to say that these people seem really nice," Ivy said.

"They are," Tink said. "Wait 'til you meet Mack."

"No, I mean they aren't making you go to school tomorrow because we're up so late," Ivy said. "And we get to see Pan and his new family and everything. They just seem to get it."

"Blane was out of doors off and on for most of his life," Tink said. "I think he gets it."

"That's good," Ivy said.

The bedsprings squeaked as Tink lay back down.

"Tink?" Ivy asked.

"Yeah?"

"I want you to know that I'm not going to blow this for you," Ivy said. "I'll stay clean and do whatever I have to. You deserve to be here, and . . ."

"I never thought you would," Tink said.

"Well, I won't," Ivy said. "And . . . thanks."

"For what?"

"For including me," Ivy said. "I haven't been feeling really . . . good lately, and . . ."

The bed groaned as Tink sat up to look at Ivy again.

"It's the drugs," Tink said. "Give it a few days — you'll feel better."

"You ever wish you had died?"

"All the time," Tink said. "But if I had died, I'd never be here. I'd never have a chance at this great life, and . . . I'm glad I made it through all of this. You will be, too."

"I miss Jeffy."

"I miss all of them," Tink said. "I figure I have to try to have a real, normal life because Saint Jude took everything from them, even their life. I kind of feel like I have to live for them — you know?"

"I like that," Ivy said. "I have to live for me and for Jeffy."

"Exactly."

Heather heard the bed shift as Tink lay down again. She stood there for a little longer and left to find Blane.

~~~~~~~~~

Monday night — 10:39 p.m.

Tanesha pressed the phone against her ear and closed her eyes. Bone tired, she stepped into the elevator to the penthouse without opening her eyes. Her mother's light, happy voice continued to tell her about their "Amazing Trip" to Paris.

Tanesha was more than happy that they were happy. Tonight, she was just exhausted. After last night's full harvest-fest, today felt like a long, long haul from lecture to lab to study group to lab to studying in the library to waiting an hour for the bus. The elevator doors opened at the penthouse.

She was finally home.

With her eyes still closed, she walked into the house. Still listening to Yvonne, she pulled off her boots and left them in the hallway. She'd gotten all the way to the kitchen before she realized something was wrong.

The loft was empty.

Jeraine had left her.

Again.

And her mother kept talking.

"Mom? Mom." Tanesha's voice cut into her mother's happy tale about how her father had met a guy who got them into a *private* part of a famous museum somewhere in the Paris suburbs.

"Yes, Tanni?"

"I've got to go," Tanesha said. "I just got home, and I've got to go."

"Okay, sweetie," Yvonne said. "I'll send today's pictures. Are you all right?"

"Just had a long day," Tanesha said.

"My medical student." Tanesha could hear her mother's smile in her voice. "Love you, Tanni."

"Love you, too," Tanesha said.

She tapped the phone against her jeans and looked around. The loft was still, silent, and empty. Even the rugs were gone.

Of course, it was still dirty. He probably expected her to clean it up before the IRS came. She made a sour face and went into her bedroom.

"Ah, great," Tanesha said.

Her clothing was gone. That jerk even took her clothes. She wondered if he had thrown it off the balcony like he had a few years back, after she caught him with some girl in their bed.

"Probably was stolen," Tanesha said. "Shit."

Not sure of what else to do, she went out to the living room and lay down on the hardwood floor. She wanted to cry, but she was simply too exhausted.

"God, if you are listening, I promise to never go through this again with that man," Tanesha said. "Never again."

She gave the floor a firm pat to emphasize her commitment to being done with Jeraine forever. Mostly, her hand fell to the floor.

And then she remembered her tea. He'd never taken her tea before. Even if she had to use hot water from the faucet, a cup of tea would be really nice. She rolled to her side and went to the kitchen.

No tea.

That man was going to fry.

She stormed out of the kitchen to get on with her life. She slid down the wall to put her boots back on. Reaching for her boot, she saw an envelope on the floor.

She scowled and muttered to herself, "More of that boy's bull." She put on her left boot before picking up the note.

"Let's see. Is it 'My music is important and you can wait,' or 'I gots to go,' or 'See you later, baby,' or 'You just ain't got it for me anymore,' or . . ."

She ripped open the envelope.

Inside was a key. She pulled the card out of the envelope.

I'm waiting for you.

She scowled. What was this? She looked at the key. The address to the yellow house was written on the side.

She blinked. Picking up her backpack, she hobbled to the elevator before realizing she wasn't wearing her right boot. She went back and put on the boot. She leaned against the wall. All she wanted to do was sit there and sleep. She closed her eyes.

Her phone rang. She looked down at it.

Jeraine.

She clicked the phone on to take the call but didn't say anything.

"Are you coming home?" Jeraine asked. "I have the night off. Dinner is warm."

"Just so tired. Don't want to move."

"Should I come there?" he asked. "We could picnic . . ."

"Wait — where are you?" Tanesha jolted fully awake. "Are you in my house?"

"Ye,s ma'am."

Tanesha clicked off the phone and got into the elevator. She wasn't sure how she made it to the little yellow house, but the next thing she knew, she was there. Jeraine had the front light on.

The front picket fence stood erect around the edges and was painted a perfect white. The house was an impeccable yellow with white faux shutters and window boxes filled with pansies under the front windows. The garden wasn't all the way in, but the brick path didn't have the big dip in it. A couple of wooden chairs and a little table were sitting on the porch next to the redwood porch swing. Behind the storm door, the front door was gorgeous antique oak with a lovely stained-glass pane where the broken window had been.

She was about to use her key when Jeraine jerked the door open.

In a breath, she was in his arms. Tears streamed down her face.

"Is it all perfect like this?" Tanesha asked.

Jeraine nodded.

"I want to see everything," she said.

Her dream had come true, and they went inside.

~~~~~~~~~

Tuesday early-morning — 12:39 a.m.

"Charlie," Sissy whispered.

Sound asleep on his futon, Charlie stirred but didn't wake. Sissy pushed on his leg with her foot and jumped back. Like he always did when he was awoken at night, he came up swinging.

"What?" he growled at her.

She gestured for him to come with her.

"Why?"

She gave him the evil "Do what I'm telling you to do" sister look, and he got out of bed. She crept down the hall to her and Noelle's room. She waved him into the room. Charlie groaned.

"Shh," Sissy said. She glanced down the hallway toward Sandy's and Aden's room. "Come on."

Charlie stumbled after her. Stepping through the threshold, he saw that Nash and Teddy were waiting with Noelle. He looked at Sissy.

"Teddy rode his bike over to help," Sissy whispered.

She softly closed the door.

"What's going on?" Charlie asked.

"Shhhh," Sissy said. "Whisper."

"Okay," Charlie glared at her and whispered, "What's going on?"

"We have a plan," Nash said.

Chapter Two Hundred & Twenty-Eight

IF YOU DO THIS THING

Tuesday morning — 7:56 a.m.

Handcuffed, Charlie nodded good-bye to his family. Nash and Teddy gave him a two-fingered salute off the nose. Charlie smiled, and got in the back of a Denver police cruiser. The officer closed the door.

"'Bye, Charlie!" Noelle yelled at the top of her lungs.

The officer looked at her and got into the car. They were already on Colfax when the officer cleared his throat.

"You're Mitch's son?" the officer asked.

"So?" Charlie asked.

"He's the reason I became a cop," the officer said. "He and O'Malley came to talk to my senior class after one of our classmates was killed."

The officer glanced at Charlie in the rearview mirror.

"And that made you want to be a cop?" Charlie asked.

"I guess it sounds pretty dumb," the officer said. "But yeah. Your Dad was so . . . cool, smart . . . such a man. My dad was a real tool. He left us when I was about ten, and I saw him only on the weekends because we had to. He moved away when I was thirteen. Never saw him again. But Delgado, man, he was so . . . tough and responsible."

"He was mostly sick when I knew him," Charlie said.

"Nah, that's not true," the officer said. "He used to bring you and your sister around. Man, he loved you guys. Sandy, too."

They pulled to a stop at the light on Pennsylvania. The officer turned around to look at Charlie.

"What I'm trying to say is that I know you're a great person because your father was a great person," the officer said.

"He's dead and my mom's a psycho. They kind of cancel each other out."

"When I heard that you were this 'Pan' everybody's been looking for?" The officer turned back around and drove through the intersection. "I thought, 'Of course, he is.' So what I'm trying to say is that you have your father inside you, and you have a lot of people rooting for you because your dad rooted for us."

The officer turned the cruiser left onto Broadway toward the downtown police station. They were in the downtown garage when the officer cleared his throat again.

"Don't feel like you're alone," the officer said. "There are lots of people around to help you, even me. You have a nice family and a lot of people who'd do anything to help."

"What are you saying?"

The officer shook his head as if he'd said too much. He came around to get Charlie from the back. Walking him into the station, the officer stuffed something into Charlie's back pockets.

"My number," the officer said in a low tone. "I'll come with an army if you need it. Any time. Any place. You're doing a really good thing, an important thing. You don't have to do it alone."

The officer gave Charlie a rough shake and pushed him into the station. As planned, Charlie howled, and the officer dragged him into booking. Another uniformed officer grabbed Charlie's other arm. They dragged him kicking and screaming into an interview room, where Detective Red Bear and Sergeant Aziz were waiting. Charlie stood in the doorway for a moment before Samantha Hargreaves came in behind him. A uniformed guard unlocked his handcuffs.

"Let's go over this again," Detective Red Bear said.

There was a tap on the door, and a man in a suit came in.

"Deputy DA Consuelo," the young man said.

He held out his hand to Samantha; she dismissed him with a

nod.

"You're 'Pan'?" the deputy DA asked. "We've been looking for you for a long, long time."

Before Charlie could say anything, Samantha gestured to the document on the table. The Deputy DA nodded and took a seat at the table.

"My client agrees to wear an ankle monitoring device," Samantha said. "He agrees to check in every day with a designated parole officer who will do a urine and breath test on him."

"Your client agrees to provide us intel on his basketball team," Detective Red Bear said. "He agrees to keep track of names, times of day, attempt to determine who purchases this crap from these monsters."

"He agrees to testify to all his knowledge regarding each of these cases," the deputy DA said.

"Pardon me," Samantha gave the men across the table a kind of scary sneer. The men leaned back a tiny bit. "It is still not clear what my client gets for all of the risk he and his family are taking."

"Attorney fees," the deputy DA said.

"Which he would not have to pay if he wasn't helping you," Samantha said.

"He gets to participate in the justice system," Sergeant Aziz said.

"Lucky Charlie," Samantha said. "Come on, Charlie. These guys are jerking us around."

Charlie stood up when she did and followed her out of the room. Samantha took his arm, and they marched down the hallway. Charlie would have freaked out if she hadn't told him she was going to do this when they'd met earlier this morning.

They were almost to the door when the deputy DA caught up with them. They walked back down the hallway to the room.

"I guess we're unclear on what exactly Mr. Delgado wants," Detective Red Bear said.

"Shall I go over the email I sent you?" Samantha gave the man a smile that indicated just exactly how stupid she thought he was. He swallowed hard.

"For the record, Ms. Hargreaves," the deputy DA said, "can you repeat your request?"

"All pending charges on all of the children are removed. All prior judgments, including Mr. Delgado's, are vacated. Mental-health support for the victims should be given prior to deposition, during the case, and continue until they are able to resolve their issues. This includes the two girls currently in inpatient treatment," Samantha said. "Salary for the time my client spends working for you to be held in a fund available to my client when the case is resolved."

"Too steep," Detective Red Bear said.

"Too bad." Samantha got up to leave again. "If you're trying to play hardball, I can assure you that my client's demands will only increase. He is a sixteen-year-old child who is risking his life and well-being for this case. His family is also at risk due to their involvement in this case. That's not to mention the effect on the girls who you'd like to testify and . . ."

"Justice is always a sacrifice," Detective Red Bear said.

"You can spare the canned speech about justice," Samantha said. "You're talking about kids who lived on the streets for years. You remember that a good half of these kids were toyed with by Saint Jude, as well as raped and tortured by these boys. They know more about justice, and who gets justice, than you ever could."

"In this economy, no one can afford these demands," Sergeant Aziz said.

"Fair enough," Samantha said. "Here's my card. Call me when you change your mind."

Charlie stood up and followed her out the door. This time, they made it to her car. When they reached the guard station, the guard gave Samantha a phone. Charlie heard a man's voice through the phone.

"Oh, I'm sorry. I didn't tell you our new requirements," Samantha glanced at Charlie.

A man's voice seemed to curse in return.

"Charlie gets to pick his parole officer," Samantha said. "Oh? That's all right, too."

Samantha gave the phone back to the guard, and they drove out.

"You have to be strong Charlie," Samantha said. "I'm not going to let them railroad you into taking all the risk."

"What about the girls?" Charlie asked. "Will they get good lawyers, too?"

"We're working on that with the Rocky Mountain Children's Law Center," Samantha said. "I know a few people there. They're scrambling to make sure that everyone has first-rate representation."

"Even the rich girls?" Charlie asked. "I mean, I know their families have money and stuff, but ..."

"Even them," Samantha said.

Charlie nodded.

"Are you hungry?" Samantha asked.

Charlie *was* hungry, but he felt too embarrassed to say anything since Samantha had been at breakfast at the Castle. He shook his head.

"You're not a very good liar," Samantha said. "Plus, I have brothers."

"Are you married to that 'Raz' guy?" Charlie asked.

"He's my partner," Samantha said. "But we're not married. Why?"

"Oh, nothing," Charlie said. "I like him. I like the way he talks to people. He really looks at them. I mean Jake and Sam, they see me. Mike and Aden, too. But ... I don't really know how to explain it. It's like Raz knows everything good and everything bad about me all at once — no pretending. Steve, um, Jill's brother, does that, too. Plus, Raz helped Nash and Teddy come up with all of this."

"He did?"

"Oh, sorry — I thought you knew," Charlie said.

"I didn't," Samantha said. "But now that you tell me, it makes sense. I wondered how Nash and Teddy came up with such a complicated plan and how they knew so much about how police departments work."

Charlie nodded. Samantha's phone rang. She looked at the caller ID but didn't answer. She drove down Market Street and pulled over at a meter across from the bus terminal.

"Let's go here," Samantha said.

They got out, and she put money into the meter. They went into the Delectable Egg and found a table.

"You used to spend a lot of time at that bus terminal," Samantha said, as she sat down.

"Begging for money." Charlie nodded.

The waitress came up to the table and took their order. Samantha ordered decaffeinated coffee, and Charlie ordered a full meal. Samantha's phone rang again. She didn't answer it.

"Is that them?" Charlie asked.

"Who?" Samantha smiled at him. "Is it weird to be back here?"

"I wondered why you picked this place," Charlie said.

"If you do this thing — collect information for the police and everything — you effectively change sides," Samantha said. "Forever. There's no going back. You won't be able to go back to this terminal and beg for change or . . ."

"I know."

"And your friends?"

"They won't, either," Charlie said. "We'll have to join the normies."

"Do you know what usually happens when kids give depositions?"

Charlie shook his head.

"They don't follow through. They go back on drugs or back to the streets or change their minds or get pregnant or move," Samantha said. "Especially street kids. So, they're asking you to make their case for them. They want you to make sure everyone shows up. It's a lot to ask."

Charlie nodded. His breakfast arrived, and he started shoveling food into his mouth. He glanced at Samantha, and she gave him a smile. He slowed down a little bit. Samantha seemed lost in thought. The waitress came by a few times, but, otherwise, Charlie ate in peace. When he was done, Samantha paid the bill. They went across the street to the bus terminal.

Charlie's eyes scanned the open area. People were moving in and out of the terminal. Right in front of them, a panhandler with a sign saying he wanted to go to Boulder got a dollar from a guy in a suit. Over there, a kid pocketed another guy's wallet.

"What do you think?" Samantha asked.

"I think this seems like a long, long time ago," Charlie said.

"You, of all people, know how brutal these boys have been," Samantha said. "If they find out you're involved, they could come after you, or worse, Sissy or Noelle or . . ."

"I know," Charlie said. "They know the risks, too. They still think it's a good idea."

"And you? What do you think?"

"I think that, sometimes, to become the man you want to be, you have to let go of the man you have been," Charlie said.

"Emerson?"

"Oddly, it's something my father said to me on my first day of kindergarten," Charlie said. "I didn't remember it until the guy who drove me downtown talked about how much my dad loved me. I don't know. Delphie would say that he was with me now. But . . ."

Charlie shrugged.

"He must have loved you very much," Samantha said.

"I wish he was here," Charlie said.

"Here they come."

She nodded toward Detective Red Bear and Sergeant Aziz. They were walking fast in their direction. The deputy DA ran to catch up. The three walked to Samantha and Charlie.

"Before you say a word," Detective Red Bear said, "we agree to your terms as stated."

"Great," Samantha said. "You have that in writing?"

The detective gave her a document. Samantha read the document and nodded to Charlie.

"We're a go," Sergeant Aziz said into his communication device.

Two police cruisers pulled up to the bus terminal. With a bit too much showy swagger, the officer who'd come for him this morning arrested him again. The officers were loud, just in case anyone was watching. Charlie played his part by resisting a little bit. In the end, he was in the backseat of the police cruiser he'd started the day in.

"Good job, Charlie," the officer said when he got into the car. "I'll take you to Probation. Did you pick an officer?"

"Aden has a friend who used to work there," Charlie said. "They're going to meet us there."

"Great," the officer said.

Charlie looked out the window. After the fuss of the arresting, the bus terminal returned to the normal ebb and flow of people. Samantha gave him a little wave. Charlie watched the terminal fade away.

He closed his eyes for a moment to mark the end of his old life.

When he opened them, he was at the parole office. Aden and an elderly black man were walking toward him.

~~~~~~~~~

Tuesday morning — 9:56 a.m.

"How are you feeling?" Valerie asked Blane as she approached Jacob's office.

"Okay," Blane smiled.

"Liar," Valerie said.

"Actually, my numbers have improved," Blane said. "Your generous gift has changed my life."

Valerie smiled. Blane nodded.

"You didn't ask about my numbers," Blane said. "I didn't get a lot of sleep last night. Tink came home last night and brought a friend."

"I heard," Valerie said. "Congratulations."

"We're pretty excited," Blane smiled "And before you tell me, I'm going home early."

"We're having another party, I think," Valerie said.

"Just the kids," Blane said. "Delphie offered to take all the kids for the day so we could rest. I think they're going to start cleaning out some of the basement rooms, but don't quote me."

"They are," Valerie said. "I'm going to help go through stuff this afternoon. You'll go home?"

"In a couple hours," Blane said. "Honestly, it's nice to just be here at my familiar desk."

"Sure," Valerie said.

She looked up when a tall, thin, graying man came out of Jacob's office. Jacob followed him.

"Let me know if you change your mind," the man said.

"I will," Jacob said.

Jacob shook the man's hand. He turned to Valerie and winked. Blane got up to escort the man out of the building. Valerie followed Jacob into his office.

"Do you know who that is?" Valerie asked. "That's the guy who's building an Old West Town in the middle of the woods. You know what his family does?"

"They donate large sums of money to politicians to get what they feel like they need." Jacob sat down in his office chair. "Yes, I know what they do."

"What did he want?" Valerie stood on the other side of his desk. "Are you going to do the rehab on his Old West Town?"

"No."

"Did he want you to donate to his political agenda? I hope you said 'No.' Mom would seriously haunt you if you started putting buckets of money into the stuff she fought to change."

"He didn't ask for money," Jacob said.

"Then, what?" Valerie put her hands on her hips. "Why was he here? And why do you look so tired?"

"Just have a lot going on, Val," Jacob said.

"Are you doing your meditations?" Valerie asked.

"Meditations?" Jacob gave her his best confused look. "What meditations?"

"Very funny," Valerie said. "You'd better do them, or you'll get all backed up. You have that look."

"What look?"

"Like you're all backed up," Valerie said.

"Good to know," Jacob said. "Is there anything I can do for you?"

"Why was that guy here?" Valerie asked.

"He wants to open the Marlowe mine," Jacob said.

"That's a great idea," Valerie said. "We could really make a difference in Leadville. It would . . ."

"Stop," Jacob said. "We're not opening the mine."

"Why not?"

"You know why not," Jacob said.

"There's got to be some kind of new technology, so you don't have to use your . . . skills," Valerie said.

"I don't have time to run another business," Jacob said.

"I could help," Valerie said.

"No, you can't," Jacob said. "You just want to start something and let me take care of it."

"What? I . . .!"

"You're leaving soon, right?"

"Uh . . . How did you know?"

"Because this is what you do right before you leave," Jacob said.

"You start a lot of work and then wander off."

"Hey!" Valerie sounded indignant.

He scowled at her.

"Well, so what if I do?" Valerie grinned. "You miss me when I'm gone."

"Right this moment, I'd *like* to miss you some." Jacob gave her a sly smile.

Valerie chuckled.

"When do you leave?" Jacob asked.

"End of the week," Valerie said. "Are you coming to my opening?"

"No," Jacob said.

"What?" Valerie's eyes welled with tears.

Jacob scowled, and Valerie laughed.

"Jill can't travel. Lipson is at a precipice, blah, blah," Valerie said. "I liked it better when I had you all to myself."

Jacob laughed.

"Okay, I didn't." Valerie grinned.

"What's the schedule?" Jacob asked.

"Premiere next weekend," Valerie said. "I'm in LA for two weeks to work on that animated thing and then back home for a month to train for the next movie. And . . ."

She looked up at him and laughed.

"You knew all of that," Valerie said.

"You've sent me ten updates," Jacob said.

"I'm going to miss you," Valerie said.

"I'll miss you too," Jacob said. "But you need to follow your dreams. You'll be miserable if you stay here much longer."

Valerie nodded.

"You'll take care of Delphie and everybody?" Valerie asked. "Watch out for Charlie?"

Jacob nodded.

"We should be home when Jill delivers," Valerie said. "I'd never leave if I didn't think I would be home for . . ."

"I know," Jacob said. "Can I help you at all?"

Valerie shook her head. Their eyes met for a brief moment in silent acknowledgement of their bond.

"Okay. Well, glad we got that settled," Valerie said.

She flipped her head and did her best flounce out of his office. She pulled his door closed because she knew it would bug him, smiled at Blane, and walked toward the entrance. She was almost to the front when she remembered that she forgot to remind him to meditate. Not wanting to give up one of her last chances to boss him around, she turned around and went back to his office.

She heard their CFO, Tres Sierra, call Blane. He got up from his desk and went to talk to Tres. She went past his desk, to Jacob's office.

She opened the door.

No Jacob.

She glanced at Blane's back and went into the office. Jacob was passed out on the floor. He was lying on his side behind his desk. He looked like he had fallen out of his office chair.

Valerie closed the door and sat down near his head. She rolled him on his back. He made the low, guttural noise he made when he was having a powerful psychic episode. Having never had one herself, Valerie always saw these as attacks of vision. She hated that her brother went away from her. She lived in terror that some day, he wouldn't come back.

"I told you to meditate," Valerie said in a low voice. She put his head on her lap. "You get backed up and . . ."

She looked up to see Blane looking into the office.

"He's having a vision," Valerie said. "A bad one."

"I'll cancel his appointments," Blane said.

Valerie nodded. Blane closed the door.

"Okay, little brother. I'm here," Valerie said. "Don't get lost coming back."

Valerie settled in to wait.

Chapter Two Hundred & Twenty-Nine

VISION

Tuesday morning—10:05 a.m.

Jacob shook his head when Valerie closed the door. She did that because she knew it bugged him. He didn't want to give her the satisfaction of seeing him get up to open it, so he waited a few minutes. This gave him a little time to obsess on his deepest fear — the Marlowe boys would kill Jill.

He shook his head. No one seemed to know. When he asked Jill, she just smiled at him and told him she wasn't Celia. Delphie was as wound up as he was about the whole thing. She was no help.

He leaned forward to get up, and . . .

He had the sense of falling out of his chair. He felt the carpet greet him before his body disappeared and he was a soul walking.

He was standing at the door of what looked like a bar. He pushed the door open and was assaulted by the stale odor of old beer, fried food, and warm bodies. The room was full of laughing drunks sitting at tables and a long bar that backed up against the right side. A woman near the back pushed a button on the jukebox and Peggy Lee's "Hey, Big Spender" came on the jukebox. The woman turned around.

Jacob took a step back. She was the secretary who had made his life hell. She winked at him and went to sit down with one of the old guys he'd kicked off the Lipson Construction board. Shaking his head, he stepped into the crowded room.

"Are you looking for me?"

A woman stood at a table near the center of the room. She looked like a comic-book gypsy. Her skin was dark and her accent was rough. Her excessive makeup was topped off by a fake beauty mark near the corner of her mouth. When she gave him a bright, red-lipped smile, the weight her false eye lashes made her eyes thin slits. She wore a bright-blue silk scarf in a turban on her head, gold rings on every finger, and a sheer, bright-orange skirt. With a jangle of at least a hundred gold bangle bracelets, she gestured to the small table in front of her, where a Tarot deck was spread. He smiled and sat down across from her.

"Hi, Mom," Jacob said.

"I am not your mother," the gypsy said. "I am Fifika, gypsy enchantress."

"Nice to see you too, Mom," Jacob said.

"Can't you just play along?" Celia waved her arm over the cards again.

"Sure," Jacob said. "Tell me why I am here, Fif . . . What was it?"

"I am Fifika." Celia jangled her bracelets as she raised her arm over her head.

"Fifika," Jacob said. "The hamster's name? Seriously?"

Celia gave him a stern look.

"Fine," Jacob said. "Why am I here?"

"You have a question," Celia continued in her gypsy accent.

"I do?" Jacob asked.

Celia gave him a frustrated look that was straight out of Valerie's playbook.

"I'm in a new place, M . . . uh . . . Fifika," Jacob said. "How 'bout you remind me? Can I have a beer while I'm here?"

"No, you can't drink beer in visions!" Celia said.

"I wonder why not," Jacob said. "Now *that's* a good question for Fifika."

Celia scowled at him.

"Why am I here, Mom?" Jacob asked. "I have a company to run

and . . ."

"You also have a few questions?" Celia asked.

"Remind me," Jacob said.

"You were wondering about the babies?" Celia asked.

"Yeah, that is weird," Jacob nodded. "Why aren't they killing Jill, like I almost killed you? I adored you, loved you always, but without Delphie's help, you would have died in childbirth, like all the women who've had Marlowe males before you. You and me — we're the only ones who've survived."

"An excellent question," Celia said in her Fifika accent. She tried to shuffle the deck of Tarot cards but wasn't able to. "Why won't you let me shuffle?"

"Because I never get much out of those cards," Jacob said. "Plus, you know the answer. Just tell me; no props."

"You've become very impatient," Celia said.

"I have this feeling, Mom," Jacob said. "It feels like everything is teetering on the top of an apex. If I change the balance in any direction, everything will crash."

Celia scowled, and her comic-book gypsy face folded into itself, with only her nose sticking out. If Jacob hadn't been so upset, he would have laughed out loud.

"I keep running from thing to thing, but I . . ." Jacob leaned forward. "I don't have any idea what the problem is or how everything got to be on this mountain. If I don't keep running, everything will fall apart. It's not logical. Everything is really fine — more than fine. It's just . . ."

"That's why you're having this vision," Celia said. "To deal with your uncertainty."

"Can't you just tell me?" Jacob said.

"I don't know everything," Celia said. "I can tell you about your boys, though."

"Okay," Jacob said.

The jukebox started to play "Hey, Big Spender" again and Jacob groaned. Celia laughed.

"The boys?" Jacob asked.

"Your vision, my darling boy. If you don't like the song, change it."

"How?" Jacob asked.

"I remember a time when you felt like you could do anything in the world," Celia said. "How did you get so . . . bound up?"

"Everything I do now affects other people," Jacob said. "If I turn that song off, that horrible woman will be upset. If I change you back to your regular self, you'll be pissed. If I . . ."

He shook his head.

"It's like my hands are tied." He shook his head. "Like I'm the puppet master. If I move too far this way, *bam* — everything falls apart."

"You don't want to lose everything," Celia said.

"I don't want to lose *anything*," Jacob said. "My life is . . . perfect and . . ."

"Very hard." Celia reached out and stroked his cheek with her red-nailed gypsy hand. "I do know something about this."

Jacob looked at her.

"You created all of this — Jill, the company, your life, your health — because it was what was good for you. Every choice you made, you made it based on what was best for you."

"I can't live that kind of selfish life now," Jacob said. "I have Jill and . . ."

Celia tipped her head to the side. Jacob was struck at how odd it was to see his mother's love and compassion on Fifika the gypsy's face.

"It's better for you to bear this burden, to feel so uncomfortable yourself, so that you don't lose everything." Celia gave him a small smile. "Is that right?"

Jacob nodded.

"Remember when we did the ice-crystal thing?" Celia asked. "It seems kind of silly right now, but . . ."

"Where Val and I loved the water and hated it?" Jacob nodded.

"Val's love was gorgeous, and mine . . . See? That's what I mean! I have to be really careful because I can't love very well."

"She'd already met Mike," Celia said. "She was in love for the first time."

"Oh," Jacob said.

"Hey, Big Spender" started up again on the jukebox, and Jacob looked over to see who was causing the racket. The evil secretary gave him a little wave and went back to sit down.

"Turn off the music," Celia said.

"She's enjoying it," Jacob said.

"You don't even like her!" Celia said. "Good Lord."

"I don't like her, but I don't want any trouble with her, either," Jacob said. "Jill was really upset when that happened, and she has the boys now and . . ."

The volume of the music rose. Jacob's ears began to ring. He dropped his head on the table.

"Your vision," Celia said. "You're in control here."

He groaned.

"You really never meditate, do you?" Celia asked.

"I have a few other things to do." Jacob snarled.

"If you meditated, you would know that you created this room," Celia said. "Do you trust me?"

Jacob sat up to look at her. He nodded.

"Turn off the music," Celia said.

Jacob raised his hand to destroy the jukebox.

"Don't do that," Celia said.

"You just said to turn off the music," Jacob said.

"With your mind, Jacob Marlowe. Do it with your mind."

Jacob rolled his eyes and lowered his arm.

"Think," Celia said. "*Music off.*"

"Music off," Jacob said.

The jukebox turned off. The evil secretary got up from her seat and smiled at him. She walked to the jukebox.

"Go away," Jacob said.

She disappeared.

"You're spending so much energy trying to hold everything together that you've become stunted," Celia said. "You're not growing. The business isn't growing. Your love with Jill isn't expanding. You're not living."

"But . . ."

"Do you remember what happened when you hated the water?" Celia asked.

Jacob nodded.

"You're too powerful to be so uncomfortable," Celia said.

"I'm uncomfortable because everything is about to change!"

"You're uncomfortable because you've told yourself that things cannot change or you will lose everything," Celia said. "Katy is not a tiny fatherless girl anymore. Jill will have your twins, and they will be wonderful. You can leave Lipson Construction in less than a year. Valerie is growing. Your Dad will continue to learn and grow."

"Why won't you tell me what's happening to Jill and the boys?" Jacob's voice rose with desperation.

"Because you already know," Celia said. "You also know what's wrong. You just won't let yourself know. You'd rather stay in this bar, listening to that horrible song, than actually risk taking a step in your life."

"But I'll lose Jill?"

"What would she say if you told her that?" Celia asked.

"She would . . ." Jacob looked up to see Jill walk into the room. It wasn't the Jill he'd married. It was when Jill was pregnant with Katy. Her long, dark hair was falling out of a braid down her back. She looked exhausted and so gorgeous. He smiled at her. She gave him a secret smile and went to take an order at one of the tables.

"Why don't the boys hurt Jill?" Celia asked in a low voice.

"Because they have each other." Jacob turned to look at her. "They're not alone."

"Marlowe men are desperately lonely," Celia said. "Even at

birth, they know they're different, unusual. Most of them spend their lives alone, in mines, and other crevices in the world. You don't meditate because the silence feels lonely."

Jacob felt her words echo through his being. He nodded and looked up to see if Jill was still waiting tables. She looked up from a table near the back and smiled at him.

"You know, she's never been angry with me for having Katy when she was so poor and . . ." Jacob smiled at Jill.

"Why do you think that is?" Celia asked.

Jacob shrugged.

"Why don't you ask her?" Celia asked.

His mother turned around and waved Jill over. Jill gave him a sweet smile and turned to Celia.

"What can I bring you?" Jill asked.

"Why haven't you been angry with my son for not taking care of you when you were pregnant with Katy?" Celia asked. "And letting you live hand-to-mouth when she was a baby?"

"Gosh — so *many* reasons." Jill looked at Jacob and blushed. "If I'd known that Katy wasn't stupid Trevor's, I wouldn't have stayed with him. I would have left and lived with Meg or . . ."

Jill gestured to Jacob.

"If Jake had known Katy was his baby girl, he would have moved mountains to find us." Jill nodded. "Right?"

Jacob nodded.

"And why aren't you mad?" Celia asked.

"Because that's just life," Jill said. "I needed to go through everything that happened so I would be ready for life with Jake. If Trevor hadn't left me and all of everything horrible, I couldn't have what I have now."

Jill nodded and moved away from the table.

"By trying to hold everything together, you're . . ." Celia started.

"Being very selfish," Jacob said. "Blocking other people from learning what they need to learn."

"From growing," Celia interrupted. "You're stopping everyone from growing, and, by being uncomfortable you're emitting waves of cosmic junk into everyone and everything around you. You're powerful enough to lock everyone in that goo."

"Like what?"

"Honey and MJ's apartment project?" Celia raised her artificially arched gypsy eyebrows at Jacob. "Tanesha's house? You didn't finish the basement, did you?"

"No but they did move in," Jacob said. "They say it's perfect."

"Their 'perfect' and your 'perfect' are not the same things, are they?" Celia asked. "How much needs to be done on Tanesha's yellow house?"

"About an hour," Jacob said. "More or less."

"And that poor apartment building has been stuck in inspection for . . ."

"Three months," Jacob said.

Celia nodded.

"You mean I'm causing this?" Jacob asked.

"You're not making all the chaos happen," Celia said. "No one can do that, but you're not making it better, either."

Jacob looked up to watch Jill move around the room with a tray full of food.

"She's very beautiful," Jacob said. "And she's not moving now, either. It's driving her crazy. She can't even get her hair done or see Tanesha's house or . . ."

Celia put her hand on his arm, and he looked at her.

"Let it go," Celia said. "Stop holding on so tightly."

"I'll lose everything," he said in a low tone.

"Or gain everything." She smiled at him. "What's wrong with Lipson Construction?"

"Ah, Mom," Jacob said. "If we're going to talk about work, can you change back?"

She nodded and transformed into her usual form. He smiled.

"Will you get us out of this bar?" she asked.

With a nod, they were sitting on a bench looking at the back side of Mount Evans just off of Guanella Pass.

"I loved it here," Celia said.

"I know," Jacob said.

"What's wrong with my company?" Celia asked.

"I don't know," Jacob said. "Everyone I trust seems really skittish about this big new job. Why did *we* get it? Those guys I fired are hovering around the site like buzzards and . . ."

"Let go, Jacob," Celia said.

"What does it matter if I know what's going to happen?" Jacob shrugged. "The company is almost half owned by employees. It's not like before, when I could change directions on a whim. Every single thing on this job looks perfect on paper. And trust me — the employees are watching the bottom line. I can't go to them and tell them the job doesn't *feel right*. Not with big money on the table."

"Show me now," Celia said. "What's wrong with my company?"

The scene in front of them shifted to the new project out by the airport.

"They want us to manage the entire creation of what will be a new town," Jacob said.

"So?"

"We're a tiny company," Jacob said. "How can we do that?"

"What did the state say when they gave you the job?" Celia asked.

"They wanted to increase opportunity for people," Jacob said. "We're moving toward one hundred percent employee ownership. The governor wanted to put that feather in his cap."

"Sounds pretty good," Celia said. "How's it going?"

"We're doing it, if that's what you mean," Jacob said.

"Any problems?"

"No," Jacob said. "But people I like and trust, like Bambi and Rodney, don't like it, either. There's just a weird feeling. Those guys who quit over the bullying Noelle thing? They're subcontractors on the job, and they're there every day. They seem so smug and superior. It's weird."

"I thought they *always* thought they were superior." Celia said. "You did, after all, sell shares to all those brown people."

"Yes, the browns." Jacob shook his head. "And the blacks. Don't forget them."

"I haven't," Celia said. "I love seeing Rodney and Yvonne together and happy."

Jacob smiled.

"What do you see that no one else can?" Celia asked him the annoying question she used to ask when he was a child. He scowled at her.

"What do *you* see?" she repeated.

"Mom, I really don't want to . . ."

"I get that," Celia said. "Do you ever want to get out of this vision?"

"Yes, but . . ."

"What do *you* see that no one else can?"

"I see . . ."

As if they were in the center of a Lazy Susan, the scene spun under them.

"Hold on!" Jacob said.

His mother laughed, and their bench spun. Soon, they had a bird's eye view of the new project and most of northeastern Colorado.

"Looks pretty good to me," Celia said.

"Who's that?" Jacob pointed to two people standing in the near distance.

"Looks like Bumpy Wilson," Celia said.

"That's Jeraine." Jacob pointed to the men.

"Should I let them do that fracking on this land in Dearfield?" Bumpy asked.

Bumpy pointed toward the Niobrara oil wells near the border of Colorado.

"There's oil and natural gas right here," Bumpy said. "And men who are going to pay big money for it."

"That's why we're building this city," Jacob said. "To house the Niobrara oil-field workers."

"Look at that," Celia pointed to the oil field.

An enormous metal tower was pushing pressurized fluid into the earth.

"That's a fracking tower, Mom," Jacob said.

"No," Celia said. "*See* it."

Jacob reached out with his senses. He could see the waves of pressure coming off the well like ripples in a river. He saw the ground rupture to release its buried treasure. The oil company stood eagerly to collect the bounty. With each injection of fluid, the ground shifted.

"The pressure's building," Celia said. "What happens next?"

Jacob shut his eyes for a moment. When he opened them, the ground was shaking. Bumpy and Jeraine were knocked on their sides like bowling pins. The Lipson project was a disaster zone. A jagged crack ran down the center of the newly paved Main Street. Equipment toppled over or fell into sinkholes. Their portable construction trailers were tossed like dice in an enormous craps game.

People were screaming in horror and pain. Some workers ran for their lives. People ran to help those stuck in upended earthmoving equipment. Rodney was screaming in rage over a man who'd been cut in half. Honey was stuck in a sinkhole. The unknown fault made its presence known in the death and destruction of the worksite.

"Enough," Jacob said. "I've seen enough."

They were back on Guanella Pass, looking at Mount Evans.

"Did you know?" Celia asked.

"I knew something was wrong," Jacob said. "I could feel a weird sense of pressure. I just . . . believed them, went along, and . . ."

"What will you do now?"

"I have no idea," Jacob said. "It will cost us millions to get out of it. A geological report will take years to complete. There's no evidence that this will happen. No one is going to believe me, and . . ."

"You'll be the weirdo."

"Again," Jacob said. "I hate being the weirdo."

"If you finish Honey's project?"

"She'll move out, and I really enjoy her living at the Castle," Jacob said.

"She never mentioned moving out," Celia said.

"If she moves to the new apartments, she can live with twenty-four hour nursing assistance, no stairs; everything is brand new."

"You should trust more," Celia said.

"Been there before," Jacob shrugged.

"You have to stop this," Celia said.

"How?" Jacob asked.

"Who did you see in this vision?"

"Bumpy. Jeraine," Jacob said.

"Maybe you could ask Jeraine when you go finish his house," Celia said.

"I have time?"

"You have some time," Celia said. "And, son?"

"Yes, Mom," Jacob said.

"You've treated people fairly and been a good person all of your life," Celia said. "People trust you. You need to trust them to think outside their wallet."

"Doesn't seem like anyone does that anymore," Jacob said.

"You'd be surprised," Celia smiled.

"Anything else?" Jacob asked.

"Just that I love you, son," Celia leaned over to kiss his cheek. "Tell Val that I love her and believe in her. Oh, and Jackie can see me."

Jacob slowly opened his eyes and smiled at Valerie.

"Mom says 'Hi.'" Jacob smiled. He started to get up, and his head exploded with pain. He lay back down.

"I'm glad you're back." Valerie kissed his forehead.

He smiled.

"I'll get you some juice." Valerie moved away from him. "Did Mom say anything else?"

"She said she loves you and she believes in you," he said.

Valerie smiled and got up. She was almost to the door when he said.

"Oh, and Jackie can see her," Jacob said.

"I knew it!" Valerie beamed at him. "Mike said I was imagining things. I knew that shadow was Mom with Jackie. Every time Jackie gets scared, the shadow shows up. Mom. I just knew it. Thanks."

She went out the door, and he lay down again. He took his cell phone out of his pocket.

"Jill?"

"Hi!" Jill said. "Is everything okay? Blane called to say you were having a vision."

"Yeah," Jacob said. "I wonder if you could come pick me up."

"But . . . you were really clear," Jill said. "Home imprisonment for the breeding stock."

"I was wrong," Jacob said. "Would you mind taking my Jeep? It has my tools in the back."

"Sure." Jill's voice relayed her glee. "Where are we going?"

"Tanesha's," Jacob said.

"Really?" Jill's voice rose with excitement. "But that's a lot of stairs and . . ."

"Have you had any bleeding?" Jacob asked.

"No," Jill said. "We're fine."

"If you do, you'll go back to home imprisonment?" Jacob asked.

"Of course," Jill said. "I would never risk the boys or myself."

"Then we're probably all right."

"Yay" Jill hung up the phone.

Smiling, Jacob lay down on the carpet. That was easy. Before he could wonder how to deal with the hard part, Valerie walked in with juice and a flood of cheerful questions about his vision.

Chapter Two Hundred & Thirty

Huge risk

Tuesday afternoon — 1:05 p.m.

Samantha pulled her car up to the Castle gate. Charlie gave her the code, and she punched it into the keypad. The gate opened.

"Those photographers would get old, fast," she said, as she parked the car.

"You get used to it," Charlie said. "If they get a photo of Jackie, they can make hundreds of thousands of dollars. And look at them."

Samantha turned to look at the photographers.

"They're just trying to feed their families," Charlie said.

Samantha smiled at him.

"Are you going to be all right?" Samantha asked.

"I think so," Charlie said. "Before you say it, I will be careful."

Samantha smiled at him.

"Why are you doing all of this?" Samantha asked. "When I was your age, all I cared about was getting nicer clothes, and what boys would ask me out, and why, oh why, was I related to the weirdo twins?"

Charlie smiled.

"I don't know if I would do it," Samantha said.

"If you had the chance to maybe save someone's life, would you have done that?" Charlie asked.

Samantha turned to look at him.

"I mean, Aden always says, 'Run the tape, Charlie. Where's this gonna go?' Mostly he means on using drugs and being an asshole, but when I run this tape... These guys... they're gonna kill someone. Maybe they won't mean it; maybe they'll want to kill that person; maybe that person will be me. But sooner or later, they're gonna kill someone. They almost killed Tink. I was there at the hospital. She was mostly dead."

Charlie shrugged.

"What would you do?" Charlie asked. "If you were my age?"

Samantha looked out the windshield. She didn't say anything for a while.

"That's what I thought," Charlie said.

"I'll do anything I can to help you," Samantha said. "And my 'anything' is pretty big."

Charlie gave her an impish grin, and she laughed.

"Come on," Charlie said. "Mrs. Valerie told me to make sure you came in when you dropped me off, and I don't want to make her mad."

"Val? She's a sweetie."

"She's really scary when she's mad." Charlie gave an exaggerated shiver.

Samantha laughed. They got out of the car and went into the house. They heard muffled laughing and loud thumps.

"What's going on here?" Samantha asked.

"Oh, Delphie's got everyone cleaning out a room downstairs," Charlie smiled.

"I thought work and teenagers didn't mix," Samantha said.

"You haven't worked with Delphie or this house," Charlie said. "There's always something spooky or weird in this house. Or beautiful. So many people have lived here. We cleaned out one room downstairs where some vagrants had stuffed all their possessions in hidden wall compartments. It was sort of gross and sort of great. Delphie was able to send the vagrants' families photos and even an old pocket watch. I wanted to keep the watch, but Delphie was sure the family would want it back. They did."

Charlie shrugged.

"You should join us," Charlie said. "We have lots of pregnant clothes here."

They heard a loud boom and a loud laugh.

"Honey and MJ are helping," Charlie smiled. "This is going to be fun. Let's take a look."

Charlie waved Samantha toward the stairs to the basement. They went down the long stairwell, turned the corner, and were confronted with a cloud of black dust. Charlie stepped back. They heard a high-pitched girl's laugh.

"That's Ivy." Charlie smiled.

"You really like her," Samantha said.

"She's just a kid," Charlie said. "She's wild and very fun. I bet she's scaring the crap out of Noelle."

"No she's not!" Carrying a box, Noelle appeared right in front of him. She punched his shoulder and walked past him. "I like her."

Noelle was down the hall before she yelled back, "Nash *really* likes her."

"Of course, he does," Charlie said. "Are you game?"

"Sure," Samantha said.

"Sandy!" Charlie yelled.

For all his maturity, in this moment, Charlie was every bit a sixteen-year-old boy. Samantha scowled at him, but Sandy appeared from a room along the hall.

"Charlie!" Sandy hugged him. "Welcome home! Samantha! Thank you so much for helping us."

Samantha smiled at Sandy.

"You need to change," Sandy said to Charlie. "Go now, before you see the girls."

"But..." Charlie's entire posture shifted. The strong, thoughtful young man was gone, leaving a grouchy child in his place.

"Now!" Sandy pointed up the stairs. "You better hurry, because Tink and Ivy are leaving in a bit, and I know you want to see them."

Charlie scowled at her. He opened his mouth; Sandy shook her head. He slunk up the stairs.

"That's impressive," Samantha said in a low voice.

"He wants to see his girlfriend," Sandy laughed. "It's all about leverage."

"He said you might have some clothes I could wear?" Samantha asked. "I thought I'd stay for a while. It would be good for me to see how Charlie and the girls interact."

"Sure. You're taller than I am, but just as huge." Sandy pointed down another hall. "Some of my old clothes are down here in the community closet."

"I got big right away," Samantha said.

"Me, too," Sandy said. "Have you seen Jill?"

Samantha shook her head.

"She's having twins," Sandy laughed. "She's taller than I am. I mean, who isn't — right? But she looks . . . I mean, she could pass for just being heavy around the middle."

"Not me," Samantha smiled.

"Me, neither," Sandy said. "Jake let Jill out of her house arrest — that's what she calls bed rest. She traipsed down the stairs. Incredible. She's due in less than two months!"

Samantha laughed.

"She was that way with Katy. She waited tables until the day she had Katy, and then she was back up a couple days later. Of course, necessity drove some of that." Sandy pushed open a swinging door. She turned on the light, and four long closet rods full of clothing appeared. "Jake made this room for all our old clothes. It's great for the kids because they can swap. Honey's smaller than I am, but she wore some of my maternity clothes. She can even wear some of the kids' clothes. Val is really generous. She leaves all her designer clothes here when she's done. Except the dresses, of course."

"Where are her dresses?" Samantha asked.

"They have their own special climate-controlled closet," Sandy said. "It's above Mike's studio."

"That's right." Samantha smiled. "I was there helping Val find something special to wear when she had Jackie."

"When she was crazy?" Sandy nodded.

Samantha nodded.

"You're a good friend. Now, let's see . . ." Sandy waded into the closet. "Everything is set up by size so it's easy for the kids. Katy's just starting to grow, so she's wearing some of Noelle's old clothes. Tink and Ivy are going to look through the closet before they go. They're welcome to anything we have, of course."

"There isn't a lot of boys' stuff here," Samantha said.

"Our boys destroy clothing," Sandy said from somewhere in the closet. "Plus, Noelle went through and took all the men's shirts. She uses them when she paints. Are you having a boy?"

"I'm not supposed to say," Samantha said.

"Here." Sandy brought out a huge muumuu-looking thing. "This should work. It's one of Delphie's old house dresses."

"This is huge!" Samantha held it up. "Delphie wore this? She's not that big."

"When she was cleaning up the house," Sandy said. "It's actually really great. It has lots of pockets that hold stuff. You'll like it."

Sandy helped Samantha put the dress over her clothing. Sandy grabbed a belt to tie up the dress.

"*Voila!*" Sandy said. "I can assure you, Val or Delphie will want the dress when you're done."

"Oh, look," Samantha said. "My purse fits right here."

"Exactly." Sandy turned to leave the room.

"Before you go . . ."

Sandy turned back to Samantha.

"I wanted to ask you . . ." Samantha's eyes scanned Sandy's face. "Is it hard for you that Charlie's taking this big risk? I mean Sissy and the girls are, too, but Charlie . . ."

"It's hard," Sandy said. "Sometimes it's hard to let them leave the house."

"That's what I mean," Samantha said. "I don't think I've ever felt this way, but now . . ."

She gestured to her baby, and Sandy nodded.

"I see a lot of parents clutch onto their kids," Samantha said. "They have to eat this specific thing and do these after-school programs. Everything is scheduled and structured and just so. Then I come over here, and your kids . . ."

"We're kind of wild," Sandy smiled.

"Paddie loves it here," Samantha said. "He's one of those kids. Julie has him on a special diet for his allergies, and he doesn't cheat. That's not what I mean . . ."

"We have a lot of space," Sandy said. "They can be kids and still do what's best for them."

"You trust them," Samantha said.

"I don't know about that," Sandy said. "You haven't seen the epic battles between Charlie and Aden."

Samantha smiled.

"To answer your question, yes it's hard for me that Charlie and Sissy and Noelle and Nash and Teddy are taking this huge risk," Sandy said. "But they really want to do it. I feel like it's my job is to help them test themselves while they're here in our house. Someday, they'll be on their own. If they don't test themselves now, how will they know what they can do?"

"My Dad was kind of like that," Samantha said.

"Did it work?"

"I still hate him for it." Samantha smiled. "But yes, I know my capabilities and my limits, especially in the wilderness."

"I have to let Charlie try to help," Sandy said. "I want to nurture his better instincts. At the same time, I'm willing and able to pick up the pieces if it all falls apart."

Samantha nodded.

"Auntie Sami?" Paddie's voice came from the other side of the door. "Mrs. Valerie is looking for you."

Samantha smiled at Sandy. She nodded, and Samantha left the

room. Sandy closed her eyes. She thought she was the only one who was worried about Charlie. Samantha's concerns made her own worries seem all the more valid and worrisome. Sandy scowled at herself and turned off the light.

"Pan!" Ivy's high-pitched voice came down the hall.

"Look — it's Charlie!" Honey said.

Sandy groaned to herself. She'd better get over there before it got too wild. She trotted past Samantha and into the fray.

~~~~~~~~~

Tuesday afternoon — 1:35 p.m.

"I think that's about it," Jacob said, as he walked into the kitchen of the yellow house. "I have to get back to Lipson."

Jeraine looked up. He had been working at the kitchen table. He pulled off his reading glasses and stood up.

"I made a list of the things we need to finish." Jill gave Jeraine a copy of the list. He looked at it, smiled, and set it down. Jill took Jeraine's hand that was holding his reading glasses and put it up to his face. She gave him the list again. He looked embarrassed but put on his glasses and read the list. "Most of it will be done by contractors, but things like those storm windows? Jake or Sam will need to put them on when they come in. Jake or I will be back to check everything when we're done."

"When do you think that will be?" Jeraine asked.

"We're going to do some planting, but we'll wait to finish things like sprinklers until the spring," Jacob said. "So, we won't be totally finished until sometime next year."

"It looks nice, though," Jeraine smiled. "Miss T is so happy. She slept like a baby last night. This house . . . It's a really big deal to us."

"Yay!" Jill clapped her hands.

"What were you reading?" Jacob asked.

"It's some stuff my dad asked me to take a look at," Jeraine said. "Our family has some land in Dearfield."

Jacob leaned over the table to take a look. Jill sat down at the table to look at the map.

"Where you got kicked by the donkey?" Jill smiled.

"I'm gettin' my teeth fixed tomorrow," Jeraine said.

"I didn't say anything about your teeth," Jill said.

"Hmm." Jeraine gave her a sour look. She had to look away to keep from laughing.

"This is a geological survey," Jacob said and stood up.

"That's right," Jeraine said. "Dad thinks there's something fishy about it. Well, actually, don't tell Miss T, but her dad thinks there's something going on out there. He talked to my dad about it, and my dad requested this stuff. 'Course it's all print, no digital. I can't make heads or tails of it either way. And I'm not stupid. I certainly don't need no white man explaining nothing to me."

Jeraine looked Jacob up and down. Jacob raised an eyebrow at him.

"How about a friend?" Jacob asked.

"Since when are you and I friends?" Jeraine scowled.

"Since you're standing in a house I own and fixed up for you?" Jacob asked.

Jeraine nodded. He thought for a moment and then laughed at himself.

"Would you take a look?" Jeraine asked.

"Sure." Jacob leaned over the maps. "I don't know if I can help..."

"Just another pair of eyes..." Jeraine said.

"Would you look at that...?" Jacob pointed to a deep underground fault zone that ran down the center of Lipson Construction's large project.

"They say here..." Jeraine picked up a book and put on his reading glasses. "They say they use those fissures... uh..." Jeraine's changed his voice to a geek voice. "To promote the expansion and release of petrochemicals."

Jeraine took off his glasses and looked at Jacob.

"What the hell does that mean? Any fool who looks at this can see that you put pressure in over here . . ." Jeraine pointed to the location of the current fracking sites.

"It's going to come out over here." Jacob pointed to the underground fault.

"That's what I'm saying." Jeraine nodded. "Isn't that where Rodney's been working?"

Jacob nodded.

"What's this?" Jill put her finger on the map.

Jacob leaned over to look.

"Isn't that the outline of the project?" Jill said. "I mean, it looks like it. It's configured here — road, buildings, area for a subdivision."

Jacob groaned.

"That isn't it." Jeraine leaned over to take a closer look. "I've gone out there to meet with my . . . uh . . . friend, Aden. Where you're pointing is about thirty miles . . ."

"Northeast," Jacob said. "Right. I wonder how it got moved."

"Probably couldn't get this land," Jeraine said.

"No, that's not it," Jacob said.

"How do you know?" Jeraine scowled. "It could be it."

"It's not," Jacob said.

"Now, how do you know?" Jeraine asked.

"I own this piece of land," Jacob said. "I bought it a few years ago along with some neighboring farms."

"Jake transferred all his property holdings into Katy's name when we got married," Jill said. "The land belongs to her and the boys."

She gestured to her belly.

"Why would you buy some farms in the middle of nowhere?" Jeraine asked.

"Dad took a contract for a sewer project out there," Jacob said. "It was before I came back to Colorado. I was helping him finish up these projects. We were working out there, and . . ."

Jacob blushed. Jeraine raised an eyebrow and gave the same look Jacob had just given him.

"You can tell a friend," Jeraine said.

Jacob pointed to the map.

"There were three houses, pretty close together, on three farms," Jacob said. "The houses are . . . gorgeous. Original fixtures, hand crafted, beautiful old-growth wood, leaded windows, everything in perfect condition . . . The families had fallen onto hard times, and they were going to lose the land to the bank. I bought them to save them from a . . .."

Jill and Jeraine looked at him. He flushed.

"They wanted to build a subdivision on them," Jacob said.

"You mean *this* subdivision." Jeraine pointed to the one Jill had found on the map.

"Probably." Jacob nodded.

"So why didn't they build it?" Jill asked.

"The owner wouldn't sell?" Jacob wrinkled his nose.

Jeraine and Jill laughed at Jacob.

"Hey, thanks." Jacob held his hand out to Jeraine. "This is very helpful."

"You bet." Jeraine shook his hand. "Any idea what I should tell my dad?"

"Hold off for now," Jacob said. "Let me see what I can figure out."

Jacob helped Jill to her feet.

"Let us know if there's anything else you need fixed," Jill said.

"You know I'm going to buy this house," Jeraine said.

"Never doubted it," Jacob said.

Jeraine walked them to the door, and they left.

"This is really a great house," Jill said.

"It is." Jacob nodded. He opened the passenger door and helped her into the Jeep. He checked the back to make sure his tools were there and got in the driver's seat.

"So, what's going on?" Jill asked.

"What do you mean?" Jacob asked.

"Why didn't they use your land?" Jill asked. "I mean, it's funny to think you didn't sell but . . ."

"They never asked," Jacob said.

"What the hell?" Jill asked.

"Exactly."

Chapter Two Hundred & Thirty-One

Tea

Tuesday afternoon — 4:35 p.m.

"I wanted to check to see you needed anything else done." Ivy said.

Standing near the bottom of the basement stairwell, Ivy's arms were full of Noelle's old clothing.

"What do you mean?" Delphie asked.

"She wants to know how to pay for everything," Honey said.

"Oh." Delphie smiled. "You helped clean out the room."

"That was fun," Ivy said.

"Fun or not," Delphie said. "You helped us move one step closer to figuring out what's in this house. Now we have some things to give away, some items to return, and . . ."

"We've finished one more room!" Valerie said, as she came down the hall toward them. "Whoo hoo!"

Valerie put her arm around Delphie's shoulders, and they went up the basement stairs.

"Can I help you up the stairs?" Ivy asked Honey.

"I can take the lift," Honey said.

She slid from her basement wheelchair to the chair lift. Remembering what it was like for her when she moved to the Castle, Honey turned back to the girl.

"Why don't you come up and help me fold Maggie's clothes?" Honey asked. "The kids will be home from martial arts soon. They go running with Jacob about five. Did you get some workout clothes?"

Ivy shook her head.

"I bet they won't go running today, since you're here," Honey said. "But don't quote me."

Ivy walked beside Honey up the stairwell. Honey plopped off the stairwell lift and into her upstairs wheelchair. When she turned around, she saw how full Ivy's arms were.

"First, let's get you something to hold all of those clothes in," Honey said.

"I'm okay," Ivy said.

Honey smiled and wheeled to the closet where they stored luggage. She rolled out a suitcase.

"I don't know where I'm going, Miss Honey," Ivy said. "I don't think I'm going to stay at Mrs. Heather's house. They're going to see if I have any family and . . ."

"That's all right," Honey said. "We can always get another."

Honey set the suitcase on the couch and unzipped it.

"I lived in the motels on Colfax when I was a kid," Honey said. She patted the couch. "It was weird when we moved. I was . . . mmm. . . eight or nine, I guess when my mom got a good job."

"I never lived in the motels." Ivy set the clothing down on the couch cushion. Honey picked up a shirt, set the hanger on the couch, and folded the shirt. "I lived with my grandmother until a couple of years ago."

"What happened to your grandmother?" Honey asked. She set the shirt into the suitcase and picked up another. Ivy copied Honey's actions.

"She died," Ivy said.

Honey glanced at Ivy with surprise.

"What?" Ivy asked.

"Didn't they take you into social services? Try to find your family?" Honey asked.

"Sure," Ivy said. "But the place was weird and . . . Everyone was a lot happier if they got the money from the state, you know for fostering me, but they didn't like me there so much."

"Wow," Honey said.

"Plus, I wanted to find my . . ."

Ivy stopped talking and focused on the clothing. In the silence, they made quick work of folding her clothing and putting it into the suitcase.

"You know, I bet you could wear some of my clothes," Honey said.

"Do you have normal clothes?" Ivy asked. Her hand went to her mouth. "I'm sorry. I didn't mean anything bad. I . . ."

"Most people in wheelchairs wear regular clothing," Honey said. "At least I do. Come on — let's look and see what I have."

Honey picked up the suitcase and wheeled to her apartment.

"Be very quiet," Honey said. "MJ and Maggie are sleeping in her room."

Honey gestured to the baby monitor hooked onto her wheelchair. Ivy heard MJ snore and gave Honey a bright nod. Honey opened the door to the apartment and wheeled up the ramp to her wheel-in closet.

"You can really have anything. Most of this stuff doesn't fit me now that I've had Maggie," Honey said. "If I were you, I'd get some of the nice stuff. You don't have anything to wear to dinner or whatever."

"Do you think I'll need it?" Ivy asked.

"If you stay around here, there's always something," Honey said. "We're virtually going to Valerie's premiere next week."

"Virtually?" Ivy asked.

"By the computer," Honey said. "It's something the movie producers set up so that family can go. We're getting dressed up. MJ's wearing his dress uniform. It'll be Jackie's first outing."

Ivy nodded. Honey took a dress out of the closet and held it up to Ivy.

"You were saying something about finding someone?" Honey tried to ask the question in the most non-threatening way possible. "Oh, here's a nice one."

Honey pulled out a pair of black silk pants and a silk top

covered in pink roses. Ivy took the hanger from Honey.

"Jill got this for me for our honeymoon. We ended up not going," Honey said.

"How come?" Ivy asked.

"I got sick," Honey said. "Try it on."

Ivy pulled off her top, and Honey went back to looking at clothes.

"My mom had an older sister, like twenty years older," Ivy said. "She told my dad all about her. My dad promised he would find her so that my mom would have some family — besides us, I mean. Then Mom died. We moved here so that my dad could keep his promise, but then he had to go to Iraq. Grannie moved to take care of me while Dad was gone, and then . . . She got kinda stuck with me."

While Honey pretended to be absorbed in her clothing hunt, Ivy buttoned the silk blouse.

"Grannie and I," Ivy's voice clouded with sorrow, "we used to have the most fun looking for my mom's sister. Grannie would do all this research during the week, online and stuff. On the weekends, we'd go on these grand adventures. We went to Leadville. We've been to almost every graveyard in Colorado looking for my mom's sister. Grannie thought it was a great mystery. That's what she would say, 'This is a mystery for the record books.' She was a lot of fun."

"You must miss her a lot," Honey said.

"I do," Ivy said. "I really do."

"Did you ever find her?" Honey asked.

"My mom's sister?" Ivy asked. "No. I don't really think she existed. I think it was just a fun game my Grannie would play with me."

Ivy pressed herself into the hanging clothing so that Honey wouldn't see her cry. Honey gave the girl her space.

"Let's see," Honey said. "I have a few running shoes. I bet we're about the same size. Do you want to try on this outfit so you can go running?"

Ivy wiped her face and nodded.

"Let's get you dressed in some of my workout clothes," Honey said. "I have a lot. You can go with them if they decide to run."

"I'd like that." Ivy grinned. "I'm pretty good at running from the police."

Honey chuckled. She took some workout clothing from her closet and gave it to Ivy.

"It's just a lot," Ivy said. "Are you sure you want *me* to have it?"

"Most of this stuff I bought with my own money from work," Honey said. "If you want, you can always babysit to make up for it or whatever."

Ivy brightened. She liked the idea of having a way to pay back. She sat down to put on the shoes. They were a little big. Honey took a look and agreed that they were okay for now. Plus, she would probably grow into them.

"You remember Delphie?" Honey asked.

"The lady with the red hair?" Ivy asked. "She's nice."

"Right." Honey gave Ivy a workout top. "You probably won't believe it, but she's a true psychic."

"Really?" Ivy asked. "Pan said she was, but I didn't believe him."

"I bet if we ask her, she'll know where your mom's sister is," Honey said.

"Do you think so?" Ivy's smiled covered almost all of her face. "Can we do it now?"

"I don't see why not," Honey said.

Ivy walked out of the closet with only a top and the shoes on.

"You have to get dressed." Honey called after her.

"Shhh," Ivy said. "The baby's sleeping."

Honey smiled at the girl. Ivy grinned and put on some exercise tights.

"Let's go find Delphie," Honey said.

Honey wheeled out of the apartment and into the Castle. She followed Delphie's laugh to the kitchen, where Delphie and

Valerie were drinking tea.

"Honey! Ivy!" Delphie said. "Would you like some tea?"

Delphie got up from the table to turn on the electric kettle.

"Is that your baby?" Ivy asked.

"This is Jacquotte," Valerie said.

"Jacquotte?" Ivy asked. "That's a big name. I wouldn't know how to spell it."

"We call her Jackie," Valerie said. "Would you like to hold her?"

Ivy nodded. Valerie pulled out a chair. Ivy sat down, and Valerie passed the baby to her.

"Do we have more of the cookies you made?" Delphie asked Honey.

"I'll get them." Honey wheeled to the pantry. "Delphie, Ivy's looking for her mother's sister. She and her Grannie weren't ever able to find her."

"She used to say it was a mystery for the record books," Ivy said.

"I like mysteries. I help my friend Seth with his detective work," Delphie said. "I don't have any mixed mint tea, Ivy — just peppermint. I do have chamomile. Does that sound good?"

Ivy nodded. She watched Jackie sleep for a few minutes before she realized that Delphie knew what kind of tea she liked. Ivy's heart filled with hope. She looked up at Delphie, and Delphie smiled at the girl.

"I don't see any souls around you, so that probably means your mother's sister is probably alive," Delphie said. "Tell me about her."

"I only know what my mom told my dad and what my dad told my Grannie," Ivy said.

Honey came out of the cabinet with a Tupperware dish full of cookies.

"That took a while," Delphie said.

"I try to hide them from the young men in the house," Honey said.

"Locusts." Valerie laughed. "Ivy was telling us about her mother's sister."

Honey wheeled to the table and set the cookies on top.

"Oh, right," Ivy said. "Well, my mom had a bunch of brothers and sisters. She was the youngest. Most of her brothers and sisters died from getting sick or hurting themselves or whatever. They were real poor and didn't have insurance or money for doctors and stuff. I guess they worked on farms or whatever work they could get."

"How do you know your mom had a sister?" Delphie asked. "Or that she's here? You know, Honey, those boys are going to blow through here in about five minutes."

"I know," Honey said.

"At least we get some first." Valerie reached for a cookie. "Ivy?"

"Oh, I don't know for sure," Ivy said. "My mom's dad died. A tractor fell on him or something gross. My mom and her mom moved here to Denver. I know that because my Grannie found the apartment building that they lived in together. We talked to the owner once during one of our adventures."

"If we can't figure this out here, we can always go to the apartment building and see if I can get something there." Delphie nodded.

"Good thinking," Honey said.

"It's kind of bad, because my mom's father *sold* her sister," Ivy said. "But it's kind of good because if he hadn't, she probably wouldn't have survived."

The electric kettle clicked, and Delphie turned around to get two more mugs from the cabinet.

"Do you know your mom's sister's name?" Valerie asked. "Maybe Delphie can call in the name."

"Chastity Bell," Ivy said.

Delphie dropped a mug.

"Anyone here?" Nash yelled from the front room. Charlie said something to Nash, and Noelle laughed.

"What did you say?" Delphie scurried to clean up the broken mug.

"My mom's last name was Bell," Ivy said. "I mean before she married my dad. Her sister was called 'Chastity,' or we thought she was."

"There you are!" Noelle said. "Hey — they're back here."

Noelle grabbed a cookie and looked at everyone.

"How come you guys are all weird?" Noelle asked.

"Did I wreck everything?" Ivy asked. "I'm really sorry."

With his arm draped over Tink's shoulder, Charlie came in. He glanced at Delphie and moved away from Tink.

"What's going on?" Charlie asked.

"I wrecked everything again." Ivy gave Jackie to Valerie and ran out of the room. Tink and Noelle ran after her.

"She's a little girl who has no one in this world," Charlie said to Delphie. "You need to fix this."

"Charlie!" Noelle said.

"No, he's right," Delphie said.

Delphie walked out of the kitchen. She looked around the living room, not sure where Ivy had gone.

"Hi, Ivy," Jacob's voice came from the front room. "Nash. Tink. What's going on?"

Delphie followed his voice.

"She's running away from me," Delphie said.

"Are you eating little girls again?" Jacob laughed. He put his hands on Ivy's shoulders. The little girl looked up at him. "Sometimes, people can't give us what we need at the exact moment we need it. That's all that happened. You surprised her."

"She broke a cup," Ivy said.

"We have lots of cups," Jacob said. "It's your heart that matters to Delphie and to all of us."

He stepped to the side to let Tink hug the little girl.

"Ivy?" Delphie asked.

The girls turned to look at her. Delphie glanced at Jacob, and he nodded to her.

"*My* name was Chastity Bell," Delphie said.

Tink gasped and stepped away from Ivy.

"You're her mom's sister?" Charlie asked.

"I don't know," Delphie said. "I could be. I left home when I was a little kid. I was the oldest, so I don't really know what happened to them after I left."

"She looks like you," Nash said.

"I do?" Ivy asked.

"I'm quite a bit older than you," Delphie said.

"She does look like you," Tink said. "I didn't notice it until Nash said something."

"We all noticed it downstairs," Nash said.

"Come on, Ivy," Delphie said. "Whether I'm your mom's long-lost sister or not, you're welcome here. Why don't we sit down, have some tea, and get to know each other? Would you like that?"

Ivy nodded.

"I would, too," Delphie glanced at Jacob. He smiled at her.

Delphie put her arm around Ivy's shoulder and led her back to the kitchen.

"Who's going running today?" Jacob asked.

He started pushing the other kids out of the kitchen.

"Charlie?" Jacob asked.

"I can only go within one square block," Charlie said.

"Good to know," Jacob said. "Let's go!"

Honey's baby monitor gave a wail as Maggie woke up from her nap.

"Have fun!" Honey waved and wheeled back to her apartment.

"I'm going to change Jackie." Valerie pointed upstairs, and Jacob nodded.

He managed to round up the rest of the children, and they left.

"It's so quiet," Ivy said.

"They're giving us time to talk," Delphie said. "Please sit."

Delphie sat down at the kitchen table. Katy came running

down the stairs from the apartment. She pulled out the chair Valerie had been sitting in and sat down.

"Katy?" Delphie asked.

"I wanted to meet your niece," Katy said.

"Is that all right with you?" Delphie asked.

"Sure," Ivy smiled at Katy.

Katy took a drink of Valerie's tea. Too uncomfortable to start, Ivy stared at her tea. Delphie was unusually quiet.

"So, where did you grow up, Ivy?" Katy asked.

Ivy chuckled, and Delphie laughed. Katy smirked.

"Katherine Roper Marlowe!" Jill yelled from the upstairs apartment. "Your bath is ready, and you're not here!"

"Have to go," Katy said. She ran up the stairs.

"She's really . . ."

"She is," Delphie laughed.

"Are you all psychics?" Ivy asked.

"Me, Jacob, Katy," Delphie said. "Everyone in the house has a special capacity. We're drawn to each other."

"Do you think I do?" Ivy asked.

"I don't know," Delphie said. "We'll have to see."

Ivy nodded and drank her tea.

"So, where did you grow up?" Delphie asked.

Ivy smiled and answered the question.

IT BEGINS

Tuesday evening — 7:17 p.m.

"Tanesha!" Jill yelled when Tanesha came through the back door.

Standing near the door, Heather gave Tanesha a hug. Jill and Sandy met their friend near the deck. In order to celebrate meeting Ivy — and the possibility of her being Delphie's niece — Honey and Valerie had put together an impromptu gathering while Jacob and the kids were running. As was typical of Denver, the recent freezing weather had broken into an unseasonably warm fall day and night. They were barbequing in the backyard.

"What's going on?" Tanesha asked. With her jaw still wired shut, her voice came out in low tones.

"How *are* you?" Jill asked.

"I don't know, Rapunzel — how did you get down from your lofty castle?" Tanesha asked.

"That's a long story." Jill smiled.

"Short version is that her husband's freak-out was unwarranted," Sandy said.

"She's a brood cow, like me," Heather said.

The women laughed.

"I love my house," Tanesha said. "I slept like a stone last night. First time since . . ."

She made a gesture, which indicated finding her mom and almost getting raped and everything good and bad. She waved to Jeraine, who was talking to Mike near the grill.

"The boy is behaving," Tanesha said.

"Why isn't he at work?" Heather asked.

"They're almost caught up," Tanesha said. "Seth's orchestra is doing longer sections, which means they can get more done at one time. That's how he was able to get everything moved yesterday. He should be done with the movie by the end of the week."

Tanesha shrugged.

"Do you love the bathroom?" Sandy asked. "Or I should say, I love your bathroom."

"My towels were warm this morning." Tanesha smiled. "How did that happen?"

"Housewarming present," Jill said.

"From all of us," Heather said.

"I love you guys," Tanesha said.

Tanesha held her arms out, and they hugged.

"Wait, that's Tink." Tanesha gestured to where Tink, Noelle, and Ivy were talking. "Isn't she supposed to be in that shelter?"

"She lives with us now," Heather said. "It's a trial run. We get six months. If it works out, then we file for adoption!"

"I love that." Sandy smiled.

"I go to medical school, and all this cool stuff happens," Tanesha said.

"It's weird, but I guess we're getting what we've always wanted," Jill smiled.

"Who'd ever believe it?" Tanesha asked.

"Not me," Heather said.

Jill and Sandy shook their heads in agreement.

"Hey," Tanesha said. "I was hoping you could cut my hair."

"Sure," Sandy said.

"What are you going to do?" Heather asked.

"That rapist guy?" Tanesha pointed to a spot of missing hair on her head.

The women shook their heads in anger.

"I want to shave it all off," Tanesha said.

"What about . . .?" Jill gestured toward Jeraine.

"He's always been such a dick about your hair," Sandy said.

"You has a nappy head." Heather imitated Jeraine in a whining voice.

"Yo' 'fro's too dry." Tanesha imitated his voice.

"You should get a weave," Sandy whined. "I can't believe yo' cheap-assed weave."

"My favorite," Jill said. She switched to a whining voice, "Get glamorous, or get left behind."

Jill imitated one of Jeraine's "cool" gestures and they laughed.

"You've noticed the man has no teeth?" Tanesha asked. "I figure I'll slide this one in while he looks a fool."

"He told me he's getting them fixed tomorrow," Jill said.

"We'd better hurry," Sandy said.

"What about the kids and . . . ?" Tanesha gestured to where Charlie, Teddy, and Nash were practicing their martial arts — or, quite possibly, kicking each other for no reason.

"They're fine," Sandy said. "Shall we?"

"Let's do it at my house," Jill said.

"I just need to grab my clippers," Sandy said. "I'll meet you up there."

"Let's check in and then go," Tanesha said.

"Good thinking," Jill said.

"Oh, look — Sissy's home," Sandy said.

Sandy went up to the deck to hug Sissy. She barely got a squeeze in before Sissy ran to see her friends. When Aden came out, she gave him a kiss. She snuggled Rachel and gave her to Aden. Sandy went into the house. Heather went to where Blane was talking to Honey and MJ. Heather caught Mack as he ran around the yard. Tanesha went to talk to Jeraine.

Jill found Jacob in the kitchen on his way out to the party.

"How was your shower?" Jill asked.

"Lonely." Jacob hugged her.

"Did Julie pick up Katy?" Jill asked.

"Katy and Paddie are at the movies with Colin," Jacob said. "I'm sure they are stuffing themselves with popcorn as we speak."

"Thanks for taking care of that," Jill said.

"No problem," Jacob said. "I'm looking forward to having Rapunzel all to myself tonight."

"I'm looking forward to being had," Jill said.

Jacob gave her a rousing kiss, and she laughed.

"Are you off?" Jacob asked.

"Sandy's going to cut Tanesha's hair," Jill said. "I thought we could take a little time . . ."

She clamped her mouth shut. She didn't want to ask his permission because she didn't want him to be a guy who needed to give her permission to hang out with her friends. Her desire to ask him if it was all right for her to spend some time with her friends pounded at the back of her throat.

He smiled at her dilemma, and she grinned.

"Great," Jacob said. "Should I bring up some barbeque?"

"We can come down," Jill said.

"I opened the red wine Tanesha likes," Jacob said.

Jill laughed.

"Have fun." Jacob kissed her again and turned to go.

Smiling, Jill watched him. Heather waited at the door for Tanesha. She jogged into the kitchen.

"Let's go before they catch up with us." Tanesha laughed.

The women went up the long stairwell to the loft. Sandy came across the kitchen a moment later.

Jacob laughed when he heard the lock turn. On his way out the door, he ran into Jeraine.

"You seen Tanesha?" Jeraine asked.

"She went upstairs with the girlfriends," Jacob said.

Jeraine shook his head.

"Anything I can help with?" Jacob asked.

"Sandy is going to cut, 'He has a small dick' in the back of her hair, so the paparazzi would know the truth about me.' Like I have a small dick, and who does she think she is telling the world that kind of thing anyway, and . . ."

Jeraine gave an indignant shake of his head. Jacob laughed.

"Yeah?" Jeraine asked. "And why is that funny?"

"She always could get you going," Jacob said.

"You don't know the woman," Jeraine said. "She's crazy."

Jacob laughed.

"Come on," Jacob said. "I'll buy you a beer."

He put his hand on Jeraine's shoulder and guided him out of the kitchen.

"You don't think she'll do it?" Jeraine asked.

"No," Jacob said. "I don't."

"Why 'zat?"

"She's pretty serious about becoming a doctor.". Jacob stopped walking and turned to face Jeraine. "And, I know it's shocking; it's hard for me to fathom sometimes, too, but sometimes our women do things that don't have anything do to with us."

Jeraine looked surprised and then burst out laughing. Jacob laughed.

"Hey, Jer," Mike yelled from the grill. "I'm on diaper duty. Can you . . . ?"

Jeraine went to take over the grill. Jacob looked out across the party. Everyone seemed to be having a great time. He noticed Aden and Sam talking near the edge of the deck.

"Jacob." Honey yelled from the grill. "Can you get the chicken from the refrigerator?"

He went back inside and grabbed the container of chicken in a dark marinade. He passed it over the railing to Jeraine and went to talk to Sam and Aden.

"Where's Delphie?" Jacob asked.

"She's praying," Sam said. "This whole . . . thing has really thrown her for a loop."

"Why?" Jacob asked.

"Oh . . ." Sam smiled. "You'd have to have known her as a child. I met her when she was a little younger than Ivy, and . . . I guess she'd just given up on her family. Celia's the one who made a family for her. Celia created all the interconnections you see now. All of these people . . ."

Sam gestured to the party.

"They're all here because of Celia," Sam said. "Now Celia's gone, and Delphie . . . She's confused — I guess that's the easiest way to say it."

Jacob nodded.

"She's not very flexible," Sam said in a low tone. "But I'll deny it if you repeat that."

Jacob and Aden laughed. Rachel made a gurgling sound as if she agreed.

"What's up with you, son?" Sam asked.

"What do you mean?" Jacob asked.

"You seem to have something big on your mind," Sam said.

"Should I leave?" Aden pointed to the party.

"No," Jacob said. "I . . . hmm . . ."

"You may as well just tell us," Sam said.

"I'm just not sure how to tell you," Jacob said.

"Try using your mouth." Sam grinned. "You psychics make everything so complicated."

Jacob and Aden laughed. When their laughter died down, Jacob felt the weight of their eyes on him.

"I had a vision today," Jacob said.

"I know," Sam said. "Blane called us."

"I asked you about it when you got back from Jeraine's, but you were kind of . . ." Aden started.

"Kind of?" Jacob asked.

"Weird," Aden said.

"Secretive," Sam said. "Like when you were slipping out to see girls when you were a kid."

"Slip out? Me?" Jacob did his best to look confused, but Sam laughed.

"Just spit it out, son," Sam said. "How bad can it be?"

"There's a deep underground fault zone under the site," Jacob said.

"What?" Sam asked.

"Right down the center," Jacob said.

"And you know this because of your vision?" Aden asked.

"The vision?" Jacob nodded. "Sure, but it's also on some geological maps the oil guys gave Jeraine."

"It's not on the maps the state gave us," Aden said.

"Why does it matter?" Sam asked. "There are lots of minor faults. When was the last time we had an earthquake here?"

"When they pushed nuclear waste into the ground at Rocky Mountain Arsenal?" Jacob nodded.

"They stopped doing that," Sam said. "Wait . . . Weren't they using pressurized towers?"

Jacob nodded.

"Oh, crap," Sam said.

"What does that mean?" Aden asked.

"Fracking," Jacob said. "Bumpy owns some family land out at Dearfield. It's on the Niobrara shale field. They are fracking along the fault lines."

"That's not good," Aden said.

"The weird thing is that the map Jeraine had showed a projection of the project north and east of where we're building," Jacob said. "You know, near that land I had to have."

"Which land?" Sam asked.

"The one with the three gorgeous handcrafted houses?" Jacob asked.

Sam groaned.

"Maybe they couldn't buy the land," Aden said.

"He owns the land," Sam said.

"They never asked," Jacob said.

"If we say we need to move it, it's going to look like Jacob is trying to bilk the state," Sam said. "If we leave the project . . ."

"People will die," Jacob said. "Plus, there's the matter of the employee owners."

"What about them?" Aden asked.

"We'd have to include them in the decision," Jacob said. "We can't just walk away from the project like we would have a year ago. Now we have to put it to a vote."

"They've voted for everything we've put forward," Sam said.

"Yeah, but . . ." Jacob looked at Aden.

"There's a faction of people who don't love the fact that any employee can buy shares," Aden said.

"The folks who tried to vote you out as CEO," Sam said.

"Yes, them," Aden said.

"You think they'll make a fuss?" Sam asked.

"I just . . ." Jacob shrugged. "I can't shake the feeling we're being set up. I asked Rodney and Bambi to take a look at it, but . . ."

"They think something's fishy too." Aden nodded.

"So do those kids Rodney got to help out," Sam said. "They think we're being punked. No, that's not it. They think we're being set up like punks. No . . . It was something about punks, and it was not a very nice thing to happen."

"No, it's not," Jacob said.

"Why do you think the project moved?" Aden asked.

"No one asked me to buy the land," Jacob shook his head.

"There wasn't an underground fault zone on the maps we approved," Aden said. "I spent two days with the geologist going over that land."

"Digital maps?" Jacob asked.

Aden nodded.

"Jeraine has a paper map," Jacob said.

"It was changed?" Aden asked.

Jacob nodded.

"I bet I know how," Sam said.

Jacob and Aden turned to look at Sam.

"You remember the woman who was your secretary when Blane was out?" Sam asked.

"Unfortunately, yes," Jacob said.

"She's a clerk in the geology division," Sam said.

"But changing a map?" Jacob asked. "They use those fissures now to increase the yields. That means that they put pressure directly into the faults and . . ."

"She seems to have a persuasive charm," Sam said.

Jacob groaned.

"What?" Aden asked.

"The Director," Jacob said. "The one she was seeing?"

"What about him?" Sam asked.

"His son works for the state," Jacob said. "He's a geologist."

Sam looked from Aden to Jacob.

"Don't worry," Sam said. "We'll work this out."

"I can't shake the feeling that it's going to be a complete mess," Jacob said.

"I like messes; so do you," Sam said. "Plus, think of it this way: If we lose everything, we'll have to couch surf for a while."

"I'm already doing that," Aden said.

"Me, too," Sam said.

"We'll all have to live with Delphie?" Jacob smiled at his father.

"That would be awful," Sam laughed at his joke.

When their laughter died down, Sam became very serious.

"People will die?" Sam asked Jacob.

"A lot of people," Jacob said.

"Then we're pulling out," Sam said. "I don't care if we use every penny — we have to do it. I will not continue knowing our folks will be injured or killed. That's just not the way I do business."

Startled by Sam's sudden intensity, Aden and Jacob turned to face him.

"I hate the selfish. Always have, always will." Sam raised his hand to the sky. "Sorry, Celia. I said the word 'hate,' and I mean it. I hate people who think only of themselves. They're so competitive they don't care what they do to other people as long as they win at whatever dumb game — which only *they* know they're playing."

Jacob nodded.

"Are you with me?" Sam asked.

"I am," Jacob said.

"Whatever I can do," Aden said.

"Then we start tomorrow," Sam said. "One employee at a time."

"I'll get the map from Jeraine," Jacob said.

"I'll call a site manager's meeting for tomorrow," Aden said. "After the sites are up?"

"Before," Sam said. "We'll start late."

Aden touched Sam's arm and left to go make the calls.

"Are you all right, Dad?" Jacob asked.

"No, I'm not," Sam said. "Those bastards said they would ruin us and now . . . We've invited all these good, hardworking people to have a little financial freedom. How hard is that? But these jerks . . ."

"Don't think about it, Dad," Jacob said.

Sam looked at Jacob for a long moment before nodding.

"Mr. Sam?" Ivy asked. "I didn't mean to interrupt, but I wonder if . . . Well, Delphie told me you knew her when she was little, and I wondered . . ."

Seeing the child's face, Sam immediately brightened.

"I sure did," Sam said. "In fact, I bet I have some photos."

"They're in your room," Jacob said. "Second shelf from the top."

"Wow," Ivy beamed. "Do you ever get used to the psychics?"

"He put them there," Sam laughed.

"We moved Dad out for a while to do some repairs on his room," Jacob said. "We just moved him back."

"And no, I've never gotten used to it," Sam said.

"Why don't I get the photos and you guys can talk?" Jacob asked.

He went into the house. Aden was talking on the phone in the kitchen. Jacob took in Aden's worried face. He nodded to Aden before going into his father's room.

This birch room had been the first room he'd discovered in this castle of a house, and it was the room his mother had died in. It had a wonderful, loving energy. For a moment, he closed his eyes and tried to let the room work on his anxiety.

"It's going to be fine," he heard his mother's voice in his head. "Trust people."

He picked up the photos and left the room.

~~~~~~~~~

Wednesday afternoon — 2:47 p.m.

Yesterday, Charlie had felt like a hero. He'd gone to the police station, dealt with probation, even hung out with his cool lawyer.

Today, he felt like a scared kid.

Wondering if he could really pull this off, he sat on the steps near the side door to the Castle. Mike came around the corner with Jacob's Labrador and Jill's childhood dog. In the last month or so, Mike had been training heavily. His sheer bulk took up much of the small room. Charlie had asked him why he was working out so much. He'd just said that Charlie would figure it out when his wife was nine months pregnant. Charlie had no idea what that meant, but he liked that Mike talked to him like a grown-up. Charlie looked up at him.

"I can go with you," Mike said.

"I'm supposed to go by myself," Charlie said.

"You really doing a great thing, an important thing..." Mike stopped talking when Charlie sneered. "Yeah, I hate that crap, too. You're doing what you have to do."

Charlie nodded.

"I have to walk the dogs." Mike gestured to the yellow Labrador and the muttish Scooter. "Jill can't walk Scooter anymore, and Sarah loves being with her old friend."

"What about Buster?"

"I figured you wouldn't be caught dead with that ugly dog,"

Mike grinned.

"Hey!" Charlie jumped up from the stair. "That's *my* dog you're talking about."

"I thought he was Noelle's dog," Mike said.

"Noelle can't do this." Charlie whistled, and Buster scrambled around the corner to him. Charlie leaned over to pet him.

"How 'bout we walk to the dog park together?" Mike asked. "It's a block from the school. I'll stay there with the dogs and you can meet me after practice."

"Yeah, that would be okay," Charlie said.

"Thanks for doing me this favor, man," Mike said. "I really appreciate it."

Charlie smirked at Mike's sarcastic comment. He took a leash from the rack near the door. Mike pointed to the stack of bags, and Charlie grabbed a few bags. Mike opened the door and the dogs jetted out to the patch of lawn. Charlie followed the dogs, and Mike locked the door. Charlie picked up after Buster and then put the leash on the dog.

They crossed the street to avoid the paparazzi and turned right on Sixteenth Avenue. One of the things Charlie liked about Mike was that he didn't believe in unnecessary chatter. They walked along in easy silence. They dodged traffic across York Street and stopped at the light on Josephine. As they set out across Josephine, Charlie remembered why he was so anxious.

Each step brought him closer to the guys who had raped and almost killed Tink. Out of the corner of his eye, he saw the other guy who was in online high school whiz by on his bike.

Mike stopped at the dog park and turned to Charlie. He held out his hand for Buster's lead. With a nod, Charlie handed over the leash and set out to walk the long block to school. He jogged across the Esplanade and plunged into the dark school. Stepping into the gym, he saw his probation officer waiting for him.

"You're late," she sneered. The probation officer held up a plastic jar for him to pee in.

The only thing Charlie could think of to say was "It begins," so he kept his mouth shut.

Chapter Two Hundred & Thirty-Three

Problem

Wednesday evening — 5:45 p.m.

"And don't be late," the coach pointed to Charlie. "I don't give a crap if you're peeing in a jar or standing on your head. You're here on time, or you don't play."

"Yes, Coach," Charlie said.

"Now get out of here," the coach said.

Charlie hung his head and slunk out of the gym. The rest of the team had already left practice. He'd had to do extra exercises and drills because he was late. Or that's what the coach had said. Charlie glanced back at the man and caught a worried look on the coach's face. He wondered if the guy knew what he was doing. He was about to turn around to ask when the coach grabbed the net full of the balls and left for the locker room.

Charlie didn't want to go to the locker room.

He continued down the hallway to the outside door. Caught up in his own world, he pushed the door open and walked down the steps. He'd already crossed the Esplanade when the other online school guy cut Charlie off with his bike.

"I don' want no trouble." Charlie didn't bother to look up. He stepped around the bike and kept walking.

"Hey," the other guy said.

Charlie looked up at him.

"I want to talk to you." The kid was following Charlie.

"Grab a number."

Charlie's voice reminded him of Eeyore. When he was first getting sober, Pete used to repeat everything he said in Eeyore's voice. Charlie smirked and stopped walking.

"What?" Charlie turned around abruptly and startled the guy.

"I . . . um . . ." The kid looked a little scared and flustered.

Charlie scowled and turned around again.

"My sister killed herself," the kid said.

Charlie turned around to look at him.

"I saw you . . ." the kid said.

Charlie took two steps toward the boy. All of his frustration, shame, and rage came forward. He was ready to kill the kid.

" . . . at the police station." The boy swallowed hard. "My parents and I. The police . . . um . . . they came to our house and said we had to come see a guy, and it was you."

Charlie sneered at the kid.

"I told them . . . I did . . . that you were okay," the kid said. "A little high strung, but okay."

"Why were *you* there?" Charlie asked.

"My sister killed herself," the kid said.

"What's that got to do with anything?"

"She was . . . you know . . . and she . . ." The boy swallowed hard. If Charlie weren't so mad, he would have felt sorry for him. "Well, you know. She never got over it."

"Oh," Charlie said. "Sorry."

"She would have died," the boy said. "You know, that night. But you found her. That's what she said: 'A kid named Pan and his friends found me, gave me a blanket, and . . . He stayed with me, held my hand, until somebody took me to the hospital.'"

Charlie looked away from the boy. He never would have thought of it, but now that the boy had said something, Charlie remembered the boy's sister.

"Was that you?" the boy asked.

Charlie gave him a curt nod.

"Will you . . . I mean . . . Can you tell me what you know?" the kid asked.

Charlie's eyes scanned the boy's face and body. The boy was

caught in the kind of desperate grief that Charlie knew all too well.

"We don't know anything." The boy's voice came out in an insistent whisper. "Nothing."

Charlie watched him struggle with his own memory.

"You're all she remembered," he said. "I mean, except for some of what happened. She would have died wherever that was, but . . . That's what the doctor said. She had brain damage and was scarred on her face."

The boy put his hand to his face.

"And . . . you know, other places." The boy put his hand on his belly and legs.

"My mom was sure she'd get better, but my dad . . . and I . . ."

The boy looked up at Charlie.

"I just miss her," the boy said.

Not sure what to say, Charlie looked over the kid's head at the school.

"I found her," the boy whispered.

Charlie's eyes jerked to the boy's face.

"Hanging." The boy nodded. "I knew she was going to do it. I did. But . . ."

The boy shrugged.

"I just miss her," the boy repeated.

"Charlie?" Mike's voice came from behind him.

The boy jerked with surprise. He grabbed his bike to ride off and then saw Buster. The shock of seeing such an ugly dog made the boy stop.

"That's one ugly dog!" the boy laughed.

Buster nudged the boy's leg and then nudged him so hard he fell over, bike and all. The boy giggled while Buster wiggled and wagged and licked the boy's face. Sarah, Jake's yellow Labrador, wagged over the boy. As if to say, "What can you do with these kids?" Scooter sat down next to Charlie.

"Okay, okay," Mike said.

Mike pulled Buster back from the boy. Charlie got his bike. As soon as the boy sat up, Buster went back to licking his face. Charlie whistled, and Buster sat down. The dog had a huge grin on his face. Sarah looked over the boy to make sure he was all right. Just in case the boy might pet her, Sarah sat right under his hand.

"Are these your dogs?" the boy grinned.

"This one," Charlie nodded to Buster.

"I know you," the boy said to Mike. "You're Valerie Lipson's husband. The artist. My sister loves her. Says she's so pretty and ..."

The boy swallowed hard. He grabbed his bike to ride off.

"Who's your friend, Charlie?" Mike slapped the back of Charlie's head.

"I don't know," Charlie said. "What's your name?"

"Tim," the boy blushed. "Tim Logan."

"Nice to meet you, Tim," Mike said. "I'm Mike Roper. This is Buster. That's Sarah and this really good dog is Scooter."

Scooter looked up at the boy.

"We were just heading back for dinner," Mike said. "Would you like to join us?"

"Sure!" The boy beamed.

"Do you want to bring your sister?" Mike asked. "It's not anything fancy, but I know Val would like to meet any friend of Charlie's."

"My sister's ... um," Tim's face fell. "She ..."

"She's one of the girls," Charlie said. "She's not here anymore."

"Oh," Mike said. "I'm really sorry, Tim."

"I wanted Charlie to show me where it happened, you know?" Tim looked at Mike. "But he ..."

"Charlie?" Mike scowled at Charlie.

Charlie shrugged.

"She had this necklace," Tim said. "She wore it every day and ... I keep dreaming about it. Like it's there waiting for me to find it."

Charlie looked at Mike.

"I play here because she thought the guys came from East because she was at a dance at East before... And... they were tall, so I thought they might play basketball and... I'm going to find them." Tim nodded.

Mike gave Charlie a wilting look.

"Charlie would be happy to help you and your family," Mike said. "Do you want to call your parents?"

Tim shook his head.

"About dinner," Mike said.

"Oh," Tim said. "Sure."

"Why don't you call your parents and invite them too?" Mike asked. "There's always plenty."

"I think they would like that," Tim said. "And then could we go...?"

Mike put his arm over Charlie's shoulder. Charlie looked at him.

"We'd love to," Mike said. "In fact, we'll all go. Right Charlie?"

"Sure," Charlie said. "Everybody gets involved in everything at our house."

"When's dinner?" Tim smiled. Charlie realized it was the first time he'd seen the kid smile.

"We're eating at seven," Mike said. "We have to wait for Sissy to get home."

"Sissy Delgado lives with you." Tim blushed.

"She's my sister," Charlie said.

"She's just... beautiful," Tim swallowed hard.

"She's my *sister*." Charlie's voice was a little sinister, and Tim jumped.

"One thing at a time," Mike said. "Why don't you go home and talk to your parents? Let us know about dinner. If tonight doesn't work, then another night will."

"But we can go tonight, right?" Tim asked. "To the place

where . . . you know? Right?"

"Sure," Charlie said.

"It's all set," Mike said. "We have to go. Charlie's on an ankle monitor. If he's not home in ten minutes, the cops come."

"Okay," the boy said. "See you later."

Tim smiled and rode off on his bike. Mike gave Buster's leash to Charlie.

"That was very nice of you, Charlie," Mike said, and set off with Sarah and Scooter.

Charlie scowled after him.

"Are you coming?" Mike asked. "We've got to hurry."

Charlie ran to catch up with Mike.

~~~~~~~~~

Wednesday evening — 5:45 p.m.

Sandy opened the side door to the Castle and stepped into the main living room. She smiled at Delphie, who was leaning against the back of the couch.

"Can I talk to you for a minute?" Delphie asked.

"Sure," Sandy said. "I need to get the kids ready for dinner. Is Aden home?"

"Aden, Jake, and Sam are meeting with the site managers," Delphie said.

"I thought that was happening this morning." Sandy hung up her coat.

"They couldn't work it out."

Delphie gave an impatient nod. Sandy grinned at her impatience.

"What's up?" Sandy asked.

"It's about Ivy," Delphie said, and then clammed up.

Sandy smiled, but Delphie didn't say anything else.

"What about Ivy?" Sandy looked up to see Honey wheeling across the living room with Maggie in her lap. Honey pointed to the kitchen, and Sandy nodded.

"Ivy?" Delphie asked.

"Are you feeling all right?" Sandy asked.

"Me?" Delphie asked. "Fine. Why?"

Sandy smiled. When she first moved here, she'd found Delphie's conversation to be very disturbing. She'd finally asked Sam about it. He told her that, until Delphie met Celia, she'd never had a conversation about herself. It was very difficult for her to talk about what was going on with her. She simply needed prodding to even remember what she wanted to talk about.

"Would you like to talk about taking care of Ivy?" Sandy suggested.

"Yes." Delphie pointed at Sandy. "That's it. Who's going to take care of Ivy?"

"What do you mean?" Sandy asked.

Delphie shook her head and started to walk toward the kitchen.

"Do you want to take care of Ivy?" Sandy asked.

"Yes." Delphie turned back to Sandy. "But I can't."

"How come?" Sandy asked.

Delphie shook her head.

"You don't want to?" Sandy asked.

Delphie shook her head.

"You don't know how?" Sandy asked.

Delphie nodded.

"Hmm," Sandy said. "I see your dilemma. I'm glad you decided to talk to me about this."

Delphie smiled.

"I bet you feel like you should take Ivy in because she's your family," Sandy said.

"You took in Charlie and Sissy," Delphie nodded.

"You took in Nash and Noelle," Sandy said.

"That's different." Delphie's voice rose with frustration. "That's not the same thing. You don't understand at all."

"No, no," Sandy said. "I get it. That's different because Nash and Noelle had daycare and a father."

Delphie nodded.

"But you took care of Nash and Noelle a lot," Sandy said.

"They went home," Delphie said. "I don't have . . ."

She raised her arms as if in a hug. Her hands moved to her chest and out.

"Hmm," Sandy said. "You feel like you don't have enough mothering capacity to help a little girl who's been hurt so much. That is tough."

"And bad." Delphie looked crushed. "Broken."

Sandy hugged her.

"Not broken," Sandy said. "Just different. We all have different gifts."

Sandy smiled at Delphie.

"You taught me that," Sandy said.

"But *every* woman should know how to . . . do . . . that," Delphie said.

"Says who?" Sandy smiled. "I think it's awesome that you know this about yourself. That's what makes you great."

Delphie scowled.

"First off," Sandy said. "Not *every* woman knows how to be a mother. My friend Heather is a great mom, but she was an only child. She doesn't have a lot of patience for . . ."

Sandy pointed upstairs, where they could hear Nash and Noelle yelling at each other.

"You handle that stuff with ease," Sandy said. "We're all different."

"What do I do?" Delphie asked. "I was just like Ivy until . . . and Celia took me in, but I'm not Celia. I *am not*. Valerie could take Ivy. She said she would, but she's leaving at the end of the week for her premiere, and then a month in LA. Ivy would be gone like Jackie."

Delphie let out a big sigh.

"I'm going to miss Jackie so much." Delphie nodded.

Sandy smiled.

"Tell you what," Sandy said. "I'll talk to my friend Heather and see what she thinks. Maybe Ivy could live with them."

Delphie nodded.

"I also think that Ivy had an aunt," Sandy said. "She was in Afghanistan when her mother died. That's why she didn't take Ivy. I bet she'd want some time with Ivy."

Delphie nodded.

"Would you like it if I found out what's possible?" Sandy asked.

Delphie nodded.

"I'd be happy to," Sandy said. "Now I'd better get upstairs before they kill each other."

Delphie nodded. Sandy touched Delphie's shoulder and left for her apartment. Lost in thought, Delphie stayed in her spot against the couch.

"Delphie?" Honey called from the kitchen. She rolled into the doorway to the living room. "Mike just called to say that Charlie's bringing a family home. I was going to make a quick pot pie for the kids with the left-over chicken from last night. Where did you put the puff pastry?"

"I think the boys made something with it." Delphie smiled. This was something she could do.

"Crap," Honey said.

"How 'bout if I make the crust and you make the inside?" Delphie stood up.

"Deal," Honey smiled.

Delphie put her arm over Honey's shoulder and they went into the kitchen.

~~~~~~~~~

Wednesday evening — 6:00 p.m.

"Ready?" Sam asked.

Jacob nodded. Aden pushed open the door to the large conference room and followed the men inside. The tension in the room was thick.

The female site managers took up the far end of the table while the black men sat closer to the front. The white men sat across from them, and the Hispanic site managers stood in the back.

Once a cohesive group, the site managers now wouldn't even look at each other.

"I'm going to cut to the chase," Jacob said. "We're pulling out of the site near the airport."

As if on fire, the site managers erupted with rage.

"I told you so," Rodney's replacement site managers screamed at the top of their lungs.

The women had a loud conversation across the table with each other. The men along the back wall argued with each other in Spanish, and the men along the side looked smug.

"Settle down," Aden said.

The white men got up and turned their backs on the rest of the room. A woman got up and knocked one of the chairs over. The men at the back were yelling, and Rodney's replacements fell quiet, almost too quiet.

"Enough," Sam said.

Everyone stopped moving.

"That is enough," Sam said.

The site managers turned to look at him.

"Get your rear ends in a chair," Sam pointed to the men in the back of the room. "Ladies — make some space for them. You — along this side. They don't have cooties. Move over. And you men! Turn your chairs around."

"But, Sam!" started a man who'd turned his chair away.

"Stuff it," Sam said. "*Now* means *do it now*."

He pointed to the black men.

"Wipe those looks off your faces," Sam said. "You're scaring . . . Jake."

Bambi chuckled. Her chuckle moved around the room until everyone was smiling. The men in the back filtered into chairs around the room.

"Now, mix yourselves up," Sam said. "We are not the 'Black Dudes' vs. 'Those Honkies' vs. 'The ladies' vs. 'Those Hispanics.'
. . .

"Honkies?" Aden looked at Jake, and he looked away to keep from laughing.

"Latinos," one of the Latino women said.

"Yeah? Did you know what I meant?" Sam asked.

She grinned at him.

"We are one company," Sam said. "We have a big problem. Everyone needs to put their differences aside and get to work fixing it."

Every eye turned to Sam.

"Now, I think you know that Jake is friends with that singer Jeraine," Sam said. "Celia and I've known Bumpy and his family for a long time."

"He's Rodney's son-in-law," DeShawn Jones, one of Rodney's replacement site managers, said.

"That's right," Sam said. "Jake went to his house last night and saw this."

Sam nodded to Aden.

"Go ahead," Aden said.

Sam pushed the button, and Jeraine's map came up on the screen behind them.

"Notice anything?" Sam asked.

"That can't possibly be right." One of the female site managers stood up. "Nate and I went through those with Aden."

"Felicia, can you show the rest of us what you see?" Sam asked.

She looked at Bambi, and Bambi gave a "go ahead" nod. She pointed to the cluster of fault lines running under the location of their big work site.

"Now you know," Sam said. He let the information sink in. When their eyes turned to look at him, he said, "It's up to us to determine what to do next."

DOWN BY THE RIVER

Wednesday evening — 8:12 p.m.

"I'm not going." Ivy screamed. "You can't make me!"

Tink and Ivy had begged Heather to take them to the Castle to help Charlie show the Logans where their daughter had been attacked. After dinner with Tim and his parents, when the niceties were over, Ivy had become more and more belligerent.

"Okay," Heather said. "That's okay. You don't have to do anything you don't want to do. Tink and Pan are going to help the Logans. They could use your help."

"No!" Ivy screamed so loud that she woke Maggie. The baby gave a screeching howl. Ivy looked horrified and ran off down a passageway into the Castle.

Tink started after her.

"Stay here," Heather said to Tink.

Heather looked at Sandy, who encouraged her to go. Heather ran after Ivy. They ran down a long passageway and into an area of the Castle that Heather had never been in before. She turned the corner to find Ivy sobbing into her knees at the end of the corridor.

Heather started toward her. Before Heather got to her, Katy sat down next to Ivy. Katy looked up at Heather and smiled.

Katy put her hand on Ivy's knee, and Ivy looked up at the little girl. Almost six years old, Katy and Ivy seemed about the same age. The two girls looked at each other for a moment.

"Are you okay?" Katy asked.

"No. Do I look okay?"

"Not really," Katy said. "Did something bad happen?"

Ivy nodded. Katy's head moved up and down in empathy.

"Right now?" Katy looked at Heather.

"No, before." Ivy's voice echoed with fear and sadness.

"Hmmm," Katy said. "Mooooooooommmmmmmmyyyyyyyyyy!"

Heather scowled at Katy. The child shrugged. Jill came around the corner.

"Anna Marie has an owie," Katy said.

"How did you know my name?" Ivy whispered.

Katy shrugged. Jill leaned down to Ivy. Heather followed Jill's lead.

"Where does it hurt, Ivy?" Jill asked.

Ivy put a hand to her heart.

"Heather knows just the thing," Jill said.

"I do?" Heather gawked at Jill.

Jill scowled at Heather.

"Mommy means that Delphie's making brownies," Katy said.

"Oh!" Like a light going on, Heather brightened. "Owies of the heart are best fixed with brownies."

Ivy looked from Heather to Jill.

"I don' wanna go," Ivy said.

"You don't have to," Heather said. "You can stay here with Katy and Jill."

"I'll go with you." Nash came around the kneeling adults to stand by Ivy. "My friend Teddy's meeting us there. We're training to be Ninjas. Our teacher's going to be there, too. We'll keep you safe."

Ivy looked at Nash and then at the women.

"You aren't mad?" Ivy asked.

"About what?" Heather smiled.

"I just ... and yelled ... and ... unacceptable." Ivy gave a sincere nod.

"We're like that all the time," Katy said.

"Katy!" Jill held her arms out, and Katy let her pick her up.

"We are." Katy gave a conspiratorial nod.

"You're not unacceptable," Heather said.

"Not to me," Jill said.

"Or me!" Katy said.

The women looked at Nash. He flushed bright red and nodded.

"Let's have some brownies to gather our strength," Heather said.

She held out a hand and helped Ivy to her feet. Heather hugged Ivy and they started back down the hallway. Jill and Katy walked next to Ivy and Heather.

"Have we met before?" Ivy asked Katy.

"No," Katy said.

"You're so familiar to me," Ivy said.

"That's just because you know Naomi," Katy said.

Jill stopped walking to let Ivy and Heather pass by. Nash followed them into the main Castle living room.

"Does she know Naomi?" Jill whispered to Katy.

"How do you think Anne Marie got here?" Katy smiled at her mother.

Jill kissed her forehead. Katy squirmed, and Jill let her go. She leaned against the door to watch Katy. Her daughter ran to talk to Ivy and Noelle. Sissy came over, and the girls laughed. In her years of living at the Castle, Katy had gone from being a small, lonely girl to a well-loved, vibrant child. Someday in the not-too-distant future, Katy would be Charlie and Sissy's age.

Jill felt a breath of cold air on her back. She shivered, and Katy turned to look at her. Katy smiled, and Jill left her corner to join the preparations for the trip downtown. All the while, Jill couldn't shake the feeling that something was coming that would change everything for Katy and the girls at the Castle.

After all that had happened, Jill knew they would get through it. She only hoped it wouldn't scar them forever.

~~~~~~~~~

Wednesday evening — 8:42 p.m.

A police officer waved for Mike to stop his Bronco on the Market Street bridge over Cherry Creek and the Cherry Creek Trail. Sandy pulled up behind them with Ivy, Tink, Sissy, Noelle, Nash, and Teddy. The DenverPpolice had blocked off Market Street and Fourteenth Avenue all the way to Little Raven. Their forensics team waited for Charlie to lead them to the scene. The darkest corners of the creek and urban trail were lit up by halogen lights, and the hum of generators filled the air.

Charlie got out of the passenger seat of Mike's Bronco and looked over the railing. These few blocks had been home to Charlie and his friends. They would work the parking lots of the Pepsi Center for change. If they had to, they sold sex for money to buy drugs and food. They'd sleep under the railway bridge behind the cement pylon or in the culvert under Market Street. As long as the urbanites in the condos up above didn't spot them on their morning jog, Charlie and his friends weren't hassled.

Charlie wrapped his arms around himself.

"You cold?" Mike asked.

Charlie shook his head.

"Come on." Mike pointed to where Tim and his parents were getting out of their sedan. "They're waiting for you."

Charlie turned toward Fourteenth Avenue and saw the mustached cop with the great hair talking to Sandy on the corner. Sandy waved to Charlie. When he got near, she tucked her arm into his elbow and held on. He looked down at her.

"We'll do this together," Sandy said, in a low tone.

Charlie let out the breath he hadn't realized he'd been holding. Sandy always knew when he was freaked out or afraid. He realized for the first time how terrified he'd been the entire time he'd lived down here. When he talked about it, living on the streets sounded like one big adventure. He glanced at Sandy again. Sandy really understood how awful it had been.

"We're on the wrong side," Charlie said to the mustached cop.

"I'd like it if you walked us through how it all unfolded for you," the mustached cop said.

His voice was so reasonable. He gave Charlie a big smile, like he was Charlie's friend. Charlie scowled. He and Sandy walked ahead.

"You know he's a dick," Charlie said, under his breath.

"I know," Sandy said. "But he's better than that twerp Aziz. Now, he's a real asshole. I could tell you stories . . . At least this one makes some effort."

Charlie chuckled, and Sandy smiled. They caught up with Tim and his parents at the down ramp to the Cherry Creek Trail from Fourteenth Avenue.

"We'd just finished working the Pepsi Center," Charlie said. "There was some game there—Avalanche, Nuggets . . ."

"It was a concert," Tink said.

Surprised, Charlie turned to see Tink and Ivy walking with Nash, Teddy, and Noelle just behind him.

"One of those bands you hear in the grocery store," Tink said. "Springsteen or The Who or . . ."

"Rolling Stones?" Tim's dad asked.

"Yeah, that's it," Charlie said. "How'd you know?"

"We went to the concert," Tim's Dad said. "Barbara was supposed to meet us here afterwards. She dropped us off and took the car. Are you're sure it was that night?"

"No," Charlie looked at Tink. She shrugged. "We just worked the parking lot. The concerts were good because people get real drunk and high. They give us more money. Sometimes, the guys get belligerent with the girls, you know . . ."

"They had their music, now they want to get off," Tink said.

"We just try to get what we need and get out," Charlie said.

"Was the concert over?" Tim's Dad asked.

"I think so," Tink said. "Remember, we had enough money for pizza?"

"Someone gave us their tickets, and we got a discount at that place next door," Charlie said. "We had enough for two extra pizzas. That's food for two days. We were pretty happy about that."

Charlie's words were spoken matter-of-factly. But the adults were startled that so little food would feed so many kids for two days. Sandy squeezed Charlie's arm.

"We were coming down here," Charlie said. "Ivy had her skateboard."

Ivy ran ahead to show them where she was. Nash ran after her.

"So, we had to go down the ramp," Charlie said. "We usually don't use this side because it's the bike side, and people are assholes. There's always some chunky guy on a fancy bike swearing at anyone who gets in his way."

"I know what you mean," Tim said.

Charlie nodded.

"I was about here when I saw something on the other side," Charlie said. "The drainpipe over there is a great place to sleep. It's quiet and pretty safe. I was checking it out because I wanted some place to put the pizza while we slept. Some frat boy might take it, you know?"

"I was behind you with the other girls," Tink said. "Like now. But Ivy was way up ahead. Pan said we should go check out what was there because maybe it was something good."

Charlie nodded. When Tim's Mom let out a little sob, Charlie looked over at them. Tim's Dad put his arm around her and she cried into his shoulder.

"Um..." Charlie couldn't take his eyes off Tim's parents. Sandy squeezed his arm, and he looked at her.

"We went back to the top," Tink said. "Ivy wanted to go down to the crossing, but Pan wouldn't let her."

"It's not a great time of the night," Charlie said. "When the concerts out, the bars fill ... It's just not great ... for any of us, but especially girls."

"We were always careful." Tink nodded. "There's enough

trouble without asking for it."

"I knew he was right," Ivy said. "But I was grumpy about it."

"What else is new?" Tink laughed. Ivy smirked and pretended to be grumpy for the reenactment.

When Charlie started up the bridge, he saw Colin Hargreaves at the top. Charlie could see his handgun in a side holster and Colin's Homeland Security badge on his belt. He wasn't sure why, but having his martial-arts teacher there made him feel a little better. Colin was taping the whole thing on a video camera. When Charlie got to the top, he saw his lawyer's boyfriend, Art Rasmussen. The tall, muscular man nodded to Charlie like he was doing a good job. Charlie blushed.

"So, we got to the top and realized we couldn't go down on the other side here," Charlie said. "We weren't really thinking straight. Then somebody said . . ."

"Jeffy," Ivy said. "It was Jeffy."

"That's right," Charlie said. "Jeffy was little. He kneeled down over there and said we should go back because it was a person. We all ran back."

Charlie ran across the bridge and down the path. He forded the creek before Tink even got to it. Tim and his parents reached Tink by the time Charlie was near the storm drain.

"It was about like that," Charlie said. "I'm fast, so I got over here before anyone else. Jeffy stayed up on the bridge."

Charlie pointed to where Ivy and Noelle were standing.

"I stayed with Jeffy," Ivy said.

"Can you wait for us?" Tim's father asked.

"Sure," Charlie said.

Tim and his father helped Tim's mother across the stream. The mustached police officer reached him about the time Tim got there.

"I found her right here." Charlie pointed to a three- foot-wide sandy triangle just below the large drainage pipe. He stepped from one large boulder to the next until he jumped down into the sand.

"She was crumpled up right here."

"Did she say anything?" Tim's mother asked.

"I don't think she could," Charlie said. "I knew there was a blanket there, so I grabbed it and put it over her. I don't know anything about medicine or whatever, but the girls caught up with me. We checked to see if she was really hurt."

"I put pressure on the cuts on her belly," Tink said.

"I know you guys say that I saved her or whatever," Charlie said. "But mostly we didn't know what to do. She was pretty hurt. Um . . ."

Charlie touched his face next to his chin and between his legs.

"We didn't want to leave her," Charlie said. "The pizza was still warm, and she was really cold, so I put the boxes on top of her. I think one of the girls got down and held her. But we were super scared."

"Why, Charlie?" Sandy asked. "Why were you so scared?"

"Because it wasn't the first time we'd seen this," Charlie said. "And she was . . ."

Charlie glanced at Tim's parents. Tim's Mom had turned into her father and was weeping.

"Ivy flagged down a car and begged the lady to take her to the hospital," Charlie said. "We didn't think she could wait for an ambulance. We helped load her in the back of the lady's SUV."

"Did she have her purse?" the mustached cop asked.

"Um . . ." Charlie scowled and looked at Tink.

"It's okay if you took it," Tim's Dad said. "I probably would have."

"I don't really know," Charlie said. "We were really scared."

"Just go through it like it happened," Art said.

Hearing his voice, Charlie jerked up to look at him. Art walked to Charlie and put his hand on Charlie's shoulders.

"You mean act it out?" Charlie asked.

"Try to be as exact as possible," Art said. "Sometimes, that jogs things loose in your memory."

Art nodded. Charlie grabbed the clipboard from a uniformed police officer nearby. He ran across the creek to the other side. He jogged up the ramp and onto the bridge.

"I'll be Jeffy," Ivy said. Nash ran over to stand by her. Ivy artificially lowered her voice, "Hey, that's a person."

"What do you mean?" Charlie asked.

"Some girl," Ivy's lowered voice said. "Nobody we know."

"Where?" Charlie asked and leaned over.

He ran across the bridge and down the ramp. He splashed across the creek. The people moved aside, and he went to the sandy bank. He set the pretend pizza on the ground and pretended to grab a blanket from the dark pipe. Out of the corner of his eye, he saw the mustached cop signal the forensics team to check out the pipe.

Charlie kneeled down and pretended to throw a blanket over the girl. Tink pretended to pull off her sweatshirt and pressed it onto the sand.

"Purse," the mustached cop said.

Charlie shook his head. Tink looked up and shook her head. Charlie looked up at Ivy.

"Did you see it?" Charlie asked Ivy.

"I remember there being something over by those rocks," Ivy said. "But I don't know if it was a purse."

"I only remember seeing her," Charlie said. "I was kinda freaked out, because I didn't know her, and she was in really bad shape. The cops had already bugged us about all of . . . episodes, and I figured they'd think we did it. And she was so hurt."

He looked at Tink and shrugged.

"Did you see anything?" Charlie asked Tink.

"Maybe," Tink said. "But I don't think it was her purse. It was more like . . ."

Tink looked at Charlie. He nodded.

"Her underwear and stuff . . ." Tink said.

"Where?" the mustached cop asked.

Tink was so surprised by his voice that she shook her head. She looked at Charlie.

"Over there." Ivy pointed.

Charlie got up and went to where Ivy pointed.

"Here?" Charlie yelled.

"Over there," Ivy said.

Charlie walked over to where boulder-sized jagged rocks stood straight up in the sand.

"Here?" Charlie asked.

Ivy nodded.

"She says it was here," Charlie said. "But . . ."

"Did she say anything?" Tim's Mom asked again.

"She wasn't really awake, ma'am," Charlie said. "She looked like she'd been bashed . . . I mean there was blood on these rocks and stuff. She opened her eyes . . . She just looked at me. That's all. Tink?"

"Pan said something like 'Wake up,'" Tink said. "And she opened her eyes. I mean, her face was all puffy and blue and she'd lost some teeth. Like me, I guess."

"She wasn't afraid of you?" the mustached cop asked.

"Me? Why would she be afraid of me?" Charlie shrugged. "But . . ."

Charlie looked down at the sand next to the rock.

"I didn't come back here after that," Charlie said. "I was too . . ."

He looked at Tink.

"It was hard on all of us," Tink said. "I think we avoided the area. I mean . . ."

Tink gestured to Ivy.

"She . . . happened here . . ." Tink looked at Charlie. "I was inside then. Did you find Ivy too?"

Charlie nodded.

"Here?" The mustache cop sounded surprised.

"It's not far from where I . . . I mean . . ." Tink shifted

uncomfortably.

"Look around," Art said. "Do you see a light? All the fixtures are broken. Zero surveillance cameras. This piece of sand? That culvert? You could do anything, and no one would see you."

"We used to come down here all the time. No one was here," Charlie said. "As long as we stayed away from the urbanites at rush hour, no one bugged us."

"How did you find Ivy if you didn't come here?" the mustached cop asked him.

"I was looking for her," Charlie said. "I thought she might have gone with Saint Jude, but Jeffy said 'No.' We went looking for her."

"And Tiffanie?" the mustached cop asked.

"Charlie was already living with us then," Sandy said.

"How did you get away?" Charlie asked Tink.

"I climbed in there when I woke up," Tink said.

"Woke up?" the mustached cop asked.

"They drugged me with something," Tink nodded. "Ivy, too."

They looked up at Ivy, and she nodded.

"They probably drugged your daughter," Tink said.

Tim's Dad looked surprised.

"I didn't know what was happening," Tink said. "Not at all — until I woke up. I'd bet that your daughter didn't, either."

"Tink?" Charlie waved her over to where he was. "Look."

He pointed to the rocks. They were all equally spaced apart except for the one he was standing over.

"They weren't like that before . . ." Charlie said.

"Come on out of there," Art said.

Charlie looked up at him. Art waved Charlie and Tink away from the rock. He held out his hand and pulled Tink up to the cement walkway. He helped Charlie out next. He pulled on latex gloves and jumped down to the sand. Squatting down, he lifted the rock.

Everyone gasped. Under the rock lay purses and wallets and

other trophies of the assaults.

"That's it! That's it!" Tim yelled. He pointed to a gold necklace on the side of the stash. "That's Barbie's necklace!"

He tried to get down to the sand, but a uniformed cop stopped him.

"Get them out of here," the mustached cop said.

Sandy and Mike hustled Tink and Charlie away from the sand bar. Charlie didn't say a thing until he was buckled into the passenger seat of Mike's old Bronco.

"What do you think?" Mike asked.

"I think there are a lot more girls," Charlie said.

"I think you're right." Mike started the car and drove back to the Castle.

Chapter Two Hundred & Thirty-Five

Trouble

Wednesday night—11:59 p.m.

Aden grabbed the note pinned to his apartment door and stepped into the apartment. Seeing the gas fireplace on, he groaned. He figured the kids must have gotten up after Sandy had gone to bed. He took a couple steps to turn off the fireplace and realized he was standing in a sea of teenagers.

Aden peered around the room at what looked like a couple girls and a couple of boys. He tried to make out their hair color to see if these were his kids to be shooed off to bed or someone else's kids sleeping over.

"Hi," Sandy's voice came from the couch in a loud whisper.

Not daring to move, for fear of stepping on someone, he glanced over to her. She got up and went around the sleeping kids. Taking his hand, she led him into the kitchen.

"Did you get the note?" she asked.

He held up the unopened note. She grinned at him.

"I thought I could read it inside," he said.

She nodded.

"How did it go tonight?" she asked in a low tone.

He shook his head and pulled off his tie. She reached up on her tip-toes and kissed him. He held her tight.

"How was tonight?" he asked.

"A lot has happened," Sandy said. "Did you eat?"

As if he were thinking, he looked up at the ceiling and then shook his head. She smiled at him and leaned into the refrigerator. His eyes followed her efforts with keen interest.

"Oh, I saved you . . ." Sandy took out a portion of the chicken pot pie. "Honey made this for the kids. It's your favorite. Should I warm it up a bit?"

He took the plate and fork from her and began eating. She smiled. After he'd had a few bites, he gestured with the fork for her to tell him about her night.

"On his way home from school, Charlie ran into a boy," Sandy said. Aden scowled. "No, not one of those boys. Mike was with him, like we'd agreed. Tim, that's the boy's name; his sister is one of the girls who committed suicide. Tim saw Charlie at the police station and wanted Charlie to tell him about what had happened to his sister. I guess her family didn't know much."

Aden nodded.

"Honey made that outstanding pot pie. Delphie made the crust." Sandy smiled. Aden nodded. "Tim and his parents came for dinner."

Aden raised his eyebrows and nodded.

"Right," Sandy said. "It was nice. They seemed relieved to have something else to think about. Anyway, it turns out that Tim and Sissy went to school in Westminster. They moved to town when all this happened and their daughter was in the hospital. Tim started online high school, like Charlie. Then they sent their daughter to a program out of town. She was home on a break when she killed herself. Can you imagine?"

Aden shook his head.

"Anyway, Sissy was *excited* to see him."

Aden furrowed his brow and gestured with his fork.

"Yes, he's sleeping out there too," Sandy said. "His parents . . . I can't imagine what they've been through. Anyway, they seemed happy to see Tim make some friends. Normal, that's what his Mom kept saying; she was glad to 'have a little normal in her life.' I guess their whole world fell apart when this happened, and now that their daughter is dead . . . Everything's kind of stopped for them. They seemed to feel relieved that things are moving, even a little bit."

Aden took a drink of milk and said, "Did you go there?"

"Right," Sandy said. "We did. It was a big deal because none of the girls have really said anything to the police and Charlie ... well, I guess we just haven't gotten there."

"Sounds hard," Aden said, and took a bite.

"It was hard," Sandy said. "Mike took Charlie so he'd have time to talk if he needed it. Charlie was so brave. Colin and Art were there, mostly to support Charlie. They took a video so that everything would be on the up and up. Charlie went through finding their daughter. It was really hard for Tim's parents. That's why Tim's here, to give them some time to work through it together."

"Where did you go?" Aden asked.

"Fourteenth and Market on the Cherry Creek Trail," Sandy said. "Can you believe it? Right in the middle of everything this horribleness goes on."

Aden nodded.

"There are cookies over there," Sandy said. "We made cookies when we got back to calm everyone down a little."

Aden smiled and opened the cookie jar.

"They found a stash of a bunch of stuff from the girls," Sandy said. "It looks like there were a lot of girls, so it was good that Colin and Art were there documenting everything. Now Homeland Security is involved. They won't take over the case, but it brings in the Feds. Colin said he'd send the video to the FBI. I bet they'll assign an agent."

"That doesn't sound like a good thing to me."

"I don't trust the cops on this case," Sandy said. "I don't know why. I just don't."

"You think they're involved?"

"No," Sandy said. "Not that. It just ... Looking at everything Charlie found, I couldn't help but wondering why these cops hadn't done anything. I mean this has been going on for a long time—at least a year. They say they don't know anything, but Tim's parents were at a concert at the Pepsi Center. Their daughter went to a dance at East and then probably came down to get them. Charlie got her to the hospital. She was in such bad shape that her parents didn't know she was there for three days. But, I mean the cops found their car in the Pepsi Center parking lot."

"That's not very far from Fourteenth and Market," Aden said.

"Right. I'm not one to bag on the cops, but even I was like, 'Come on guys!'"

Aden nodded.

"You should have seen Art's face when he lifted this rock and saw all the trophies," Sandy said. "If eyes were lasers, that detective would be missing a body part or two."

Sandy took a bite of a cookie while she remembered.

"We got home and everyone was brave and happy," Sandy said. "Heather stayed because Blane was with you?"

Aden nodded.

"As soon as they lay down, one by one, the kids lost it," Sandy said. "Heather was so great with Tink and even Ivy. I tried to help Tim. When everyone was really asleep, Charlie was upset. I finally got him to sleep on the couch. I . . . I don't know how they're going to get through this."

Sandy shook her head.

"It's one thing to have to go through the assault," Sandy said. "And then go through the process of getting better. Tink was probably beaten the worst. She still has a lot of physical healing to do. Well, I mean, Ivy has missing teeth and stuff, too. After all of that, we ask these kids to relive it for these cops like, 'Oh, it's a school night. Come walk us through your worst horror.' They all stand around watching. Just gross."

Sandy shivered.

"Awful," Aden said.

Sandy nodded.

"Are they going to school tomorrow?" Aden asked.

"I think they have to," Sandy said. "We have to keep things as normal as possible."

Aden nodded.

"I missed you," Sandy said. "We could have used your ... stability."

"I wish I had been there," Aden said.

"How did it really go?" Sandy asked.

"Not great and okay," Aden said. "I think we can see the fractures in the company and, I don't know, maybe what's going on in our country right now is playing out here. No one trusts anyone else. They've formed these little coalitions and don't trust anyone outside their little group. Everyone's out for himself because he thinks the other guy is out for himself. It's like the more opportunity they have, the more sure they are that they're being screwed out of something better."

"I think that's everywhere," Sandy said. "It's like shopping. Do I buy this now? Maybe I'm missing a coupon or the deal that the guy in front of me is getting, or there's some insider thing. And even when I know I've gotten a pretty good deal, I feel like I've been cheated. It's hard."

"Right," Aden said. "It feels like we're all mice scrambling for crumbs."

"We can't even pick our meal," Sandy nodded. "Just whatever falls from the table. It doesn't feel good."

"I guess that's what gets to me," Aden said. "I see being able to buy into Lipson as a way to get ahead and help my family. But the first thing people want to know is how they can get a better deal. A bunch of families pooled all of their money, like everybody and grandma gave money, to buy in. So, the big question tonight for Sam was: why did he give them a better deal? I mean, obviously, they got a better deal because they own more shares. Sam was so mad that I thought he was going to stroke or something."

Aden shook his head.

"I think we made progress," Aden said. "But... Sam's really discouraged. He wishes he'd closed the place rather than let Jacob take over and sell it to the employees."

"I'm sure it's just growing pains," Sandy said.

"It's hard to have these growing pains when we're really in the middle of a crisis," Aden said.

"Did they see that?"

"Yes." Aden nodded. "They could tell we were in trouble. Just... there's no easy fix and ..."

Sandy reached up and kissed his lips. He smiled.

"You've had enough worry for the night," Sandy said. "Let's try to get some rest."

"Would you like me to stay out here tonight?" Aden asked.

"No," Sandy said. "I'll stay. Heather's here, too."

Aden nodded.

"Where's Rachel?" Aden asked.

"I left her upstairs at Jill's," Sandy said. "She was asleep, and I didn't want to wake her. I'll go up in a bit to see if she'd like to nurse. It's our last few nights with Val."

"You need your rest," Aden said.

"We'll get there," Sandy said. "One step at a time."

He smiled.

"With all these kids... I was thinking about making something yummy for breakfast," Sandy said. "Are you due at start-up?"

Aden nodded.

"Then off to bed with you!" Sandy said.

He leaned down to kiss her, and she looked away. He laughed. He was almost out of the kitchen when he turned and looked at her.

"Love you," he said.

"Go." Sandy pointed.

He nodded and left for bed. Lost in thought, Sandy stood in the kitchen. She jerked to the present when she heard Aden's shower water turn off. Nodding to herself, she got out the ingredients to make quiche.

~~~~~~~~

Wednesday night — 11:59 p.m.

Jacob lay on his back in the living area of the loft. Using his psychokinetic skill, he juggled an apple, one of Sarah's mangy tennis balls, and a balled-up piece of paper. Every once in a while, he'd reach up to grab the apple, take a bite, and return it to its rotation in his juggling act.

"Jake?" Jill's sleepy voice came as a whisper across the loft.

Everything fell out of the air. He managed to catch the apple.

"I'm here," Jacob said and took a bite of the apple.

Jill's head appeared over the couch. He smiled.

"I'm meditating," he said.

"I thought I saw some things flying through the air," Jill said.

"Oh?"

"Very funny," Jill said. "Will you show me?"

Jacob lay back. Soon the ball of paper, Sarah's mangy ball, and the apple core were rotating through the air.

"Pretty exciting," Jacob said.

"I thought you didn't meditate," Jill said.

"I did this as a kid," Jacob said. "Mom said it counted, so I thought I'd try it."

"How was the meeting?"

"Awful," Jacob said. "I should have stayed in Maine."

"You'd be awfully lonely in Maine." Jill smiled and crossed her arms over her expanded belly. "Katy would miss you so."

"I wish I were lonelier here," Jacob snarled.

Jill smiled and went to the kitchen. She returned with an apple. She waited until the apple core was near her to grab it. She tossed the apple into the mix. It dropped and then was caught by Jacob's mind direction.

"Was it really that bad?" Jill asked.

"It was . . . honest," Jacob said. "I don't know why I thought we could protect our little company from all the anger around now."

"I can't go to the grocery store without someone sneering at me," Jill said. "I'm glad I'm not in school this semester."

"I thought all this negativity would end when the election was over," Jacob said. "Mercury went direct or whatever. But everyone was sure angry tonight."

Jill came around and sat on the couch.

"Dad was furious," Jacob said. "He actually said that he wished he had closed the company. I've never, ever heard him say something like that."

"What did they say to that?"

"One of those jerks got right in his face and said that Dad should have closed the company instead of ripping off his employees for all those years."

"Wow."

"Yeah — wow," Jacob said. "You know we pay average or above salaries, have great benefits, promote from within regardless of gender or whatever, provide daycare for every employee's child, and . . . Anyway, Bambi took the guy on. Aden told him that he should just quit if he felt ripped off. But Dad was just crushed. He's worked so hard to be fair . . . "

"People feel like they're being ripped off," Jill said.

"Well . . . I was just sitting here trying to decide if I should close the company," Jacob said. "I still own more than half the shares. What would you think about that?"

"I think it's not something you should decide after one angry meeting," Jill said.

"You know that whole *Atlas Shrugged* thing?" Jacob asked. "The hyper-responsible go on strike and let everyone else suffer."

"Mmm," Jill scowled.

"Maybe we should quit," Jacob said. "We'd have to sell a few things to have income and, gosh, we could move to some beach and sleep for a month. You'd have the boys, and we'd have time to enjoy them. I never feel like I get enough time with Katy."

"You'd last a day, maybe two," Jill said.

"It sounds really nice."

"I want to get this straight," Jill said. "You're going to let this one singularly irritating site manager change the plans and vision you've worked on for more than five years?"

"Uh . . . "

"Sounds like you're easily manipulated," Jill said.

"When you put it like that . . ." Jacob said.

"Maybe I should wake Katy," Jill said. "She found her pony bags tonight and remembered that she really wanted a pony."

Jacob made a noise that was somewhere between a growl and a groan. Jill grabbed the piece of paper out of the air and sat back down on the couch. She unraveled the wad of paper to read it.

"These are the numbers for closing the company tomorrow," Jill said. "You had Tres run the numbers?"

"I did," Jacob said. "We'd have to sell a house or two, but I think we can pull it off."

"What did Tres say?"

"He said I was an ass," Jacob said.

"And your father? Aden?"

"I didn't tell them," Jacob said.

"That's nice of you," Jill said.

Jacob glanced at her, and the ball fell on his forehead. The apple hit his chest.

"What's going to happen to the site manager?" Jill asked.

"Aden told him to leave before he did any more damage," Jacob said.

"Are you going to fire him?" Jill asked.

"Aden is going to meet with him after start tomorrow," Jacob said. "I guess that's today."

"And fire him?" Jill asked.

"Probably not," Jacob said.

"So . . . people can act out like crazy folks, cool off, and everything's all right," Jill said. "But you keep a permanent record?"

"Uh . . . maybe," Jacob said. "I . . .

He was about to justify his position when he glanced at her face. She was scowling at him. He looked away.

"He's going to get a note in his file," Jacob said.

"Uh, huh," she said. "What's this about?"

"I hate selfish people," Jacob said.

"Hate?" Jill asked.

"Yes, hate," Jacob said. "Here we are, living in the great city, in this awesome time, in the amazing country, and all some people can do is whine about how they're not getting what they should. They've won the lotto! You know what he said?"

"What?"

"He told Dad that he bet he didn't pay any taxes," Jacob said. "'Rich assholes like him just let his kids starve,' that's what he said. Dad pays for all kinds of things for the Lipson kids. Shit, I've supported that stupid school for years. I should just close it and then see what he thinks."

"That would sure show him," Jill said. "And since he goes to school there, I bet he'll really pay the price for being a jackass."

"He doesn't go there," Jacob said.

"Oh? Who does?" Jill asked.

Jacob glared at her.

"When Trevor and I went to counseling, the lady told us that anger was like a hot potato," Jill said. "I'd get angry about something and throw my hot potato at Trevor. He didn't want to sit with a hot potato ,so he'd throw it back. Anyway, our life didn't exactly work like that, but it seems to me that you're making decisions based on someone else's hot potato."

"It pisses me off," Jacob said.

"Okay," Jill said.

"What? You're not going to defend him again?" Jacob asked.

Jill scowled at him.

"Sorry," Jacob said. "I know you're just trying to help."

"What are you really mad about?" Jill asked.

Jacob looked away. The apple went around in a circle in the air.

"I can't imagine anyone being mad at Dad," Jacob said. "Or saying those awful things."

"Sounds to me like the site manager was mad at himself," Jill said. "He just took it out on your dad."

"You mean like Katy and Paddie do? He's not five!"

"Maybe you can add *hating immature people* to your list," Jill said.

Jacob didn't say anything for a while. Jill crumpled the piece of paper and threw it at him. He added it to the rotation along with the nasty tennis ball. After a while, Jill got up and went back to bed.

About twenty minutes later, Jacob came to bed.

"Sorry," he kissed her lips.

"Are you all right?" she asked.

"I just needed to think it through," he said. "Thanks for trying to help."

"Are you going to fire the guy?" Jill asked.

"No, but I'm going to ask him about his kids," Jacob said. "I bet something's going on there to make him hurt so much."

"Good thinking," Jill said.

"Just because he says we're jerks doesn't mean we have to start acting like jerks," Jacob said.

"There *is* that," Jill said.

"You're brilliant," he said.

"You're due at work in three hours," Jill said. "The girls are going to be here for breast feeding in a half hour; you should sleep."

Just then, Katy cried out in her sleep. Jill got up to check on her. When she was done, Sandy was there to get Rachel for breastfeeding. Jill went downstairs with her to join Honey and Val. When she got back into bed, Jacob was sound asleep.

~~~~~~~~

Wednesday morning — 6:19 a.m.

"So, I need to ask you something, but I don't want you to make fun of me." Nash blocked Charlie's entrance into their bathroom.

"I have to pee," Charlie said.

Nash didn't move out of the way.

"What?" Charlie asked.

"Did you . . . you know . . . with Ivy?" Nash asked.

"Did I what?" Charlie's voice rose.

"Shhh," Nash said. "Did you sleep with Ivy? Was she your girlfriend?"

"No." Charlie's voice was indignant. "She's a little kid. That's just gross."

"Good." Nash moved to the side, and Charlie went into the bathroom.

"At least I don't think I did," Charlie said from inside. "You know, it's all kind of fuzzy. Maybe I did. Yeah, I'm sure I did."

"She was a little kid!" Nash flew into the bathroom.

Charlie laughed.

"Very funny," Nash said.

"I thought so," Charlie said.

"Stop talking and get dressed!" Sandy yelled from the front room.

"You won't tell her I asked, will you?" Nash asked.

"Not a word." Charlie smiled and got into the shower.

Chapter Two Hundred & Thirty-Six

Something New

Wednesday morning — 9:19 a.m.

After getting everyone ready and out the door, Delphie had gone back to bed. The late nights and worry had left her feeling worn out. And today she had to be on her game.

Ivy's aunt was coming in a few hours.

Delphie heard the door to her apartment open and footsteps move across the living room. She sat up in bed.

"Sam?" Delphie asked before he entered the room.

"Sorry to wake you," Sam said. "I know today's a big day."

"Did you come home to rest?" Delphie asked. "I don't think you slept at all last night."

Sam gave her a slight nod and sat down on the bed.

"I need to ask you something," Sam said. "At least I think you're the person to ask. I wasn't sure this morning, but then we got started, and I thought, 'I should ask Delphie; she won't mind.' But then I see that you're resting, as you should be after such a late night and today being such a big day. Plus, I know that I must have kept you awake with my tossing and turning and . . ."

Delphie put her hand on his leg, and he stopped talking. He looked at her for a moment. They had what Delphie called, "The Standard Agreement." She agreed not to read his mind without permission, and he agreed to ask when he wanted to know something. Of course, like most couples, she didn't tell him when she was reading his entire essence, and he expected her to tell him when there was something wrong.

They sized each other up.

"You have to ask," Delphie said, just because she knew she should.

He smiled at her deception.

"You've never asked me about the business," Delphie said.

"I know," Sam said. "I just . . . I miss Celia."

Sam winced at his words. He closed his eyes to avoid seeing what he assumed he would — Delphie's pain.

"I miss her, too," Delphie said.

Sam opened his eyes to look at her.

"I loved her absolutely," Delphie said. "I don't mind that you did, too. I would expect you to miss her because I do, too."

"You're not offended?" Sam asked.

"No," Delphie said. "I tell you that all the time, but you . . ."

"You're not second best to her, you know," Sam said. "Our life, this relationship, it's different . . . Celia was . . . and we're . . ."

"More like friends," Delphie said. "I know."

"I don't ever want to diminish you or our life," Sam said. "Because you mean the world to me. Our life is really wonderful. You make everything . . . work. I couldn't do all of this without you."

Delphie smiled.

"But you're not Celia," Sam said. "You're softer, kinder, more fragile, and less . . ."

"Bossy," Delphie nodded.

"And right now . . ."

"You could use Celia's help," Delphie said.

Sam looked at Delphie with sorrow-filled eyes.

"I'm sorry for hurting you," Sam said.

"You're not," Delphie said.

"I'm not?"

"You're not hurting me at all," Delphie said. "Now, let me freshen up a bit, and we'll see what we can figure out."

"You're sure? Because . . ."

"I'm sure," Delphie said. She got up and went into the

bathroom. "You have to trust me more, Sam."

"I'm . . . discombobulated," Sam said.

Delphie washed her hands and came out.

"Did the kids get to school?" Sam asked, because he knew he should.

"Did the sites open?" Delphie smiled.

"You're right," Sam said. "I'm off the point."

Delphie went to her kitchenette. She filled her kettle and put it on the gas burner.

"What do you need to know from Celia?" Delphie asked.

"Celia . . ." Sam started. He leaned close to Delphie. "Is she here?"

"She's always around you or me," Delphie said. "She leaves only to watch out for Katy or Jackie."

"I guess I knew that." Sam nodded.

"What's going on, Sam?" Delphie asked.

Just then, the kettle squealed, and Delphie got up to make tea. When she came back with two steaming mugs, Sam seemed to have made a decision.

"We started this business, this construction thing, together — Celia and I," Sam said. "I wanted to be a carpenter. I'm a pretty good carpenter, but . . . We would have starved. Celia taught me everything I know about running a business. Her family has successfully run businesses since . . . well, the beginning of time."

Sam nodded. He looked up and took the mug of green tea that Delphie offered him. She navigated them into her living area. He sat down on the couch, and she took the soft chair she enjoyed. She had just sat down when Cleo, Sandy's cat, scratched at her apartment door. She got up to let in the cat.

"What's this?" Sam asked.

Cleo gave him a regal look and sauntered across the room.

"Miss Cleo comes in the mornings to sit on the windowsill," Delphie said.

Cleo looked at Delphie and jumped up onto the sunny

windowsill.

"That's a good spot," Sam said. "I might take it from her."

Cleo gave a loud *meow* as if to complain, and Delphie smiled.

"Can we talk about this in front of...?" Sam discreetly pointed to Cleo.

Delphie smiled. With the cat in the room and his tea in his hand, Sam felt more grounded and whole.

"What is it that you want to know?" Delphie asked.

"Celia would know just what to do with this whole mess," Sam said. "She'd have known what to say to those awful site managers last night. She'd have had just the solution to make everything better. Hell, she probably never would have gotten into this mess. But Jake and me, we're..."

He fell forward with his elbows on his knees.

"We're not Celia," Sam said. "I can't shake the feeling that this is the big test. We have to commit to being employee owned."

"That's why it has been presented to you," Delphie said.

Sam looked at her for a moment.

"They want your little experiment to fail," Delphie said.

"The old board members?" Sam asked.

Delphie nodded.

"They always have to be right," Sam said.

Delphie nodded.

"I can feel it in my bones," Sam said. "This is the moment that will mean either a long life to this company or the end of it. I don't know what to do, and..."

"Celia would." Delphie nodded.

"She'd have told off that so-and-so site manager, and... I don't know what," Sam said. "I feel beaten down. I want to crawl into a hole and hide."

"You felt like that when Jake bought the company," Delphie said.

"I hadn't thought of it, but yeah," Sam said.

"Well, that's some of it," Delphie said. "Decisions made in a moment of desperate grief carry that same quality."

"That's good," Sam said. "Celia?"

"Me," Delphie said.

"You *are* wise," Sam smiled.

Delphie grinned.

"What would Celia make me do that I won't want to do but is the exact right thing to do?" Sam asked.

"She would take the entire situation with the site to the employees," Delphie said. "Celia was absolutely fearless. She believed secrets only aid existing power structures. She was hell bent on breaking those . . .

"*Archaic, misogynistic power structures*," Sam and Delphie said together.

"Yes," Sam said. "I remember that."

"She believes . . . "

Sam jerked at Delphie's use of the present tense. Delphie gave him a slight nod.

"Celia believes in the goodness of people," Delphie said.

Sam groaned.

"You know I'm right," Delphie said. "She wouldn't put up with this chaos and bullshit. She'd tell the site managers to bring it to their employees . . ."

"And fire anyone who didn't." Sam nodded. "Yes, that's what she'd do."

"Rather than put up with crap, she'd tell them to ask their employees what they wanted to do and bring the answers back to her. Employees are the true stakeholders in any company because their lives are on the line. They're more invested in the company's well-being because of it."

Delphie nodded.

"It sounds good to me," Delphie said.

Sam gave her a long wry look and she grinned.

"What will happen if I do that?" Sam asked.

"You're asking me?" Delphie asked. "It's kind of close to me so

I . . ."

"Oh, come on," Sam said. "You don't give a crap about the company. You get fuzzy only over stuff you really care about — like whether Ivy's aunt is a decent person."

"Valerie's going to help me with that." Delphie nodded.

"You're avoiding my question," Sam said.

"Because I think you should try it to learn for yourself," Delphie said.

"Celia told you to say that," Sam said.

Delphie smiled. He shook his head at her.

"What will happen?" Sam asked.

"You'll find that your employees trust you," Delphie said. "If Jake thinks the site should move, then it should move. Period. They don't care about the power politics. They want to make sure they have jobs tomorrow and the next day."

Delphie's eyes went vague for a moment.

"In fact, many of them do know something's wrong," Delphie said. "By asking them, you'll give their worry form."

"That doesn't sound good," Sam said.

"Think of it this way," Delphie said. "Your site managers can leave at any time and get jobs anywhere in the country at the same or equal pay, right?"

Sam nodded.

"Most of your employees aren't in that same position," Delphie said. "For many of them, their job feeds their families. Their kids go to the Marlowe school. They need and value Lipson medical insurance. Their Lipson stock is the first big financial investment they've ever made. If the company folds, they're the ones who have the most at stake."

Cleo jumped down from the warm windowsill onto Sam's lap. She rubbed her head against his chest.

"You have to ask them," Delphie said.

"How?" Sam's big carpenter's hand rubbed Cleo's black-and-white head.

"Start with the site managers who support you — like Bambi or Jerry or those kids taking Rodney's place," Delphie said.

"Jerry walked out of the meeting last night," Sam said. "Said he was going to kill someone if he didn't."

"He's a good person to ask, then," Delphie said. "Get the site managers to survey their crews. Tell Jake and Aden to talk to the other site managers. They have more pull with the younger employees."

"If they won't do it?" Sam asked.

"Get rid of them," Delphie said. "Let them go somewhere where bosses are king and employees don't matter. There are lots of places like that."

Sam nodded.

"I bet Honey would help you," Delphie said.

"She's on maternity leave," Sam said. "I couldn't . . ."

"She would tell you how the people who work for you need their jobs," Delphie said. "Plus, she's going stir crazy."

"She is?"

"She'd be happier working a few hours a day." Delphie nodded. "Between Rosa and me, we can watch Maggie."

Sam nodded. Delphie got up to make more tea. They drank their tea in quiet company.

"Well, I need to go read Celia the funnies," Sam said.

"She'd very much like that," Delphie said.

Delphie got up to show him out. He kissed her and whispered, "Thanks," into her ear before leaving. She smiled.

"Well, Miss Cleo — what's next?" Delphie asked.

Cleo meowed and sauntered into the bedroom. She heard the cat jump onto the bed.

"Good idea," Delphie said.

She went back to bed.

~~~~~~~~~

Wednesday afternoon — 2:19 p.m.

"She's not coming." Ivy slunk away from the front windows of Heather's and Blane's home.

"She's just late," Heather said. "She'll be here."

"She called when she got stuck in traffic," Delphie said. "She called when she got lost."

"If you want to be somewhere, you just get there," Ivy said. "You're not late or . . ."

There was a knock on the door. Ivy's eyes went big. She ran to Delphie, and Delphie hugged her.

"I'll get the door," Valerie said. "Put her off her game."

Heather nodded. Valerie opened the door to a medium-sized thirty-year-old woman. She had reddish hair, a pleasant face, and a tight military body. She was wearing an Air Force dress uniform. Seeing Valerie, she gaped.

"Hello?" Valerie smiled her brightest and most intimidating smile.

"Val! Um, Ms. Lipson, um," Ivy's aunt said. Her mouth moved up and down like a fish out of water.

Delphie edged Valerie out of the way.

"You!" Ivy's aunt scowled. "I know you. You're that psychic lady. And you're Valerie Lipson, and . . .

Ivy opened the door wider. Heather stood right behind the girl, with her hands on her shoulders.

"I'm Ivy," she said. "I mean Anna Marie. But everyone calls me Ivy."

"I'm Second Lieutenant Grace McDonald," Ivy's aunt said. "Most people call me 'Gracie.'"

Ivy's aunt stood very still. Her eyes scanned Ivy's face. She glanced at Delphie.

"You were right," she said.

"I was?" Delphie asked.

"You told me that my brother wouldn't come home; that his child would suffer unspeakable horrors until she made her way home; and that I would make it back to love her all of my life,"

Ivy's aunt said. "I know we're just meeting, Ivy, but I feel like I've known you all my life."

Ivy glanced up at Heather, who squeezed Ivy's shoulders.

"When Grannie was alive, we would read your letters together." Ivy nodded. "You were Gran's favorite child."

"She was so angry with me for going into the military," Ivy's aunt said. "I never heard . . . not one word . . . and then . . . I thought you were in foster care, and . . ."

Ivy's aunt looked from Delphie to Valerie and then to Heather.

"Would you like to come in?" Heather asked.

Gracie took off her hat and stepped into Heather's house. She looked at Valerie again.

"How did you get Valerie Lipson here to introduce you?" Gracie smiled at Ivy.

Unsure of whether to hug her aunt or not, Ivy moved closer to Heather.

"My good friend Delphie is Ivy's aunt," Valerie said. "We think."

"You are?" Gracie asked.

"It's definitely possible," Delphie said. "People say we look alike."

"I can see it," Gracie said. "Did you know when I saw you?"

"Unless I saw you in the last couple of days — no, I didn't know," Delphie said.

"We think Mom was Delphie's little sister," Ivy said.

Gracie gave Delphie a long look before she nodded.

"I have this feeling that everything is going to work out really, really well." Gracie smiled.

"Me, too," Delphie said.

"*Aunt power!*" Gracie raised her fist, and the women laughed.

"My husband made a buttermilk chocolate cake for us," Heather said. "And Val brought some of her awesome coffeecake. We have coffee. Would you like to come in?"

Heather made a vague wave toward the back of the house. They walked toward the den. Jackie, Mack, and Maggie were sleeping in cribs along the wall of the living room.

"Oh, look at the babies!" Gracie said. She glanced at Heather. "Are they all yours?"

"No, just the one," Heather smiled and gestured to Mack. "I'm prolific but not that much."

"I didn't know if you were fostering or . . ." Gracie blushed.

"I'm babysitting Maggie." Ivy stood a little taller at the mention of her responsibility.

"That's very nice of you," Gracie said.

"And this is Jackie." Valerie went to where Jackie was sleeping.

"I guess I read that you had a baby," Gracie said. "You and Sergeant Roper, right?"

"Mike," Valerie said.

"The painter," Gracie blushed. "I hate to say it, but I think I've read everything there is to read about you."

"I wonder why?" Valerie asked.

"Nice girl makes good," Gracie said. "Meeting you . . . It's like it's meant to be."

"It's nice to meet you, too." Valerie smiled. "We've really enjoyed the chance to get to know Ivy a little bit. I'm glad you'll be in the family."

Grace smiled.

"Did you say that your husband baked a cake?" Gracie asked.

"He was a chef," Heather said. "It's kind of a long story."

"I'm on emergency family leave, so I have time." Gracie nodded. They moved into the house to talk.

~~~~~~~~

Wednesday afternoon — 3:49 p.m.

Heather pulled her Subaru into the dog park near the school. While they lived close enough to walk, Heather preferred to pick up Tink from school. Heather had this vague feeling that all this stuff with Charlie was going to pour over onto Tink. She wanted to make sure she would be there to help. She'd left everyone at her house to pick up Tink.

Of course, Tink didn't love the fact that Heather picked her up. As a compromise, they'd agreed to meet at the dog park a block away. Seeing Mike and the menagerie of Castle dogs, Heather got out of the car. She watched Charlie saunter toward the school. Tim Logan, the boy she'd met last night, skidded his bike to a stop and started walking with Charlie.

Mike stopped with the dogs to chat with Heather. She was on her way to him when she noticed Charlie and Tim going into the school. A few seconds later, Tink came out. Tink was by herself, because Sissy was at an all-day ballet training with some Russian somebody or another and Wanda was home sick. Tink jogged down the few steps. She had just made it past the red "E" when five boys surrounded her.

Heather couldn't tell what was happening, but Tink was upset. She tried to get out from the middle of them, but a boy grabbed her arm. The boy put his face right near Tink's, and Tink closed her eyes. Even from a distance, Heather could see the boy making kissing lips to Tink. The boys around them were whistling and jeering at her.

Tink was crying.

Heather ran toward the entrance to the school. Mike and the dogs ran past her. An SUV blocked their view and movement as it went past on the Esplanade. Heather had just caught up to Mike when they heard Tink yell, "*Let go of me!*"

The boy screamed and then screamed again.

The SUV moved out of the way. Tink was standing in the middle of the boys with a small personal Taser. Her face was red with rage and wet with tears. The boys scooted back with their hands up.

"*Get away from me!*" Tink yelled.

The school security officer grabbed Tink's arm, and she tasered him. Heather had almost reached her when the second security guard tackled Tink and took her down to the ground.

The boy lay screaming just inches away.

"Knock it off," Mike said to the boy. "You're fine."

Heather tapped the security guard with her foot.

"Get off my daughter," Heather said. He looked up at her. "*Now* — or I'm pressing charges."

"I saw the whole thing," said a young mother nearby. "You're arresting the wrong person. That boy was sexually assaulting that young girl. He was groping her privates with his nasty hand and . . ."

Police cruisers squealed to a stop in front of the school. The boys were screaming that they had been victimized by Tink. Other kids and parents voiced their opinions on what had happened. When the boy who'd been Tasered began to howl again, Scooter and Buster growled at him.

But all Heather cared about was Tink.

Heather knelt down and rolled her over. Tink looked at Heather.

"I . . ." Tink started. Her eyebrows furrowed. She tried again. "I . . ."

Tink was having a full-blown seizure.

CHAPTER TWO HUNDRED & THIRTY-SEVEN

NO DRAMA

Wednesday evening — 5:19 p.m.

"Here's what's going to happen," Aden said.

He was standing in the living room of their apartment. The kids, scowling and surly, were begrudgingly standing with him.

"There will be no drama from you," Aden said.

"But, *Dad*!" Noelle whined at the same moment Sissy said, "She's my *best friend*!"

"No drama," Aden said.

"Yeah, whatever," Charlie said. "You just want to get laid."

"I've said this before, but you're not listening," Aden said. "Sandy is exhausted. She was up all night with each of you, all week! Today, she's been running to work to help Heather help *you*, Sissy, with your big ballet day. She was up all night with Rachel."

"Sandy's fine," Nash grumped from the couch.

"How would you know, Nash?" Aden asked. "You haven't pulled your head out of that stupid computer in months."

Nash looked up at him.

"It's not like *you're* any better," Charlie said.

"Yeah!" Nash said. "You're always whining about your company and stuff."

"Fair enough." Aden pointed his finger at himself. "No drama tonight. See, that was easy."

Sissy grinned at him, but the boys sneered. Noelle looked heartbroken.

"Do you remember what happened the last time Sandy was this tired?" Aden asked. The kids all looked at the ground. "Anyone?"

The children were painfully silent.

"Do we want that to happen again?" Aden asked.

"No, but . . ." Noelle started. "This is really *big*!"

"Bigger than last night? Or last weekend? How about when you ran out of paint and the world was going to end?" Aden asked. "Sandy ran all over town to get you exactly the right paint from precisely the right place. That was Monday!"

None of the kids would look him in the eyes.

"All I'm asking for is one night of no drama," Aden said. "I'm taking Sandy to a nice dinner. We need to look at her apartment and decide what we want to do about with it. Boring stuff. We'll be back to tuck you in."

The kids were so quiet that he looked at each of their faces to make sure they were even awake.

"We can't go if any one of you goes off the deep end again," Aden said. "Okay? No drama!"

"How's dinner going to make it better?" Charlie sneered.

"She needs time to talk about herself," Aden said. "She needs to get dressed up, eat food that's way too expensive, and unwind. She'll relax and feel better. You'll see."

"Why does she need that, Dad?" Noelle asked.

"I don't know why," Aden said. "I just know that she does."

"How do you know?" Sissy asked.

"I've known Sandy a long time; I'm her husband," Aden said. "Plus, I've received no less than ten texts from the girlfriends informing me that Sandy's near her breaking point."

Aden smiled, and the kids laughed.

"This is Valerie's and Mike's last night here," Aden said. "They want to spend some time with you tonight."

"Is Ivy coming over?" Nash asked.

"Tink?" Noelle asked, because Charlie was too cool to ask.

"As you know, Tink had a seizure today," Aden said. "She's at home resting. Ivy is staying with them until they work out where she's going to live."

"So, they're coming over?" Charlie asked.

"No," Aden said. "You're stuck here with a world-famous actress and her incredibly talented painter husband. He and Jake are taking you and Nash to play hockey, by the way."

"Oh," Charlie said.

Aden laughed to himself. They heard movement on the stairs.

"Let's go over this one more time," Aden said. "What's going to happen?"

The kids wouldn't look at him.

"Anyone?" Aden asked. "Sissy."

"No drama," Sissy grumped.

"Noelle?" Aden asked.

"No drama, but . . ." Noelle started. She caught the look on her father's face and confirmed, "No drama."

"Boys?" Aden asked. "Charlie?"

"No drama," Charlie said. "I'll take Rachel."

"You can't take Rachel!" Noelle said. "*I'm* taking Rachel."

"Kids!" Aden growled.

"Okay — we've got it," Nash said. "No drama."

"Good," Aden said.

"I'm taking Rachel," Nash said.

The girls started screaming. Charlie snatched Nash's computer away, and he started screaming. Aden looked up to the heavens for help.

The door opened. Sandy came into the apartment with Rachel on her hip.

The kids stopped moving.

"What's going on?" Sandy asked.

The kids scattered like mice.

"Wait — what just happened?" Sandy asked. "I could hear them yelling downstairs."

"They're fine," Aden hugged Sandy. "How would you like to go to a quiet dinner with me?"

"Quiet dinner?" Sandy asked. "What about homework? What about..."

Sandy leaned forward.

"Drama," Sandy whispered.

"We're practicing our *no drama* skills," Aden said with emphasis.

Sandy smiled.

"Why don't you get dressed?" Aden smiled. "We have reservations in an hour."

"Where?"

"Beatrice and Woodsley," Aden smiled.

"Ooooh!" She was almost to the bedroom when she said, "Are we taking Rachel?"

"Rachel is staying with her friend Jackie tonight," Aden said in a loud tone. "It's Val's last night, and she wanted some quality Rachel time."

A general moan came from the direction of the kids rooms.

"Val brought a dress up for you," Aden followed her to their bedroom. Sandy had set Rachel on the bed and was holding a dress. "She said her French dressmaker made it. She made it for some curvy mistress in Paris, but the lady got dumped. The dress is paid for, but the lady couldn't 'possibly wear it' and the man who paid for it doesn't want his wife to find it. They sent it here because it matches your hair — or something like that."

"It's mine?" Sandy squealed and clapped. "I have just the shoes!"

"I know," Aden smiled.

"Out!" Sandy pushed him out of the room.

"We only have an hour," Aden said.

"I'll be ready in time," Sandy said. "You'll see."

Aden smiled. When he looked down the hall, the kids' heads were sticking out of their bedrooms. He gave them some silent applause.

When he turned to go into the living room, he heard their bedroom door open. He crept into the hallway. When Sandy waved the kids into their bedroom, he pointed at them. They nodded and crept into her bedroom to talk to her while she got dressed. Smiling, he left the apartment to arrange the rest of their evening.

~~~~~~~~~

Wednesday evening — 6:59 p.m.

"Wha . . ." Tink sat up and looked around. She was lying on some kind of a table in the basement of the house she was living in.

"You had a seizure," Blane said. He came to the side of the table. "Lie back. We're almost done. How do you feel?"

"Awful," Tink said. "Why are there all these needles in me? Are you torturing me?"

"Do they hurt?" Blane asked.

"No," Tink said.

"It's acupuncture," Blane said. "I'm a doctor of Chinese Medicine."

"How come you work as that guy's secretary?" Tink asked.

"That's a long story," Blane said. "And I'd like to know about you."

"What do I do?" Tink asked.

"Just lie there." Blane smiled.

He picked up her wrist to listen to her pulse.

"You seem better, stronger," Blane smiled. "What do you remember about today?"

"Um, I woke up here, at your house," Tink said.

"Our house," Blane corrected. Tink smiled.

"We had breakfast, and Heather took me to school," Tink said. "Wanda texted me that she was sick, and I knew Sissy was at a ballet thing. She's probably going to leave in January."

"Nothing's happened yet," Blane said.

"If she doesn't go soon, she'll be too old." Tink nodded. "They're coming from all over the world to check her out. That's where she was today."

Blane smiled.

"How was school?" Blane asked.

"Okay, I guess," Tink said. "Just school. I'm starting to get the hang of it."

Tink nodded.

"I think I'm going to do okay this term," Tink said. "That feels kind of unbelievable. Of course, I couldn't do it without Sissy's tutoring. But even she says I'm starting to get it."

"Do you remember meeting up with Heather?" Blane asked.

"No," Tink said. "Did I have a seizure then?"

"It was a little more complicated than that," Blane said.

"What did I screw up?" Tink asked.

"Nothing," Blane said. "Let me take these out."

He started taking the needles out. Tink lay very still to be the best patient she could possibly be, but her heart was racing, and her stomach was turning over.

What if they wouldn't let me stay anymore?

Did they figure out what a horrible girl I am?

"Huh, that's weird," Blane picked up her wrist. "Your pulse is racing."

He looked at her face.

"What's going on Tink?" Blane asked.

"You'd tell me," Tink said. "You'd just be straight, right?"

"About what?" Blane asked.

"About whether I get to stay or not," Tink said.

"Stay . . . here?" Blane asked. "Why wouldn't you be able to stay here?"

"I had a seizure and . . . whatever happened that I don't remember . . . and . . . whatever's wrong with me . . ."

Blane nodded.

"What?" Tink asked.

"I get what you're saying, that's all," Blane said. "I've felt like that for a ... for a long time. I know there's nothing I can say that will make it better. I know that you feel this way because you feel this way. I can tell you, Tink — someday, you won't feel like this."

Tink snorted, and Blane smiled.

"I probably would have responded the same way," Blane said.

He kept pulling needles out. In his warm, compassionate company, Tink began to calm down. He snuck a few needles in while he was taking a few out.

"What changed it?" Tink asked.

"How I felt?" Blane asked.

Tink nodded.

"A couple of things," Blane said. "One was connecting to people who loved me no matter what — like Jake, Sam, and, eventually, Heather and Mack. Loving them, caring for them — it changed me. Probably the next thing was learning that bad things happen."

"Everybody says that." Tink artificially lowered her voice and added, "Bad things happen to everyone, Tiffanie. Stop whining."

"Stepdad?" Blane asked.

Tink nodded.

"I'm not saying you should give up your own suffering." Blane snorted. "If I'd given up mine, you wouldn't be here. We wanted to adopt a teenager because of my suffering."

"Wha'j you mean then?" Tink's eyes drooped.

"I think what's hard is feeling like I suffered because of something inside of me, like it was personal," Blane said. "Seeing that so many people suffer made me realize that suffering *isn't* personal. My suffering is mine, belongs to me, and I can do whatever I want to with it. I can feel bad about myself. I can hate the world. Or I can accept that it happened and move on to a better life."

"How do you move on?" Tink asked.

"I think that, first, you have to get through it." Blane smiled.

"You're still in the middle of it all."

He squeezed her arm.

"Why don't you rest for a minute?" Blane asked. "I know Heather wants to see you. Mack's been trying to get in the whole time we've been down here."

"Ivy?" Tink slurred.

"She's upstairs," Blane said. "She wants to tell you all about meeting her aunt, but she's scared you might be too sick. She's a wreck. I guess we've all been."

"Why?"

"We love you and were worried about you," Blane said.

Tink was asleep. He touched her shoulder and left the room. He found Heather playing with Mack in the den.

"How's Tink?" Heather asked.

"She doesn't remember anything," Blane said. "She got upset, so I put her out. She'll wake up in a few minutes."

"They told us she might not remember," Heather said.

"Where's Gracie?" Blane asked. "Ivy?"

"Gracie went to get settled in her hotel," Heather said. "She'll be back for dinner. Ivy went with her to get a little time together."

"Is that all right?" Blane scowled.

"It was either that or dissolve into a puddle while waiting for Tink," Heather said.

"Do we know what . . .?" Blane asked.

"The boy's parents and their lawyer are meeting with Max and Samantha right now," Heather said.

"Max, too?" Blane asked.

"Max does civil law; Samantha does criminal law," Heather said. "We're keeping her pretty busy."

"I guess," Blane smiled. "What are the police doing?"

"The police confiscated his phone. He had the video of Tink being assaulted. His friends do, too. They are preparing to charge them with possession of child pornography."

Blane nodded.

"They're pretty mad," Heather said. "The parents, I mean. Tink's Taser is considered a concealed weapon. They've asked the district attorney to charge her and the school to ban her from the premises."

"Well, I'm pretty mad." Blane held out his arms, and Heather stepped into them. "It's going to be all right."

"How do you know?" Heather asked.

"I don't," Blane said. "I just know you, and you will not rest until this is worked out."

"*Ta! Ta! Ta!*" they heard from the basement.

They stepped back from their hug.

"Forgot to put the baby gate back up?" Heather asked.

"I'll get him," Blane said.

"I'll go," Heather said. "You can shower. It's going to be a long night."

Blane nodded. Heather jogged down the stairs where her baby boy was jumping at the doorknob to the acupuncture room. She picked him up and went inside.

"Oh great, you're awake," Heather said. "Do you mind?"

"Not at all," Tink said.

Heather took out Tink's last few needles and set Mack on the table.

"*Ta!*" Mack smiled.

"Mack!" Tink said.

Heather smiled.

"Is everything okay?" Tink asked.

"It will be." Heather smiled. "Are you ready for some dinner?"

"What are we having?" Tink asked.

"I thought you were making it," Heather said.

"Me?" Tink looked so surprised that Heather laughed.

"Crockpot soup, homemade bread, and some cake for dessert," Heather said. "How's that sound?"

"Great," Tink said. "And ..."

Heather turned to look at her.

"Thanks," Tink nodded.

Heather smiled.

"Come on," Heather said. "We can't hide in the basement forever."

Tink picked up Mack and followed her up the stairs.

~~~~~~~~~

Wednesday evening — 7:59 p.m.

Aden's phone buzzed.

"You can check," Sandy smiled over her glass of red wine.

"I'd rather just be here in this fairy tale of calm and beauty," Aden said.

He looked around at the Aspen tree trunks, which marked the edges of the room. Sandy smiled.

"Did you notice every eye was on you when we came in?" he asked.

She smiled. He leaned forward and kissed her.

"You should look," Sandy said. "Find out what's waiting for us at home."

He gave her a slight smile and took out his Blackberry. He'd received an email.

"I'm going to freshen up," Sandy said.

He nodded and clicked the email icon.

Dear Parents,
    I have been informed by the Denver Police Department that there is a video or possibly a series of videos being distributed to mainly boys in the Denver Public School District. These videos depict girls being physically attacked and violently sexually assaulted by multiple assailants.
    Possession of these videos is a Federal Crime.
    The videos are extremely violent. These assaults have led to at least one death and

long-term health consequences for more than one girl. For your reference, the youngest girl assaulted was nine years old, and the oldest was sixteen years old.

The Denver Police are cooperating with the FBI and the Department of Homeland Security in this matter. The District Attorney has made it clear that he will not hesitate to prosecute any individual who has any of these videos in his or her possession.

The Denver Police have asked us to ask you to check your child's computer, phone, and mobile device for this video. Should you find the video, please contact the Denver Police at (303) 555-1234. They are willing to work with any family who voluntarily turns in a device with this video on it. They will confiscate the device and interview your child. The devices will be returned to you. The District Attorney's Office assures me that they will not prosecute the children and families who voluntarily come forward to assist this investigation.

Starting tomorrow, the Denver Police will confiscate any phone, computer, or mobile device entering our schools. If your child's device contains this video, you and your child will be prosecuted to the fullest extent of the law. The Denver Police have informed me that they can detect the video if it has been deleted. Those who have deleted the video will have the additional charge of obstructing a criminal investigation.

If your child was assaulted or knows someone who was assaulted, please contact the Denver Police as soon as possible. If you or your child has any information on this matter, please contact the authorities, your teacher, principal, or counselor.

This is an active police investigation. Any information will help the police bring these

criminals to justice.
  Please join me in supporting the victims
and their families and bringing the
perpetrators to justice.
Thank you for your help.
Superintendent of Schools
Denver Public School District

Aden put his Blackberry in his pocket. Like every man in the restaurant, he watched Sandy walk back from the bathroom. The fabric of the dress clung to her full breasts and round hips. Her step was jaunty and inviting, but her eyes were focused only on him.

"What was it?" Sandy asked.

"The Superintendent has asked every parent to check for the videos," Aden said.

Sandy's relaxed face pinched with worry. He put his hand over hers.

"We still have a couple hours," Aden said. "I thought we could stop by your old place . . ."

Sandy beamed at him.

"We need to figure out what to do with it," Aden said.

"You mean now that Lizzie's in LA?" Sandy asked.

"Sure." Aden lifted his coffee cup to cover his sly smile.

"We'd probably have to check my bedroom and maybe the shower," Sandy said.

"To make a good decision, we should probably try the kitchen and living room, too."

Sandy giggled, and he smiled.

"I'm not missing out on an offer like that!" Sandy stood up.

Aden dropped money on the table and followed her out of the restaurant.

CHAPTER TWO HUNDRED & THIRTY-EIGHT

FAMILY PROBLEMS

Wednesday night — 9:59 p.m.

"Dog, what did you do with the phone you used to send On-Line the video?" a voice on the phone said.

"I *told* you," the boy replied. "I got rid of it Monday night when all those cops came to school. Why you hasslin' me 'bout this?"

"They's sent out a notice to all parents to look for those videos," he said.

"Shit," the boy said. He looked at his brother, and his brother scowled at him.

"You sure it's gone?" the voice on the phone asked.

"I took the battery out and threw the phone in the lake," the boy said. "I tol' my mom it broke and anyway I was getting lots of wrong numbers. She bought another one at Walgreens with a different number. You calling me on the new line, ain't you?"

"And that phone?"

"It's clean, dog," the boy said. "Don' worry so much. We gots this covered."

"You're not going to chicken out and tell your brother, are you?"

"No," the boy said. "My brother don' know nothin'"

"Better stay that way."

The phone went dead.

"Give me the god damn phone," his brother said.

The boy gave him the phone he'd used to send Charlie the video.

"You promised me you'd stop doing this," his brother said.

"They'll kill me if I don' go along," the boy said.

"I'm going to kill you if you do this again," his brother said. "What's wrong with you? Can't get a girlfriend without gang raping and beating them?"

"It ain't like that," the boy said. "They'll kill me if I don't go with them or if I stop. I tol' you. I stayed home that time you tol' me to. They threw a brick through the window and lit our trash on fire. Scared Mom to death."

"Can't you just get a girlfriend? Go to a dance?" his brother asked. "You have to hang out with rich white boys playing gangster instead?"

"It ain't like that," the boy said. "They ain't all white."

His brother raised a disbelieving eyebrow.

"Plus, girls like me," the boy said.

"Girls like you, so you rape them with your friends?" his brother screamed.

"They told me they'd take Mom!" the boy said.

"You disgust me," his brother said. "And if anyone finds out you're in this thing? I'm going to lose my job. You know what that means?"

"Mom's gonna lose the house, and I'm going back to juvie," the boy said.

"Is that what you want?" his brother asked.

"No," the boy said. "It's just . . . I can't roll on my boys! They'll kill me."

"The DA's talking about charging you as adults. Your little brown ass is going to adult prison," his brother said. "And you can't roll on your boys?"

"It's called loyalty," the boy nodded. "You should try it."

His brother raised his fist to hit the boy. He punched the wall instead.

"Shit," his brother stalked toward the front door. "Keep your dick in your pants, and stay in the house. If we're lucky, you'll weather this thing. If not . . ."

"We all go down," the boy said. "I know. You're like a broken record."

His brother pointed at the boy and walked out the door. The boy watched Sergeant Aziz walk to his dark-blue sedan. He waited for his older brother to drive off before turning into the house. He went straight to his room and closed his door.

He leaned against the door, and his phone rang again. Seeing the number, he closed his eyes. He set the phone on the end of his bed.

He went to the desk and wrote a note to his mom. She'd probably find him when she got off work in a couple hours.

He didn't want her to think he didn't love her.

Like he planned, he went to the closet and got the belt his father had given him when he was ten, the last time he'd seen his father. He put one end over the clothing rod and pushed it through the buckle. He closed his eyes for a moment before he found the resolve to step onto the box lying on the closet floor. He put his chin into the loop.

He stood on the box with the only present he'd ever received from his father tight under his chin. He stood there for what felt like an eternity.

He kicked the box out from under him, and for a moment, he felt only air.

He wished for the box.

He wished for death.

He wished he'd never been born.

Like a television on the fritz, everything blinked and blinked again. He saw his brother rush into his bedroom and scream something.

He was falling. His brother clutched him to his chest. He rocked back and forth.

"Why?" his brother was screaming and crying. "Why would you do this?"

"They'll kill me," the boy whispered.

"Don't you die on me," his brother screamed. "Don't you do it. I will come to the gates of hell and kick your ass."

For the first time in more than a dozen years, the boy began to cry.

~~~~~~~~

Thursday morning — 5:59 a.m.

"Okay," Heather said. "Yes, I understand. Thanks, Risa."

"What did she say?" Tink asked. "Can I go today?"

"Not today," Heather said. "We've scheduled a conference with the principal this afternoon."

"Oh," Tink said. "Did I get kicked out of school?"

"Like we talked about," Heather said. "The Taser is considered a concealed weapon, and you aren't supposed to have those on campus."

"Even if guys are going to be creeps?" Tink asked.

"Sadly, there are rules about Tasers and no rules about guys being creeps," Heather said.

"Why is that?" Tink asked.

"I think everyone expects guys to be creeps," Heather smiled.

Tink laughed.

"Go back to bed," Heather said. "I'll wake you and Ivy in a little while. We have to check in with your doctor first, and then we're meeting Gracie for lunch. If we have time, we can go shopping."

"What about your work?" Tink asked.

"I have the day off," Heather said. "Blane took Mack to school so we would have some time together."

"Because of me?" Tink asked.

"You had a medical emergency yesterday," Heather said. "You need to see the doctor."

Tink nodded and went back up the stairs. She was near the top when she panicked. She ran back down the stairs.

"I'm not in school," Tink said. "I broke our agreement!"

Surprised, Heather blinked at Tink.

"You're sending me back! Just say it. You're sending me back!"

Tink grabbed Heather by the arms.

"You made me go up to bed so you can call them."

"Uh . . ." Heather started.

"I didn't mean to do it. I really didn't. He was grabbing me, and you saw the bruises on my privates and . . ." Tink said. "Don't send me back. Please. I'll try harder. I'll . . ."

"I was going to make some coffee," Heather said.

"Don't lie to me," Tink said. "You're going to call as soon as I'm upstairs."

Heather held up the coffee filter in her hand.

"Coffee," Heather said.

"You can't have coffee!" Tink said. "You're just covering up . . ."

"Decaf. I'm making decaf," Heather said.

"Oh," Tink looked at her.

While Tink watched, Heather got the beans out of the cabinet and filled the grinder. She ground the beans and put them in the coffee filter.

"What are you going to do when the coffee's done?" Tink crossed her arms over her chest.

"Drink it," Heather said.

"Oh."

Tink turned on her heels and went upstairs. She slammed the door to her room. Ivy groaned. Heather listened until she heard Tink get into bed.

"You get the child you deserve," Heather chuckled, and went to read her email.

~~~~~~~~~

Thursday morning — 6:59 a.m.

"How was dinner?" Jacob asked Aden.

He leaned against the seat of the restaurant booth.

"Dinner was food," Aden said. "After dinner was heaven. Thanks for the suggestion."

Aden waved Blane over to their booth.

"What's a friend for?" Jacob smiled. "And the apartment?"

"God, I love that place," Aden yawned.

"Mmm," Jacob smiled.

"Why do you look like the Cheshire Cat?" Blane asked.

"I had a date night with Sandy," Aden said.

Blane took Jacob's coffee cup away from him.

"It's decaf," Jacob reached for the cup. Blane took a drink.

"It's not," Blane said.

"Okay, it's not decaf," Jacob smiled. "But . . ."

Blane gave Aden a sly look, and Aden laughed.

"Any ideas why we're here?" Blane asked.

"None worth sharing," Jacob said. "There's Dad."

Jacob stood up so that his father could see him. Sam came over to their booth. The waitress appeared to take their order.

"What's going on, Dad?" Jacob asked.

"You know I asked our site managers to ask their employees and get back to me personally," Sam said.

"I remember you fired a bunch of site managers." Jacob gave him an irritated look.

"Yeah, I guess that caused a crunch," Sam said. "But your mother . . ."

He glanced at the men's faces and laughed.

"Oh, hell — they were assholes," Sam said. "You're just irritated you didn't get to fire them yourselves."

They laughed.

"So, as the kids say, here's the word," Sam said.

"I don't think anyone says that anymore," Jacob said.

Sam scowled at Jacob, and he shrugged.

"I'm sorry, Dad," Jacob said. "Too much coffee."

"Coffee or no, you're going to want to hear this," Sam said. "The employees out at the site are saying they've been approached by a couple other contractors. They've been offered jobs."

"Doing what?" Aden asked.

"Their same job," Sam said. "That's what's crazy. They've offered our employees their same job on the same project. They were told we're going out of business."

"Us?" Jacob looked at Aden and at Blane. "Know anything about this?"

"No," Aden said.

"Nothing," Blane said.

"Anyway, we're meeting with everyone in a couple days," Sam said. "I just thought you should know that people are pretty... mad, I guess. They feel like we're going to pull the rug out from under them."

"Why wouldn't they just ask me?" Jacob asked.

"That's the thing," Sam said. "These other companies tell them they won't hire them if they talk to you about it."

"We could lose our entire crew," Aden said.

"We could. The employees said they asked their site managers — you know, those guys I let go yesterday? You know what they said?" Sam looked from face to face. "They told the employees to keep their mouths shut."

Jacob, Aden, and Blane were quiet as they thought it through. The waitress bought their breakfast, and they started to eat.

"You know what I think we should do?" Jacob asked.

The men looked up from their plates at him.

"I still own around fifty percent of the company," Jacob said. "Val owns about fifteen. Dad, how much do you own?"

"About ten," Sam said.

"Aden?"

"Maybe two percent," Aden said.

"Blane?"

"About the same," Blane said.

"So that's enough, I think," Jacob said.

"To do what?" Sam asked.

"I think we should pull out of the job," Jacob said. "Tell the state, 'Thanks, but no thanks,' we changed our minds. If we want to, we can tell them about our concerns over fracking and the fault lines."

"And then what?" Aden asked.

"And then we build the same job on my land," Jacob said. "After I move those houses, of course."

"What about the employees?" Aden asked. "We've killed ourselves this year trying to teach everyone how to run a company. We've sold them shares. If we do that, we really are pulling the rug out from under them."

"No, we're not," Jacob said. "We need to ask them what they want to do, but only after we know what we can do."

"What?" Blane asked. "You're not making any sense."

"We send out our teams to the other site, where the original city was planned," Jacob said. "We survey, map out, and get everything set. We can do that based on our ownership of the company. When we have the information, we can present it to the employees."

Aden and Blane nodded. His father scowled.

"We don't hide anything from anyone," Jacob said. "We do it all out in the open — clear communication and transparency, like we promised. We tell the site managers that we're looking into an expansion project, something a little extra. That site is not so far from this one, so, eventually, it would be developed anyway."

"We line up every duck, have a meeting to vote, and pull the trigger," Jacob said. "We'll be out of this project before those other guys know what hit them."

No one responded. Jacob scowled.

"We have to do something," Jacob said. "We've wasted a lot of time, energy, and resources in this stupid conflict that gets us nowhere. We have to get out of the cycle. This is a way."

"It just might work," Sam nodded.

"Aden?" Jacob asked.

"It's crazy," Aden said. "But it's worth a try."

"Blane?" Jacob asked.

"It's going to look like you set the whole thing up," Blane said.

"Who cares? I *will* set it up so that Lipson could make a killing," Jacob said. "What do you think? Are you in?"

"I am," Sam said.

"Me, too," Blane said.

Aden stared off into space.

"Aden?" Jacob asked.

"It's so Aikido," Aden said. "We're kind of sidestepping all this hostility. I like that. So, I'm in."

"Great," Jacob said. "So, you'll tell Tres?"

"No," Aden said.

"Not me," Blane said.

Sam gave Jacob a long look.

"Fine," Jacob said. "I'll tell him when we get back."

"Good man." Sam clapped Jacob on the back.

Jacob swallowed hard and concentrated on eating his breakfast.

"What's hard for me is that they always seem one step ahead of us," Blane said. The men turned their attention to Blane. "I mean, what if the whole point was to pick off the high stock owners or . . .? I don't know. I guess, I'm tired of playing a game I don't know I'm playing and one where never seem to know the rules."

The men went back to eating their breakfasts. After a while, Jacob looked up.

"You know what? You're right," Jacob said. "Let's come up with our own plan, based in our own ideas and our own values."

"Going back to us making decisions and everyone following is just us owning the company again," Sam nodded.

"Right," Jacob said. "I'll talk to Tres. Dad, you can call a meeting of the employees this afternoon. We'll get their ideas and make our own plan."

"It's risky," Aden said.

"Blane's right. We're losing the business as it stands," Sam said. "If we don't make our own plan — not what the state wants, not what we think someone else is going to do — we've already lost."

On that grim note, Sam got up and left the restaurant. Jacob grabbed the check, nodded to Aden and Blane, and left.

"You ready?" Blane asked.

"I don't know if I can get out of this booth."

Laughing, Blane got up and dragged Aden to his feet.

"Sandy gave you a tough workout?" Blane asked.

"Oh, yeah," Aden said.

Blane laughed.

~~~~~~~~~

Thursday mid-day — 11:59 a.m.

Sandy's last client hugged her and left the shop. On her own cloud after last night's adventure, she wandered to the back of the shop to get her lunch. She'd just pulled a yogurt container from her little refrigerator when she heard the bell to the door.

She peeked out of the back to see who it was.

Sergeant Aziz was standing at her door. He cupped his hands and peered in to try to see her through the mirrored glass. She scowled and was about to go back when she saw a young man peer out from behind his back.

She'd always liked his little brother. Groaning to herself, she went to the door.

"What do you want?" Sandy asked.

"You have every right to be like that," Sergeant Aziz said. "But . . . we need some help."

Sandy caught a look of desperation on his face. She stepped back and let them in.

"It's my lunch hour," Sandy said.

"I know," Sergeant Aziz pushed his brother forward. "We brought you a salad."

When the boy got close to her, Sandy saw the bruising around the boy's neck.

"What's going on?" Sandy took the salad and guided them to the back.

"Tell her," Sergeant Aziz said to his brother.

In a low tone, his brother told Sandy his whole story, from going along the first time, to trying to get out of it, to sending Charlie the video. He didn't look up until he was done.

"Why are you telling me all of this?" Sandy asked.

"Because I don't know what to do," Sergeant Aziz said. "I've been trying to protect him, but by saying nothing, I've left him . . . in the hands of these . . . monsters."

"It sounds like he's a little monster himself," Sandy said.

"Yes, ma'am," the boy said.

"Why do you think I know what to do?" Sandy asked.

"Because you're O'Malley's goddaughter and you know that Homeland Security guy, the big one, and the blond guy," Sergeant Aziz said. "Nothing would be happening if he and the blonde guy hadn't gotten involved."

"Why is that?" Sandy asked.

"Red Bear is a weirdo," Sergeant Aziz said. "And I . . ."

He gestured to his brother.

"You'll be suspended," Sandy said.

"Better than," Sergeant Aziz gestured to his brother's neck. "And I don't care anymore. He's really in trouble. He tried to tell me, but I was too scared of losing everything to listen."

"And now?"

"I'd rather lose everything than lose my brother," Sergeant Aziz said. "He screwed up, and this is bad, but he can't get out of it. Not on his own, and I don't know how to fix it."

"Why should I help you?" Sandy asked. "Why should my friends help you?"

"They gonna kill me, Sandy." The boy looked up at her. "I know I deserve it. I tried to stop — I really did, . . . ever since the first time. And I don't . . . you know, I can't . . ."

He gestured to his lap.

"I just take the videos," he said. "I'm still . . . a monster."

"Why not tell Detective Red Bear?" Sandy asked.

"I don't trust him," Sergeant Aziz said.

Sandy looked at Sergeant Aziz and then at his brother.

"Think of it this way: if I hadn't been such an asshole, you wouldn't be married to that Aden guy," Sergeant Aziz said. "So you owe me a favor."

"That's just pathetic," his brother looked at him and shook his head. Sandy scowled.

"Please," Sergeant Aziz said.

"I'm only going to do this if you call your Mom," Sandy said. "She deserves to know what's going on and to be here when it happens. I won't do it otherwise."

Sergeant Aziz looked at his brother, and he nodded. Sandy raised her eyebrows, and Sergeant Aziz called his mother. When he was done, Sandy got her iPhone and placed the call.

"Raz?" Sandy asked.

"Hey, Sandy," Raz said. "Sami was just reminding me to make an appointment."

"Yeah, it's about that time," Sandy said. "Um, something's come up, and I wondered if you and Colin could come over to the studio."

"One of the boys contacted you like we talked about?" Raz asked.

"Uh, huh," Sandy said.

"Should we come guns blazing?" Raz asked.

"Hearts open." Sandy reached out her hand and touched the boy's shoulder.

"You'll call O'Malley?" Raz asked.

"I will," Sandy said.

"Give us a half hour," Raz said.

"Come on," Sandy said. "Let's get you cleaned up."

"But . . ." the boy said.

"You want to change your life," Sandy said. "The first thing to change is how you look. You want a different life — right?"

The boy nodded.

"Come on," Sandy said.

She guided the boy out into the salon. She helped him out of his cap and his gangster coat.

"Wow — when was the last time you showered?"

"Couple of days," the boy said. "Maybe a week."

"Go get cleaned up," Sandy pointed to the shower. The boy slunk toward the bathroom. "I have some clothes here. Toss yours out, and your brother will wash them."

Sergeant Aziz took the clothing and went into the back. Sandy brought the boy a pair of Pete's jeans and a long sleeved T-shirt. When the boy came out, he looked like a tiny boy in a grown man's body. She knew that he was going to be the key to ending these brutal crimes. She only hoped he was up for the task.

Sandy smiled to encourage him and began cutting his hair.

CHAPTER TWO HUNDRED & THIRTY-NINE

MEETING OF THE MINDS

Thursday afternoon—3:35 p.m.

"Before we start," FBI Special agent Angela Montiz gave a hard look at the Homeland Security Agents Colin Hargreaves and Arthur "Raz" Rasmussen. "I'm wondering why Homeland Security is involved in this situation at all. It's way out of your jurisdiction and, although I can't quite determine what team you're on, you don't appear to be on DHS's High School Sex Crimes Team, because there isn't one."

Raz smiled at Agent Angie, and she sneered back. They were sitting around a small table in the office above Sandy's hair salon. Colin was sitting between the Deputy District Attorney in charge of District Court and the Commander in Charge of Major Crimes for the Denver Police. Raz was sitting next to the Denver Police Commander and Agent Angie.

"I know the charming smile of a snake when I see one, Agent Rasmussen," Agent Angie said. "You're going to have to come up with something a lot better than that."

The men chuckled, and Raz looked down at his large hands.

"I teach martial arts to a boy who was sent a video clip of a girl being beaten and raped. I brought the video to the attention of the Denver Police," Colin said. "We discovered that the assigned detective and his Sergeant didn't appear to be functioning in this case."

"I spoke with the investigative supervisor," said the Commander in Charge of Denver Police Department Major Crimes. "Because we weren't certain what was going on, I requested DHS assistance. DHS has assisted with other cases, and we've found Agent Rasmussen and Agent Hargreaves to be helpful."

"Our primary assignment is flexible enough that, if we have time, we're happy to assist where we can," Raz said.

The door to the room opened, and Seth O'Malley stepped inside.

"Sorry I'm late," Seth said. "What did I miss?"

"I just found out why Homeland Security is involved in this, "Agent Angie said.

Seth put his hand on her shoulder, and she looked up at him.

"I'm glad you're here," Seth said.

"Were you going to tell me why *I'm* here and not someone from the large Denver FBI office?" Agent Angie asked.

"In our review of the case, we discovered that there is an FBI agent already assigned to this case," Raz said.

"An FBI agent, a DPD investigative team, a slew of forensic professionals, plausible leads, solid forensics, and . . ." Seth shrugged and sat down next to Agent Angie.

"No action," Raz said. "That's what concerned us. Prior to our initiation into this case, the investigative team has done exactly nothing to pursue these cases."

"Not *nothing*, Raz," the Denver Police Commander said. "They've obstructed the investigation where they can."

"All right," Agent Angie said. "Why me?"

"You were assigned to a case with us last year," Seth said. "We found you to be extraordinarily competent, smart, and efficient."

"We have two problems, Agent Angie," Raz said. "One is the brutality of these crimes. They are not date rapes or even violent attacks. These girls are drugged and brutally assaulted in every way. Their lives are assaulted through the sale or malicious distribution of the videotapes of their assault to every sick mind with a keyboard."

"There's money in the middle of all of this," Seth said. "We're concerned the money had perverted the course of the investigation both at the Denver Police and at the FBI."

"Any proof?" Agent Angie asked.

"Only the lack of activity," Colin said.

Agent Angie nodded.

"Today, a member of the investigative team stepped forward with his younger brother," the Commander in Charge of Major Crimes said. "He admits to delaying the case because he knew his brother was involved. With the agents' help, he and his brother have turned themselves into me, personally. The young man in question was the videographer for one of these crimes. He has turned in more than thirty video recordings of the group. He's given written testimony as well as interacted with the District Attorney's office."

"Is he willing to testify?" Agent Angie asked.

"He appears to be," the Commander in charge of Major Crimes said. "He states that this situation 'just happened' one night and then became a regular thing. He tried on a number of occasions to get out of this thing, but either he or his mother were threatened with violence. He saw them perpetrate violence against a mother as a reprisal for one of the boys leaving the group."

"And the mother?" Agent Angie asked.

"She never came forward," Colin said. "We found evidence that, around the dates of her assault, she went to one of the larger free clinics in town, but that's all we have."

"And this boy — the brother of your investigator," Agent Angie said. "Do we believe him?"

"He makes no excuses for himself or his actions," Raz said. "He seemed . . . in over his head. He lives with his single mother. His brother is the only male in his life. This thing was like a rolling stone he couldn't stop. The boy has made serious suicide attempts on at least three occasions."

"You liked him?" Agent Angie asked.

"I believed him," Raz said. "He participated in something that goes way beyond the meaning of the word 'wrong.' But I believe this is a case of a kid getting in over his head and almost drowning. He also seems redeemable."

"I believed him too," the Deputy DA said. "And I like his brother. I think they're credible witnesses."

"So we know why one party of the investigative team slowed the investigation down, but not the other," the Commander said. "We've allowed the Sergeant to stay in his role in the investigation to see if we can get to the bottom of what's going on there. He will resign from duty as soon as the case is resolved."

"I'm still not sure how I can help," Agent Angie said. "Why don't you gentlemen just work your case?"

"The bottom line, Angie, is that we believe that the young men are using the distribution channels that were created by other perpetrators," Seth said. "We're hoping, with a little luck, we'll be able to finally put this distribution channel to rest."

She scowled at Seth and then looked from face to face around the table. Her eyes leveled at Seth again.

"You realize I was pulled from that case," Agent Angie said.

"Not by anything we did," Seth said.

"That's correct," Agent Angie said. "I have a full caseload of my own. I don't want to get involved here and then . . ."

"I understand," Seth said. "But if you were involved, what would you do first?"

She squinted at Seth, and he smiled. Her eyes went up to the ceiling as if to implore God himself before leveling her eyes at Raz.

"Good-looking man like you, I'd go to the free clinics, put the word out that you want information about any woman who has been assaulted," Agent Angie said. "Whatever happens, you're going to need *a lot* of credible witnesses, because what usually happens in these cases is that the community closes ranks. What are a few raped and brutalized girls in comparison to the entire future of our star football players? Our basketball stars? Those girls were sluts and whores; our boys have athletic scholarships, and you know, *boys will be boys*, and crap like that. I don't want to spend my free time on this case and find out that the City and County of Denver would rather cover over the ugly in favor of a few privileged boys."

Raz nodded.

"And you, blondie." Agent Angie nodded to Colin. "Isn't your daddy a Senator?"

"He's retired, but yes," Colin said.

"I'd get my famous father to start making noise about this case," Agent Angie said. "Give the case some public clout so that this scum can't crawl into their holes."

"Good idea," Colin said. "My mother has been looking for a cause to champion."

Agent Angie nodded.

"As for you," Agent Angie pointed to the Deputy DA and the Denver Police Commander. "You need to find people in your departments who are willing to prosecute and investigate this case, because, when the media gets a hold of it, they are going to take the heat. Look for men, not just women."

"Why not women?" the Deputy DA asked.

"Have someone in mind?" Agent Angie asked.

The Deputy DA nodded.

"If you have a woman lead, the case will be marginalized as a woman's problem," Agent Angie said. "It's hard to believe that this is the world we live in, but it is. And, there are plenty of men who are disgusted by this type of crime — men who *like* women, men who were raised by single mothers and understand the pressure that your investigator's brother lives with every day. These men exist and are chomping at the bit to do something to help protect women, but no one asks them; the woman haters are loud."

The Denver Police commander nodded.

"Anything else?" Seth asked.

"You need someone to put some money behind this." Agent

Angie looked at Seth. "Money gets attention and shifts the focus. Set up a reward for information. Make a show of hiring private investigators. Better yet: You're the famous Magic O'Malley — investigate this thing yourself. You need to change the dialogue about this case before it ever hits the media."

The men nodded.

"Officially, I'm not involved," Agent Angie said. "I'm going skiing for the weekend and then home to Arizona. But when it comes down . . ."

"We'll put you front and center," Raz said. "Because after all, this is out of Homeland Security's jurisdiction."

"I'm starting to like you," Agent Angie said.

He smiled.

"One more thing," Agent Angie said. "You need a PR person on this. I know it sounds crazy, but if you really want to prosecute, you're going to have to manage the jury, starting right now."

"Any ideas who?" Colin asked.

"No, but I bet he does." Agent Angie gestured to Seth.

He nodded.

"You know where to reach me." Agent Angie gave each of them a hard look. She got up and left the room.

The men sat around the table for a moment, looking at each other.

"I guess that's it," Seth said. "Thanks. I really appreciate it."

The men nodded to Seth and left the room. Colin lingered to talk to Seth.

"How goes the movie-making?" Colin asked.

"Good," Seth nodded. "Done."

"And Lizzie?" Colin asked.

"She and Schmidty are staying in California for now," Seth said. "Ava and I are home for a while."

Colin nodded.

"How is Connor?" Seth asked.

Colin gave him a broad smile.

"I'm thrilled for you," Seth said.

Colin nodded.

"What would you do if it was your son?" Seth asked.

"I . . . only hope my sons would never get involved," Colin said. "But if he was? I'd stand by him while he felt the consequences. That's kind of my job as his parent."

"I feel for the parents who are finding out that their sons are involved in this in any way," Seth said.

"Heartbreaking," Colin said.

Seth nodded and they left the room.

~~~~~~~~~

Thursday afternoon — 4:05 p.m.

"I don't know why you even bothered." Melinda flipped her hair, and Nash scowled.

"You said to meet you after school," Nash repeated what he'd said three times. "We were going to walk to my house, do our homework, and go to a movie."

"That was before I saw you," Melinda said.

Nash looked behind him.

"Right now?" Nash asked.

"At the Fifteenth Street Bridge," Melinda crossed her arms. "My mom said, 'Isn't that Nash?' and I saw you."

"Looking over the bridge?" Nash asked.

"With that girl," Melinda said.

"What girl?" Nash asked. "My brother Charlie was helping the police with something and . . ."

"And what's all this with your *brother* Charlie?" Melinda shook her head. "You don't have a brother. I checked."

"With who?" Nash asked.

"With everybody," Melinda said. "You only have a sister — Noelle. That's all. One sister."

"My dad . . ."

"Sure, go ahead. Blame your lies on your dad," Melinda said.

Nash squinted at Melinda.

"What?" Melinda asked.

"What what?"

"Why did you look at me like that?" Melinda asked.

"Because I don't know what's going on. You seem to know what's going on, but for whatever reason, you aren't telling me."

"Hmpft." Melinda turned slightly away from him.

"What's going on?" Nash asked.

"I saw *you* and *that girl*," Melinda said.

"What girl?" Nash asked.

"I don't know what girl," Melinda said. "Are there more than one? What? Are there ten girls? Twenty? What's wrong with you?"

"What girl did you see me with?" Nash asked. "My sister Sissy? Noelle? One of Sissy's friends? Noelle's friends? Uh . . ."

"Oh," Melinda said. "She's one of Noelle's friends?"

"I don't know what you're talking about, so it could be *any* girl," Nash said.

"There are lots of girls?" Melinda gaped at Nash. Her face went bright red, and tears sprang from her eyes.

"In the world? Yes, there are lots of girls," Nash said.

"I don't want to go out with you anymore," Melinda said.

She spun in place and stomped off in the direction of her house. Stunned, Nash watched her go. She walked two blocks before meeting a group of her girlfriends. The girls' angry and accusing faces turned to glare at Nash. Still not sure what he'd done, Nash blushed bright red. The girls flipped their hair in unison and walked toward Melinda's house. Nash stared at them until they turned the corner. He began the slow walk home. Alone.

~~~~~~~~

Thursday afternoon — 4:45 p.m.

Bumpy opened the exam-room door and went out into the hall.

He scowled. Usually his wife, and nurse, Dionne was waiting here to tell him which exam room to go to next. Dionne was nowhere to be found.

He looked into his office. He glanced into the kitchen.

He looked at his watch. He hadn't left work before seven in more than twenty years. Hard-working people needed doctors who could see them early and late.

Hearing voices, he went toward the front of the office. Dionne was standing in the doorway to the waiting room. He came up behind her and put his hands on her hips.

She looked up and scowled at him.

"What did I do?" he asked.

She shook her head.

"There he is," a woman's voice came from the lobby. "You go on. You go on and tell Dr. Bumpy what you did. Go on."

A medium-sized woman dragged her glaring son from a chair and pushed him toward the door. Bumpy glanced into the waiting room.

The chairs were filled with boys and young men. Dressed in low-riding jeans that put their boxer shorts on display and jackets two sizes too big, none of the boys looked up at him. Their mothers circled around the room like sharks. He could almost taste the anger in the room.

"Uh, huh," another woman said. "You ain't going to talk to Doctor Bumpy before he does."

The woman kicked the chair out from under her son. He fell onto the ground.

"Get yourself up," the woman said.

"Scum like them deserve to slither on the ground," another woman said.

The mothers started kicking the chairs out from under their sons.

"Whoa!" Bumpy said. "Stop. Everyone, stop. Stop."

He grabbed a tiny woman who was kicking her son's chair over and over again in an attempt to knock it out from under him. When she looked up at him, he saw her rage and heartbreak. He nodded in acknowledgment and let her go. The moment he did, she started kicking the chair again. Dionne went to her and hugged her. The mother started to weep.

"What's going on?" Bumpy asked.

"This *creature* used *my* money to purchase videos of poor girls being raped..." The mother kicked her son. "...and beaten...and...who knows what else. The Denver Police said to bring them in to the police station, but Dr. Bumpy said if this *creature* ever got in trouble to bring him to talk to you first."

"Mmm, hmm," the mothers made a sound in general agreement.

"What are you going to say, Dr. Bumpy?" the mother said.

"Should we just kill them now?" another mother asked.

"Once a rapist, always a rapist," a mother near the corner of the room said.

"I d'n't rape nobody," one brave boy's voice cried out in the middle of this.

"You did just the same," his mother said.

"Just the same," the mothers agreed.

"And I want you to know, Dr. Bumpy," a mother near the door to the street said. "Most of the girls are white girls, but it don't matter to me. These are precious children of God's being violated and abused by scum."

The woman swallowed hard before turning to her son.

"I did not struggle and suffer to bring this boy into this world so he could get his jollies watching any girl — white, black, or purple — get abused like that."

Like a fish out of water, the mother gasped for breath.

"Mmm, hmm," the other mothers agreed.

"I know that, in other cities, they cover it up and say 'Not my good son — it's the girls' fault.' But I won't do that. My son has done wrong, and I won't stand by and blame some poor defenseless girl for his trouble. He's going to jail."

"I won't, either," a mother near the middle of the room said.

"No way," a mother near the front said.

"Then that settles it." A mother near the door grabbed her son's jacket and dragged him to his feet. "You're going to jail."

The mothers started hauling their boys toward the door.

"Stop!" Bumpy said.

The women stopped moving.

"You remember my friend Seth O'Malley," Bumpy said. "He came by this afternoon to speak to me about this very situation."

"And what did he say?" a large woman near the center of the room said.

"He said that what they mostly want is information," Bumpy said. "They want to know who sold the videos, how much they paid, and when. This is a big deal, ladies. The FBI and Department of Homeland Security are involved. No one is going to sweep this under the carpet."

"I ain't gon' say nothin'," a boy near the front said.

"Me, neither," the boys mumbled around him.

His mother picked him up by the back of his collar and carried him to Bumpy. She dropped the boy at his feet.

"You can castrate him now," his mother said.

"Castrate?" The boy scooted back from Bumpy.

"That's right," his mother said. "You're my son, and I say, castrate him."

"Cut it off," another mother said. The women nodded in agreement. The boys squirmed in their seats.

"Gentlemen!" Bumpy pointed to the back. "Now!"

CHAPTER TWO HUNDRED & FORTY

SONS

The boys scurried through the door to the exam rooms.

"You can keep him," a mother called from the hallway.

"You got that right," the other mothers agreed.

Bumpy pointed to the largest examination room, at the end of the hallway. A grim line of young men shuffled and squeezed into the room. Bumpy went in after them and closed the door. The boys sat next to each other on the exam table. A few sat in the chairs, and others sat on the floor.

Not one dared looked up at him.

"Any of you involved in this thing?" Bumpy asked. "You'd better tell me now, because, if I find out later, it's going to be bad for you."

The boys pointed to a boy named Solomon. Despite his regal name, the boy was a simpleton. Solomon was a sweet kid who volunteered at the library twice a week after school and worked on the sign team at Lipson Construction the rest of the week. He spent his nights and weekends keeping up in school by sheer force of will and his mother's dedication. It was unlikely the boy even knew what they were talking about. Bumpy scowled at the boy; Solomon gave him a bright smile.

"Why?" Bumpy asked.

"Don' really know," the boy said. "It's kind a fun. We get high, and . . ."

Bumpy shook his head and looked away.

"Dallon, would you show the video to Solomon?" Bumpy asked.

The boy sitting next to Solomon took out his phone and played the video. Solomon closed his eyes after the first few seconds. Bumpy touched Dallon's arm, and he took the phone away. Bumpy turned to the rest of the boys.

"What about the rest of you? You don't need me to tell you that it's sick and wrong to watch those videos. Real men can't take the violence and cruelty. And you know, just having the video means you're involved in a sex crime."

"Not me!" the boy closest to him yelled. The others nodded in agreement.

"What's it going to be?" Bumpy asked. "You going to do the right thing and help find the scum responsible for these assaults?"

"You mean like him?" A boy near the middle of the room pointed at Solomon. He hadn't opened his eyes yet.

"Don' do that, man," Dallon said.

"Everybody knows he's involved," another boy said. "Setting the girls up with his sweetness and knocking them down for his bros."

"Come on," Dallon said. "How's he gonna . . . ?"

Bumpy looked from Dallon to the other two boys. Bumpy put his hand on Solomon's shoulder.

"You were invited to go with them?" Bumpy asked.

Solomon nodded.

"Did you go?" Bumpy asked.

"Don' have time," Solomon shook his head. "Have to help the library, and my team needs me."

"I threw up when I saw it," Dallon said. "Twice. I couldn't sleep for a week after the second video."

"Me, too," a young man in the corner said. "I like the girl in the video I got. Wanted to take her out, but now . . ."

"Now what?" Bumpy asked.

"She's not in school anymore," the young man said.

"Happened to me, too," a boy near the back said. "There's this girl in my math class. She was out for a month or whatever. When she came back, she wouldn't even look at me. Come to find out, she's in one of these videos."

"So, they're beating and violating your women," Bumpy said. "I don't think I need to tell you what I'd do to anyone who hurt Dionne or LaTonya."

The threat in Bumpy's words hung in the room like a sword.

"Real men don't watch crap like this," Bumpy said. "They don't hurt, rape, maim, or beat on their women."

"Lots of men beat their women," a middle-school boy near the wall said.

"Those aren't men," Bumpy said. "They're cowards who never learned to deal with their own demons. Think about it — they'd rather take their anger out on someone they love than deal with their own darkness. That's no man in my book."

Bumpy saw the boys' heads move slightly up and down.

"How 'bout you all?" Bumpy asked. "You going to be cowards, or are you going to start acting like men?"

The boys stared at the ground.

"What's the holdup here?" Bumpy asked. "Your big fat egos in the way?"

"I don't want to go to jail," a handsome boy sitting against the wall said. "I've worked my ass off to get into college. Momma and I... we have a plan. I'm going into the Army, so they'll pay for medical school. I already signed a contract. I've got two months and..."

"You'd rather be a coward?" Bumpy asked.

"I'm no coward. I..." The boy looked up at him. "It would kill my mom."

"She's going to kill you now," Bumpy said.

"What do they want from us?" a tall boy sitting near Bumpy asked.

"They need you to get over your ego to see that you screwed up by not reporting this," Bumpy said.

"Who we gonna tell?" a boy with an orange mohawk asked. "I tried to tell my counselor. I thought he was cool, but he... Uh, uh — no way."

"They got everyone on the payroll. We talk, and we go down," the tall boy sitting near Bumpy said. "You should see what they're planning for this kid they call On-Line."

Bumpy swallowed hard.

"I heard they going to do his sister," another boy said. The boys nodded.

"That's my friend Sissy!" Solomon said. "She's on my team at work. They can't do that, can they Dr. Wilson? Are they going to hurt my friend?"

"And make you take the fall for it," Bumpy said. He looked at the boys in the room. "Are you going to let that happen?"

"I ain't going to sign my sisters and mom up for getting raped because I squealed," said a large football player taking up an entire corner of the room. "No way, no how."

"But you'll consign other girls to this fate?" Bumpy asked.

"Who we gonna tell?" the boy with the orange mohawk asked again. "They got to everyone."

"I can take care of the who," Bumpy said. "My question is: are you the type of men who own up to your mistakes and take what's coming to you? Because this moment, this very one, is the moment when your entire life will be decided. Own up to your mistakes, take your lumps, you'll be just fine. But lie about it? Cover it up? Let this poor boy take the rap?"

Bumpy shook his head.

"God have mercy on your soul," Bumpy said. "Because this train is coming, and, one way or another, it's going to run you down."

~~~~~~~~~

Thursday night — 10:15 p.m.

"What are you doing up?" Aden asked Nash as he entered the apartment.

Nash was sitting on the couch. staring off into space. His laptop was closed and sitting next to him on the couch. Nash looked up at Aden, shook his head, and went back to staring into space. Aden picked up the computer, set it on the coffee table, and sat down next to Nash. He waited to see if Nash would respond.

"Are you okay?" Aden asked.

Nash shook his head. Aden felt woefully unprepared. He wished Sandy were there, because she always knew the right thing to say, or Jacob, who seemed to connect so easily with the kids. Nash glanced up at him.

"What's going on?" Aden put his arm around Nash. They sat like that for a few minutes before Nash leaned into his father.

"Couldn't sleep," Nash said.

"Usually when you can't sleep, you're up playing games with your friends on Facebook," Aden said.

Nash looked at the laptop and back at his father. Aden pulled on his tie and slipped off his shoes.

"Hard day?" Nash asked.

"Long," Aden said. "Confusing."

Nash nodded.

"Sandy told me what happened with Melinda," Aden said.

"Really?" Nash shrugged. "I don't have any idea what happened with Melinda. What did she say?"

Aden smiled.

"I really don't need the 'relationships are hard' speech," Nash said. "I need to know what happened."

"Sandy said Melinda saw you on the Fifteenth Street Bridge the night you were out with everyone," Aden said. "She said that Melinda didn't know why you were there, and that made her feel uncomfortable. She'd talked to you earlier that night, and you hadn't mentioned it."

"Didn't know we were going," Nash said. "I was going to tell her all about it when I saw her today."

Aden nodded.

"She told me she never wants to see me again, or something like that," Nash said. "She and all of my friends unfriended me on Facebook. Every single person who knows me and knows her unfriended me. She's blocked me so I can't even see what she said to make everyone hate me."

Unsure what all the unfriending meant, Aden looked at Nash. His son's eyes held the stunned look of someone who'd experienced something horrible.

"So, you're right, Dad," Nash said. "I'd play games, but I don't have any friends anymore."

"Not even Teddy?" Aden asked.

"Teddy doesn't count," Nash said.

"Why?"

"He's like a brother," Nash said. "I mean, she wouldn't even listen to me. It's like her mind was already made up and she knew everything."

"She's been invited to a dance by another boy," Aden said.

"Why didn't she just say that?" Nash's voice was angry and loud. Sandy peeked out of their bedroom. Seeing Aden, she smiled and closed the door.

"Maybe she didn't know how," Aden said.

Nash sniffed. Aden looked over to see a tear roll down Nash's face.

"I felt so connected, popular. For the first time in my life, I was popular," Nash said. "I mean, these kids are cool, rich, and . . ."

Aden waited to see if Nash would say more.

"Before you ask, I don't want to be like them," Nash said. "But when I think about it, I have been like them. I've spent so much time on the computer that I haven't really been here and . . . Ms. Valerie left today, and I haven't seen her in months. Mike, too. And Charlie's going through this big thing. You heard that Bumpy said that Sissy's going to get attacked."

"I don't think it's a big surprise to anyone that they might try to hurt Sissy," Aden said.

"It was to me." Nash's head bobbed in a nod. "It was to me."

Aden waited again. When Nash didn't say anything, he said, "It sounds like a drug."

"The 'being popular' drug," Nash said. "Suddenly, I'm not loser Nash Norsen anymore. I'm 'Cool Nash' with cool friends and . . ."

Nash turned to look at his father.

"I didn't like 'Cool Nash' very much," Nash said. "I'm sorry I've been such a butt."

"I'm sorry I didn't realize what was going on," Aden said. "It sounds like you've had a tough time."

"The whole thing," Nash said. "It's hard to pretend to be someone I'm not, and it's hard now not to be friends with the people I pretended to be like, and it's hard to find out that the people you love are struggling, and you don't have a clue, and . . ."

"That's a lot of *ands*," Aden said.

Nash nodded.

"What did Sandy say?" Aden asked.

"She said that she loved me," Nash said. "That's it. Sissy and Noelle, too. They said they weren't mad at me and that they understood. Noelle said we all go through it and that Nuala had the same trouble. And she's right. I've been just like my jerk of a mother."

"I think Sandy would really hate it if you called her a jerk," Aden said.

When Nash didn't respond, Aden looked down. The boy was crying. Aden pulled his head to him, and the boy cried against him. Aden heard a sound and looked up as Sissy and Noelle crept into the living room. Noelle squished in between Nash and the arm of the couch. Sissy sat next to Aden. Buster the ugly dog flew out of the hallway and launched himself onto the couch. He landed on Aden's and Sissy's laps. Charlie was not far behind. He sat at Nash's feet.

"You can come out, too," Nash said in a tearful voice.

Sandy came out of the bedroom with Rachel. She set the baby on Nash's lap and ruffled his hair. He looked up at her.

"Sorry for calling you a jerk," Nash said.

Sandy kissed his wet cheek and sat down on the arm of the couch. The little family leaned in together in a kind of hug. Nash tickled Rachel, and the baby giggled.

"I think the point of having a family is to have a place to fall back on," Aden said. "You have to go out in the world and try new things. Even though we seem really far away, we're still right here. We're your roots—whether it works out or it doesn't, we're here."

Charlie looked up at Aden, and Aden smiled at him.

"That seems like a good cue to make something yummy," Sandy said. "What's a yummy root? Beets? Turnips?"

The kids groaned, and Aden laughed.

"How about we start with some hot chocolate?" Sandy asked. She got up to move to the kitchen. "Welcome home, Nash."

"Now you can be Ivy's girlfriend," Noelle said.

Sissy gave a little clap. Nash scowled at them.

"What about the rest of my friends?" Nash asked.

"They don't seem much like friends," Charlie said. "They just made you feel stupid and insecure all the time. You were always watching to see if someone unfriended you or whatever. Who needs that? I'd rather be alone than have to deal with that."

Nash scowled at him.

"Sweet potato pie!" Sandy yelled from the kitchen. "That's rooty *and* yummy!"

The family turned to look at the kitchen.

"She's really . . ." Nash started, and everyone laughed.

~~~~~~~~~

Thursday night—11:15 p.m.

Jacob pulled their new, ready-for-the-twins SUV up to an old house north and west of the airport. There were two almost-identical houses near this house. Jill looked at him and turned around to check on Katy. She was sound asleep in her car seat in the back.

Jacob nodded and started to get out of the car. Jill touched his arm.

"Why are we here?" Jill asked.

"I wanted to show you the houses," Jacob said. "The other two are rented, but this one's empty right now."

"Okay," Jill said. "Why are we here?"

Jacob settled back in his seat. He glanced at Jill, and she raised her eyebrows to repeat the question. He sighed. With his sigh, he crumpled forward and put his head on the steering wheel. She touched his back.

"Tough meeting?" Jill asked.

"Stupid meeting," Jacob said. "Want to walk?"

"What about Katy?" Jill asked.

"What *about* Katy?" the little girl asked from the backseat.

"What are you doing awake?" Jill asked.

"What are we doing here?" Katy gave her big-Katy-smarty-pants smile. Jill laughed. "I can walk. I wore my *trainers*—that's what Paddie's sort-of-uncle calls them."

She lifted her feet to show her new exercise shoes.

"Walk?" Jacob asked.

"Sure," Jill said.

She fussed with Katy's heavy coat and wool hat before letting her get out of her car seat. Jacob helped Katy out of the SUV while Jill stepped out on the passenger side. Jill pulled her jacket around her round belly. Jacob took Katy's hand and held out a hand for Jill. They walked toward the large, handcrafted farmhouse.

"I bought this place right after I moved to Colorado." Jacob stopped walking. He let go of Jill's hand to point. "This house and the other two. Mormons built them around 1900. They farmed here, raised families here…for decades. The last generation moved on to Utah around the time I moved back to Denver. The houses aren't extravagant — not in any way, really — but they are gorgeous inside, solid, and . . .built with love."

Jill watched his face in the moonlight.

"I dreamed of living here with my family," Jacob said. "My daughter would keep her horses in the barn."

He waved in the direction of an empty field near the house.

"My sons would run across the open fields," Jacob said. "And you . . ."

He leaned into her, and she kissed his cheek. Jill knew that he was telling her something important, so she didn't respond. He looked out across the field.

"We'd grow corn or soy," Jacob said. "I wasn't sensitized to the whole GMO thing and pesticide thing then. Now, I think I'd grow sunflowers and . . . organic corn, and kids; maybe a cow or two, some goats . . . I'd give it all up for a patch of land, a lovely wife, and a few kids."

Katy tugged on his hand, and he let her go. She ran out into the moonlight and twirled in place.

"I'm sorry," Jill said. "I don't know if you're sharing a very sweet dream with us or if you're seriously thinking about giving everything up and moving to this farm."

Jacob nodded.

"I see." Jill watched Katy in the moonlight. "Rough meeting?"

"I'm tired," Jacob said. "Tired of the fighting. Tired of being tired. Tired of working so damned much that I never see you or Katy. And the boys . . . I thought this Lipson crap would be long over before the boys were here. Now, I'll be lucky to live long enough to get away from the company."

"You're distraught," Jill said.

He turned to give her an exasperated look. Shaking his head, he looked away.

"What?" she asked.

"You don't understand," Jacob said. "All I ever wanted was a quiet life."

"What do we have?" Jill raised an eyebrow at him.

Jacob moved away from her, picked up Katy, and carried her to the car.

"We may as well go," he said.

Jill came up behind him and held him for a moment.

"Why don't you show me the inside?" she whispered in his ear.

He looked back at her. For a moment, with the twins between them, their eyes held. He gave her a partial smile.

"I'm sorry," he said. "I'm just . . ."

"Worn out," Jill said. "Can we stay here tonight?"

"No beds," Jacob said. "The house has been empty for a couple of months."

"Let's go take a look," Jill said.

CHAPTER TWO HUNDRED & FORTY-ONE

CRUX

"But . . ." Jacob started.

"I put the sleeping bags in the back this afternoon and some blankets," Jill said.

"You did?" Jacob asked.

"Of course, I did," Jill said. "I bet we could camp out here for days if we wanted to."

Jacob smiled. He put Katy on his hip and held out his hand to Jill. They walked onto the solid porch. Jill noted the signs of Jacob's small repairs. Jacob opened the heavy oak front door, and they went inside. The home smelled like wood, cinnamon, and love. Jacob flicked on the light and Jill smiled. The house was just as he'd said — solid and beautiful.

"The other houses are rented by a couple of Amish families," Jacob said. "But they've already told me they want to move to the San Luis Valley or maybe up by Craig. There are large Amish communities there. They want to be with their own people. The family who was renting this house has gone to buy a farm for them. The way the world is now, I don't blame them for not wanting to be out on their own like this."

"This is where the new city is supposed to go," Jill said.

Jacob gave a curt nod.

"The rooms are small, of course, for heating," Jacob said. "Unlike the Castle, the house has all of the original fixtures."

He nodded to the glass-paned doors and the sliding doors in the living room. There were stained-glass windows on either side of the fireplace mantel, and every transom featured the same happy stained-glass theme.

"The fireplaces work, and there's a cord of wood in the back," Jacob said. They walked toward the back. "I replaced the furnace a couple years ago. It needs a new kitchen, but what house doesn't?"

Jill nodded.

"You feel like you have to give up your dream in order to create the new city," Jill said.

"I feel like I've lost myself in work," Jacob said. "I don't know if I'm too scared to really have the dream — you, me, a bunch of kids, a nice quiet life — or . . ."

"The dream has changed?" Jill asked.

"Maybe," Jacob said. "I'm bound up with Delphie and the Castle and the drama of this stupid company and all the people who . . . expect something for nothing because they imagine that the other guy is getting something for nothing or . . . I don't know what."

"You're tired," Jill said.

"I'm tired of defending my right to sell the company," Jacob said. "I'm tired of defending my decisions to the people in the company I sold to. I'm tired of seeing my father look so old and exhausted. And mostly, I'm tired of living without you and Katy and our boys in the center of every minute of every day. I want a quiet life."

Jill smiled.

"You think I'm crazy," Jacob said.

"I think you're tired," Jill said.

He leaned against her for a moment.

"I also think you're a person who needs a lot of stimulation," Jill said. "A person who has a lot of energy. Sure, you'd love living here for a while, but once the farm was set up, the cows and goats purchased, and the people hired to work the fields, you'd get restless. It wouldn't happen right away, but soon you'd want to fix up this house or someone else's house, and you'd be away from us again."

"I hate that about me," Jacob said.

"I love you, Daddy," Katy said. "Just the way you are. Would Delphie live in one of those other houses? Would Mr. Colin and Ms. Julie take the other one so Paddie could live next door?"

Jacob kissed Katy's forehead and closed his eyes. Jill watched him breathe in their daughter's sparkle and let it go. Katy put her hands on his face, and he opened his eyes.

"What's wrong, Daddy?" Katy asked.

"I don't know," Jacob said.

"Can you take tomorrow off?" Jill asked.

"I've already told Aden I couldn't do any more," Jacob said. "He *told* me to take tomorrow off. Blane's going in. Dad's not leaving until the afternoon. They'll survive without me."

"Then let's just rest here tonight," Jill said.

"What about dinner?" he asked.

"It's in the cooler in the back of the SUV," Jill smiled.

Not sure what to say, he smiled.

"Go on now," Jill said. "I'll get us settled while you move things inside."

"We have to be back for Val's cyber premiere," Jacob said.

Jill smiled.

"What?" Jacob asked.

"Nothing," Jill said. "Would you mind getting the things from the car?"

Nodding, he set Katy down and left to get their overnight gear. Jill turned to Katy.

"What do you think?" Jill asked.

"I think our plan was perfect," Katy smiled.

Chuckling, Jill gestured toward the staircase, and they went up.

~~~~~~~~~

The next morning
Friday early-morning — 5:15 a.m.

Jacob kissed the back of her neck and her bare shoulders. Even after all this time, and in her bulging condition, his strong hands brought her waves of bliss. To her surprise, she continued to enjoy the gentle movement and deeper probing of his skin tight against hers. She turned her head for one last kiss before she got up.

"If you think I haven't noticed that this house has recently been cleaned," Jacob said , "I noticed last night."

"Clean?" Jill feigned ignorance. She went through the bathroom to check on Katy. The little girl was sound asleep in the room adjoining the bathroom. She used the bathroom.

"Is everyone coming here?" Jacob asked.

"Yes," she said, standing in the doorway to the bathroom.

"When?" Jacob asked.

His eyes followed her. She dove into their makeshift bed of sleeping bags and blankets.

"After five," Jill said.

"Caterers?" Jacob asked.

"Two," Jill said.

Jacob lay on his back staring at the ceiling. She rolled over to rest her head on his shoulder.

"Are you mad?" she asked.

Jacob shook his head and stared at the ceiling.

"It's the crux of my problem," Jacob said. "I don't want to miss Valerie's premiere. She's taking this huge risk by taking Jackie to the premiere. Sure, she has her co-stars' support, and they're bringing their kids, but it's a big deal. She needs my support, *our* support. I would never miss that, but man, I want to."

"It's a web that ties you down," Jill said.

He nodded.

"What weighs so heavily on your heart?" Jill asked.

"When I was a kid, Dad used to say that my actions had consequences," Jacob said. "There was no way to know how the ripples of my actions would affect others. I had to just do my best and . . ." He shrugged.

"I guess I feel the weight of all that responsibility. Whatever I do now affects so many people — at home, at Lipson, you, Katy, the boys," Jacob said. "I long to shrug it off like a cloak and...I don't know, move back to Maine, open a wood shop in the forest, and..."

"Would you be happier there?" Jill asked.

"Would you move to Maine with me?"

"Sure," Jill said. "But that's not what I asked."

He didn't respond. After a while, she leaned up to look at his face, and he was sound asleep. She moved to get up but he held her in place. She looked at him again.

"Just tired," he said.

She smiled and lay down against him. For this moment, they could just lie here, together, in peace.

~~~~~~~~~

Friday afternoon — 2:15 p.m.

Delphie turned on the electric kettle and sat down at the table in the main Castle kitchen. For the last few months, she'd met Valerie at this very table every day at 2:30 p.m. for tea and chat. They would talk about nothing until Jackie woke up or the kids came home from school.

But today, Valerie was in Los Angeles, and she was alone.

She could have gone with Valerie. In fact, Valerie had almost begged her to go, but Delphie felt like she was needed at home. After all, the rapists had threatened Sissy, and Jill would be having her grandsons soon. No, she was needed at home.

Plus, there was the cyber celebration of Valerie's new movie tonight. Delphie knew she should be calling the caterers and checking on everything. It was her job to make sure everyone was ready for the party. But today, she didn't feel like taking care of anything.

Today, she wanted to have tea with Valerie and talk about nothing.

The kettle clicked off at the same moment she heard the side door to the Castle open. She got up and went to the counter to make some green tea. Out of habit, she took a mug down for Valerie.

"Are you making tea?" Sam asked.

She turned to look at him. He was wearing the new tux and tails Valerie had bought for him for the cyber premiere.

"You're dressed up," Delphie said.

"Yes," Sam said. "Wonder why?"

"Probably something out in the world-ish," Delphie sighed.

"Yes, Eeyore, I have an 'out in the world-ish' event to attend," Sam said. "Curious as to what?"

Delphie gave a small shrug, and Sam smiled. He came up behind her and put his hands on her shoulders.

"I'm here to pick up my princess for the ball," Sam said.

"Celia's gone, Sam," Delphie said.

Sam raised his eyebrows in amused surprise. He kissed her cheek and whispered in her ear: "You're my princess."

She shrugged him off and finished making her tea. She slumped back to her seat at the kitchen table. She set her tea on the table. She was about to sit down when she saw a lovely purple gown hanging on the coatrack. The bodice was tight, and the skirt was long and flowing. The purple matched his purple cummerbund. Unwilling to give up her gloom so easily, she glanced at him and sat down.

"What's this?" She nodded to the dress and took a sip of her tea.

"This is your day gown — or that's what they said it was called," Sam said. He came around the kitchen counter to stand on the other side of the table. "I know you miss Val and Jackie."

"And Mike," Delphie said.

"And I know that putting on another party is just a lot of work," Sam said. "Especially since Val's not here and Honey's with Maggie and Jill's pregnant with the twins and Sandy's . . . busy. The whole burden falls on your shoulders."

A little hiccup of a sob escaped Delphie's guarded mouth. She lifted her cup over her betraying mouth.

"So, we came up with a plan," Sam said.

"We?"

"We, the unpsychic," Sam smiled. "Me, Honey, Sandy, and Jill, too. She's only visiting your team. She's still on my team."

Delphie couldn't help but smile at the idea of "Sam's unpsychic team."

"And Valerie," Sam said. "Of course."

Delphie looked up at him.

"You're going to the premiere," Sam said.

"But how?" Delphie's sorrow hit her full force. "Val and I went over this a million times. She can't come back today, and I'll never make it through security."

"They've changed airport security," Sam said. "It's been all over the news, but Val didn't realize it until she left. Seth and Ava are coming with us. They have a house in Malibu . . ."

"Val and Mike are staying there," Delphie said.

"Exactly," Sam said. "All you have to do is get up and come with me. We have a limousine and everything."

"But my clothes and . . ."

"Jill packed them last night," Sam said. "They're in the car. I picked up your dress from the laundry."

He nodded to the dress.

"You can change here and wear it all day," Sam said.

"But . . ."

"There's another dress waiting for you there." Sam looked at his watch. "But we have to get going, or you'll miss the whole 'getting dressed with Val' thing that you love so much."

"But what about the cyber party?"

"They're having it out at the house by the worksite," Sam said. "Aden and Blane couldn't get there otherwise."

"But . . ."

Sam held out his hand to her. She looked at her teacup and

then at his hand.

"But..."

"But?" he asked.

"Oh, hell." Delphie got up from the table. "Why not?"

"That's my princess," Sam said.

"I'll get dressed in the limo." Delphie went to look at the dress.

"We're picking up Seth and Ava," Sam said.

"Then they'll get a quite a show," Delphie said. "Did you get shoes?"

"Your Birkenstocks don't work?" Sam asked.

Shaking her head at him, she took the dress down and walked to the front door. Sam watched her go.

"Coming?" Delphie yelled before opening the door.

Laughing, he ran to catch up.

~~~~~~~~~

Friday afternoon — 3:15 p.m.

Heather tried not to run over any kids in her haste. She pulled up to where Tink, Sissy, and Wanda were waiting for her outside East High.

"Come on! Get in!" Heather yelled through the passenger door. "We'll be late if you don't hurry."

"What's going on?" Sissy asked.

The girls scooted into the back seat of Heather's Subaru.

"We're going to the cyber premiere," Heather said, "and we don't have a thing to wear!"

"We get to go?" Tink asked. "I thought all the seats were taken, and..."

"Close the door. I'll tell you everything," Heather said. "We're getting dressed up and we're going to be on the large-screen television at the premiere of Val's film."

"What about Ivy?" Tink asked.

"She's already on her way there with her Aunt Grace," Heather said. She glanced in her rearview mirror and pulled out. "We have exactly an hour to get you girls something to wear."

"I get to go, too?" Wanda asked.

"I talked to your mom. She seemed excited for you," Heather said.

The rail-thin girl smiled.

"She wants you to call her. But . . ." Heather jerked to an abrupt stop at Seventeenth Avenue. "We're not going anywhere if you don't have your snacks."

Sissy diligently pulled out her protein bar and water. Wanda took out an apple and a small slice of cheese. Tink looked at her friends and then at Heather.

"I know, right?" Heather asked. "No snack for Tink. Sandy made chocolate-chip cookies. I have them up here — *but* you have to eat your apple first."

Heather tossed an apple into the back. Tink smiled.

"All right, ladies," Heather said. "We're going to have some fun tonight!"

Heather turned left at York Street.

"But we have to be fast!" Heather said.

~~~~~~~~
Friday afternoon — 4:15 p.m.

"Hey," Aden said.

Charlie looked up from his book.

"Where's Mrs. Anjelika?" Aden asked.

"She leaves at four on Fridays." Charlie turned his attention back to his book.

"Great," Aden said. "Ready to go?"

"Where?"

"We're going to Val's premiere," Aden said.

"I thought that was here," Charlie continued to stare at his book.

"What are you reading?" Aden asked.

"*Oliver Twist*," Charlie said.

"School?"

"Mrs. Anjelika," Charlie said. "She thinks I can learn something from it, or that's what she says. I have to finish by Monday so we can talk about it."

Aden nodded.

"Well, come on," Aden said.

With his nose still in the book, Charlie stood up. He grabbed his jacket and blindly followed Aden out of the house. He was sitting in Aden's sedan before he looked up. Aden started the car and left the driveway.

"Where are we going?" Charlie asked.

"Out near the airport," Aden said. "Jill moved the cyber premiere out there."

"Isn't that close to your work?"

"It is," Aden said.

"Why are you here?" Charlie asked.

"I'm here to take you to the party," Aden said.

"And to talk to me," Charlie added before Aden could. "What did I do?"

"Nothing," Aden said.

"Then why . . . ?"

"Tink is going to be at the party," Aden said. "It's a small house, and everyone's staying there tonight."

Charlie raised his eyebrows but didn't say anything.

"That's exactly right," Aden said. "Heather and Blane asked me to talk to you."

"About what?" Charlie made an effort to be nonchalant.

"About Tink," Aden said.

"What about her?" Charlie asked.

"You're really not going to make this easy, are you?" Aden asked.

Charlie smiled. Aden stopped talking, and Charlie returned to his book. After they pulled onto I-76, Charlie looked up at Aden.

"You may as well spit it out," Charlie said.

"What is it you think I'm going to tell you?" Aden asked.

"Don't be a jerk." Charlie shrugged. "Don't embarrass us too much, stuff like that."

"I'm actually going to talk to you about sex," Aden said.

"Knock yourself out," Charlie said. "Need some pointers? 'Cuz I'm not going to talk to you about having sex with my sister."

Aden laughed, and Charlie smiled at himself.

"I know that you like Tink and that she likes you," Aden said. "I even know that, if something happens, it won't be the first or even the tenth time you guys have ... been together."

"But?"

"It would be the first time since she was assaulted," Aden said.

"Oh," Charlie said. "Is that a big deal?"

"It can be," Aden said. "Her own physical sensations and feelings — you know, they can make her remember what happened and ..."

"Wow," Charlie said. "I would never want to hurt her."

"I know," Aden said. "I think we just want you to be careful — both of you to be careful."

Charlie grunted, and they drove for a while in silence.

"What do you think 'be careful' means?" Charlie asked.

"Good question," Aden said. "I think you have to go slower. Be aware that she might want to stop at the drop of a hat. If she gets upset, be comforting."

"What if I can't stop?" Charlie asked. "Sometimes things get going and ..."

He made a fist and then splayed his hand out.

"I mean stop touching her," Aden said.

"Oh," Charlie said. "How do you know?"

"I was single most of my life," Aden said. "If you stay single, you'll date girls who've been raped and assaulted. That's just how it is."

"That really sucks," Charlie said.

"It really sucks," Aden said. "And you know about Mr. Blane — right?"

Charlie nodded.

"It happens less to boys than girls, but it still happens a lot," Aden said.

"Even to girls who live at home?" Charlie asked.

Aden nodded.

"That really sucks," Charlie said.

"It really sucks." Aden nodded.

"What do I do?" Charlie asked.

"Be careful, mostly," Aden said. "Ask her if she's all right at every step of the way, and let her stop anytime she wants to. And, if she gets upset, be comforting. This is part of the package of being with a great girl like Tink. Some guys get really angry and blame the girl."

"Some guys are assholes."

"Don't be like that," Aden said.

"I'd be okay if she didn't want to." Charlie nodded. "But I don't want her to think that I'd hold it against her or anything."

"That's right," Aden said. "You have a condom?"

Charlie shook his head.

"There are a couple in the glove box," Aden said.

"Why do *you* have condoms in *your* glove box?" Charlie asked.

"I got them for you," Aden said. "Sandy wanted to make sure you and Tink were protected. None of us is so stupid as to think that if you and Tink want to get together, you won't find a way to do it. Blane talked to me about it today. Heather talked to Sandy, and she wanted to make sure that, if it happened, it was all right."

"For Tink," Charlie said.

"And for you," Aden said. "Sometimes things go . . . off the rails. It's the kind of thing you never forgive yourself for and never forget."

"So, all the adults know that Tink and I might do it tonight?" Charlie asked. "That's just . . . embarrassing."

"Realistic," Aden said. "Don't you think?"

Charlie shrugged.

"What was your first thought when you heard that everyone, including Tink, was going to stay at the house tonight?" Aden asked.

Charlie blushed.

"Exactly," Aden said. "We'd be fools to think otherwise."

"Does this count as my agreed-upon date?" Charlie asked.

Aden laughed and pulled into a long driveway. The end of the driveway was packed with cars.

"Sandy has our clothes," Aden said. "The only thing I ask is that you help out where you can and try to be gentle with Tink."

"I can do that," Charlie said. "What about the babies? Tink really likes the babies."

"Honey and MJ are already here." Aden pointed to MJ's truck. "They brought Maggie. Sandy's picking up Rachel, Mack, and everybody else. Maybe you could help out with them."

Charlie nodded.

"Wanda's coming, too," Aden said.

"So?"

"I just thought you should know," Aden said. "Are you nice to her?"

"Nice?" Charlie asked. "Whatever. I don't really get what's going on with *her*, but I think it would totally suck."

"Yes, it would," Aden nodded.

Aden pulled the car to a stop. Charlie took the condoms out of the glove box and stuffed them into his pocket.

"There's Sandy." Aden pointed behind him. "Let's help her bring everything in."

Charlie picked up his book and got out of the car. He was unloading the suitcases when Heather pulled up. Out of the corner of his eye, he watched Tink, Sissy, and Wanda glide into the house. He swallowed hard.

"You can do this." Aden picked up two suitcases and a

backpack and went into the house.

Nodding to himself, Charlie followed.

CHAPTER TWO HUNDRED & FORTY-TWO

GOLD HEART

Friday evening — 5:05 p.m.

"I know it's not much." Jill gestured to the small porch she had set aside for Honey and MJ. "I thought it would offer you guys some privacy from the teen horde and ..."

"We're happy to be included," Honey said in a soft tone, so as to not wake Maggie, who was riding in a Mozy carrier on her chest. "It seems like everyone is sharing space. We're lucky to have even a little privacy."

"And tomorrow morning?" Jill asked.

"I'll be okay." Honey smiled. "MJ can help me."

"I know how — it's just better for our relationship if I don't." MJ grinned.

"Why?" Jill asked.

"Keeps the mystery alive." Honey smiled.

Jill smiled.

"Actually," MJ said. "Steve checks Honey's health while he helps her get up. He has a more consistent sense of where she is."

"And where is she?" Jill scowled.

"I'm doing really well, Jill," Honey said. "Don't worry. This is really fun."

"At least it's on the main level," Jill said. "It's just ... small. I ..."

"It's like camping out," Honey said.

MJ looked puzzled, and Honey laughed.

"Without the tent," they said in unison and laughed.

Jill smiled.

"I'm glad you were able to come," Jill said. "I know Val wants you to be there at the premiere, and Jake . . ."

"How is Jake?" MJ asked. "He seems . . . gloomy."

"I think all the stuff going on in the world is hard for him," Jill said.

"People are so angry," MJ said. "I live in this little bubble of work, rank, duty, assignment . . . everyone does what they're supposed to, at least most of the time. When I step off base and see all this . . . It's shocking to me. I can't imagine what it's like for Jake to live in the middle of it all."

"Jake's more open," Honey said.

Jill nodded.

"Plus, he's trying create change," MJ said. "That's got to be tough."

Jill smiled. Maggie made a sound, somewhere between a yawn and a cry. She smacked her lips and rooted toward Honey.

"Maggie's up," Jill said.

"Did you bring the breast milk?" Honey asked.

Maggie made the little sound again.

"It's in the cooler," MJ said. "Frozen. Sorry, I . . ."

"Shit," Honey said.

Maggie began to scream. Although she was very tiny at birth, she was growing fast. She spent most of her days sleeping or eating. Honey tried to console Maggie, but once the baby was upset, she only got more upset, especially when she was hungry.

"Stupid," MJ said. "I'm sorry. Delphie usually has it if we don't."

Honey and MJ looked so desperate that Jill wanted to hug them.

"Listen, it happens to everyone," Jill said. "MJ, why don't you grab a bag of milk and we can warm it up fast? Just takes a couple minutes. I'll show you how."

MJ looked at Honey and shook his head. Honey nodded. She gave him Maggie, and he took the baby inside.

"He wants so badly to be a good dad that any screw up sends him around the bend," Honey said. "And every time she's upset, he checks her for Crohn's symptoms."

"Nothing so far?" Jill asked.

"She's perfect," Honey said. "It doesn't stop him from getting anxious, though, and . . ."

Honey shrugged.

"His TBI kicks in?" Jill asked.

Honey nodded and rolled her chair across the little porch. She took a bag of frozen breast milk from the cooler.

"He forgot," Honey said.

"Poor guy," Jill said.

Jill followed Honey as she rolled into the kitchen. They heard the baby's crying move through the house.

"*That's Maggie!*" They heard Ivy's high-pitched voice carry from the front of the house. "Come on, Aunt Grace! You have to meet her and Honey and MJ and . . ."

"Ivy's here," Honey smiled.

"I can stay here," Jill said. "Why don't you go?"

"Thanks." Honey wheeled out of the kitchen.

Jill turned the water to hot. She let it run for a while before she realized there was no more hot water.

"Teenagers," she said under her breath. She filled the teapot and put it on the gas stove.

"Maggie!" Jill smiled at Ivy's high-pitched enthusiasm. "This is Maggie and . . ."

"Michael Junior?" Ivy's Aunt Grace asked. "MJ?"

Jill could feel the heavy silence.

"What's going on?" Ivy asked.

"I thought you were dead," Grace said.

Jill flipped on the burner and hurried out of the kitchen. She found Honey halfway to the front of the small house. Honey looked like she'd been punched in the gut. Jill knelt down.

"You have to help him," Jill whispered to Honey.

"You don't have anything to say to me?" Grace's voice rose above Maggie's screams.

"He ... that ..." Honey swallowed hard.

"You know he can't do this," Jill said.

"But he ..." Honey said.

"He's your husband," Jill said. "He's loved you all of his life."

"And I suppose this is your child?" Grace's voice was angry and hard.

"But what if ... he loved her more and ... just forgot," Honey said. "I hadn't seen him in ... years and ..."

"Tough," Jill said. "He's married to you now. You have to fight for him."

Honey shook her head and started to turn away.

"Come on, Sweet Honeybee," Jill said using MJ's high-school nickname for her.

Honey's sad eyes looked up at her.

"You do it, or I will," Jill said. "And you know that's not going to go well."

"What's going on?" Sandy's voice came from the front. "Who are you, and why is Maggie crying? Ivy, the kids are downstairs. Why don't you go ...?"

"But ..." Ivy started.

"Or Sandy will." Jill raised her eyebrows to challenge Honey.

"Go," Sandy said.

They heard Ivy stomp off and Gracie's low and angry voice.

"I don't care," Sandy said. "This baby is hungry. That kind of takes precedence over your little drama. You're adults. Get over yourselves."

"Go. Fight for your man," Jill said. "Would you put up with this at work?"

"But ..."

Jill gave Honey's wheelchair a push, and she rolled toward the front of the house. Jill followed close behind.

"There's Honey," Sandy said. "Why is Maggie out here with

MJ?"

"*Honey?*" Gracie's voice rose a notch. "You've got to be shitting me. You had a baby with the Honeybee? What the . . ."

"Enough," Honey said. "That's enough. I know you're upset. This man can make anyone crazy. But this is not the time or the place."

MJ turned to look at her. His eyes reflected his panic and despair. Hearing her mother's voice, Maggie's screams increased. She flailed against MJ.

"Sandy, can you get Maggie?" Honey asked. "We forgot to defrost some milk."

"But he . . ." Grace pointed to MJ.

Sandy pushed past Grace, took the baby from MJ, and carried her to the kitchen.

"He has a traumatic brain injury," Honey said. "It affects his speech."

"But . . ." Grace said.

"He can't talk to you or me or anyone," Honey said. "Look at him."

MJ's panicked blue eyes looked from Grace to Honey, and back at Grace.

"Go for a run," Honey said. "We'll be here when you get back."

MJ shook his head and pointed to the ground. Honey shook her head.

"Go." Honey pointed at the door. "Do you have your phone?"

MJ nodded.

"Call me when you can," Honey said. "Go."

"I was just heading out with the boys." Jacob pushed Charlie out of the basement. Nash and Teddy came up behind him. "The boys are feeling a little . . . wound up. Want to come with us, MJ?"

Jacob gestured to the boys, who were punching each other.

"We have to go now, or we'll miss Val's big moment," Jacob said.

MJ nodded and followed Jacob out of the house. Grace went to follow them.

"Where are you going?" Honey asked.

Grace turned in place.

"There's nothing out there that's going to answer your questions," Honey said. "You want to know? You've got to stay."

Grace stared at Honey for a moment.

"But I . . . you . . ." Grace pointed at Honey.

"I'm staying here," Honey said. "My baby is hungry, and I need to feed her."

Honey turned in place and wheeled back to the kitchen. She winked at Jill as she passed. Grace stared after Honey. She glanced at the door and then squared her shoulders. She stomped past Jill to the kitchen. Jill raised her eyebrows and followed Grace to the battleground.

~~~~~~~~~
Friday evening — 6:45 p.m.

"There she is!" Jill pointed to Valerie stepping out of the limousine on the big white screen in the front of the room. The cameraman moved closer to get a picture of Jill, Sandy, and Heather.

"Look at Jackie!" Sandy said.

Jackie turned her head so her blue-hazel eyes could take in all of the activity and people on the red carpet.

"Go, Jackie!" Heather yelled.

"Ready to take over." Honey laughed.

"That's my girl," Tanesha said.

The women laughed. On the screen, Mike stepped out of the limousine. He took Valerie's hand, and they started the red-carpet walk.

Everyone was sitting in the living room. watching the screen. The cameraman and sound crew had arrived at the same time as Jeraine and Tanesha. Because Jeraine had more experience with video production, he helped everyone get ready. Because Jeraine was Charlie's pal, he stuck Charlie and Tink in the back.

Charlie put his arm around Tink. She looked up at him and gave him a nice, warm kiss.

"Awww," the adults said when the son of another star ran up to give Valerie a yellow daisy for Jackie.

"Can you believe that whole Gracie-and-MJ thing?" Tink whispered. "MJ totally dumped Gracie when he got injured. She thought he'd *died!* Now he's married to Honey and . . . Well, Honey told Gracie that they would talk about it later, that now is not the time, but . . . It's a big mess!" Tink shook her head.

"How's Ivy?" Charlie whispered.

"Hysterical," Tink said. "Heather stayed with her, but Ivy says she can't deal. She's heading out tonight."

Charlie shook his head.

"We won't let her go," Charlie said.

Tink nodded. She looked up at him, and he grinned. He was about to kiss her again when Noelle hit his shoulder.

"We're on," Noelle said in a terse voice.

"Go," the video director said.

"Hi, Val!" everyone yelled.

Valerie beamed at them and waved. Jackie giggled. An announcer asked Jacob a question, and they had to be super quiet. Jacob was handsome, charming, and funny. Charlie felt a wave of jealousy toward Jacob. Then he remembered how goofy Jacob had been when they were out running. He had done this girlie voice and gushed about how MJ was so hot. Charlie had joined in and got Teddy and Nash to do it too. When Jake knelt down and begged the hotness of MJ for some loving, MJ finally laughed and was able to talk. Charlie chuckled at the memory. Aden turned around and shushed him.

"When the movie starts, you wanna . . ." Charlie gestured away from the room.

Tink gave an emphatic nod, and Charlie smiled. They waited through more interviews and more pictures. The movie stars were so perfect that they looked weird. Even Valerie looked strange in her get up.

"That's it, folks," the video crew chief said. and they were able to move around. "We need you back here in a half hour for the movie."

Charlie bided his time. He knew that as soon as the movie started he would have Tink to himself. He and Tink found Ivy to see if she was all right. Ivy was very upset by everything. Mostly, Charlie thought she wanted Honey to adopt her, and not Gracie, but Ivy was like that. She always wanted impossible things. If it was impossible, Ivy was sure to want it. But, Ivy had promised Tink that she wouldn't leave. Heather walked in as she said this, and they stopped talking — like it was a secret.

There was a loud noise, and they went back to the room. When Charlie went to sit down, he noticed Nash was trying to sit next to Ivy. Since Jeraine had helped Charlie out, he thought he'd extend the favor. He called Ivy over and had her sit next to Nash. Completely oblivious to anything but her own inner turmoil, Ivy acted like she was just meeting Nash. By the time the movie started, their heads were pressed together. Charlie smiled, happy he'd helped Nash out.

After the opening credits, Tink pulled on his hand, and he followed her out of the room. They slipped downstairs to the corner they'd staked out in the basement. She kissed him.

"You want to . . ." Tink's eyes held a glazed look he didn't recognize.

"We could if we want to," Charlie said. "But I thought we could also talk and stuff first."

"Oh," Tink said. "Talking is okay?"

"Sure," Charlie said. "A lot has changed, and I . . ."

He scowled and tried to remember what Aden had told him to say. He shrugged. She kissed him, and they kissed for a while. Tink was a really good kisser.

"I got something for you," Charlie said.

"You did?" Tink looked really surprised, which made him happy.

"Aden said we could go on a date tonight," Charlie said. "Since we're here, I asked him if we could get something for you instead."

"Oh!" Tink beamed. "That was really nice."

Charlie nodded. He reached into his jeans pocket. The kissing had made his pants super tight, so he had to squirm to take the small jewelry box out of his pocket.

"It's not rich, but . . ."

Charlie held the box out to her. She set the box on her hand and looked down at it. She was looking at the box when Charlie remembered what he wanted to say.

"I wanted you to know that I care about you," Charlie said. "Whatever happens, wherever you go, I care. There's a lot of hard stuff we have to do, but this way, you'll have something to help you remember that at least one person really cares just about you."

Tink opened the box to find a small gold heart on a chain. She flushed bright red, and her eyes filled with tears.

"Plus, you can take off your Saint Jude," Charlie said. "He didn't really care about you."

Tink hugged him tight. He lost focus and felt some wetness in his underwear. He cleared his throat, and she smiled. He could never pull anything over on Tink. He grinned.

"Will you help?" Tink asked.

"Sure," he said.

He helped her take off the old Saint Jude pendant and put on the new shiny gold heart.

"How does it look?" Tink asked.

The heart sat in the hollow of her neck. Between the smile on her face and the heart, Tink looked very pretty. When Charlie told her so, she got teary again. She hugged him.

"There you are!" Sissy said. "You have to come up."

Charlie sneered at her.

"Ivy's in trouble," Sissy said. "She got super upset and argued with her aunt and . . . You just have to come."

Charlie looked at Tink, and she nodded. He let Tink go first so he could adjust himself.

"Did you see what I got?" he heard Tink ask Sissy as they went up the stairs.

Sissy squealed and clapped the way she did when she was happy.

Charlie smiled. He hadn't remembered quite the right thing to say, but Tink was happy anyway.

That felt really good.

Chapter Two Hundred & Forty-Three

Honest life

Saturday morning — 9:12 a.m.

"The property ends just over here." Jacob pointed to a dirt road on the rise ahead of them.

Jacob, Aden, and Sam were walking Jacob's farmland to get a feel for whether moving the large construction project made sense. Sam and Delphie had returned on an early plane so that Sam could participate in this review. Jacob glanced at his father. He was glad Sam had made it.

Sissy, Tink, Wanda, Ivy, Charlie, Nash, and Teddy were flying kites in the middle of the autumn-bare field in front of the house. From where the men were standing, the children looked like an oil painting against the bright fall sky.

"We can see the whole expanse from right here," Jacob said.

He turned around and gestured to the fields and houses behind him.

"The farms on either side are for sale," Aden said.

"I'm sure everything went up for sale the moment we started the other project," Sam said. "Most small farmers have one foot out the door."

"If they can get top dollar, why not sell?" Jacob shrugged.

"Would you buy?" Aden asked.

"I wouldn't be able to swing it," Jacob said. "With everything — and the babies coming — we're pretty tapped out right now."

"We could probably put our resources together," Sam said. "Get Val and . . ."

"Just more to do," Jacob said. "Don't you think we have enough to do?"

Sam and Aden turned to look at him. Jacob shrugged. They turned their backs to the open fields and looked at the homes. The oldest son of the Amish family on the nearest farm came out of the barn with a pail of milk. They watched the young man carry the milk to the house. Jill opened the door. From where they were standing, they could tell Jill made a fuss. The boy turned to go back, but Sissy yelled to him. He nodded and went back to the barn. A few minutes later, the older boy came out with two kites and four younger siblings. The kids joined the teenagers.

"I always wanted this life," Aden said.

Jacob turned to look at him.

"A quiet, safe place to raise my kids," Aden said. "No gang rape or whatever. Just land, a farm, someone to love . . ."

"Open air and sunshine," Sam said.

"Wake up, deal with what's right in front of you, work all day, back to bed at sundown," Jacob said. "Sounds like bliss."

The men watched the kids play. The oldest Amish boy laughed at something Sissy said. He responded, and Sissy laughed.

"It's a way of life," Jacob said. "Maybe that's what gets me."

Aden and Sam turned to look at him. Jacob collected his thoughts.

"This way of life seems so much better than what we do — get up at the crack of dawn, work until your brain is oozing out of your ears only to have people tell you what a spoiled and lazy son of a bitch you are."

"Honest," Sam said. "It seems like a more honest way to live."

Jacob nodded.

"Would you move out here?" Aden asked.

"Jill says she'd move," Jacob nodded. "But, honestly, I can't imagine it." He shrugged.

"I am what I am," Jacob said. "I'm the guy who works until my brain oozes out of my head. If it's not Lipson, it would just be something else."

"I was going to say that we could join you," Aden said. "It would be really good for our boys to spend their summers on a farm like this, and . . ."

Aden scowled and turned back to watch the kids.

"And?" Sam asked.

"Charlie's going to have to get out of town," Aden said. "No one's said it yet but . . . After talking to Bumpy, we decided to let Sissy take a ballet contract. and Charlie . . ."

Aden shook his head.

"The kid only tried to help," Aden said. "He saw those girls and . . ."

Aden shook his head.

"It's like he's doomed," Aden said. "Doomed to live on the streets; doomed to live in the shadows . . ."

Sam put his hand on Aden's shoulder.

"You weren't doomed," Sam said. "Why should Charlie be?"

Aden scowled.

"What's that?" Jacob pointed to a battered orange work truck as it pulled off the road and stopped. A burly man wearing overalls got out.

"Wade?" the man yelled.

"We should go," Jacob said.

Jacob ran down the hill with Aden and Sam behind him. He saw Sissy push Wanda behind her and Charlie come between the man and Sissy. The Amish kids edged back toward their house.

"What's going on here?" Jacob asked.

"I just want to talk to my son," the man said. "And this kid won't . . ."

"It's okay, Charlie," Aden said. "We've got this."

"But he . . ." Charlie started.

"Why don't we head back into the house?" Sam asked. "Sandy was baking when we left. I bet she has something wonderful waiting for us."

Jacob's eyes fell on Wanda. Her face was blotchy and her eyes fixed on the ground. She clasped her hands in front of her. Jacob could see that, if she could have erased her existence at that moment, she most certainly would have. She looked at him and then ran to catch up with Tink.

"I don't get to see my kid," the man was telling Aden. "I haven't seen him in three years. I was driving to work and I saw him. and ..."

The man tried to get around Aden.

"Wade?" The man's voice was almost as desperate as Wanda looked. The man turned to Jacob. "You're that rich kid, that Jake Lipson, right?"

"I'm Jacob," he said. "What can I do for you?"

"You're running that job down the road, aren't you?" the man said. "I'm on the plumbing crew."

"We run the job," Jacob said. "This is Aden Norsen and my father, Sam Lipson."

Jacob gestured to Sam, who was walking back from dropping the kids at the house.

"I don't want any trouble," the man said. "I just want to see my kid. He's had a lot of problems and I didn't handle it really well. I mean, when I was a kid. we didn't talk about problems. I thought if I was tough with him, he'd toughen up — like my Dad was tough with me. But his mom ... I ... I just want to see my kid."

Wanda made it to the house before turning in place. She ran across the field toward the men. Sissy and Tink took off after her, but Wanda was too fast. Her dad barely had a moment before Wanda hugged him tight.

"I ..." the man said. "Oh."

Wanda let go. She met Sissy and Tink in the field, and the girls ran to the house. The dumbfounded men could only watch.

"He's always been the sweetest kid." The man gave an exaggerated sniff.

"He's a *she* now," Jacob said.

"I read that in the report the ex has to send me." The man nodded. "You think he'll get over that?"

"No," Sam said.

The man nodded.

"Is that a problem?" Sam asked.

"Who cares?" the man asked. "That's what I said the first time his mom talked to me about it. I don't care if he wants to be a girl or a boy or a Martian. But . . . That was definitely not the right thing to say."

Jacob and Aden smiled.

"Listen," the man said. "You should know — there's something going down on that project."

"Oh?" Sam shifted forward.

Aden and Jacob took the cue. Sam would handle whatever this man had to say.

"Yeah." The man nodded.

"Any idea what?" Sam asked.

"Sure," the man said. "My buddy's in the middle of it. He says if we don't get involved, we'll get screwed, and who cares if those rich kids get screwed, you know?"

"Would you like to tell us?" Sam asked.

"Can I see my son?" the man asked.

"Daughter," Sam corrected.

"Right, my daughter," the man said.

"I think it's up to her mom," Sam said.

"She won't mind," the man said. "She's always bugging me to see . . . What's his name now?"

"Her name is Wanda," Jacob said.

"Wanda." The man smiled. "That was my grandmother's name."

"Why don't we go inside and call her?" Sam asked.

The man looked like someone had handed him an ice cream cone.

"Did I mention my name?" the man asked.

"Nope," Aden said.

"I'm not housebroke," the man said. "That's what the ex used to say. Anyway, I'm Erik Le Monte."

He held out a beefy hand, and Sam shook it. Jacob nodded to the house, and the men started across the field. Aden and Jacob fell in behind Sam and Erik.

"I think we can manage the farm," Aden said.

Jacob turned to look at him.

"There's enough land with the adjoining farms to start the project," Aden said. "We can create a farming zone like they have in Boulder, or just keep the farms the way they are. By the time the city is up and running, our kids will be grown."

Jacob stopped walking to turn and look at Aden.

"Don't give up, Jake," Aden said. "That's what I'm saying. It was only a few angry people. The rest of Lipson just don't know what to do. You have to lead the way."

Jacob nodded, and they went into the house.

~~~~~~~~~
Saturday morning — 10:00 a.m.

"It's just this way," MJ said.

He pointed down a long hallway in the basement of a building at Buckley Air Force Base. Gracie had never been anywhere near the building. MJ used his ID card and thumbprint to get into this hallway. That was after they had gone through a body scanner and given their IDs to the building guard. When she saw the nameplate on the door, she groaned.

"You're on the Fey Team?" Gracie said, in a terse whisper. "You don't think you could have told me? Shit. Shit. Shit. I can't believe you got me into this."

Gracie turned to leave, but Honey was rolling behind her. She sneered at Honey.

"You didn't ask." MJ opened the door.

The door opened to a small office. The sergeant at the desk

smiled at MJ. The young man looked like he was trying to swallow a laugh.

"This is Dusty," MJ said. "He goes by 'Sergeant Dusty.'"

"Ma'am," Sergeant Dusty said. "They are waiting for you. Do you want to wait with me, Honey, or do you want to go in?"

"Why would she wait with you?" MJ asked.

"Because this is military business," Sergeant Dusty said.

"It's probably better that I go," Honey said.

"Suit yourself," Sergeant Dusty said.

He got up from his desk and opened the door behind him. From where they stood, they could see a long conference table, a comfortable seating area, and a wide mahogany desk near the windows. There were two people standing and one person sitting behind the desk. The bright light from the windows made the people into dark silhouettes.

"Please." Sergeant Dusty gestured for them to go inside.

"You know I . . ." Gracie said.

"Oh, no, you don't," Honey said. "You started this; in you go."

Gracie turned in place. Moving further into the room, she could make out the people behind the woman at the desk. A dark-haired man who looked like an accountant was standing at her right hand. His fatigues insignia tab indicated that he was a Captain in Special Forces. His assignment patch was a large black Vivaldi "F." The man on the woman's left was Gracie's superior officer. Gracie groaned.

"Please come in," the woman at the desk said.

Gracie looked at her for the first time. She was in her mid-thirties. She had a pleasant kind of face that looked like it was mostly used for smiling. Her short brown hair stuck straight up in a military cut. Oddly, her fatigues insignia tab indicated she, too, was in Special Forces, a Lieutenant Colonel. Gracie popped to attention next to MJ.

"I'm Lieutenant Colonel Hargreaves," the woman said. "This is Captain Mac Clenaghan."

MJ bristled at the formality in his superior's voice. Even though he knew this formal ruse was designed to cut through bullshit, he found the whole thing unnerving.

"I believe you've met Captain Handon?" the woman asked.

"Yes, ma'am," Gracie said.

"Sir," Captain Mac Clenaghan said. "You will address the Lieutenant Colonel as sir."

"As you may have noted, we are a highly classified intelligence team," the Lieutenant Colonel said. "In order to maintain the classified nature of our work, personal disruptions require our immediate attention."

"Yes, sir," Gracie said.

"At ease," the Lieutenant Colonel said.

"You may be seated," Captain Mac Clenaghan said.

Gracie and MJ sat down in the chairs in front of the desk. Honey rolled around to MJ's side. He glanced at her, and she smiled.

"Hi, Honey," the Lieutenant Colonel said.

"Alex," Honey said.

"Sergeant Scully?" the Lieutenant Colonel said. "Can we get directly to the point?"

"Gracie and I went out for a while before I was injured," MJ said. "I think you'll remember that I went from Walter Reed to Mologne House and was assigned from there."

"I remember," the Lieutenant Colonel said.

"I think you'll also remember that I joined the Marines . . ." MJ started.

"You what?" Gracie's voice rose with surprise.

"Second Lieutenant, being at ease is no excuse for being disrespectful," her superior officer said.

"Yes, sir," Gracie said. "Sorry, sir."

"I joined the Marines just after being assigned," MJ said. "I met Honey while on assignment after returning from basic training."

"Yes, Sergeant," the lieutenant colonel said.

"I forgot a few things along the way," MJ said.

The Lieutenant Colonel nodded. She looked at Gracie. Her brown eyes seemed to penetrate her very soul. Gracie instinctively put her hand over her heart.

"Second Lieutenant?" the Lieutenant Colonel said. "Would you like to tell us what this is about?"

"I . . . um . . ."

"From the beginning," Captain Mac Clenaghan said. "That's the best place to start."

Gracie's eyes flicked to her superior officer. He gave her a look that reminded her to do what she was told. She nodded.

"I met MJ at my brother's funeral," Gracie said. "He tried to save my brother when he . . . he . . ."

Gracie cleared her throat.

"Do you remember that?" Honey asked MJ.

MJ shook his head.

"That would be Ivy's father," Honey said, and Gracie nodded. MJ shook his head.

"Sergeant Scully has a traumatic brain injury," Captain Mac Clenaghan said. "He has blank spots in his memory. I can assure you that if he says he doesn't remember, he does not."

"I don't know if that's not worse." Gracie looked at him.

"I remember you," MJ said. "I don't remember your brother or his injury. How did he die?"

"Sniper shot through the helmet," Gracie said. "You kept him alive all the way to the field hospital and then . . . he . . . he didn't make it."

"I'm sorry, Gracie," MJ said.

"Anyway, we dated for a while," Gracie said. "We talked about getting a place together, but he was SF, and I was a pilot. We spent leave together all over the world for about a year. Do you remember that?"

MJ nodded.

"We were supposed to meet in Greece," Gracie said. "No

phones, no computers, just the beach. I didn't find out about your team until a month later. I thought you'd stood me up. You'd done it before. I figured you were freaked about settling down. Then I thought you were dead. Now, come to find out, you're not dead, but you have settled down. You're not dead! You're settled down!"

She gestured to Honey. MJ shook his head.

"What happened?" Gracie asked.

"As near as we can put together, his team hit an IED, probably some kind of land device," Captain Mac Clenaghan said. "MJ helped save his teammates, but on a trip back to the Humvee, the second explosive blew. He placed a tourniquet on his own leg and went back to working on the rest of his team."

"You lost your leg?" Gracie looked horrified.

MJ gestured to his calf.

"After that, he was in Germany, and then at Walter Reed," Captain Mac Clenaghan said. "During the time MJ was there, the wards were extremely overcrowded. A lot of things fell through the cracks. That may be why you weren't notified."

"We had twelve guys in our room," MJ said. "When I first got there, I couldn't talk at all, so they let me be. I couldn't tell anyone to call you, Gracie. With all the pain, and trying to walk, and get another job and stuff, I forgot almost everything."

"After Walter Reed, he was placed in Mologne house," Captain Mac Clenaghan said.

"We recruited him from his hospital bed," the Lieutenant Colonel said. "He's been on active deployment since then."

"Honey, why are you here?" Captain Mac Clenaghan said.

"MJ and I really like Ivy, Gracie's niece," Honey said. "I want to make sure we resolve this without a problem, so MJ can keep his job and we still get to see Ivy."

"Why would MJ lose his job?" Gracie asked.

"We are an elite intelligence team," Captain Mac Clenaghan said. "This kind of interpersonal strain is disruptive to our work and leaves us open to security risk. We either work this out today, or MJ will be replaced."

"Sir," MJ said. "May I say something?"

YOUR TRUTH

The Lieutenant Colonel nodded.

"I wanted to say..." MJ cleared his throat. He glanced at Honey, and she smiled to encourage him. "I'm sorry, Gracie."

Gracie scowled at him.

"I wasn't a very good friend to you," MJ said. "I'm sorry for it. You deserved a lot better. But I wasn't...that."

"And I suppose you are now?" Gracie sneered.

"I've changed a lot since we were together, Gracie," MJ said. "I don't treat people like I did. Not because of my job, but because I realized that people matter. I don't have fighting relationships anymore—not with anyone. I even made up with my mom."

"*Fighting relationship*." Gracie nodded. "That's what we had."

MJ nodded.

"You're a great girl, Gracie. You probably think I'm just saying this because..." MJ gestured to the officers in front of them. "But you are. I'd like to be your friend now, if I could. Honey would too, I think."

Honey nodded.

"You broke my heart," Gracie said.

"I did," MJ said. "You're right. I'm really very sorry. I was good at breaking hearts, took great pleasure in it. I don't break hearts anymore."

"Why?" Gracie asked. "I get that you were injured and in the hospital. And I get that you didn't remember us and everything. I understand that. I don't get why or how you're so different. I mean, you never ever wanted to even be in the same room with Honey, and now you have a baby and..."

Gracie gestured to Honey.

"And you're *nice*, so nice," Gracie said. "You made sure last night that I was taken care of and a part of the whole Hollywood thing. You even brought me a blanket so I wouldn't be cold. You weren't nice like that before."

MJ nodded.

"What happened to you?" Gracie asked. "And what happened to Honey? Did you do that?"

"I think that's our cue." The Lieutenant Colonel stood up. "Captain Handon, I believe I promised you a good cup of coffee."

"And a pastry." Captain Handen followed her out of the room. "You promised pastry."

"That I did." The Lieutenant Colonel came around her desk. She touched Honey's shoulder and winked at MJ before leading Gracie's superior officer out of the room. "We have pastries — not Parisian, you understand. They are good, though."

They waited until the superior officers were gone.

"What was that?" Gracie looked at MJ.

"Second Lieutenant, this matter is not resolved," Captain Mac Clenaghan said.

"Yes, sir," Gracie said and swallowed hard. She hadn't realized that the Captain was the hard-ass in the room.

"Sergeant Scully, I believe the Second Lieutenant asked you a question," Captain Mac Clenaghan said.

Gracie gave a partial smile. At least, he was a hard-ass to MJ, too.

"I know death now," MJ said. "That's the easiest way to say it. Me, Honey — we both almost died; by all rights, we should be dead, both of us. I used to keep death 'over there' some place."

He gestured to the far corner of the room.

"Death was something I mocked, cheated, played with," MJ said. "It was all just a game, one I wanted to win at all costs. Then, I was on assignment, and Honey got stabbed, and . . ."

He glanced at Honey and she smiled.

"She almost died on the kitchen floor," MJ said. "And I realized that life isn't a game that you ever win. And I realized that, by not valuing death, I didn't value my life or anybody else's. I was playing a game with everything that mattered. At first, I just wanted her to live, and then . . ."

MJ shrugged and looked at Honey.

"She's the love of your life," Gracie nodded. "I always knew that. I guess I . . ."

Gracie's head went up and down as she worked through what he'd said.

"You broke my heart." Gracie's eyes welled. "I . . . I thought you were dead."

"I'm sorry," MJ said.

"What do you need to make this right, Second Lieutenant?" Captain Mac Clenaghan asked.

Looking down at the desk, Gracie crossed her arms across her heart and shook her head.

"I understand, that two years ago, you requested through your command, a training day with the Jakker — then again last year, and again this year," Captain Mac Clenaghan said. "I assume you'll be putting the request in again in January?"

Gracie looked up at him. Her hand flew to her throat. She glanced at MJ, and he smirked.

"Sergeant Scully has arranged for the Jakker to be available to you for the rest of the day," Captain Mac Clenaghan said. "When you've finished here, you may begin."

The Captain gave Gracie and MJ a nod and walked out of the room. Gracie turned to MJ.

"Did you love me so much?" MJ asked. "Was I the love of your life?"

"I . . ." Gracie shook her head.

"What can we do to make this right with you?" Honey asked.

"Spending the rest of the day with the Jakker?" Gracie smiled.

Honey smiled.

"How did you pull that off?" Gracie asked.

"He flies the Fey," MJ said. "You met his son last night. The kid with the great eyes and black hair, boyfriend of Noelle?"

"Teddy." Gracie nodded.

"His son," MJ said.

Gracie looked down at the ground for a moment. When she looked up, she gave MJ a long look. She glanced at Honey and then back at MJ.

"It's different," Gracie said. "Here. In country. People have kids. The Jakker has kids."

"Four," Honey said.

"Who knew?" Gracie asked. "It's like my heroes are real people. You're a real person, MJ — not a monster or a victim or a hero or anything. Just a person. It's . . . different."

"War," MJ said. "All you think about is your next mission. There's a lot more to think about here."

Gracie nodded. She looked at MJ and then at Honey.

"I'm kinda glad you found each other again," Gracie nodded.

MJ nodded.

"Do you mind if I . . ." Gracie pointed to the door.

MJ smiled and glanced at Honey.

"He's an asshole," MJ said.

"Rapist?" Gracie asked.

"No," MJ said. "Just an ass. The only person he's nice to is the LC. She's the only one who holds the end of his chain."

"He's an amazing parent," Honey said.

Gracie nodded. She had the impatient look of a child waiting for permission to eat her special treat.

"Go," Honey said.

Gracie looked at her. Her face broke into a smile, and she ran out of the room. MJ looked at Honey, and she smiled.

"Good idea to ask Zack," MJ said.

"I thought so," Honey said. "She's happy. You?"

MJ took her hand and they started toward the door.

"I feel bad," MJ said.

"Sure," Honey said.

"But not that bad," MJ said.

"Sure," Honey said.

"Wanna get our baby and go home?" MJ asked.

"Sure," Honey said.

He grinned at her, and they went to get Maggie.

~~~~~~~~~

Sunday morning — 5:22 a.m.

Jacob let the dogs out the front door of the farmhouse. He watched them wander, sniff around, and eventually settle into doing their business. Scooter came right back to him. Jacob rubbed the old dog's ear and he looked up at Jacob. Scooter did not want to miss out on a chance to snuggle with Jill and Katy in bed.

"I hear you, boy," Jacob said.

Jacob opened the door to let Scooter into the house. Scooter raced up the stairs. He heard Jill open the door to the room they were staying in and Katy giggle. He smiled and closed the front door. He put a leash on Sarah, his yellow Labrador, and Buster, the ugly dog. He started running on the dirt road that ran along the back of the property. Used to this morning activity, the dogs fell in beside him.

He couldn't be happier. The weekend had been fun. The kids didn't argue. Charlie and Tink didn't end up putting on a show. Everyone had a great time. Sam and Delphie showed up early Saturday morning from LA and made the weekend with their stories of their red-carpet adventures. Last night, the adults stayed up long after the kids were asleep, watching the stars under thick wool blankets and drinking cocoa.

He loved having everyone together.

He loved it when everyone laughed and enjoyed each other.

He loved that Ivy had a chance to enjoy his father.

He loved that Delphie got to be with everyone at the farmhouse and go to the premiere.

The problem was that right now, he hated people.

Right now, he wanted to be left alone.

For the briefest moment, he imagined never coming back. He would run to the airport, take a plane to somewhere foreign, and never return.

Relief coursed through his veins. No more Lipson. No more people telling him what an asshole he was. No more Jill?

That was always about as far as he got with this little fantasy.

He stayed because he couldn't imagine taking even one breath without Jill in his life.

He stayed because his sons were coming and his daughter was amazing.

He stayed because that's who he was.

He plodded on down the road.

"The problem is that no one believes you," Wanda's father Erik had said. "I mean, who gives away their business these days? Especially to their employees. Today, it's all about 'Grab what you can and stick it to the next guy.' I mean, think about it — would you believe it?"

The words made Jacob so angry that he sped up. He wanted to throttle the cynical world that would rather cling to its own misfortune than see the bounty presented to it. The conversation continued to play in his head.

"What do they think we're doing?" Sam had asked.

"What rich people always do," Erik had said. "Shift the burden onto the little guy while they run away with all the goodies. I mean — look around you? You don't think people notice the roads are falling apart? The schools suck? People like me drive those roads. Our kids go to those schools. But rich people, they drive on perfect roads and send their kids to schools where the teachers know their kids' names."

Jacob wanted to hate the man. He wanted to blame him for his words. But every cell in his body told him that Erik was honest to a fault. The plumber was telling him what no one else would. He was telling him the truth.

Jacob ran for a while. Erik had gone on to tell them what they already knew. The men Sam had fired had told everyone that he was selling Lipson Construction because it was broke. The rumor was that the employees were buying at prime rates but that the company was worth only a third of that.

Jacob snorted. Since taking the larger contract, Lipson Construction was worth almost double what the employees were paying.

Why didn't anyone believe him?

He just couldn't fathom it. He never lied. He never cheated. And still no one believed him!

He had come full circle.

He hated people.

He wanted to run away.

He increased his pace to do some speed work. The dogs loped along beside him.

"Don't let it get to you, Jake," Aden had said. "No one believes those jerks."

His father had just looked at him. He hadn't said a word. He'd just watched him with worried eyes.

Jacob reached a bend in the road and took it to the right.

He should take the company back. It wouldn't be hard. He already had the figures from Tres. He'd say he changed his mind. He was allowed to change his mind, wasn't he?

He nodded at his reasoning and kept running. Up ahead he saw the Brighton home Valerie had purchased for the Marlowe School. Out of curiosity more than anything else, he ran up to the doorstep. He used his psychokinesis to open the door and went inside.

This was a gorgeous house.

The morning sun filtered through dusty windows to show off

gorgeous woodwork and antique fixtures. Jacob went to the spot where Aden and Seth and the police officers had stood while he and Delphie were fighting the demon.

He couldn't get over how pretty this house was. Feeling something behind him, he turned around. He was standing face to face with an apparition of a woman. She was wearing a Victorian dress. Her hair was up in the style of the time. She had a pleasant face and pretty eyes. When she realized he could see her, she smiled.

"Who are you?" Jacob asked.

"I own this home," she said.

"Why aren't you . . .?" Jacob gestured to where they had laid the family to rest.

"I love this home," she said. "You were going to fill it with children and I didn't want to miss it."

"Are you stuck here?" Jacob asked.

"No — thanks to you, we are all free." She smiled. "Thank you." He nodded.

"I don't have a lot of time for ghosts," he said. "And I'm pretty grumpy."

"Good to know," she said. "Why are you here?"

"I was just out for a run," he said.

"Yes, the dogs told me," she said. "But why are you here? You dropped the house here, and probably haven't given it another thought. Suddenly, you're grumpy and here. Why is that?"

He shrugged. Everywhere he looked, he saw things he could improve. A little buffing here, some color there, sand the floors and . . .

"You're making a list of how to improve the house," she said.

"What if I am?" Jacob asked.

"I just wondered — does the wood like it when you sand the floor?" she asked.

"No idea." He looked at her.

"Do walls appreciate the feel of wet, cold paint?" she asked.

He scowled.

"Walls and floors are made of the same stuff as people," she said. "Why would people appreciate the transitions any more than the floors appreciate being sanded?"

His eyes flicked to her.

"Maybe, Mr. Tough Guy, you should tell your employees why you're selling," she said.

"So, they won't believe me?" Jacob asked.

"What if they do?" she asked.

Jacob squinted at the woman.

"No, your mother didn't put me up to this," she said. "She told me about your situation. I guess . . ."

She gazed at him, and he felt her eyes drift over his sweaty skin. It was such a weird sensation that he shivered.

"There was so much I never said," she said. "To my love, my children, my brothers, my sisters, my darling parents. You can hear people's thoughts. You can read their energy. But people cannot read your thoughts. They can't read your energy. They can only believe what they hear, and they hear less than half of what they are told."

"Why didn't you tell your family what you thought?" Jacob asked.

"I wasn't supposed to," she said. "When I was alive, women were weak and stupid creatures who didn't have feelings or thoughts. At least that's what I was told all my life. It never occurred to me to tell my family how I felt or what I thought. Like you, it never occurred to me that they would care."

"Why are you telling me, then?" Jacob asked.

"Your mother asked me to," she said. "People will die if you do not move the project. And this . . . problem is nonsense compared to that."

"Nonsense?" Jacob asked. "You're dead, and you're telling me my problems are nonsense?"

"For an honest man, you tell very few people your truth," she said. "It's time to tell your company everything. They know you. They'll listen."

"You're sure you're not my mother?" Jacob asked.

"She is with your sister." The woman smiled. "But you knew that."

The woman faded. Jacob watched her for a moment before moving toward the door. His hand was on the doorknob when she reappeared in front of him.

"Yes?" he asked.

"Tomorrow, you must run with the dogs in the afternoon," she said. "The little painter needs you in the park."

"I'll be there," he said.

"Good," she said and disappeared.

"Thanks, Mom," he whispered.

At the bottom of the steps, he stopped to look at the house again. Nodding to himself, he ran back to the farmhouse and his life.

~~~~~~~~~
Sunday night — 9:42 p.m.

"Yo," the voice on the phone said.

"Yeah? Whatchu want?" he responded.

"Tomorrow, just after the start of b-ball practice, we're gonna take care of our On-Line problem."

"Gotcha."

"We all gonna be there," the voice said. "You?"

"I'll be there."

CHAPTER TWO HUNDRED AND FORTY-FIVE

IN THE AIR

Monday morning — 7:42 a.m.

"Wasn't the weekend fun?" Noelle's bright chatter made Sandy turn to look at her. Sandy gave Noelle a probing look, and the girl blushed. Rachel gurgled from her spot on Sandy's hip.

"Sissy! We have to go!" Sandy yelled down the hallway.

"We're riding our bikes," Nash said.

Nash and Teddy walked by her with their bike helmets on. Teddy stopped to smile at Noelle.

"Good morning," Teddy said.

Noelle beamed at him. Teddy glanced at Sandy, and Sandy scowled. He nodded and jogged to catch up with Nash.

"What's going on with you and Teddy?" Sandy asked.

"Nothing new." Noelle twirled back and forth.

"Uh, huh," Sandy said. "Sissy, if you don't hurry, we're going to leave you here. You'll have to drag all your ballet crap to school yourself."

"I'm coming!" Sissy hustled down the hall with a duffle bag full of her dance gear.

"Charlie!" Sandy yelled from the living room.

Charlie turned the corner from the kitchen and looked at Sandy.

"Oh, good — you're here," Sandy said. "Mike's not here to walk you to basketball . . ."

"So, Jake's taking me," Charlie said. "Yes, I remember from the last forty times you told me."

"Good." Sandy smiled, and he scowled.

"Noelle's right, you know," Charlie said. "Last weekend was great."

"God, not you too," Sandy said. "Yes, I know. Young love is in the air."

Charlie wiggled his eyebrows, and Sandy shook her head at him. Sissy caught up with her, and Sandy gave the girls a nudge out the door. She followed Sissy and Noelle down to the enormous SUV. Noelle helped Sissy put her stuff in the back. The girls sat together in the back because Rachel, her diaper bag, and her command-center car seat took up the middle seat. Sandy got into the driver's seat.

"Anything you want to talk about, Noelle?" Sandy asked as she started the car.

"What do you mean?" Noelle asked.

"She wants to know if you and Teddy did it this weekend," Sissy said.

"What?" Noelle looked horrified. "Why would you think that?"

"You're all glowy," Sissy said.

Sandy turned up Sixteenth Avenue toward East High School.

"Oh," Noelle said. "I'm just really happy. I get to spend the afternoon with Teddy's stepmom, and . . . I just feel . . . really happy."

"Yeah," Sandy said. "How'd you get so happy?"

Sissy giggled, and Noelle blushed.

"I would never betray the trust you place in me and in Teddy by having sex at my age." Noelle nodded. "We agreed and shook hands and everything."

"But?" Sandy asked.

"I hear the 'but' too," Sissy said.

"But kissing doesn't count, does it?" Noelle asked.

Sissy squealed and laughed. Sandy looked at Noelle in the rearview mirror.

"What are you doing with Teddy's stepmom this afternoon?"

Sandy asked.

"We're going to the park," Noelle said. "I'm going to paint her portrait. She's very beautiful. Have you met her?"

"I have," Sandy said. "And you're right — she *is* very beautiful."

Sandy pulled up in front of East High School.

"Sissy, you remember what Dr. Bumpy said, right?" Sandy asked. "You'll be super careful?"

"Ivan's picking me up at noon," Sissy said. "I should be gone all afternoon. Then he's dropping me off at home for dinner. I'll be with Ivan until I'm home."

"You have your phone?" Sandy asked.

"I promise. I'll be okay," Sissy said. "You'll see. Those guys are just begging to get caught. We'll laugh at them tonight."

Sandy gave a worried nod. Noelle hopped out of the car and helped Sissy carry the heavy duffle bag to the office. Sandy called Tanesha on her iPhone and spoke to her until Noelle came back. Noelle got into the passenger seat.

"How's Tanesha?" Noelle asked.

"Her parents are back from Paris," Sandy said. "I think she's a little overwhelmed with them and school and Jeraine, but you know Tanesha."

"Tanesha can do anything," Noelle said. "She's Wonder Woman."

Sandy gave a slight nod. She started down the East High Esplanade and turned right on Seventeenth Avenue.

"I wanted to talk to you about . . ." Sandy asked.

"What's going on?" Noelle asked.

"Jake talked to Aden and me last night after you went to bed," Sandy said.

"Oh?" Noelle asked.

"He was warned that something might happen to you today," Sandy said. "In the park."

"I'll be with Teddy's stepmom," Noelle said.

"You'll be safe?" Sandy asked.

Noelle nodded.

"You have your phone?" Sandy asked.

Noelle nodded.

"I just . . ." Sandy started. She pulled into the parking lot of the Marlowe School. "I don't want anything to happen to you."

"I'll be careful," Noelle said. "I won't be reckless. I promise."

Noelle grabbed her backpack and got out of the car. Sandy watched her go inside the building before getting Rachel from the back. She couldn't shake the feeling that something horrible was going to happen. Sandy shook her head at herself. Her past was not Noelle's present. She hoped.

Sandy cuddled her baby for a moment before taking her into the nursery. She chatted with Anjelika and went back out to the car. Sitting in the driver's seat, Sandy nodded to herself.

"Everything is going to be fine," Sandy said, out loud.

Anxiety shot through her gut. Sandy scowled and started the car.

~~~~~~~~~
Monday mid-day — 12:05 p.m.

Jacob cleared his throat and walked to the front of the room. The site managers had gathered everyone for a noon meeting. In order to avoid confusion, they were waiting to distribute lunch until Jacob had finished talking. As he walked, he saw men and women he recognized. Some had worked for his parents. Some he'd hired himself. Rodney touched his shoulder in a gesture of support as Jacob passed.

"I apologize for disrupting your day," Jacob said. "I called this meeting because I have a few things to say, and we as a company need to make some decisions. I am going to speak for a few minutes, and then we'll have lunch. My father, Aden, Blane, and Tres are in the back. They will be available to answer your questions until the end of the hour."

He looked out at the employees in front of him and smiled.

"I'm sure you're aware of the tension that's developed within our company," Jacob said. "I realized this weekend that some of the strain stems from the fact that you don't know why my father, Valerie, and I are selling Lipson Construction."

He saw heads instinctively move up and down.

"My mother and father started this company," Jacob said. "They ran it out of our basement. As some of you remember, Val and I worked every day after school and all summer. I can't tell you how many nights, weekends, birthdays, and dinners one or the other of my parents missed because they were on a backhoe, up all night writing a bid, or just trying to make ends meet. My father worked side carpentry jobs to support the company the entire time I was in grade school. And then something miraculous happened: Denver needed a new airport, and we got the bid."

Jacob nodded.

"My family had a lot of problems," Jacob said. "And my mother died."

Jacob's voice caught with emotion. He could never utter the words without feeling his heart squeeze.

"And Lipson continued to grow," Jacob said. "My mother's dying wish was that the people who had made Lipson Construction great — her employees — could one day reap the benefits of their hard work. It was *her* dream, what *she* wanted."

"That's exactly right!" Bambi yelled out from the back.

"Told me that herself," Jerry said.

"It's taken a long time," Jacob said. "My father was plagued with people who wanted to gut the company for its cash value. I bought most of the company from him and have been fighting with the same men ever since."

Jacob swallowed hard.

"It comes down to this: They don't want you to own this company," Jacob said. "They don't want you to own any company."

"No, they do not!" DeShawn yelled out.

"They want the money that selling this company to the highest bidder will bring them," Jacob said. "As you've learned in the last six months, there's a lot more to running a company than making money."

There was a general rumble of people agreeing with him.

"We believe the company should belong to you," Jacob said. "And we want you to be successful. But if I had allowed people to buy the entire company at the very beginning, like some of the more vocal employees have proposed, it would have failed within a year. That's what has happened to every single company in which employees have assumed one hundred percent ownership right away. This company — any company, really — is too complicated. By slowly selling shares, we hold the responsibility and risk while you learn the ropes.

"People have asked me — 'Why are you doing it, Jake?' We're doing this so *you* can succeed. We're doing this so the company my parents sacrificed so much for doesn't fail. In fact, the only people we're sticking it to is ourselves!"

Jacob felt a wave of anger and his heart raced. He put his hand on his chest against the angina he still felt when he was very angry.

"Today, I received the current evaluation of Lipson Construction." Jacob nodded to Tres, and he put the chart on the overhead. "I want you to see that the *value* of Lipson has risen significantly. We do not intend to change your share price. You, and your hard work, make this company successful. You made the value rise. You deserve to purchase the company at the original offer price."

"We are aware that a number of you are unhappy with your situation," Jacob said. "We've heard that more than a few of you feel cheated. In response to your feedback, my father and I have decided to launch a buy-back. This is your opportunity to sell back your ownership shares for what they are currently worth. Selling your shares will not affect your employment, but you will not be able to repurchase your shares at the original price. If you choose to repurchase shares, and we choose to offer them to you, you will pay the current market price."

Jacob looked at the men and women in the room.

"Now is your chance," Jacob said. "We'll give you the rest of the hour to have lunch and arrange to sell back your shares. Tonight at six, the Lipson Construction owners will meet back here to make some important decisions. For the next hour, you have the option not only to rid yourself of what many of you now think is a scam but also to make a profit. If you still own Lipson Construction stock at six this evening and decide you no longer wish to own it, the only way to unload your stock will be to end your employment with the company. The terms are non-negotiable. Thank you."

With that, he left the room. He walked to the parking lot and got into the passenger seat of Jill's SUV.

"How did it go?" Jill asked.

"I don't know," Jacob said.

"Okay," Jill said. "Lunch?"

"Lunch with my girl sounds fabulous," Jacob said. "I need to be back around two to take Charlie to basketball."

"We have plenty of time." Jill smiled.

"Smile like that, and I'll want to go home."

Jill laughed and drove out of the parking lot.

~~~~~~~~~
Monday afternoon — 2:05 p.m.

"I like this area of the park," Noelle pointed to a quiet grove of trees. "No one ever comes over here anymore. I mean, the running path is over there, and the fields, but no one can see you here."

"Is that safe?" Bestat Beher, Teddy's stepmother, asked. She pulled her Mercedes sedan next to the running path. She was a stunning woman with almond-shaped, rust-colored eyes, long, jet-black hair, and golden skin.

"I don't know why not." Noelle gave her a bright smile. "I

mean, if there's trouble, there are people around, you know. Plus, I thought it would be good to have some privacy."

Bestat looked at the girl for a moment before asking, "Why?"

"I saw you." Noelle gave Bestat such an innocent smile that the woman scowled.

"When?"

"When we were in Brighton, and everything was turning for the worse," Noelle said. "You fought the demon."

"And you know this?" Bestat asked. "How?"

"I see things how they actually are," Noelle said. "Like your baby. She's like you, even though she has Mr. Zack's eyes."

Bestat sat very still.

"No one will ever believe me," Noelle said. "You can stand there, and I'll still be able to paint you as you are."

"Have you always had this . . . capacity?" Bestat asked.

"Dad thinks Nuala, the lady who had me, took drugs when I was inside her," Noelle said. "Well, we know she did because I was high when I came out, but . . . maybe she was like this, too. Maybe she just didn't understand it. Anyway, I've always been like this. Mike, my teacher, he says I have 'the sight,' whatever that means."

"Do you see anyone else?" Bestat asked.

"I know that Mrs. Alex is a fairy; I can see her wings. Her husband has a blue fairy that follows him around," Noelle said. "I don't think he trusts his fairy very much; I don't trust her, either."

"Fairies always have their own agenda," Bestat said.

"But not Mrs. Alex," Noelle said.

"No, Mrs. Alex is very special," Bestat said. "What about Teddy or my Zackary?"

Bestat's voice seemed to purr when she said her lover's name.

"Your Zack is a dragon rider. But *my* Teddy?" Noelle mimicked Bestat's words, and Bestat smiled. "He has a kind of glow about him. Mike says it's his shining armor, but I don't know."

Bestat nodded.

"Sandy?"

"Sandy?" Noelle nodded. "That's easy. She has the warm glow of an earth mother or something. Just watch when everyone's around her. They kind of melt. Tanesha's Wonder Woman. Everybody can see her cape. Heather is a connector, like a bridge or a highway. And Jill is the happy elf meddling in everyone's life."

"I think you're right," Bestat said.

"Will you still model for me?" Noelle asked. "No one will ever, ever, ever believe it's you. They will just think it's me being my silly self."

"Delphie and Jacob will know," Bestat said.

"Yeah, but they know everything anyway," Noelle said.

"How about this?" Bestat asked. "You will do one of me here. I will commission Michael to do another of my family. At that time, you will agree to paint me as a woman."

"I'll do it," Noelle said. "I'm just learning, though. I'm not like Mike or anything. I'm just a kid."

Bestat put her hand on Noelle's leg.

"We all start somewhere," Bestat said.

"You can just be invisible," Noelle said. "So that no one will see you in the park. But I'll still see you, right? You can do that, right?"

Bestat gave her a slight nod.

"Will you have another baby?" Noelle asked.

Bestat gave her a sly look, and Noelle giggled.

"Can I ask you something?" Noelle turned to look at her directly.

Bestat nodded.

"Do you see the future?" Noelle asked.

"I see the river of life," Bestat said. "Why?"

"Will Teddy and I . . .?" Noelle's forehead wrinkled, and she looked like a very little girl.

"You don't need me to answer that question," Bestat said. "He is your knight."

Noelle beamed.

"Shall we?" Bestat asked.

Noelle got out of the passenger seat. Looking out across the grove of trees, she saw one of Charlie's basketball teammates. She sneered. The boy didn't appear to see her, so she went to the trunk of the car.

"What is it?" Bestat asked and opened the trunk.

"One of those boys who've been hurting girls," Noelle said.

Bestat cast her eyes in the boy's direction.

"Let's not let him spoil our fun," Bestat said.

Noelle beamed. She grabbed her portable easel and paint supplies.

"Over here!" Noelle yelled. She ran into the grove of trees.

Bestat's eyes followed the boy until he was gone. She made a mental note and followed Noelle into the grove.

~~~~~~~~~

Monday afternoon — 2:25 p.m.

"We know what we wants to do." The leader stood in the middle of the circle. "We jus' can't today."

Their leader had a joint hanging out of his mouth. His eyes were glassy and his pupils large. He paced back and forth in the middle of the circle of boys in the East High School parking lot.

"Why?" the boy Noelle had seen asked.

"'Cuz On-Line's sister ain't here," Sergeant Aziz's brother said. "She left before lunch."

"I thought you liked that girl," the boy Noelle had seen said to the captain of the basketball team.

"Dis is more important," the captain of the basketball team said. "Somebody's been talking to the po-lice. Dat somebody's sister is gonna pay."

"So, we agree," the boy in the middle of the circle said. "We get this tomorrow?"

"He has another sister," said the boy Noelle had seen. "She's just over there."

He pointed to the park.

"Who she with?" the boy in the center of the circle asked.

"I didn't see nobody," the boy Noelle had seen said. "I went back to check. She set out her art crap and started painting. No one was with her. She's in that hidden place in those trees over there."

The boy Noelle had seen realized everyone was looking at him. He stood a little taller.

"I say we hit that," the boy said. "She's younger and fresher."

"Good thinking," the leader in the center of the circle said. "You know how much I love how the virgins scream."

"We gonna kill this bitch," another boy said. "Teach On-Line a lesson."

"We mess her up, have our fun, and then kill her," the boy in the center of the circle said. "On-Line won't fuck with us anymore."

"Where she at?" one of the boys asked.

The boy Noelle had seen pointed toward the park. The boy in the middle of the circle gave him a nod of appreciation, lit his joint, and then headed into the park. The boys followed in his drifting smoke. A couple boys passed around joints laced with meth like they always did before these events. The boys were hopping with excitement. Sergeant Aziz's brother didn't follow them. He stood staring at his car.

"You better get your ass over here," the leader said.

"Yo Momma's next." The boy next to him pushed Sergeant Aziz's brother.

The boy nodded and made a move to follow. In his pocket, he texted his brother one word:

"Help!"

Hitting "Send," he said a silent prayer that this would be over today.

The boys started across Seventeenth Avenue, and Sergeant Aziz's brother ran to catch up.

CHAPTER TWO HUNDRED AND FORTY-SIX

IN THE PARK

Monday afternoon — 2:45 p.m.

Wanda was on her own because Tink was still suspended from school, and Sissy was pursuing her dream. She'd crossed the street to the Tattered Cover at lunch so she wouldn't have to eat alone. While she missed her friends, she'd spent most of her life in the silence of her secret. She was used to being alone. She finished her last class and followed the line of kids out the front door of the school. Standing on the top step, she looked for her mom's car. As usual, Mom was late.

Looking out, she noticed a group of boys moving from the parking lot to the park. Just then, a senior boy walked into her. They jostled, and his papers went everywhere. She helped him pick them up while they laughed. The boy patted her shoulder and went to the bike racks. When she looked for her mom again, she realized that the pack of boys were the same ones who'd hurt Tink and threatened Sissy.

A flush of rage shot through Wanda. She took off running toward the boys.

When Wanda was Wade, she'd competed in boys' track in elementary school and junior high. Wanda was really fast. She just missed catching the boys at the light on Seventeenth Avenue. With her eyes on the boys, she waited until all the cars had passed and raced across the street.

Closing the distance, she saw her best friend from elementary school running up ahead. Of course, he was too cool to be her friend now. Even though he didn't acknowledge her presence most days, she still thought of him as her friend. The last time he'd even looked at her was when she'd given him cream for the burn on his neck left by the belt. He didn't have to tell her he'd tried to hang himself; she just knew. She'd just set the cream on his desk and gone back to her desk in the front of the class. The next day, his neck looked a lot better.

Was he one of the boys who'd hurt Tink? Unsure of what to do, she slowed.

"Whatchu doing, freak?" A boy jumped out from behind some bushes.

"What are *you* doing?" Wanda's voice was indignant.

The boy circled her like a dog stalking prey.

"I have to go," Wanda said.

"You ain't going nowhere," the boy said.

Before she could move, the boy hit her in the face.

Wanda screamed and fell to all fours. In her mind, she went through everything Mr. Colin had told her. She was going to fight these jerks. She was strong.

Mr. Colin hadn't told her it would hurt so much or that she would be so scared.

When she looked up, she saw that a circle of boys had closed around her. Before she knew it, they were kicking her. She covered her head.

"Frankie!" she screamed.

Up ahead, Sergeant Aziz's brother skidded to a stop.

"Frankie!"

No one called him that anymore. Most people called him by his middle name, "Brutus," or "Brut" for short.

"Help me!" Wanda screamed.

Only one person called him "Frankie."

Unable to stop himself, Frankie spun in place and ran back to where five boys were beating up Wanda. His rage and shame flushed through him. He threw himself at the group. He yanked one boy away from Wanda while kicking another in the rear. He was so angry that he didn't feel it when they hit him back. He punched a boy in the face and kicked another boy hard in the nuts. He vented his rage with each point of contact.

Frankie didn't fight fair. He didn't even try to protect himself.

He just wanted to save Wanda.

He fought with all his might. And then, something weird happened.

"It's okay, son — I got this," a man's voice said.

He looked up and saw Wanda's father. The boys who'd attacked Wanda were running in all directions.

"It's okay, Frankie." Wanda's dad held out his arms and hugged Frankie tight. Frankie felt like crying his eyes out, but the man let go.

A boy crept toward Wanda

"Get the fuck away from my daughter." Wanda's dad bent down and picked up a clod of dirt. He threw it at the boy. The boy ran away. "Good to see you, son."

"We have to go," Wanda said.

Wanda's dad helped her up. Her dress was torn, and her face was bruised. She was holding her ribs like they hurt. Her left leg was beginning to swell. Frankie took off his hoodie and gave it to her. She put it on over her ripped dress.

"You okay?" Wanda's dad asked.

"We have to help!" Wanda wiped the tears and blood from her face with the back of her hand.

"They goin' to get some girl." Frankie gestured in the direction of where the pack of boys had gone. "On-Line's sister."

"I need to get Wanda to the hospital," her dad said.

"No, Dad," Wanda said. "Listen to me. We have to help!"

Her dad looked at her. His eyebrows scrunched together like he was thinking about something.

"Your mom's going to kill me," he said. "This is just provisional and . . ."

"Dad!" Wanda said. "Some other girl is getting beaten up and raped and whatever else."

"They was goin' to kill the girl," Frankie said.

"What happened to your vocabulary, Frankie?" Wanda's dad asked. "You're a smart kid. Why are you talking like a thug?"

"Dad!" Wanda said. "Focus. We have to save the girl. They will kill her. They almost killed Tink."

"Your little friend?" Wanda's dad asked. "The one I met last weekend?"

Wanda and Frankie nodded.

"What are you doing hanging out with people like that?" Wanda's dad asked.

Frankie took off in the direction of the other boys. In order to make his point, Wanda's dad followed him.

"You used to be on the honor roll with Wade!" Wanda's dad said.

"Wanda!" Wanda limped along at his side.

They ran until they reached a quiet grove of trees.

"Holy crap," Wanda's dad said. He gave Wanda his phone. "You call the police."

"I'm not going to sit this out," Wanda said.

"Girls leave the fighting to the men and boys," Wanda's dad said.

"Not this girl," Wanda said.

Frankie smirked, and they entered the grove.

~~~~~~~~~
Monday afternoon — 2:45 p.m.

Jacob let the dogs play at the dog park for a while after Charlie had sauntered off to basketball. He liked to see his puppy Sarah play with Buster, the ugly dog. Buster treated Sarah like his personal princess. They romped and played all over the fenced area while Scooter stayed close to Jacob's side. Jacob leaned down to rub Scooter's ears. The old guy was slower now but still liked to be with the other dogs.

Jacob whistled for Sarah. She ran straight to him, and Buster followed. He clipped the leashes onto their collars and checked that Scooter was attached. He started a slow jog down Josephine Street past the East High parking lot and into the outer edge of the park. His plan was to jog along York Street and turn up Twenty-Third Avenue near the zoo. If Scooter seemed too worn out, they would walk the rest of the way.

Buster pulled toward the east side of the park.

"Nah, we're going this way." Jacob assumed he wanted to follow their usual morning route.

Buster pulled again to the east, but Jacob kept him on track. He glanced down at Scooter. The old boy trotted at his side with a big smile on his face.

Jacob smelled it first.

Rage.

He stopped short. Buster jerked his leash and took off into a grove of trees.

"Buster!" Jacob yelled.

He used his psychokinetic ability to stop the dog before he got too far. Uncharacteristic for the gentle dog, Buster turned around and snapped. He gave a loud bark and lunged at Jacob. Sarah jumped in front of Jacob. The dogs snarled at each other for a moment before Sarah looked up at Jacob. She gestured with her head that they should follow Buster.

"All right, boy — we'll follow you," Jacob said.

They started across the grass. Jacob slowed. A couple boys ran across their path toward York Street. The boys looked like they were running for their lives. Buster pulled, and Scooter barked. Jacob sped up, and they ran deeper into the grove.

And he saw . . .

He wasn't sure what he saw.

He blinked. The dogs scooted closer to him.

An enormous blue-and-green dragon lay in front of them. Her eyes were almond shaped and a beautiful shade of rust. Her eyelashes were like long tree branches. The dragon's mouth was as big as a fire truck. Fire came from the dragon's mouth in a stream and made a circle around Noelle.

Lit up in the fire's orange and red, Noelle focused on her painting. As if they couldn't see the fire, a group of twenty or more young men stood frozen just inches from Noelle. Lust and rage emanated from the boys like exhaust fumes. One of the boys held a baseball bat just inches to the side of Noelle's head. Another boy held a knife just inches away from her.

A taller boy, clearly the leader, stood to the side. A joint was dangling from his mouth, and his pants looked worn, but his eyes held the pure, dark emptiness brought by the joy of extreme violence. The boy was strategizing how to rape and kill Noelle.

In the corner of the clearing stood Wanda, her father Erik, and some boy. Wanda looked like she'd already had a run in with this gang. Erik's mouth hung open as if to shout, and the boy next to him had the stunned look of someone waking from a nightmare.

"Jacob Marlowe," the dragon said.

"Ma'am." Jacob swallowed hard. Not sure what to say, he added, "Uh, what's going on?"

"What does it look like?" the dragon asked.

Jacob groaned. Ghosts on Sunday. Dragons on Monday. How much could he really deal with? For a brief moment, he thought about leaving, but there was no way he'd leave Noelle like this. He tried to remember what Delphie always said about dragons.

"Delphinium always says that dragons can't answer questions," the dragon said.

"It's very rude to read someone's mind without his permission," Jacob sniffed.

The dragon laughed.

"I am not reading your mind," the dragon said. "We're out of time. Surely, you recognize the feeling of being out of time. You've been here before."

Jacob blushed. Once, in a fit of desperation, he'd pushed Jill out of time. He'd done it only once.

"No shame, young Marlowe," the dragon said. "You cannot help who and what you are any more than I can."

Scooter tugged, and his leash slipped from Jacob's hands. The old dog went to the dragon. He greeted her with his head down. He rubbed his head against the dragon's shoulder. She seemed to smile, without ever letting up on the fire. Scooter lay down at her shoulder.

"Scooter and I are old friends," the dragon said.

Unsure of what to say or do, Jacob shifted back and forth. His mind threw out question after question. He tried to slow down and think.

"Noelle's in danger," Jacob said.

"Noelle's in imminent danger," the dragon said. "They intend to kill her."

"You can deal with them," Jacob said.

"I cannot deal with them," the dragon said. "I'm with child. My powers are limited, and I cannot fly. I can, however, eat them. While they look like tasty snacks, I believe Denver would notice a few chewed-up boys. I've been hunted before. I'd like not to repeat that."

"You want me to do something," Jacob said.

"I want to use you as a channel," the dragon said. "I will add my power to yours. You will toss these boys away from Noelle so that her friends can save her."

"I don't want to be hunted, either!" Jacob said.

"Noelle will think it's me," the dragon said. "Her friends and the boys are unable see our power. They are too caught up in themselves. We have to stall long enough for the police to get here."

"Noelle will be hurt," Jacob said. "Even with your power, I can't hold them all off. There are too many, and they are too . . ."

"They are on drugs," the dragon said. "They enjoy this sport of blood and lust."

Jacob shivered with disgust.

"And yes," the dragon said. "I'm sorry that Noelle will be injured, but she will."

"It will destroy her," Jacob said.

"You can't destroy a child like Noelle," the dragon said. "But she will be hurt. So will you and Noelle's friends. There's simply no other way."

"You're sure?" Jacob asked. "And the dogs?"

The dragon gave him a wry smile. Jacob groaned.

"The dogs will be injured, too," Jacob said.

"Less than the humans," the dragon said. "This is a human battle. Now, let the dogs off leash."

Jacob unhooked Buster and Sarah. The dragon seemed to speak to the dogs. Buster got between Noelle and the boy with the bat. Sarah refused to move from Jacob's side.

"She loves you very much," the dragon said.

Scooter got up and encouraged Sarah to move toward the center. Sarah and the dragon stared at each other for a long moment. Jacob wasn't sure what was going on, but Sarah looked up at him and then moved into the fight.

"Are you ready?" the dragon asked.

For a moment, he wished he were back in bed with Jill. He remembered her face in the moonlight. He remembered what she looked like when a tear ran down her cheek. He saw her in the silly mask from the party in Santa Monica. He wished he could transport himself to Jill.

He glanced at Noelle. She was the bravest girl he'd ever met.

"Wait," Jacob said.

The dragon turned her attention to Jacob.

"Delphie says that dragons cannot affect the course of human-to-human interaction," Jacob said.

"That's correct," the dragon said.

"I'm no dragon," Jacob said.

Jacob went to the boys around Noelle. He pushed down his

sleeves to cover his hands and jerked the baseball bat out of the boy's hands. He set the baseball bat where the boy with Wanda would find it. He took the knife from the boy near Noelle and threw it, blade down into the grass. Jacob thought for a moment.

"You've done all you can do?" the dragon asked.

Jacob scowled. The dragon wanted him to do something else — but couldn't tell him. Jacob looked from boy to boy. He looked at the dogs. Glancing back at the dragon, he saw that she was staring at Noelle.

Of course.

Noelle had been taking martial arts since her mother, Nuala, had broken her cheekbone. He had spent long hours teaching her Brazilian jujitsu. The boys joked that she was particularly ruthless. Jacob dropped down and crawled under the fire ring.

"Noelle." Jacob shook Noelle awake.

Noelle's eyes focused, and she looked up at him. She gave him a confused look before noticing the fire ring and then the boys. She gave a tiny squeal. She grabbed onto Jacob in fear and then pushed him away.

"Okay, okay," Noelle said. "I'm okay."

Jacob helped her to her feet.

"They *are* going to attack you," Jacob said. "What do you do first?"

"I assess the strengths and weaknesses of my opponents," Noelle said. She looked at the boys closest to her.

"What do you do next?" Jacob asked.

"I prepare myself because this is going to hurt like hell," Noelle said.

"Exactly," Jacob said.

"Um, why are they frozen?" Noelle asked.

"The dragon cannot affect human interaction," Jacob said.

Noelle nodded as if that were obvious.

"Are you ready?" Jacob asked.

"I'm ready," Noelle said.

Jacob slipped out of the fire ring. He repositioned the dogs.

"You know, the boys are high. Anything they say will be suspect, especially if they say they saw something as crazy as a dragon."

"Duly noted," the dragon said. "Are you ready?"

"Noelle?" Jacob asked.

"Ready," Noelle said.

Jacob nodded to the dragon

And time returned.

CHAPTER TWO HUNDRED & FORTY-SEVEN

ENOUGH

For a brief moment, everything stood still, and Jacob's mind raced. He hoped he wouldn't die. He hoped Noelle wouldn't be injured. He wasn't sure what happened if you injured a pregnant dragon, but he was fairly certain it was not good. He felt a nudge against his leg. He glanced down; Scooter was now standing next to him.

When he looked up, everything was in motion, and his mind was still. He felt the dragon's power like a heartbeat. All sound disappeared except for the heartbeat.

Beat. He raised his hand, and the leader of the group flew back against a tall pine.

Beat. He moved his fingers back. The leader slapped against the branches as he rose up the tree truck.

Beat. Jacob touched his index fingers to his thumbs and flicked the boys away from Noelle.

Across the grove, he saw Wanda reach Noelle. The girls turned back to back to fight with the boys nearest them. The boy with Wanda picked up the baseball bat.

Erik, Wanda's father, yelled something at the boy, and he nodded. He hit several boys' legs with his bat. Erik was attacked by two boys at once.

Wanda and Noelle were overrun with boys.

Jacob had been so focused across the grove that he didn't see the punch coming at him until he was struck in the face. Jacob weaved a second too late and felt the impact of a second punch. He rotated, turned in place, and pushed the boy to the side. Thrown by Jacob's unchecked power, the boy flew ten feet before hitting the ground. Jacob took a step, and another boy confronted him.

His human mind panicked. He was overwhelmed with the rage that was pulsing through each of these boys. The dragon beat marched forward, but Jacob had lost his focus.

The boy in front of him hit him once more in the face, and Jacob fell to the ground. Through the chaos of running legs and fighting, he saw that Wanda was getting pummeled. Noelle fell next to Wanda. A boy kicked Buster out of the way to get to Noelle.

His mind flooded, and his entire life felt futile.

How had his world become like this?

Why were young boys trading away all of their opportunity for rage?

Why was being right more important than getting along?

Why did the world give in to violence and power games?

Somewhere deep inside, Jacob heard a human heartbeat. He heard his mother tell him that, someday, he would know just exactly what he was. He heard the dragon laugh.

One word came to his mind.

Enough.

"Yes," he heard the dragon say.

He knocked the boy in front of him off his feet and stood.

"Enough!" Jacob yelled. "I have had enough!"

He raised his hands and the boys in the grove rose twenty feet off the ground. The young men looked horrified.

One young man opened his mouth and pointed to him.

"Imma get you." Jacob read the boy's lips.

He dropped the boy to the ground. The boy's legs broke like toothpicks and terror moved through the rest of Jacob's hostages.

He felt a hand on his right shoulder. He turned to find his father standing behind him.

Jacob blinked. He had no idea if his father was actually there or if he was looking at a dragon-induced illusion.

"I love you, son," Sam said.

Without releasing the boys, Jacob hugged his father tight. He felt more than saw Sarah rub her head against his leg.

"I can't do it anymore," Jacob said.

"I know," Sam said. "Every man has a moment when he realizes he has to fight for what he believes in."

"One tiny inch at a time, they've taken so much," Jacob said. "Now we're fighting with each other over stupid stuff because the bullies refuse to talk about real issues."

Sam gave him a wry look. He looked around the grove.

"Maybe it's time for the powerful few to stand up and say, 'Enough,'" Sam said.

"But you said . . . You said never, ever . . ."

"I had no idea the world would become like this," Sam said. "Girls assaulted by thugs their own age. Drugs, guns . . . hard work that means very little in the face of bullies disguised as businessmen . . . I don't think anyone could have predicted this."

Erik ran over from across the grove. Sam turned toward the street.

"The police are almost here," Sam said.

Jacob watched his father. The boy Wanda was with helped Wanda and Noelle up.

"How are you here?" Jacob asked. "Why can I hear you?"

"You needed me here. You willed it." Sam smiled at him. "I'm having my afternoon nap with Delphie at home. After all, we have a long night ahead of us."

Wanda, her friend, and Noelle jogged over to Jacob.

"But . . ."

"Set them down on my count." Sam turned to Bestat. "You need to change."

"I can't hold them without her!" Jacob said.

"You've never needed me," the dragon said. "You only needed to decide you were in the game."

The dragon faded. The woman appeared. There was not a hair

out of place on her head and her linen suit looked freshly pressed. She gave Sam a bright smile. She kneeled down to pet Scooter.

"You've been in a fight," Sam said.

"Good point," Bestat said. Before their eyes, her hair was ruffled, her shirt torn, and her face bloodied.

"Girls, you need to go back to where you were," Sam said. "Son."

Noelle and Wanda nodded. They ran back to where they were. The boy with Wanda jogged back to where he'd been standing.

"Erik," Sam said.

The plumber nodded and followed the girls back to where he'd been.

"Now," Sam said.

Jacob set the boys on the ground only seconds before the first police cruiser drove up onto the grass. An unmarked car approached from the other side. Sergeant Aziz ran in front of a swarm of police officers. He found his brother and hugged him tight. The boys scattered, and the uniformed officers chased them down.

Jacob felt another fist slam against his face.

"Seriously?" he asked the boy in front of him.

He shot the boy across the grove in front of a uniformed officer. The officer slipped zip ties on the boy's arms and legs, and moved on. Jacob whistled for the dogs. They trotted over to him, and he clipped on the leashes. He saw that Bestat had walked over to him. He gave her a sly smile. She flagged down a uniformed officer.

"Officer," Bestat said. "I'm a diplomat from Egypt. I was here with my son's girlfriend and we were attacked. We were separated and I haven't been able to find her."

"There are two girls over here," the officer said.

Jacob followed Bestat to where Noelle and Wanda were being treated by paramedics. Wanda reached for Frankie's hand. He grabbed on. Bestat knelt down next to Noelle. Erik shook off a uniformed police officer and ran over.

"How are they?" Jacob asked the paramedics.

"Are you their father?" the paramedic asked.

"I'm Noelle's uncle." Jacob glanced at Noelle and she smiled. "Wanda's father is . . ."

"Right here," Erik said.

"They seem to be mostly bruised," the paramedic said. "They both have defensive wounds. They said they were fighting this bunch. We won't know if they broke any bones until they get to the hospital. You have insurance? 'Cuz the trip to the hospital is pricey."

"Of course," Jacob said at the same moment as Erik said, "Uh . . ."

"We've got this covered." Jacob put his hand on Erik's shoulder.

The paramedic nodded and helped the girls onto stretchers. Bestat stepped into the ambulance with Noelle. The paramedics took off with a scream of sirens toward the hospital. Jacob looked back at the grove. The police were rounding up the boys. Sergeant Aziz walked over to him.

"Did any of you see a young man about this big, low-slung jeans . . .?" Sergeant Aziz asked. "We've been told he's the leader. No one remembers him leaving, but we can't find him."

"Haven't seen him." Erik looked at Jacob. "You?'

Jacob shook his head.

"That's a shame," Sergeant Aziz said. "He's wanted in two states. I guess he goes from school to school, gets the boys hooked on meth and violence, and then disappears to let them take the rap."

Jacob turned his right hand over. The boy screamed on his way down the tree trunk. He landed on his rear at the bottom of the tree and began to wail. Jacob raised his eyebrows at Sergeant Aziz.

"Is that him?" Jacob asked.

Sergeant Aziz looked across the grove at the boy and then back at Jacob.

"Must have climbed the tree to watch," Erik said. "Fell out."

"Imagine that," Sergeant Aziz said. "Just a second before we got here, I could have sworn I saw these boys floating above the ground."

Sergeant Aziz looked at Erik and then at Jacob.

"Nothing?" Sergeant Aziz asked.

"Where's Detective Red Bear?" Jacob gave the Sergeant a bright smile.

"On leave," Sergeant Aziz said. "But I would guess you knew that."

Jacob nodded. They watched a uniformed officer arrest the boy who was with Wanda.

"My brother," Sergeant Aziz said.

"Why are they arresting Frankie?" Erik asked.

"He's been a part of this." Sergeant Aziz cleared his throat and swallowed hard.

"I need to go to Wanda," Erik said. "When we're done, we should talk to the police, because Frankie saved my Wanda today."

"Frankie and Wade," Sergeant Aziz said. "They were always so close."

Erik nodded. He held his hand out to Jacob.

"Thanks," Erik said. Jacob shook his hand, and Erik walked to his truck.

"What was that?" Sergeant Aziz asked.

"He works for me," Jacob said.

"Uh, huh," Sergeant Aziz said.

"I need to call Noelle's father," Jacob said. "Get the dogs home and . . ."

"You're around?" Sergeant Aziz asked.

"You can reach me here." Jacob gave him his card.

Sergeant Aziz nodded. Jacob turned back to look at the police officers and the boys. His mind replayed the whole odd event. He grinned. He gave Sergeant Aziz a nod before jogging off with the dogs.

At the dog park, Jacob knelt down to check the dogs. Somehow, they had made it through everything without a scratch. Before walking to the school to get Charlie, he called Aden, who was already on his way into town. Charlie and Jacob ran back to the Castle to pick up his car. There was a note on the door from Jill saying they had gone to the hospital. Jack let the dogs into the Castle and took Charlie with him to the hospital.

They found Delphie and Jill in the waiting area. Erik joined them a moment later. They settled in to wait.

~~~~~~~~~

Monday evening — 6:00 p.m.

Jacob stepped up to the podium in front of the Lipson employees. His face was a mess of bruises, and his right hand was wrapped in gauze, but he was there. It took a moment, but the employees stopped talking.

"Thank you for being here this evening," Jacob said. "I'm sure you've heard that Aden's daughter and her friend Wanda, Erik Le Monte's daughter, were attacked this afternoon."

He saw a group of employees whisper to each other near the back.

"Erik's on our plumbing crew," Jacob said. "If you'd like to call, feel free to do so. We'll hold the vote until you get back."

The men and women talked to each other, and one of them got up.

"Wanda, Erik's daughter, has some broken ribs and a broken leg," Jacob said. "Noelle, Aden's daughter, broke her hand on a boy's thick head. Both girls have some internal damage and facial bruises. They're staying at the hospital overnight, but the doctor's expect them both to fully recover. As you can see, I was there."

Jacob grinned. The employees laughed.

"We have an entire presentation ready," Jacob said. "But I'm tired and bruised. I'd like to cut to the chase."

Jacob looked out across the crowd of employees.

"We need to end Lipson Construction's involvement in the project by the airport," Jacob said.

There was a stunned silence.

"Blane and Tres will walk you through the reasons," Jacob said. "They will also share with you the expected cost of abandoning the contract. It's going to cost us, but it's the right thing to do."

"For who?" a voice near the back yelled out. "You?"

A few employees chuckled.

"Please stand up," Jacob said.

No one moved. The mood of the employees shifted. The people nearest to him whispered to each other.

"Yes, that's what we've turned into," Jacob said. "We fight with each other over nothing. How do the rest of you feel about the constant back biting, toxic cynicism disguised as intelligent comment, and arguing?"

Jacob shook his head.

"I've had enough," Jacob said. "You want to grumble and gripe? Find yourself another job. I've had enough of it. Site managers? Do you agree?"

"Fuck, yeah!" Jerry said.

"Absolutely," Rodney said.

"We're with you, Jake." Bambi stood up in the middle of the room. She turned around and pointed to a man. "You're fired. I've heard you whine enough to recognize your voice anywhere. Get out of here."

"You can't do that to me!" the man said.

"Out," Bambi said.

A few employees near the front began to clap. The man glared at Jacob and stomped out of the room. Jacob waited for a few minutes for everyone to settle down.

"We need to come together to work together," Jacob said. "Or we will not survive. Period. If there's anyone else who would like to leave, I encourage you to do so now. Remember what we said at noon: Leave and your employment is ended. And trust me, I'm dead serious about this. I'm sick of the cynics destroying any forward momentum. We're destroying ourselves from the inside. I'm done tolerating it."

About five people from around the room slowly got up and left.

"And the rest of you," Jacob looked out at the employees. "Are you ready to get to work?"

"Let's get it done, Jake!" Jerry yelled out.

The employees cheered.

"Let's get to work," Jacob said.

Chapter Two Hundred & Forty-Eight

Scared Kids

Monday evening — 7:13 p.m.

"Mom?" Noelle whispered.

Sandy got up from her chair and sat on Noelle's bed.

"Mom?" Noelle whispered again.

"I'm here," Sandy said.

Noelle's head rolled over to look at Sandy.

"The boys?" Noelle croaked.

"They went home," Sandy said. "Charlie and Aden are at the police station. Alex's husband, John, you remember him? He's very handsome?"

Noelle nodded.

"He took Teddy and Nash home to their house," Sandy said. "Sissy and Tink were here with Wanda for a while. Auntie Heather took them home for the night. Sissy said she would be here first, first, first thing."

Noelle smiled.

"She wanted to stay with you, but we can have only one person," Sandy said. "We thought you'd want me here."

"Where's Rachel?" Noelle sat up in a panic. "Did you forget her? Leave her?"

"Rachel is with Auntie Jill for the night," Sandy said. "Jill picked her up from school when she got Katy. She and Katy are having a trial run of what it's like to have a baby. Rachel is their practice baby."

"Rachel is a really good baby." Noelle gave a sincere nod. "I bet Jill's boys won't be as good of babies."

"I'm sure you're right." Sandy smiled. "But we'll be there to help."

Sandy patted Noelle's shoulder, and the girl lay down again. Noelle stared at the ceiling for a while.

"Mom?" Noelle whispered.

"I'm here," Sandy said.

"I was so scared," Noelle whispered. She scooted around so that her head was on Sandy's lap. "So . . ."

Noelle began to sob. Throughout this entire ordeal, Noelle had laughed, told big stories, and even bragged to her brothers. The doctors had marveled at how well she'd come through the terrible experience.

But Sandy knew her daughter. When the boys were gone, and the excitement wore off, her terror would return. Sandy stroked Noelle's back and hair, and let her cry.

Through the tears, Noelle told her story. It wasn't a big story of "whupping up on those jerks" like she'd told her brothers. It wasn't even the horror-filled story she'd told the police. Noelle told a smaller story, of a little girl who went to the park and was all alone when a lot of scary boys attacked her.

Noelle hiccupped and sobbed her way through her story, and Sandy held on to her. Sandy had never felt so inadequate and ineffective in her entire life. She had no idea if she was healing or helping or even being kind. She just listened and loved. It was all she could think to do.

When Noelle's story was over, the little girl fell silent. Sandy kept stroking her back.

"I think she's asleep," the nurse said. "Let me help."

Together, they set Noelle back against her pillows. The nurse fussed over Noelle's covers and checked her IV lines. Sandy stayed next to Noelle on the bed.

"You can get in the bed with her," the nurse said. "That's what I'd do."

"You would?" Sandy

"Of course," the nurse said. "I'll help."

The nurse moved Noelle over a bit.

"Just lie down with her," the nurse said. "It'll help."

Sandy lay down in the bed next to Noelle. She opened her eyes for a moment and closed them again.

"After such a big ordeal, you can't give a child enough snuggling," the nurse said. "Especially as brave a child as Noelle."

When the nurse left the room, Sandy lay on her side next to Noelle and stared at the wall. Sandy knew exactly how horrified Noelle had been. Images of her own terrifying experiences flashed across the cheery hospital wallpaper. Sandy wouldn't wish that horror on anyone, especially not Noelle. She bit her lip to keep from crying.

"Mom?" Noelle whispered.

"I'm here," Sandy said.

Sandy gave Noelle a soft hug. Noelle turned her head to look at Sandy. For a moment, the girl just looked at her. Sandy felt the child's gaze travel over her forehead, her nose, and her lips. Noelle gave a little nod and settled back on her pillow.

"Love you, Noelle," Sandy said.

"Mom?" Noelle whispered.

"I'm here," Sandy said.

Noelle nodded. Sandy's words echoed in her own ears.

"I'm here."

She'd said it over and over again tonight because it was all she could think to say. Noelle was calling for her mother; Sandy was there, right there. Sandy hadn't been there in the horror-filled past. But, now, she was right there with a little girl who loved her.

Noelle had miraculously escaped the horror and violence that had almost killed Tink.

Sandy had also miraculously escaped the horror and violence that had been her life to — by some miracle — wind up right here. Overwhelmed with gratitude, Sandy began to cry.

"It's okay, Mom," Noelle said. "I'm right here."

"I'm glad," Sandy said.

Noelle grinned and fell into a sound sleep.

Sandy knew it wasn't over for Noelle. There would be hearings and, eventually, a trial. Noelle would have to repeat her story over and over and over again. Long after her physical wounds had healed, she would continue to deal with the mental ones. She'd probably have nightmares and need to see her therapist again.

But when all was said and done, Noelle was there.

Sandy was there.

That was all that really mattered.

~~~~~~~~~

Monday evening — 8:25 p.m.

"Hey," Frankie said, when he entered Wanda's hospital room.

He was wearing an orange jumpsuit and his hands were handcuffed in front of him. A uniformed police officer stood by his side. Wanda's mom, Edith, looked at Frankie and then at Wanda before getting up out of her chair.

"Why don't I wait outside for a minute?" Wanda's mother asked. "Officer? Would you like to join me?"

The uniformed officer looked at Wanda's mom and at Frankie. He unlocked one of Frankie's hands and locked the handcuff to the rail on Wanda's bed.

"Don't go anywhere," the officer said.

"I won't," Frankie said.

"This is a special favor," the officer said. "Screw this up and you're back in with the pack."

"Yes, officer," Frankie said.

"All right, then," the officer said. He followed Wanda's mom out of the room.

"What's going on?" Wanda asked.

"I have to go to Gilliam tonight," Frankie said. "Juvie. I'm 'sposed to go to the Children's Home, you know, 'cuz of the stuff with my stepdad. But I can't go there 'til there's a bed."

"Why?" Wanda asked.

"It's part of my sentence," Frankie said. "I went to court and stuff last week. This is a pretty good deal. I got it mostly 'cuz of my brother."

"You turned in all those videos," Wanda said.

"How'd you know that?" Frankie asked.

"Your mom came by," Wanda said. "She said you gave those big Homeland Security guys enough evidence to figure out what's going on from top to bottom. She said she's really proud of you. I am, too."

Frankie furrowed his eyebrows and scowled.

"Listen, I wanted to tell you," Frankie glanced at Wanda and looked down, "if you're doing all of this because of me, you don't have to. I already told my mom."

"What did you tell her?" Wanda asked.

"That I'm gay," Frankie blushed. "And that you and I ... when we were in junior high, and ... Well, she's okay with it."

"Are you sure you're gay?" Wanda voice rose with anxiety.

"Well, there's that stuff with my stepdad," Frankie said. "And you. And I could never... I mean the guys made fun of me because I ..."

"Just because you're not a rapist doesn't mean you're gay," Wanda said.

"What about you?" Frankie asked.

"I'm a girl," Wanda said. "I told you over and over again. I knew I was a girl when I was three or four. I told my mom but she and dad thought I'd grow out of it. Then ..."

"Is that why you starved yourself?" Frankie asked. "I always thought it was 'cuz you didn't want to be gay."

"I wanted to control my body," Wanda said. "When you're starving, you don't go through puberty. And ..."

"You almost died," Frankie said. "I don't like that."

"If you're gay, then we can't be together." Wanda didn't want to talk about her eating disorder.

"Why?" Frankie shrugged.

"Because I'm a girl," Wanda said.

"But . . ." Frankie shook his head. He leaned in. "Are you going to . . . you know?"

"Eventually," Wanda said. "I have to live like a girl for at least a year. But even my dad thinks it makes sense that I'm a girl."

"Oh," Frankie said. "Your mom?"

"She doesn't like it," Wanda said. "She thinks she did something wrong. Or that I'm doing this because I love you, but . . ."

"You love me?" Frankie blushed.

"You know that," Wanda said.

"Even after everything and all of this?"

Wanda nodded.

"You love me, too?" Wanda asked.

Frankie nodded, and Wanda smiled.

"It's pretty weird to love a girl like me," Wanda said.

"Don't think there's anything I can do about it." Frankie shrugged.

Wanda smiled.

"Are you going to get better?" Frankie asked.

"Yeah," Wanda said. "You?"

"I don't know," Frankie said.

"How 'bout if we both promise to get better?" Wanda asked. "I'll do everything I can, and you do everything you can."

"Okay," Frankie said.

"I don't know if we'll be together forever, like some movie or something," Wanda said. "But, at least, if we get better together, that's really good. That seems like a really good way to love someone."

"So you're saying you won't starve yourself anymore?" Frankie asked.

"And you'll work hard to get better," Wanda said.

"For you," Frankie said.

"They'll tell you that you have to do it for yourself," Wanda said.

"I am," Frankie said. "If I get better, and you get better, then we stand a chance at . . . life."

Wanda nodded.

"I'm glad you're okay," Frankie said.

"I wouldn't be if you hadn't helped," Wanda said.

Frankie smiled. The police officer came in.

"Kiss the girl good-bye, dummy," the officer said. "That's why we're here."

Frankie leaned over and kissed Wanda's lips. She touched his face, and he smiled. The officer re-handcuffed him, and they shuffled out the door. Wanda's mom came back in.

"So is this being a girl . . . Is that about Frankie?" Wanda's mom asked.

"No, Mom," Wanda said.

"Just checking," Wanda's mom said. "Because he's pretty cute."

"He is." Wanda smiled.

"So are you," Wanda's mom said.

She leaned over and kissed Wanda's forehead.

"I saw you and Dad talking," Wanda said. "Are you . . .?"

Wanda's mother raised a stern eyebrow at her and sat down in her chair. She started flipping pages in a magazine.

"Okay — the excitement's over," the nurse said when she came into the room. "Time for you to sleep. You have surgery for that leg tomorrow. You need rest."

The nurse fussed over Wanda and flipped off the overhead lights. Wanda's mom turned on a floor lamp, giving the room a warm, yellow glow. Wanda lay quiet for a while.

"Dad's been really great," Wanda said.

"He has," Wanda's mom said.

"He's pretty cute, too," Wanda said.

"Mm-hmm." Wanda's mom pretended to read her magazine.

"And he doesn't have a new family like you thought."

Wanda's mom scrunched up her face and said, "You think . . .?"

Wanda nodded. Her mom smiled.

"Maybe you could have another kid," Wanda said. "A real boy this time. He can have all that stuff you bought for me."

"Don't push it," her mom said in a strong voice, but she smiled. "Go to sleep."

"Okay," Wanda said.

It was pretty hard to fall asleep when she was still all tingly from being kissed by Frankie. She was just about to say she couldn't sleep when she dozed off.

~~~~~~~~

Monday night — 10:23 p.m.

"Hi," Jill said in a low tone.

Jacob was sitting on the couch, with his back to her. Hearing her voice, he turned to look at her. She came around the couch and sat on his lap. She tugged on his tie and kissed his bruised mouth. He grimaced as he kissed her.

"Whatcha doing out here in the dark?" Jill asked.

"Thinking," Jacob said. "I'm dead tired and feel like I've been hit by a bus, but my mind is . . . crazy."

Jill smiled.

"Can I bring you some dinner?" Jill asked.

He shook his head.

"Bath?" she asked.

"Only if you can join me, and I don't think you can," he said.

"Probably not a good idea," Jill said. "I'm starting to dilate and . . ."

He smiled.

"You knew that." She smiled.

He nodded.

"Why don't you stay right here on my lap?" he asked. "Do you mind?"

"Not at all," Jill said.

"Today, before everything happened, you know, I... I just wanted to run away... to you," Jacob said. "I wanted to just look at you. And... that's all I wanted."

Jill smiled.

"I feel... guilty for wanting to leave Noelle, for not thinking of Katy, for..."

Jill put her fingers over his mouth.

"You're taking something very sweet and making it bad," Jill said. "Did you think that maybe you thought of me to gain strength to do something really hard?"

Jacob gave a sad shake of his head.

"Plus, you didn't leave Noelle," Jill said. "You've never left Katy."

Jacob gave a sad nod.

"What happened tonight?" Jill asked.

"Oh, tonight." Jacob pulled on the knot of his tie and pulled the tie off. "Tonight was good. Bambi had to fire a guy who was whining, but, after that, everyone worked. Most of our people are very reasonable, smart. They knew what was going on, but the curmudgeons shouted so loud, they couldn't get a word in edgewise. They just focused on their jobs and hoped it would work out."

"So, you're leaving the site?" Jill asked.

"I'm going downtown in the morning to talk to the state inspector's office." Jacob nodded.

"That's really great news," Jill said.

"Everyone worked hard," Jacob said. "You should have seen them. When tempers flared, someone made a joke or they talked it through. We were able to get there, together. I was... blown away. Dad came late after checking on Noelle and Wanda. He... was really proud. That's what he said."

"Nice." Jill smiled.

Jacob nodded.

"So, what leaves you out here and not in bed?" Jill asked.

"Just a feeling." Jacob touched her face. "I've given up so much, one tiny bit at a time, and . . . I . . ."

He leaned forward and kissed her.

"We have to be careful not to let the cynics and scowlers take everything precious to us — hope, love, joy, faith, grace — one sarcastic comment at a time," Jill said.

"Yes," he said. "That's what's happened to me — one tiny word at a time, I've lost hope and faith and joy . . . It's like fluid depression, with no beginning or end. And . . . Scowlers?"

"You know what I mean." Jill shrugged.

"Well, this deal should be done before we have the boys," Jacob said. "I can leave Lipson in good conscience."

"You're going to take time off work?" Jill grinned.

"I know — it's unlikely," Jacob said.

"Probably," Jill said. "We'll have fun anyway."

Jacob tugged her a tiny bit closer.

"Are you okay?" Jill whispered.

"I am," Jacob said. "I just had to say 'enough' and stand up for hope and faith and joy and love and grace and . . . life."

"And the fluid depression?" Jill asked.

"I'm okay," Jacob kissed her. "I have such a wonderful life. I need to say 'enough' more often so I can enjoy my life more."

Jill got off his lap.

"Come to bed." She held her hand out to him.

He looked at her hand for a moment before taking it. They walked to the bedroom. She helped him undress and get into bed. She had just slipped in beside him when she realized he was already sound asleep. She kissed his cheek and lay back. She stared at the ceiling for a moment before whispering, "Thanks" to whatever had helped Jacob shake off the funk he'd been in. As if she'd heard a reply, she nodded and fell asleep.

~~~~~~~~

Tuesday early morning — 12:23 a.m.

"Charlie!" Aden came into the living room. "What are you doing up?"

"I . . ." Charlie started.

Aden took in the boy's red, swollen eyes. His handsome face was blotchy with emotion. Aden sat down next to him on the couch.

"I . . . all of this . . . and . . ." Charlie tried to express himself.

Aden tugged on his shoulder and Charlie fell over into his lap. The boy began to weep. When Charlie stopped weeping, the boy stared straight ahead.

"What is it?" Aden asked.

"It's all my fault," Charlie whispered. "They attacked Noelle because she was *my* sister."

"None of this is your fault," Aden said.

"But Noelle . . ." Tears ran down Charlie's face. "Jake and, God, poor Wanda."

"Only the boys who decided to beat up your sister and her friend are at fault," Aden said. "Not you."

"Why does it feel like it's my fault?" Charlie asked.

"Because, if it's your fault, you can control it," Aden said. "Make it stop."

"They told me at the police station that only I could make it stop," Charlie said.

"Art and Colin didn't say that," Aden said. "Did they?"

Charlie shook his head.

"Why do you think that is?" Aden asked.

"They're our friends." Charlie shrugged.

"I think they didn't say that because they are honest men," Aden said. "They told me that you were very brave and that, without you, none of this would have happened."

"That's what I mean!" Charlie said. "None of this would have happened!"

"None of the arrests would have happened," Aden said. "These boys would have kept getting high and hurting girls. You made that stop. That's a pretty big deal. They even caught the leader. He's wanted in other states for doing the same thing."

Charlie didn't know how to respond, so he didn't.

"That's the truth," Aden said. "You can believe you screwed up, or that you set things right. It's up to you."

"What do you think?" Charlie asked. "Sandy? Noelle?"

His voice caught with Noelle's name.

"We think you're pretty wonderful," Aden said. "Noelle told Sandy that she didn't realize how brave you were until she saw how scary those guys were."

"Sounds like Noelle," Charlie said. "Do you think this is over?"

"God, I hope so," Aden said. They sat in silence for a while before Aden repeated, "God, I hope so."

"Me, too," Charlie said.

Denver Cereal continues at DenverCereal.com.

Glossary of Characters

Aden Norsen:
CEO at Lipson Construction; single father of Nash and Noelle; boyfriend of Sandy.

Alexandra Hargreaves:
Identical twin to Max Hargreaves; "The Fey"; the leader of the Fey Team; wife of Dr. John Drayson; sister to Colin and Samantha Hargreaves.

Andrea Menendez or Andy Mendy:
Mother of Sandy; Seth's love & lover from the time he was 12 until he lost her when he was 30.

Anjelika:
Mother of Megan, Mike, Steve, Candy and Jill; grandmother to Katy; wife of Perses.

Arthur Rasmussen:
Member of the Fey team; boyfriend of Samantha Hargreaves.

Ava — Amelie Vivian Alvin:
Denver Police Crime Lab Technician; fiancée of Seth O'Malley.

Beth Barnes:
Ava's best friend since childhood; child psychologist; murdered by Saint Jude.

Blane Lipson:
Jacob's "cousin"; raised in foster care; either the child of Sam Lipson's father or brother; assistant to Jacob Marlowe at Lipson Construction; husband of Heather; father of Mack.

Bob aka "Blood Spatter Bob":
Former expert forensics instructor with the FBI; currently a laboratory technician in Ava's Denver Police Department lab.

Bree or Briana Lipson:
Stepchild of Sam Lipson.

Becky Lipson:
Stepchild of Sam Lipson.

Candace or Candy Roper:
Daughter of Anjelika; sister to Jill; partner to Jazmyne.

Charlie Delgado:
Stepbrother of Sandy; street kid; drug addict; has been out of school for a long time; comes to live with Sandy in Cimarron.

Celia Marlowe:
Wife of Sam Lipson; mother to Valerie Lipson and Jacob Marlowe; died of cancer nine years before *Denver Cereal* begins.

Cleo:
Black-and-white cat belonging to Sandy.

Colin Hargreaves:
Brother of Alex, Max, and Samantha Hargreaves; Homeland Security Agent; Fey Team member; father of Paddie Hargreaves.

Dale:
Boyfriend of Beth, Ava's best friend; housemate of Amelie; handyman.

Delphinium or Delphie:
Psychic; beekeeper; master gardener; best friend of Celia Marlowe; girlfriend to Sam Lipson.

Evette:
Secretary of Jacob's for one week. Tells press of romantic relationship between them.

Fran:
A laboratory technician in Ava's Denver Police Department lab.

Frankie:
Brother of Sergeant Aziz; boyfriend of Wanda

Heather Lipson:
Jill's childhood friend; one of Jillian Roper's group of best friends; mother to Mack; wife to Blane Lipson.

Honey Lipson:
Second daughter of Tiffanie; stepdaughter of Sam Lipson; wife of Sergeant MJ Scully.

Jacob Marlowe:
Son of Sam Lipson and Celia Marlowe; boyfriend of Jillian Roper; brother of Valerie Lipson; president of Lipson Construction; owns his own house rehabilitation business; carpenter; hockey player.

James "Jammy" Schmidt V:
Seth O'Malley's music agent; partner to Lizzie O'Malley

Jeraine Wilson:
R&B star; childhood sweetheart and husband to Tanesha Smith; father of Jabari and Jeraine Jr.

Jillian or Jill Roper:
Daughter of Anjelika; mother of Katy Roper; girlfriend of Jacob Marlowe; ex-wife of Trevor Mc Guinsey.

John Drayson, MD:
Vascular surgeons; husband of Alex Hargreaves.

Julie Hargreaves:
Mother of Paddie Hargreaves; wife of Colin Hargreaves.

Julie Ann O'Malley:
Seth O'Malley's second daughter with his first wife; Marine.

Katy or Katherine Anjelika Roper:
Daughter of Jillian Roper and Jacob Marlowe.

Leslie:
A laboratory technician in Ava's Denver Police Department lab.

Leslie Roper:
Wife of Steve Roper; mother of infant Elisa Roper.

Levi Johansen:
Won Delphie in a card game when she was 5-6; held her as a slave/The Oracle Tabor; gets out of prison and wants Delphie dead; evil.

Lizzie O'Malley:
Seth O'Malley's eldest daughter by his first wife; biological mother of Connor Hargreaves; partner to James Schmidt V.

Mack Lipson:
Infant son of Heather and Blane Lipson.

Margaret Peaches or Sergeant Margaret Peaches:
Fey team member; partner of Sergeant MJ Scully.

Max Hargreaves:
Identical twin to Alex Hargreaves; brother to Colin and Samantha Hargreaves.

Megan Roper:
Daughter of Anjelika; partner of Tim; mother to Ryan and two other boys.

Melinda:
Daughter of one of Sandy's clients; Nash Norsen's romantic interest.

Mike Roper:
Son of Anjelika; husband of Valerie Lipson; hockey goalie; painter.

Mitch Delgado:
Sandy's stepfather, whom she called "Dad;" father of Charlie and Sissy; Seth O'Malley's best friend; died of lung cancer 8 or 9 years ago.

MJ or Sergeant Michael Scully Jr.:
Fey Team member; partner of Sgt Margaret Peaches; husband of Honey Lipson.

Molly:
Bookkeeper for Jacob Marlowe's rehabilitation business.

Nash Norsen:
Son of Aden and Nuala Norsen.

Nelson Weeks, MD:
A laboratory technician in Ava's Denver Police Department lab.

Noelle Norsen:
Daughter of Aden and Nuala Norsen.

Nuala Norsen :
Ex-wife of Aden Norsen; biological mother of Nash and Noelle Norsen.

Patti Delgado:
Mother of Sissy and Charlie; aunt to Sandy; wife of Mitch Delgado.

Paddie Hargreaves:
Best friend of Katy Roper; nephew of Alex and Max Hargreaves; son of Colin Hargreaves.

Pete:
Husband of Molly; father of her children; friend of Aden Norsen.

Perses:
Paid assassin; rescuer and biological father of Jillian Roper.

Rodney Smith:
Father of Tanesha; imprisoned for 26 years for a murder he didn't commit; husband of Yvonne Smith; site manager at Lipson Construction.

Ryan:
Oldest son of Megan Roper and Tim.

Sam Lipson:
Husband to Celia Marlowe; married to Tiffanie Lipson; boyfriend of Delphinium; father to Valerie and Jacob Marlowe-Lipson; stepfather to Brianna, Becky, Honey and the "stepwhore."

Samantha Hargreaves:
Sister to Alex, Max and Colin Hargreaves; girlfriend of Art Rasmussen; best friend of Valerie Lipson; criminal defense attorney.

Sandy:
Best friend of Jillian Roper; one of Jill's group of best friends; girlfriend of Aden Norsen; hairdresser.

Sarah:
Yellow Labrador belonging to Jacob Marlowe.

Scooter:
Gift from Celia and Delphie to Jillian on her marriage to Trevor McGuinsey; taken care of for last 4 years by Delphie after Trevor put him up for adoption; Katy's constant companion.

Sergeant Aziz:
Denver Police detective assigned to investigate rapes; does nothing to protect his brother, Frankie.

Seth O'Malley:
Godfather to Sandy; best friend of Sandy's step father; Denver Police detective; talented composer and pianist.

Stepsister or "Stepwhore":
Eldest daughter of Tiffanie Lipson; sister to Honey, Brianna, and Becky Lipson; stepdaughter of Sam Lipson; second wife of Trevor McGuinsey.

Steve or Stephen Roper:
Son of Anjelika; middle child of Roper family; medical nurse; husband of Leslie.

Sissy Delgado:
Stepsister of Sandy; anorexic; talented ballet dancer; comes to live with Sandy in Cimarron.

Tanesha Smith:
Childhood friend of Jillian Roper; one of Jill's group of best friends.

Teddy Jakkman
Son of Captain Zack "The Jakker" Jakkman; best friend of Nash Norsen; dates Noelle Norsen.

Tiffanie Lipson:
Second wife to Sam Lipson; mother of Briana, Becky, and Honey Lipson and the stepwhore.

Tim:
Partner to Megan Roper; father of Ryan and two other children.

Trevor Mc Guinsey:
Ex-husband of Jillian Roper; assumed father of Katy Roper; fiancé to the stepwhore.

Valerie Lipson:
Daughter of Sam and Celia Marlowe; wife to Mike Roper; soap opera and movie actress.

Wes or Wesley Kapanski:
Hollywood producer; was engaged to Valerie Lipson at the beginning of Denver Cereal.

Zack "The Jakker" Jakkman
Father of Teddy Jakkman; "The pilot" to Sissy and Charlie; Sandy's childhood pen pal; friend of Sandy's.

Denver Cereal.com

eBooks and Paperback available

everywhere you purchase books.